Gone I

Copyright & Thanks

Copyright© 2021 by Louise Murchie
All Rights reserved

This is a work of fiction. Names, characters, wealth or incidents are not genuine. No part of this story/book may be reproduced in any form or by electronic/mechanical means, including information storage and retrieval systems, without written permission from the author, unless for the use of brief quotations in a book review.

*To Kirsty,
Here's to worthwhile second chances!
All the best,
Louise Murchie*

Gone Dutch

Copyright & Thanks 1

One 5

Two 12

Three 17

Four 24

Five 40

Six 49

Seven 55

Eight 61

Nine 70

Ten 84

Eleven 92

Twelve 104

Thirteen 110

Fourteen 119

Fifteen 125

Sixteen 131

Seventeen 138

Eighteen 154

Nineteen 169

Twenty 171

Twenty-One 184

Twenty-Two 196

Gone Dutch

Twenty-Three	202
Twenty-Four	207
Twenty-Five	215
Twenty-Six	230
Twenty Seven	237
Twenty-Eight	251
Twenty-Nine	257
Thirty	267
Thirty-One	287
Thirty-Two	297
Thirty-Three	306
Thirty-Four	313
Thirty-Five	338
Thirty-Six	355
Thirty-Seven	375
Thirty-Nine	385
Forty	391
Forty-One	412
Forty-Two	420
Forty-Three	445
Epilogue	466
About The Author	469

Acknowledgements:

For my husband, kids, Tina, Aoifa, my sister, parents, in-laws and friends who I consider family, who genuinely know me; thank you!

Gone Dutch

One

"Have you got everything?" her mother asked. Despite her being in her mid-thirties, Elspeth McInnes knew her scatter-brained daughter would forget something. Either forget it on the way to her destination, or on the way home. It was always the way and had been since she was a toddler.

"I think so. If I haven't, it's just tough, isn't it?" She turned to grin at her wise, white-haired mum as she clicked the case shut.

"Now, Shauna" Her mother's Scottish accent got stronger and became the tone she used for unruly children. A tone she'd no doubt be making at her grandsons once they returned from school that day.

"Mam, I'm done. Make-up is packed, the dress is with Helene in Rotterdam. I've got the shoes that match, spare clothes, matching knickers and bras, cash… there's nothing else I need."

Elspeth smiled. Shorter than her daughter at five foot nothing but just as Celtic in their roots as the other. Both were strong women, physically. Elspeth's figure was now rounded, but homely, whilst her dark chestnut eyes were now a contrast for the white hair that had once been ebony black.

Gone Dutch

Shauna stood at her full five-foot-eight. She had what can only be described as an athletic build. She was slim, perhaps more than she ought to be, but it didn't bother her. She slid her feet into sensible shoes. She'd be driving herself and Ruth, her friend, to the airport and from there, flying to Utrecht before getting the hire car to drive to Rotterdam and their friends' wedding.

At that moment, the doorbell rang and Shauna could hear Ruth's Black Country voice carry up to her.

"Are you ready, our gal?" said her friend who had climbed the stairs to find her. Ruth's curly light red hair was washed and treated; lest it went frizzy in the heat or the air conditioning of the flight that they were due to take in two hours.

"Nearly" replied Shauna, turning to her mother.

"Now, don't let Mike or Drew try and pull the wool over your eyes. They're getting crafty with how they're *asking* for things."

Elspeth smiled. "Yes, you said. Already." Elspeth sighed. "You know we've raised the four of you? They're not going to try something that's new to me. I have been here before." Shauna smiled at her mother.

"Aye, I know YOU have mam, but I havenae. Their tricks are all new to me since they play Bryce and I off against each other. Wee scroats!"

Elspeth chuckled. "No more than you and Bryce did to yer dad and I. And if it wasn't you two, it was either Isobel or Cait. One of the four of you were always

Gone Dutch

playing me up. You four never did it for yer dad though!".

"Oh aye they did!" said her father James, coming to join them at the bottom of the stairs. "I just didn't tell you about all their antics."

He smiled at his eldest daughter. "Listen, darling, we've been there, bought the t-shirts, caps and ripped them all as well. We're auld hats at looking after kids". Her father's blue eyes danced as he smiled. Even in her flat shoes, Shauna was taller than her father's now five-foot-six. His number one crew cut tried to hide the bald spot at the back of his head, but it didn't really. His white beard was short but would soon be grown full and bushy so that he could once again play "Santa" at the end of the year for the Rotary Club he was a member of.

"Just, I've not…" Shauna let the sentence hang. She'd hardly been out since her husband Matt had died in a freak motorcycle accident three years before. Her boys, Michael and Andrew had been nine and six when they were left fatherless.

"We know, honey," her father said, hugging her. His slim physique was evident in his four children; whilst his wife's rounder nature was more homely.

"Have you not gone yet, sis?" Bryce asked incredulously as he came down from the loft bedroom. Since his divorce at around the time Matt died, Bryce had lived with his sister and two nephews in their attic en-suite room. Helping to provide a father figure for her

Gone Dutch

boys as well as his own daughter when he had her for the weekends, his sister helped him keep access to his daughter, much to his ex-wife's disgust. Standing at six-foot-three, he was the tallest of the four, second eldest and his sisters had claimed he was spoiled for being the only boy.

Shauna chuckled. "No, trying to! Come on Ruth, let's go!"

"Finally!" Ruth declared as she took her case to Shauna's older Seat Leon on the drive. It didn't take long for the car to be loaded, for the engine to be started and both ladies on their way to the airport with waves and grins in their wake.

"So," Ruth said as they finally hit the motorway to go to Birmingham International. "What do you think of all this with Helene then?! And did you bring them?"

Shauna signed. "To be honest, I don't know. I've met the man twice?" She paused, a frown coming over her face. Then she nodded. "Yes, twice before we got the invite. She didn't give us much notice. Thank heavens mum and dad could look after the boys; Bryce is working all weekend!" Shauna looked across to Ruth quickly. "And yes, I did bring them. Special bride request!" they grinned at each other.

"I can't even pronounce his name properly." scoffed Ruth.

"You can't?" Shauna glanced across at her friend as they changed from the M5 to the M42. "It's Fons, but

Gone Dutch

not like Fonz from Happy Days, so don't start doing that impression, please? It has a softer S at the end." Ruth was hot on TV shows, or at least she had been. Now caught up as a lawyer in Birmingham for Child Services, Ruth claimed she had no time for a serious relationship. However, if she could rib someone up about things that amused her, Ruth would.

"Think the cards will hint that I'll meet a hot Dutchman at their wedding?" asked Ruth. Men loved her strawberry-blond curly hair but even Shauna knew Ruth would enjoy a chase, a party in the sheets and then leave them by dawn. The notches on the bedpost were getting fewer and fewer, but that didn't deter Ruth. If she wanted someone, she was getting him.

"I'm just happy to be away for a weekend for the first time since Matt died" she replied, honestly. Shauna was Scottish, born in Stirling but moved to the Black Country by her parents for job prospects, Ruth and Shauna, with Helene and Ellen had known each other since they were nine. Forging a friendship in primary school that was still strong, the four of them had vowed to be there for each other no matter what.

When Matt had died it was Ruth, Helene and Ellen that had helped the family get through the first horrible weeks, the funeral, the getting on without daddy and life partner. Her parents and Matts were beside themselves, lost, angry and confused. There were still moments of that for them all, though it was less now.

Gone Dutch

Helene had been the only one of them not ever wed. Ruth who was only ever with a guy for a few dates but divorced after a few weeks, Ellen with a divorce and a daughter under her belt and Shauna widowed, they often called themselves a right motley crew. Through thick and thin, these women had stuck by each other. Now that Helene had been swept off her feet by, what she called, a Viking hung like a long-boat, the other three went to bid her good luck. A small party was organised for the evening for the four of them. No mothers, no mother-in-law, Helene had insisted. She was seeing out the second to last night of single-dom with her best forever friends.

They travelled through airport security with little to no fuss. Their cases secured in the hold, the car locked into the car park, they chose to chill out in the departure lounge just before their gate. Ruth was going to have a "loosen up" drink until she was reminded that Dutch driving laws had a lower alcohol tolerance for driving than the UK. Ruth mumbled but relented on an orange juice and lemonade. Something with a bite, she said. Shauna wondered right there just how much alcohol Ruth was putting away each day. She'd have to have a word with her friend about that later, away from the others and after this weekend.

Shauna was nervous; her boys could be wild and whilst she wasn't looking for *any* excuse to dirty any

Gone Dutch

bedsheets, she was both looking forward to the weekend of celebration and anxious for leaving the boys at home in her parents' care.

"They'll be fine! Your parents practically raised the four of us and your three siblings," remarked Ruth, guessing what was going through one of her life-long friend's mind. Shauna relaxed her shoulders. "Not to mention Cait…" Ruth let the sentence die. "Just, chill out Shaunie!"

Aye, I should chill out." She smiled. "I'll try!" she grinned, taking one long slurp of her lemonade and lime.

Gone Dutch

Four

The morning of the wedding started the same as the day before; the gentle rocking of the boat, the smell of food cooking. What was different was the sound of someone moaning about the world spinning. Shauna had to grin; Helene had over-done it last night. Quickly getting dressed into something light, she went to check on her friend.

Helene was indeed, slightly worse for wear but there was time for Helene to recover.
"What did I do?" she wailed as Shauna handed her some paracetamol and a glass of water. Shauna laughed. "You did a good Freddie!"

Helene looked at her aghast. "I didn't mean to… Oh heck, I get married in…"

"Five hours, we've time, dear bride," sang Shauna in reply. The knock at the door announced Ruth and Ellen's arrival with a maid behind them, bearing breakfast for them all.

"Okay, food. That's the first thing, then, showers / bubble baths etc." said Shauna, taking charge. They worked getting the breakfast for the four of them into Helene's room whilst dresses etc. were fetched from their respective rooms. After breakfast had been cleared

Gone Dutch

away, they took turns to shower and get themselves ready. An hour before they were needed, they began to braid Helene's hair, just as they'd practised the day before.

It was five to the hour when Helene's father knocked on the door.
"You've got a chance to back out, if you want?" he said, gently as he stood admiring his beautiful daughter. It was traditional that the bride was given an out.
Helene shook her head. "No daddy, I'm good. I'm ready."
Shauna smiled at Helene's father, Nathan. "Happy to make him wait a few minutes, though," she grinned. He nodded in reply. Turning back to his daughter, he said: "You look amazing my gorgeous girl!"
Helene smiled. "Thank you, dad. Where's mum?"
"Waiting for you," he watched as Shauna and the others gathered their bouquets, double-checked their tiaras, veiled Helene and taking a big deep breath, Helene nodded. They were ready.

The wedding march was the cue for the gathered guests to stand and welcome the bride. Fons stood at the front with his best man, nervously watching Helene

Gone Dutch

slowly strode towards him. He gasped as he saw her in the figure-hugging white satin dress.

Shauna paid attention to the bride but cast her eyes around the front row to Helene's mother, sister, the groom's family. The best man smiled at her then focused on the groom. Shauna cast her attention back to the job at hand and the duty she and her friends still had to perform.

She sighed happily a few hours later. The duties for the day, for the bride, were now mostly complete. Shauna smiled as she watched one of her closest and life-long friends dance with the man she'd fallen in love with. She was breathless after the first Waltz and was glad for a rest, even against the bar! She noticed a woman in red being escorted from the reception by two, no three of the groom's entourage. She watched until the woman left, but not before they'd made eye contact. 'What's her issue?' thought Shauna, because if looks could kill . . . Shauna turned her gaze back to the dancers, away from the trouble.

At the slightly "old maid" age of nearly thirty-five, she was finally happy. At least Helene had the rest of her life before her; Shauna did not feel the same about her own life, despite what the cards had hinted at last night. She smiled at a waiter as he swerved past with a tray of champagne. Being a year older and a widow with

Gone Dutch

two kids, was hard. Most men (and she used that term very loosely) left or suddenly stopped calling when she revealed she was a mother to two boys.

The sight of the best man smiling at her made her jump. Why was he smiling at her? She knew she would soon find out, as he was making a bee-line straight for her.

"That was a beautiful service," he declared as he grabbed two glasses of drink from another passing waiter, handing her a fresh one.

Shauna smiled. "Yes, it was. I'm surprised that the wedding service in our two countries is pretty similar," she replied, playing with her empty ring finger.

He smiled at her. "Wait until you see the Kransekage," he smirked.

"The what?" she replied, frowning, not quite sure what he'd said.

"Wedding cake," he smiled, almost downing the glass in one go.

"Err, is everything okay?" she asked him, tentatively. Champagne wasn't usually something a person drank in one go, especially when they were glasses as tall as these.

He nodded. "It will be. Old . . . acquaintance decided to drop by." He grabbed another drink and asked the barman for something far stronger.

Gone Dutch

"Oh? Was that the angry-looking woman in red who swept through about ten minutes ago?" she asked, sipping her drink.

"That was her," he said, his Dutch accent getting stronger. Shauna smiled; her own accent got stronger when alcohol was involved too. "She has gone," he said.

"I'm glad of that, and I'm sorry but I've totally forgotten your name," Shauna admitted, taking a slightly bigger drink of champagne than she intended to hide her embarrassment.

"Harek, at your service," he said, sliding a strong, warm hand around her waist and leaning in close. She had to admire how his smell, touch and proximity somehow made her skin tingle. His mouth was suddenly very close to her ears. "And you, my dear widow, are beautiful," he whispered.

In one sentence, he'd both inflated and deflated her. She turned her head and began to alight from the stool.

"Did I say something . . ." he asked, grabbing her by the elbow before she managed to bolt.

Lady Gaga would have been proud of her poker face. "My marital status seems to be far more important to you than anything else." Her soft Scottish accent was starting to get stronger as she got more annoyed, her face and narrow eyes betraying her emotions. "Thank you for reminding me my husband is dead."

Gone Dutch

He let go of her arm and looked deflated. "I apologize," he said. "I did not mean to make you... uncomfortable." His jaw clenched, then softened as he motioned towards the outside deck of the boat. Shauna wasn't sure she wanted to follow, but his strong warm hand around her waist again was guiding her to the outside deck. The hot sensations he made her feel just by touching her angered her even more. 'Damn neanderthal!' she thought as he guided her outside to the deck.

"You don't seem to realise how alluring you are," he said, closing one of the sliding doors behind them, drowning out some of the noise from the party.

"How can my being a widow be alluring?" She folded her arms. *'This Dane is a pig!'* she thought.

"Because you have something I fear I may never have." He turned to stand before her, but at a pace apart. She caught sight of the lights from the other side of the river reflecting in his eyes, which were now huge, hiding the hazel colour she'd seen a few moments before.

"Oh? And what's that?" she asked, placing her weight onto her back foot. Was she going to have to kick him to get away?

"Children," he said, simply. "You have children, a family. That is something I now... only wish I had." He turned to look out across the river. Shauna was stunned. She was attractive because she had children? That just had to be a first.

Gone Dutch

"I have always wanted children: three or four. My sister has two, one of each. But, it seems I cannot find the right person to be by my side." He turned to Shauna and she was aware that he was baring his soul. "Fons told me about his fiancé's friends, but I dismissed his now wife's description of you. I should not have."

He stepped closer and gently touched the side of Shauna's face. "I have had my hopes for a family dashed, played with and thwarted too many times. And here, at least, finding someone with integrity is… hard." His accent was enticing and she felt her heart flutter. When was the last time it had done that?

"Given my status here in this country" he continued, "my name, people throw themselves at me for lots of reasons. But, I can never seem to find anyone who is not focused on what I am," he sighed. "They do not see me. They see the success but resent the hard work, long hours, and the interrupted family moments that go into being successful. The ones that do get it," he nodded back into the party, to the angry woman in red from earlier, "Are not ones I want to spend the rest of my life with."

Shauna lifted her chin and squared her shoulders. "So, let me get this straight. You wanted to meet me because I have children already, not because of anything else?" she was starting to feel a-fronted. Was she not attractive in her own right? What kind of maniac wanted

Gone Dutch

a ready-made family already? She was now cautious and glad she wasn't holding a drink.

He smirked. "It was a reason, but I saw you arrive, and yesterday at the rehearsal…" His lip curled into a small smile as he remembered seeing her for the first time. "I just could not get you out of my head and I knew I had to get to know you." He closed the gap between them, wrapping an arm further around her waist and ever so gently, expertly kissed her.

It was like kissing Matt back in the school gymnasium all over again. Only, this was twenty-five years later, on a boat, in Rotterdam, with a very good looking Netherlander who had an action movie star's figure. Why was her heart all-a-flutter again? Surely she was past that now, being a widow. The little voice inside her head said: *You're no dead yet, hen!*

Harek ended the kiss, slowly. Shauna stood still, eyes closed, clearly lost in whatever thoughts he'd invoked within her. Slowly, she opened her eyes and he smiled at her.

"I . . ." she breathed and stopped talking.

He leaned in again to kiss her and this time, she responded more openly. Whether it was the alcohol, the champagne, his brutal honesty, her reaction to him or a mix of all four, she wasn't sure. What she was sure of was this: She wanted more of this. At least for tonight, she wanted to be more than a mother, a provider, a carer, a businesswoman, cleaner and business admin.

Gone Dutch

Harek groaned lightly as he reacted to her stepping in slightly, to the touch of her warm hands on his chest. In places she was soft and as he wrapped his free hand around the one on his chest, he felt her strength as well as her determination to do whatever was needed. The calluses on her hands weren't tradesman rated, but they certainly knew what hard work was! He nearly forgot where they were and why they were there.

He pulled back again, not wanting the moment to end but knowing that the Kransekage still had to be cut and shared. It was a tradition Fons had wanted to follow, since the recipe was from his deceased grandmother's cook-book. He'd told Harek that he wanted it done; before he swept his bride off to the honeymoon suite.
"We have one more duty to perform."
"Duty?" she mumbled, forgetting why. "Oh!" she breathed, recalling everything. "The cake," Shauna shook her head slightly, trying to clear the kiss-induced-fog. "Helene said Fons was determined to cut it and serve it to her?"
Harek nodded. "Come, let's do these last things, then we can do what we want to."
Shauna nodded. "More talking," she said, smiling. He grabbed the door and slid it open, allowing her to step through back into the noise.
The other men from the groom's entourage were starting to mill about and upon seeing Harek, smiled,

Gone Dutch

grinned, said something in Dutch that was clearly a tease and began moving a few tables around. A few moments later, the Wedding cake, or Kransekage, was bought in.

Rings and rings of almond cake were stacked up to almost three foot in height. The bottom layer was almost two-foot-wide in its own right. The decoration was in iced light blue swirls, with white sugar flowers, forest fauna and leaves. It was truly a work of art.
Shauna turned to Harek and whispered: "That's gorgeously unbelievable!"
Harek smiled and nodded as Fons gently guided Helene to the front of the table where the knife was. Taking it and placing it in her hand, they cut the bottom layer. Fons cut a slice out of the cake and fed it to Helene, saying something in Dutch.
Shauna turned to Harek as he called out with the other Dutch guests a reply, her face holding a confused look.
"He's promised to always feed, protect and cherish her," he answered, aware that the language was something of a barrier. He hoped it would be one that wouldn't stand between them for long.
"And what did you all reply with?" she asked, as a glass of champagne and cake were handed to her by Harek. How had he moved to obtain these so quickly?
"That we witnessed the promise" he said smiling. "It's a Norwegian tradition that we Netherlanders

Gone Dutch

sometimes use, especially if like Fons, your family hails from Norway." He took a piece of cake from his plate and offering it to Shauna's mouth.

Shauna understood exactly what Harek wanted when he gently offered her a slice of the wedding cake. She took the piece into her mouth, ensuring that her lips touched Harek's fingers.

As she had to keep reminding herself, she wasn't dead yet! She saw his reaction in his eyes as his pupils dilated and she smiled inwardly. She was getting a reaction from him for sure!

He leaned in and whispered: "Temptress" into her ear. She turned whilst he was still in earshot. "You started it. Sure you can finish it, *lad*?" She emphasised the lad word, implying that he was being too youthful and acting like a child. His grin got wider, revealing some of his teeth.

She had to admit, they were Hollywood standard, like everything else about him.

"I'll show you, lad, later" he whispered, touching her jawline gently.

"Promising things already, huh?" she asked, sending him a warm smile. His warm hands on her back pulled her towards him a little.

"Most certainly," he whispered, his mouth very close to her ear. He stepped back and looked up as his name was called by another person from across the bar. Harek waved and bent to Shauna.

Gone Dutch

"There are two more things we need to do before the groom and bride depart. Are you ready?" he asked, taking her hand.

She nodded and he led her to the dance floor, where Fons and Helene were standing. Someone shouted something in Dutch and Helene with all the male guests, left the room.

Shauna wasn't sure what was going on, until someone nudged her and told her she had to be the first to kiss the groom good luck!

"I what?" she said. The tradition was explained that every female guest now had to kiss the groom good luck and it started with the maid of honour. Fons looked at her expectantly, but a tradition was a tradition. Shauna walked up to Fons, bid him good luck in his married life and issued a warning.

"Treat her well, or else!" and she gently kissed the groom on his cheek.

Fons grabbed Shauna's hand. "I promise," he said, nodding and smiling. Shauna saw the sincerity in his eyes and was sure he would keep that promise too.

When all the kissing, good luck and hugs were over, the bride and the male guests returned. Helene's makeup didn't look out of place, but she went to Fons and embraced him. Shauna laughed. They needed to get a room!

Gone Dutch

She felt a presence behind her and she didn't need to turn to know that it was Harek. He bent down to speak lowly in her ear.

"Shall we dance?"

Shauna shrugged. "I'm no really one for dancing, but I'll try!" she said, allowing Harek to take her to the dance floor.

Once Fons and Helene had danced, others were allowed onto the floor and despite Shauna saying she couldn't dance, Harek thought she was pretty good at following his lead.

Shauna dipped out of the reception and found her way onto the deck a while later. Needing some cool night air around her, she had grabbed her cardigan and slid onto the deck Harek had taken her to only a few hours before. She breathed in deeply, holding onto the rail and closed her eyes. When was the last time she had danced like that? She couldn't recall Matt ever wanting or being able to dance anything that resembled ballroom, cha-cha but Harek could.

"Man, he can move!" she whispered to herself, not hearing the steps behind her until a jacket was draped over her shoulders.

She snapped open her eyes and turned to see Harek smiling. His tall frame hid the lights behind him, but it was hard to see much of anything else.

Gone Dutch

"Hey, you," she asked, turning to him. He looked down at her and smiled. "Thank you! I hadn't realised how much cooler it was out here. You can dance!" she said, smiling broadly.

He grinned. "My mother told me it was a way to get to the girls, so I took lessons for a few years," he said with a shrug. "It didn't pay off, until now."

"I never learned, but with you for a partner, I would!" She reached up onto her tiptoes and he leaned down to embrace her in a hot, passionate kiss.

She had to admit, he was an excellent kisser as well as a dancer. He didn't just thrust his tongue down her throat the way boys do, and this wasn't tonsil tennis. It was sensual, asking, gentle but above all, enticing. Every tongue stroke, lip nibble, sigh or groan gave way for the next. It was quite a few minutes before Harek stepped back. He was sure Shauna could feel just how much this kiss was affecting him. She smelled beautiful, a mix of ocean and Jasmin. If the alcohol wasn't enough to let down their guards, the dancing and feeding each other with food certainly did.

She opened her eyes and smiled as she looked up at him.

"You're a great kisser and dancer!"

Harek felt pleased as her compliment reached his ears. If he could swell with pride and pleasure, he would. However, he broke the kiss because he was feeling the

Gone Dutch

cold, which meant that it was time to go in. He motioned back to the party and Shauna visibly sighed.

"We both have duties for the bride and groom, unless they've snuck out early. Which, I hope Fons has. Then we are all on our own and we can leave too."

That made Shauna smile. Another kissing session would be great!

'Oh lord, I'm thirty-six and acting like I'm on the edge of seventeen' she chided to herself. However, when Harek held out his hand and opened the door, she smiled.

Fons and Helene had indeed, ducked out to their suite, as Harek had predicted. He spoke with some of the other guests and mingled. Shauna decided to do the same when it became clear that he wanted to tie his duties up before anything else. He was conscientious certainly, she thought. She wondered what was beneath that shirt. His tuxedo jacket smelled of sandalwood and spice. She breathed it in deeply, hoping that she'd be able to do more than that later on. A waiter brought over a drink of single whisky with a note to her table and left, smiling.

"Shona, will be back soon. H."

She'd correct him on the spelling of her name later on, but for now, she grabbed the whisky, settled back into the seat with his jacket around her, and enjoyed a few moments alone.

Harek saw one of the other best men and enticed him away from the pretty lady he was clearly getting

Gone Dutch

intimate with. "Lend me your key for our room. I need to grab a few things before you head into there."

Jon smiled. "Saw you dancing with the maid of honour. Things getting serious?"

Harek grinned. "As serious as they do at weddings. But time will tell."
Jon grinned back. "Here," he said, fetching his key out of his trouser pocket. "Bring it back to me though. Where's yours?"

Harek looked back towards Shauna. "In my jacket." Jon followed his gaze and realised that Shauna was wearing it. "Ah. Ok. Don't take too long, I can't wait all night!"

Harek grinned and headed off to their room in the quayside hotel. Ten minutes later, he was back with his bag and was returning Jon's key and asking a cabin boy which room was Shauna's.

Gone Dutch

Five

It was nearly twenty minutes, a single whisky and some watch checking before Harek returned. Shauna smiled.

"There you are! I was beginning to think you'd gotten lost!" she said, standing. Harek motioned for her to sit back down and produced another whisky for her and a much larger one for hims

"My roommate needed me to take more than a few things out of our room. That took longer than I thought to gather my things together."

Shauna suddenly wondered where he'd moved his things to.

"So, where's the bag?" she asked, looking around his huge feet.

"It is behind the bar, for the moment," he sipped his whisky and peered at her over the cut glass. "May I leave it in your room, for a while?"

Shauna laughed and her eyes sparkled. "So that's how it starts, huh? You move your things into my room and I never get them out?" She brought her glass to her mouth. "Starting as we mean to go on?"

She nudged Harek playfully, a smile in her eyes and on her lips. She sipped at the whisky, not taking her eyes off him.

Gone Dutch

Harek noticed she wasn't falling for the thrown out line he'd come up with. The truth was, Jon was taking the girl back to their room and he had grabbed more than clean clothes and his toiletries. So, he decided to her the truth.

"Ah, so he's going to take a pretty girl to his bed; what are you going to do?" she asked, knowing full well that his intentions were exactly the same, but in her room.

He leaned in and began kissing her on the jaw, just where her ear began. "I was hoping a very pretty lady would do the same, but in a very different room". He bestowed gentle kisses along her jaw and worked his way to her mouth, gently kissing and caressing as he went.

"Good job that's a possibility, isn't it?" she breathed out huskily. He loved how her accent made her words purr in reply.

"Shall we?" he whispered, taking his glass in one hand and extending the other towards her.

"Bold fella, aren't you?" she said playfully. She'd decided before she'd left for home, if there was a way to break the three-year sabbatical she was under, she would. She was ready for this. Heck, even the cards had hinted at this! The question was Harek aware of what he was getting into?

It didn't take long for them to grab his overnight bag from behind the bar and reach Shauna's cabin.

Gone Dutch

"The staff wouldn't let me bring this in here," he said as she unlocked the door. He smiled as she stopped in the doorway, gaping at the state of her room.

State implies that it was messy. It was far from that. On the side, two candles that hadn't long been lit, stood in front of the mirror. The sheets had been changed and the bed turned down.

The drapes were half-open with the voile curtain closed over the slightly open sliding door to a private deck. It moved gently in the late evening breeze. Upon the bed sat a tray, containing a dish of strawberries, some chocolate in a fondue with two wooden skewers. A bottle of sparkling wine in an ice bucket sat in a stand with the glasses hanging over a holder on the side.

She turned to look at him. "You organised this?" she asked. Just who the hell was he to arrange this on his friend's boat *and* at his friend's wedding?!

Harek nodded and motioned for her to go further inside. Shauna draped the dinner jacket on the back of the chair and looked around. The candles were scented, she wasn't sure what scent but the room smelled heavenly and floral as a result.

"You're conniving," she said, giving him a slightly incredulous look. Harek looked confused. Shauna chuckled. "Someone that likes to plan things on the quiet, usually bad things," she said.

Harek shook his head. "Not bad things," he said, picking up his jacket and hanging it up. He went to undo

Gone Dutch

his bowtie but Shauna went to him and stopped him. "Here, let me," she said as she gently tugged two different ends of the tie. In less than thirty seconds, the tie was loose and she had undone his top button.

"Thank goodness that is off. I dislike them but they're necessary with these suits." Shauna smiled and wondered where she could sit. The bed and the table were now covered in stuff, not all hers. Harek saw that she was looking around. Removing his bag from the chair, he pulled it out and motioned for her to sit. He should have got a chaise bought in, but it would be too crowded by the time it was in this small cabin.

"I'm sorry I forgot how little space these standard rooms have."

He smiled and went to move the tray from the bed to place it by the side table. Shauna quickly moved the candles a little to allow the tray to move and she moved to sit on the bed. Harek grabbed her hand and swung her back to the chair, like a move ending a dance from Strictly Come Dancing.

Shauna chuckled as he moved her to the chair and watched as Harek went to pour a drink, moving quickly and quietly for a man his size. A few seconds later he turned around to her and presented her with a small bowl of strawberries and a glass of champagne. Shauna smiled and settled the glass down, thinking that she'd had enough champagne for one weekend, or

Gone Dutch

maybe a lifetime. The strawberries though, were a lovely option.

"So, we're finally alone," she whispered as she bit into a strawberry. Harek grinned but the strawberry didn't last long. He watched as she seductively bit into it, devouring it in a few bites. He looked around, found the biggest strawberry that he could, and offered it to Shauna's mouth.

With a grin that would rival Morticia Addams, she gently took it in her mouth and slowly bit little pieces out of it. Harek chuckled as Shauna nibbled the last of the large strawberry then waved her hand between them.

"Enough! I'm pretty full from the dinner and the champagne!" Harek grinned and then turned to the open deck. "Come, let's sit outside."

From somewhere else in the room, he produced the two cut glasses of whisky they'd brought with them. Shauna grabbed a cardigan and her coat as they went to sit on her private deck. It was wide enough for two chairs, a small table and a trail of fairy lights.

"Where'd the lights…" she turned to Harek who smiled and shrugged. She chuckled but she held his gaze, softly. "You are full of surprises, Netherlander."

"I aim to please," he said as he guided Shauna into the tighter spaced chair. She crossed her legs and Harek averted his gaze slightly as the dress revealed the slits up to her thigh. Shauna saw him look away.

Gone Dutch

"You can look, ya know. Touching is for later."

Harek smirked. "You're a temptress," he said as he placed their strawberry picnic on the small table.

"I'm just enjoying the attention, it's been a while," she said, reaching across for another strawberry.

"I want to know so many things, but . . ." He let the question hang.

"You don't know how to ask?" Harek could only nod in reply..

Shauna sighed. "I haven't got something prepared as an answer; it's not something that's come up in conversation on the two dates that got to a second date I've been on since Matt died." She drank some champagne from her glass. Harek had seen where she'd placed it and brought it out. He sat back and waited patiently for her to start talking.

"Matt died in a motorcycle accident. His bike slipped on some oil in the wet and he broke his neck as he crashed into the kerb. It was instant. The poor woman behind him managed to stop and call the services, tried to help. She was traumatised when she was told he was already dead." She drank some more champagne, mainly now for courage.

"In the time since he died until tonight, I've been on exactly three dates; two made it to a second and that's as far as it has gotten." She shrugged.

Gone Dutch

"Three? Is that all?" Harek looked incredulous, as if he couldn't believe that anyone let this gorgeous creature go.

Shauna nodded, smirking. He knew how to react. "Three. The first one ran when I told him I had two boys; they were six and nine when Matt died, but a wee bit older by the time I started trying to date again. The second one wanted the boys to call him dad by the second date. Again, *that* ended there and then. The third wouldn't commit to anything after the second. After the third attempt to organise the third date, I told him to just not bother. I might have been more forceful than that though!" she laughed.

"That was about nine months ago. So I came here with an open mind, though I did put a wish up to the powers . . ." She looked up at the stars that shone brightly above them, "to let there be for someone who could love me, would find me, before I left." She decided that revealing the Tarot reading with her friends wasn't necessary.

Harek reached across and touched her arm. "I am sure your prayers were answered," he said, smiling gently. The same question ran across his mind yet again: How can anyone turn down this woman?

Shauna grinned, but it did not reach her eyes. "So, there you have it. My boys, Michael and Andrew, are twelve and nine now, but going on twenty! They

Gone Dutch

miss their dad. We have bad days, which are getting fewer, but mostly good days."

Harek nodded. For the next half an hour, they spoke about their families; she learned that Harek had a sister, Vayenn who was married to a Ruben with a daughter and a son, who Harek doted on. He'd been in a few semi-serious relationships over the years, the most recent had ended only six weeks ago.

"You saw her earlier" he grimaced as he shared some of the details. His face fell as he spoke of the betrayal and lies he'd encountered at her hand.

Shaun placed her smaller warm hand into his, connecting with him to remind him why he'd sought her out. That, and even at the wedding rehearsal, he couldn't believe his eyes.

Shauna nodded. "Bullies come in many shapes and forms. If it's that serious, you take it to the authorities or get lawyers involved. If it's not, block the crazy lady and go live life. It's way too short for stressing out about someone who doesn't have your interests at heart."

Harek smiled at her. She was right but he had needed to hear it from someone else too.

"I never like to hurt people," he said. "But I tend to be bull-headed." For the size of him, he could wrestle a tiger and not be bothered by it. At least, that's how Shauna saw him.

Gone Dutch

"No one in their right mind does. If they can't take a hint, be direct. If they don't get it then, well, show them the door."

"I like your direct approach. We Netherlanders, we try to be. It's not that easy sometimes."

"Amen!" muttered Shauna as poured out the last of the champagne. "I have a proposal, for us both," she said, handing Harek his glass back.

He lifted his glass slightly and waited. "To being honest, direct and to talking with each other." They clinked their glasses together and drank.

Once the last of the drink was consumed, Harek glanced at his watch. It was nearly one a.m. and they hadn't noticed the time slipping by. Talking with her was so easy, it made him calmer.

"Come, let us go inside, it's warmer and I think it might rain a little soon," he said, glancing at the small swells of water on the river.

Shauna nodded. "Yeah, it's a wee bit colder now!" Harek stood and helped Shauna out of her small corner and guided them both back inside.

Gone Dutch

Six

Shauna gasped as her ankle gave way as the sliding doors were closed. Harek somehow managed to wrap an arm around her to stop her from tumbling and close the door.

"Thank you," she said, very aware just how close he was to be able to kiss her; again. She looked away and tried to focus on her ankle, but instead, glanced to watch him move. He smiled and helped her to the bed, then sat her down upon one edge. The candles were only a third liquid and cast an even softer glow across the room.

Carefully, Harek slipped Shauna's shoe off, but didn't let go of her ankle. He massaged it carefully, firmly and after a few seconds, he looked up as she gasped.

His hands were warm, firm and sending electric currents through her. How can someone's touch on her ankle be so good, she thought? He smiled and removed the shoe on the other foot, doing the same. She moaned gently. That felt good! Shauna wasn't much for wearing heels but today, she had, for hours. Even though they weren't super high, only an inch, her feet were glad to be out of them.

Gone Dutch

She gasped as Harek's hands went further up her leg, behind her knee and back down. The touch was light, sensual and made Shauna's breath hitch again. He knelt between her legs, facing her and reached in for a kiss.

It was electrifying! The nibbles and tongue dancing sent sensations through them both. As Harek kissed her, his hands reached behind her and began unzipping her dress. Gently, he removed the fabric from her shoulders to reveal a lacy light blue slip. He removed that from her shoulders and slid it down to meet her dress.

He gasped as her hands suddenly began undoing the buttons on his shirt. Not once did their kiss stop and when her cold hands found his warm chest, he broke away.

"You did not say you were cold," he said, taking her hands in his and blowing warm air onto them.

"I didn't feel cold, until now. They'll warm up soon, I'm sure," she said, taking in the sight before her. He was broad, muscular and with a ripped chest and stomach, he was enticing! The chest hair wasn't overtly stated, its light brown colour matched that of his hair. His arms were broad, reminding her of wrestlers or bodybuilders but in a good way.

She uncoupled her hands from his and leaned forward, aiming to begin kissing his chest, but Harek had

Gone Dutch

other ideas and met her mouth with his own. He stood her up, which allowed her dress and slip to fall to the ground, revealing a very fine figure of a woman. Her breasts were full, her stomach flattish but not ripped as he was, though it was clear she exercised. The stockings were held up with a matching garter as was her lacy knickers. As he looked at her he forgot to breathe.

"You are incredible," he said as he reached in to kiss her again, taking her head in his hands and expertly kissing her until she too, forgot to breathe. She placed both her hands on his chest, feeling the muscles and entwining her fingers around his chest hair. Slowly, she moved the shirt aside, or tried to. He broke the kiss and undid his cuffs. He stopped removing his shirt when he felt her begin to do it for him, kissing his chest as she did so.

"I thought you'd have muscles on your back too," she muttered, kissing him in places he'd never been kissed before. If he were prone to swooning, he would have. She dragged her fingers across his shoulders and upper back, feeling each muscle as she went whilst mumbling gently and bestowing kisses upon him. As she came back to the front of him, he grabbed her gently by the shoulders, determined to root her to a spot. Gently, he walked her backwards to the bed and began his own worship of her strong, lithe body.

It was all Shauna could do to moan. His kisses sent hot sensations through her as he not only found

Gone Dutch

kissable spots (she knew the spot by her ears, it had been one of Matt's favourite places to kiss her as it made her ears ring) but new ticklish spots that turned into writhing spots of pleasure. She moaned as he began kissing her through her knickers, before removing those and the garter belt, which did not seem easy.

Shauna laughed. "It's a bugger to put on too," she said, "but I joined Helene in wearing one." Harek raised his eyebrows and said something in Dutch, but she recognised Fons' name.

"What did you say?"

Harek grinned as he kissed the inside of her thigh, making Shauna gasp in delight.

"I said Fons was a very lucky man."

Harek's tongue and fingers brought Shauna to a climax. As she calmed down, his kisses up to her breasts to remove her bra made her just moan. She rose against him as he gently took one breast in his mouth whilst he stroked her side, sending ripples down her spine. When she thought she couldn't take any more, he did the same to the other breast, laying on her other side and pinning her down just slightly.

She somehow managed to free an arm and drag her nails across his back. It didn't hurt, but it added to the pleasure he was feeling, and he knew when he'd hit a particular sweet spot as her nails would dig in slightly.

Gone Dutch

He stopped for a moment, realising he was still partially dressed. He began undoing his trousers but her hands reached for his and stopped him.

"Please," she whispered, taking his buckle, slowly undoing it and unfastening him. Her eyes never left his until she heard the flump of the fabric as it hit the floor. She tucked her fingers into the fabric of his underpants and gently pulled them down, making them follow his trousers and she grinned.

"Well, hallo laddie!" she said, grinning broadly. Harek chuckled a little in response but gasped as she firmly grabbed him and began licking the length of him. His hands found the back of her head and he ran his hands through her hair as she slowly enticed his erection to a fuller state.

Harek managed to break away before she could bring him to a climax. Even in Dutch, his obvious delight in her touch was clear. He held out his hands and moved her further onto the bed, lying between her thighs and kissed her deeply. She moaned as his kisses became deeper. He raised her hands above her head and held them there. He couldn't believe how right she felt, lying beneath him. He broke the kiss to look at her as he entered into her. She moaned and she raised her head to grab his mouth. Within moments, he released her hands as he began to make love to her. Her nails scratched his

Gone Dutch

back as he bought her to a climax and as she cried out, he joined her.

He lifted his head when he was spent, noticing she was quietly crying.

"Did I hurt you?" he whispered, kissing her. Lord, he hoped not!

She shook her head. "It's… been a while since…" He leaned in to kiss her tears away, grabbing the covers as he did so. He waited until she stopped weeping before he withdrew from her, rolled onto his back and swept her half across him in a fluid movement.

He stroked her head, her face and kissed her head as she settled down. Her breathing settled and with a smile on his lips, he too joined her in sleep.

Gone Dutch

Seven

Shauna awoke to someone next to her and she froze.

'Who? What?' she thought, then she remembered Harek, their talking, their lovemaking. She sighed happily. She looked upwards to see him still asleep and she drifted her hand over his chest, down his stomach and found his appendage, slowly responding to her touch, even if he himself wasn't awake. She smiled as she stroked the length of him and she kissed his chest. It didn't take long for him to respond, though sleepily.

"Good morning," she said, coiling a leg around one of his as she continued her ministrations.

"Good morning," he replied, his voice slightly hoarse. He grabbed her by the waist and hauled her on top of him. She felt so good as she lay on top of him. She moved from kissing his chest to kissing his mouth and she shifted her legs so she straddled him.

"Are you sure?" he asked, feeling himself get harder by the moment.

She pulled out of the kiss and looked at him with raised eyebrows and a light in her eyes. "Am I sure? You want to check in with me on that now?" she said as she ran kisses down his jaw.

Gone Dutch

"Yes," he breathed as he reached up to tenderly touch a breast.

She chuckled. "I just woke you up to ravage you again and you want to know if I'm up for it, consent to it?" She wiggled herself right over him and sighed happily as the full length and breadth of him entered into her again.

He arched backwards. God, she felt so good! He grabbed her hips as she began to ride him, slowly at first and he had to show her how he needed her to move so that he could enjoy their coupling.

He sat up after a few moments, changing how she sat on him, but it meant he could nibble her breasts, her neck and her ears. He loved that she moaned differently when her ears were played with. He could tell she was close to coming again but he was a little further off.

"Not yet…" he whispered, trying to get her to hold back for a little longer.

She answered him by reaching down between them, behind her, and stroking his testicles and she found the sweet spot beneath his scrotum. She stroked it, gently and it didn't take long for him to explode inside of her as her climax shook her.

"You…" he chuckled, holding her as the waves of their lovemaking subsided.

"What about me?" she said, accepting his deep kisses.

Gone Dutch

"You're a temptress!" he chuckled. "A gorgeous one," he mumbled between many kisses.

"Aye, I might be, but I'm a hungry one now. Someone's used up all my energy!" she chuckled. Harek smiled. He reached across to the phone and waited a few moments, then spoke rapidly to whoever was on the other end.

"Room service will be about twenty minutes," he said, hanging up the phone and pulling back the covers.

"How can you organise that at your best friends' wedding?" she asked, astounded by his ability to get what he wanted.

"It's easy," he said, smiling at her, kissing her as he went to the bathroom. "I built this boat".

Shauna's mouth dropped, and she had to consciously close it again. So that's what he did. No wonder his name was well known in certain circles in Rotterdam.

"I see," she said, smiling as she jumped back into the bed, waiting for him to finish. He popped his head around the bathroom door.

"Come, join me," he said, holding out a hand.

"I've never done it in a bathroom before," she said, giggling like a schoolgirl. Harek's face lit up and he dragged her into the small bathroom, before enjoying more kisses in the shower.

He was glad that they'd mostly cleaned up before breakfast arrived, though the timing could have been

Gone Dutch

slightly better. They were both still in the bathroom when the trolley was wheeled in, but they emerged a few moments later and dressed in clean clothes

"How much food did you order?" Shauna gasped. There were plates with toast with bacon, egg and cheese on top. Then there was all the fresh fruit and a large pot of coffee.

"I didn't ask if you liked coffee, I'm sorry."

Shauna smiled. "I have two boys; you bet I start with my day with a coffee," she poured a cup, added some milk and sipped it appreciatively. "I tend to drink camomile or herbal tea for the rest of the day," she said, sitting down at Harek's invitation on the private deck. She had to smile as he served her food, juice, fruit and as much coffee as she could take.

He smiled at her. She'd chosen a white and purple floral dress that whilst it swayed in the breeze, hugged her figure perfectly.

"So, tell me about your family. We skipped that part last evening."

Shauna smiled as she told him about her brother, his divorce, and her two sisters, one of whom drove her crazy. "I love Cait, but most of the time she riles me up. She has standards no one can meet and it's not the first time we've had to tell her to butt out of things that do not concern her. She likes to poke her nose in an awful lot!" They spoke about her other sister, Isobel, her parents and

Gone Dutch

the business Matt had that she was still working for, though part-time.

"So, what are your plans for today?" he asked as they cleared away the breakfast dishes.

"I was meant to spend the day with Ruth and Ellen, but I'd need to check what their plans are now. I suspect they have had their plans messed up a little as a result." She grinned as she went to find the phone and she quickly sent a text to the others. After ten minutes, only Ruth had responded with a "Sorry, change of plans. Spending the day with a hunk!"

Shauna grinned: she was expecting Ruth to bail, Ellen and herself had worked out what they'd do without Ruth. Ellen text back only a few minutes later, feigning a headache. Shauna replied with: "Does he have dark hair?" and Ellen replied back with a pokey out tongue and a "have fun yourself!"

Shauna grinned and laughed at the messages appearing on her phone. "Looks like I'm now free for today."

Harek grinned. "Perfect! Let me go grab an outdoor jacket and I'll show you Rotterdam".
Shauna smiled. "Okay. I'll put on some flat shoes and meet you out front in about ten minutes? I want to check in with home first." She checked her watch. It was early enough and this nagging feeling that something wasn't quite right had kicked in. The last time she had this

Gone Dutch

particular sensation as strongly as she did, was when Matt had died.

She was sure the boys would be up and her parents wouldn't be. She sent a text to her parents and her eldest as she put on some flat shoes. She then grabbed her coat and made the room as presentable as it could be, before heading out.

Her eldest replied as she walked through the boat, and she stopped walking to read it and reply before continuing.

Gone Dutch

Eight

She walked to the gangway and looked around for Harek. Where was he? She sighed as her feet touched solid ground, the knot in her stomach getting worse, and saw a catering van at the side of the building Helene had said belonged to Fons' family. The party had been on the boat, so why was the van parked over one hundred metres away from where the kitchen was? The bus-boy with the baseball bat was the first hint that something was seriously amiss.

"Oi, what are you doing!?" she called out, marching towards the waiter. Only, he turned to reveal a Vendetta mask on his face. Shauna slowed her march as two others turned towards her. They said something in Dutch, jumped into the van and drove away. Shauna rushed over to see who was being beaten up, to find Harek, bloody and unconscious on the floor.

Hours later, Shauna stood to work the creaks out of her back and sides. She couldn't tell the police why, even with some of the other wedding guests who had responded to her calls of help, what had happened. The CCTV that was usually on at the side of the building had been cut, meaning that the police had not many clues. A

Gone Dutch

woman came to sit down next to Shauna and she began speaking in Dutch.

"I'm sorry," she shook her head. "I don't know your language," she said and stood to move away.

"You helped my brother," she said, switching to staggered English. "Thank you."
Shauna sat back down again. "You're Vayenn," said Shauna, introducing herself and extending her hand.

"Yes. You were with my brother last night, at the wedding," she said. Shauna blushed. "And afterwards!" Vayenn laughed. "I'm glad. He needed some intimate company last night, he's been tense for weeks because of large contracts. It will keep his company afloat for years once they are signed."

Shauna could see the family resemblance. Vayenn was just over a year younger than Harek, with the same hazel eyes but much fairer hair.

"Did the doctors tell you how he was doing?" she asked, turning to Vayenn.

"Not really. I'm hoping that they'll come and talk with me soon. Mamma is worried."

It was another hour before a doctor came to talk with Vayenn. "You can tell us both at the same time. This lady is the reason he's here at all."

The doctor nodded. "He has a few cracked ribs, a concussion, a few other fractures in his left radius, a few broken fingers and a black eye. His retina isn't

Gone Dutch

dislodged, so he'll be able to see once the swelling goes down. Until then, he's resting."

Vayenn stood, nodding. "I'd like to see my brother."

The doctor nodded. "Yes, you may see him but only for a little while, please."
Shauna motioned for her to go through. She was family. So far, Shauna was just a one-night stand. Vayenn came out after a few minutes.

"He's asking for you," she said, motioning for Shauna to follow her.

Dutch hospitals were pretty much like English ones. Except that this wasn't the NHS, this was a private hospital and Harek had a room bigger than the cabin they'd shared only hours before.

The beeping of the monitors was the only sound in the room, but the rise and fall of his chest told her that he lived. She went to his side and gently took one of his hands in hers, the one that wasn't broken.

She looked at him and tried not to show how upset, frustrated and angry she was. It took her a few moments to compose herself before she gently called his name.

His eyes flickered open and he tried to smile as he looked at her. He'd felt her hands take his and hold it.

"Hej!" he said, trying to reach up to wipe away her tears.

Gone Dutch

"Hi, you!" she said. "Doctor says you need time and rest to get better. I'm sorry I wasn't there sooner…" She fought back the tears. He squeezed her hand and tried to speak.

"It's okay," she said. "Take your time. I'm here for now."

The doctors finally had to tell Shauna to leave as the evening shift began. Vayenn and Shauna had swapped numbers and Vayenn had put her number on her brother's phone.

"Your sister will keep me posted," she said as she gently kissed his cheek. He'd been in and out of consciousness whilst she'd been sat with him and given the beating he'd suffered; Shauna wasn't surprised he wasn't lucid a lot of the time.

She emerged from the hospital and immediately wondered how she'd get back to the boat. A car honked its horn and its lights flashed, but Shauna ignored it. Why would anyone in a foreign country be honking at her? The occupant left the vehicle and walked towards her. It was Vayenn.

Shauna smiled. "Thank you!" she said, glad that she had someone be able to help her get back.

"I'll keep you posted about my brother. But you, I think you need some food," Vayenn looked at her as mother's do with teenage children. "When did you last eat?" she asked matter of factly.

Gone Dutch

Shauna's stomach growled in reply. "This morning, when... Harek ordered room service."

Vayenn nodded, grinning. "He's a charmer, my brother, but he's stubborn and stupid. I think you will be good for him, though not quite in the way he anticipates."

Vayenn smiled as she guided Shauna to her car and set off to the Harmony Sea. Less than fifteen minutes later, they were back. Shauna felt alone but was soon greeted by a few of the guests, including the bride and groom.

"How is he? How are you?" gasped Helene as she hugged Shauna.

Ruth and Ellen were on hand too and in a second, Shauna found herself in a group hug, crying.

It took Vayenn and Jon to guide her back to her cabin. Helene wanted to stay but Shauna insisted she go to her now-husband. Nothing else could be done tonight for Harek. Her on the other hand...

She returned to the cabin and smiled. It had been tidied up, the sheets replaced again. Harek's suit was nowhere to be seen but everything else was as she'd left it that morning.

"So much for seeing Rotterdam," she cursed as she sat in the chair. However, everywhere she sat, reminded her of the evening before. Of Harek, his touch, the kisses, the lovemaking...

Gone Dutch

She grabbed her key and headed to the function suit. Someone else still had to be on board, someone else could help her chase away the feelings that now coursed inside of her like a tempest.

    Ellen and Ruth were amazed to see her and quickly offered her a chair as their pair became three.

    "Just like school," she reminced, taking a chair. It had been an action very similar to this, all those years before that had started their friendship.

    "How are you holding up?" asked Ellen.

    Shauna shrugged. "I keep thinking about what I could have done differently," Shauna ran a hand through her hair, "but the truth is, there wasn't much I could change. I think they were waiting for him, but he was maybe earlier than planned." She ran a hand through her hair again, changing its direction. "Being honest, I don't know why him or why today of all days. Doctors say he'll get better, but cracked ribs and broken fingers don't heal overnight."

    Ellen and Ruth looked at Shauna. "You spent the night with him, didn't you?" asked Ruth, practically bouncing in her seat. "You got a hot Dutchman. We all got hot Dutchmen!"

    Shauna scowled at Ruth. "Is that all you think about?" Shauna knew she was being mean to Ruth, but now was not the time to go on about the latest conquest, even if it was meant to lighten the mood.

Gone Dutch

Ruth sulked. "Sorry Shaunie, it's just…"

Shauna sighed. "I'm sorry. Just, I'm not being very good company right now."

A waiter brought over a large tray of food under a silver dish and placed it before the three of them. Shauna looked around and spied Vayenn near the kitchen, who smiled and waved.

Underneath it was a huge savoury pancake. "Pancake?" asked Ruth "With meat on it?"
Shauna smiled and helped herself to some cutlery.

"Pancakes aren't for breakfast here in the Netherlands, Roo. Eat up or starve girl." Shauna cut herself a large slice, slid it onto the side plate that had been left for each of them and tucked in. The others followed suit and before too long, it was finished with.

The tray was taken away and some cake with a pot of coffee was left in its place. Shauna looked around for Vayenn again, but she was nowhere to be seen. Shauna checked her phone, but nothing new had come through.

"He's not going to text you yet, dummy," said Ruth, scoffing.

"No," said Ellen, facing Ruth and squaring her shoulders. "But his sister might have heard something and shared it. So, shush."

Roo recoiled slightly. Ellen hardly ever told her friends off for anything, being the quiet one, she hardly

Gone Dutch

ever confronted anyone, but was often given the last card to settle arguments.

A few hours later, Shauna decided she needed sleep. "Are you coming back with me tomorrow Roo?" she asked as she gathered her things. The catering staff had cleared away their dinner and beyond a refill of drinks, had left them pretty much alone.

"I don't know yet, it depends on Dirk," she said, smiling. "See ya!"

Shauna and Ellen shook their heads. There was no stopping Ruth when she had a quest between the sheets.

Ellen and Shauna bid each other good night as they returned to their cabins.

"Shaunie," said Ellen, before they departed. "Do you want to share?"

Shauna shook her head. "No thanks El, I'll be OK."

Ellen nodded. "You know where I am if you need me," she said, and hugged her friend tightly. "No matter when."

Shauna nodded. "Aye, I ken." She made her way back to her own cabin and sighed as she closed the door. In a few moments, she was in bed, dressed as she would have been at home, not with Harek, in a t-shirt and a pair of shorts. Eventually, sleep claimed her, but not before

Gone Dutch

her mind had raised a maelstrom of emotions, should have, would have, could haves and guilt at her.

Nine

The alarm went off the following morning and Shauna forgot where she was. When she remembered, she sighed. She checked her phone and found a message from Vayenn. "He's doing better. Told him you had to return home today. Said he'll message you when he can hold his phone."

Shauna smiled. She wondered what kind of night he'd had, how he was feeling. She sent a message back, asking. It didn't take long to get a reply.

"Morphine helped. It'll be a few days before they'll let him out. He says Hej back (and I'm sure he sends you one of these)." One of those, as it turned out, was a kissing emoji. It wasn't much, but it would have to do.

S: Tell him I'll see him soon, somehow.
V: I know my brother, he'll make sure he does.
S: Tell him to rest up first.
Shauna paused before adding: I don't think he knows what that is.

Gone Dutch

V: Haha! So true! He's asleep now, will tell him your message when he wakes. Wees voorzichtig

Shauna had to look up the last words to understand them. "Take care."

Ruth didn't join Shauna for the travel home. Shauna was left to her own devices more as she travelled the Dutch motorways, then the airport. By the time she was at her own front door early that evening, she was emotionally exhausted. She tried to keep an upbeat voice due to the boys, but it didn't take much for her mother to work out something was amiss. Once the boys were sent to bed, Elspeth spoke with her daughter.

Shauna told all to her parents and Bryce, who had returned from a late shift at work. Shauna sipped some cocoa as her parents took turns to hug her. She jumped as her phone pinged and she read out a message from Vayenn.

V: He says hi. Hope you got home OK. He can see better, now and should be able to message you tomorrow himself.

S: Tell him I say hi back. (She also included a kissing emoji). And yes, I got home.

V: You can share those with him yourself later.

S: Looking forward to doing so!

V: So is H. BYE!

Gone Dutch

Shauna inhaled deeply. "We'll be off darling," said her father. "I'm going home for a rest!" Shauna grinned as she said goodbye to her parents.

Even though James and Elspeth only lived five streets away, it might as well be Rotterdam. It was going to be a long few weeks.

The knotted feeling Shauna felt disappeared three days after she returned home from work. It didn't take long to work out why when her phone rang with Harek's name flashing up on the screen. Her heart jumped.

"Harek?" she shrieked, excited to finally hear his voice.

"Hej, gorgeous!" She could hear that his voice wasn't great. It croaked but it was him.

"How are you?" she asked, finding a seat on her sofa and perching to talk with him. The housework could wait.

"I'm getting better. Slowly. I'm sorry about what happened."

Shauna gasped. "You've nothing to be sorry for. You didn't ask to get beaten up, did you?"

Harek chuckled but she heard him wince and guessed he had moved slightly.

"See, didn't think so," she said, answering for him. "I am the one who should be sorry. If I'd listened to my gut, if I'd been a few moments quicker to catch you up..." Harek shushed her as best he could.

Gone Dutch

"You couldn't have done anything," he said. Shauna smirked. There's more to her than even Harek had been told so far.

"So you say. Still, if I had been a few minutes quicker" she sighed, trying to let go of the guilt she felt. She pulled her shoulders back. "But it doesn't matter, it didn't happen that way, no sense in wondering what could have. I've done enough of that."

Harek winced. "Have you? Why?" he asked. On his side, he moved slightly to ease the pain in his ribs.

Shauna sighed. "Guilt, I guess. Wishing I hadn't been so helpless or been a few minutes earlier...."

Harek sighed. "You couldn't have done anything. So, let's stop going over what we'd change about that day. I'm looking forward to going home later. Though, my home will be empty now I've met you."

Shauna smiled. "Well, you'll have to get yourself better so I can come back and we can get that tour of Rotterdam done," she said.

"I know," he said. "I have work things here to take care of, admin stuff," he said, before Shauna could admonish him again. "So I won't be doing anything heavy with fibreglass," he assured her.

Shauna smiled. "Good. How's the hospital food?" she asked.

They talked about silly things for a while. Then Shauna noticed they'd been talking for about an hour.

Gone Dutch

"I'm going to let you go and rest up some more, so they don't keep you in again tonight."

Harek chuckled. "I'm all packed, waiting on Reuben."

"Ah," she said, not quite sure who Reuben was. He guessed she was curious. "Vayenn's husband, my brother-in-law."

"Ah, yes. You did tell me." she waited a moment, not sure if she should say what he was feeling. "I miss you" she whispered. How can she miss someone with who she'd only spent one night? The truth was, she did. She was sure he felt the same way, since he had called her.

"I know. I miss you too" he whispered.

"Take care, speak soon?" She whispered. She just wanted him to be near her, but it wasn't possible. Not right now.

"Yes!" he said, maybe more forcefully than he wanted to. "Reuben is here. I'll call you later tonight," he said, a matter of factly. Then the line went dead.

Shauna held the phone for a few moments.

He said he'd call later.

He'd be calling later.

That spurned Shauna on to finish the house chores and the few hours of work that she needed to attend to.

Gone Dutch

By the time Michael, Andrew and Bryce had returned from work and school, the house was gleaming. Shauna wasn't going to allow any distractions and by the time the boys came home, she was tired but very happy.

"What's up, sis?" asked Bryce as he walked into the place he called home. Everything chores wise, was done. Usually, Shauna procrastinated over chores, she always had. Today though, was very different.

"Ach, nothin'," she said, far more cheerily since her return from Rotterdam. Bryce closed the door to the hall once he made sure his nephews were out of earshot.

"Okay, where's my big sis and what have you done with her?" he asked, leaning against the door frame.

Shauna chuckled. "Harek called, that's all. He's getting out of the hospital today and it made me happy." Shauna smiled again and Bryce chuckled.

"I spend nine hours at work and you're happy you got a phone call from a beat-up Dutchman?" He was teasing, she knew he was, but that didn't stop her from scowling at her younger brother.

"That beat-up Dutchman made me smile and more the weekend gone," she said, waving a wooden spoon at her brother's chest. "And he got beat up for some stupid reason. But call him Dutchman again brother," she grabbed a wooden spoon and waved it in

Gone Dutch

his direction. "I'll shove this spoon where the sun disnae shine."

Bryce chuckled. "The sex was that good, huh?" he said with a straight face. Shauna whirled around at him and she poked him hard on his chest. "Aye, and I got to be happy for the first weekend since Matt died. Well, one evening. Don't knock it," she said, knowing full well Bryce's luck in the sex department was as long as hers had been. Now it was longer.

Bryce held up his hands. Standing nearly seven inches above Shauna's five-foot-eight, his six-foot three frame matched Harek's, though his body wasn't quite the Jason Momoa build Harek had going for him.

"Aye, okay! I hear ye," he said, chuckling. It was good to see the fighting spirit back in his sister.

"I have a question," she asked and continued as Bryce raised his eyebrows in reply. "Do you think Chris would let me train again?"

"Why?" he asked, allowing his face to show his puzzlement. "Because of what happened?" Shauna nodded.

"Aye," she sighed and bit her lip. "I don't think that what happened at the weekend is quite the end of it. It rather feels like it's the beginning." She looked at her brother. "You ken how my spidey sense kicks in." He nodded and folded his arms.

Gone Dutch

"I'm sure he'd love to have you back," he said, pulling his phone out of his back pocket. "I'll text and ask him, but I'm sure he'll be fine with that."

A few moments later, he pushed himself off the door frame. "He said he'll call you to discuss. And I'm going to grab a shower, work was a mare!" he said, grabbing an apple from the fruit bowl and calling up to his nephews as he made his way up to his room.

A few seconds later, Chris's number came up on her phone.

"Hey, Chris," Shauna greeted her old martial arts sensei and Bryce's friend heartily. She took a seat at the breakfast bar.

"Hey, Shauna," Chris sounded upbeat. "Bryce said you were interested in coming back to train. You okay?"

"Yeah, just, had a run-in with some idiots at the weekend and someone got hurt. It reminded me I've gotten a bit lax on my training over the last few years."

She could hear Chris smirk. "That happens, lovely," she could hear pages in a book being turned. "We have a ladies' night on a Tuesday, Julie would love to have you back in that group. Was there anything, in particular, you wanted to start with?" Chris remembered that Matt and Shauna had been quite the martial arts duo. If there was a style, they wanted to try it. Chris was never stuck on one style, he always encouraged his

Gone Dutch

students to try things, to blend them and make all the different aspects of the styles work for them.

"These guys were more into swinging baseball bats than anything, but disarming for sure."

Chris winced. "They can make a mess of people," he said, unaware of how much of a mess Shauna had seen on Harek.

"Aye, they do that" she agreed. "So you're OK if I turn up on Tuesday with the subs etc. The boys might have to sit and watch their mum get her butt kicked."

Chris chuckled. "We have got a waiting area and your boys will soon remember where things are around here. I'm sure they've not forgotten," Chris chuckled as he remembered her boy's energy and antics.

"Sweet. I'll see you Tuesday then, sensei," she said, aware that one of her boys was on the stairs now. Chris bid his goodbyes and Shauna turned to see her eldest, Michael, standing in the kitchen doorway.

"What's going on mum?" he said, sitting on another of the breakfast chairs.

"Just, got a stark reminder to keep up with my training." she smiled. Michael gave her a knowing look.

"Huh, Mum," Michael tilted his head as she stared at his mother. "I wasn't born this morning". Shauna chortled. The Greatest Showman was a favourite movie of theirs.

"And eighteen will be just fine," she answered.

Gone Dutch

"What happened, mum? I know you've told gran and gramps."

Shauna sighed. Michael was too perceptive. "Someone from the wedding got beaten up the morning after. Someone that… that I was going to spend the day with."

Michael nodded. "You've been smiling since I came home from school so I'm guessing he called?"

Shauna looked at her son, aware that he was as empathically attuned as she was, if not more so due to his age. He was just the spit of Matt at that age. The Matt she'd fallen in love with. Booted with her perception, she was sure he was going to break some hearts and stand for no-nonsense.

"Yes, he did. He's mending. And his name is Harek," she said as she went to make herself a cup of tea and begin preparing dinner.

"Who is Harek?" asked her younger son as he too came into the kitchen. She heard their stomachs growl, so she pointed to the fruit bowl.

"The man who I shared time with at Helene's wedding and who got beat up the morning after." Andrew stopped and looked at his mother.

"Did you kiss him?" he asked, slightly more grossed out than Michael about his mother kissing someone.

Shauna snorted. "Yes. What is this?" she looked between her sons. "The Spanish Inquisition?" she

Gone Dutch

chuckled. She'd always been honest and open with the boys about who she was going to date and how it had gone. Michael and Andrew then sat opposite where she was standing and waited.

"This IS the inquisition," she exclaimed in a chuckle, but told the boys the main part. Spending the night with Harek was left out but Michael, being an almost teenager now, worked out that is what had happened.

"Just, make sure he makes you happy mum," he said to her, later on after dinner. Andrew had gone up to get ready for bed and as usual, he'd read a little before going to sleep. Michael helped clear the kitchen down and load things into the dishwasher.

"I will." she smiled at her son. He reminded her of his dad. "Oh, I'll be going back to training from Tuesday," she said. She watched Michael's response over the edge of her cup.

Michael nodded. "Given what happened, that's probably a good idea, mum." He went to go to his room, then turned to face her. "I've been wondering if you'd be OK with me going back too. Is that okay?"

Shauna nodded. "I'll check with Chris, see if we can get the same times but in different areas."

Michael nodded. "Good night, mum!" he said as he went up to bed. She listened as he went up to the top floor, called goodnight to Bryce, and went down to his

Gone Dutch

room.   She sent a text to Chris about Michael joining her, then went to find her favourite sparkly wine glass, some red wine and settled on the sofa to wait.

At around nine o'clock, Harek called her.
"I'm in bed," he told her, confirming that he was indeed taking it easy. "I've taken refuge for a time at my parents' house, but I might only stay for a few days."
Shauna smiled. "Did you get much sleep or haven't you had a chance yet?"
Harek humphed. "I have ordered around like a naughty child," he replied, somewhat indignantly. "But my parents mean well." He sighed. "The pain is easing each hour and I can see colours properly again, so that is good."
Shauna smiled. "What's your room like?" she wondered what his childhood home looked like.
"Let me show you," he said and turned the video on for the rest of their conversation.
"Oh wow!" she said as he slowly swung the camera around the room.

From what she could see, he was resting on a large low level bed. At the foot of the bed was a chaise lounge. To his left, were tall windows with floor to ceiling curtains. Between two of the windows was a chest of drawers, an en-suite bathroom door was left open slightly, sliding wardrobes to the right of that. He

Gone Dutch

swung around slowly and she saw a desk and bedside tables. His entire room looked to be as big as a floor in Shauna's house.

"Do you live in a mansion or something?" she asked, somewhat awestruck.

Harek laughed. "No, but this is the retirement home I bought for my parents. Their room is like this, but on the other side. This is just the guest room as they have friends all over the world coming to visit them."

"You bought that house?" she asked. Harek flipped the video back to him and he smiled.

"They raised Vayenn and me. The old house, where I usually live, was too much for mamma now, too many floors between the styles of building. I found this single storey house and had the work done that mamma and pappa wanted. Then I took over the family house. The renovations there aren't yet complete. I'm going to love showing it to you and the boys when they are."

Shauna smiled. Her and the boys. The 'and' part wasn't missed, not by her.

She flipped her camera around to show Harek her house, or part of it. The living room, the kitchen, some of the office.

They talked for a little while longer until Harek yawned.

"I'm sorry," he said, shifting position in the bed. "These painkillers…"

Gone Dutch

"Time for you to go and sleep," Shauna said, blowing him a kiss.

He blew her one back, bid her goodnight and ended the video chat.

Harek leaned back and sighed. Damn, it hurt to sit up but he did not want to end the call. How could she blame herself for not being there? He was sure he was alive because of her intervention. He hadn't updated her with what the Politie had said. He hadn't told her that the Marechaussee, the military part of the Politie, had asked him more questions than he was able to answer. Whoever had wanted him hurt, had really wanted to make sure they weren't found.

He sighed and made himself comfortable in the bed. What he had found with his prospective contracts, wasn't great either. How can one part of his life start to go well and other aspects fall apart? He leaned on the side that wasn't broken, placing the other pillows behind him as best he could. Closing his eyes, he fell asleep almost instantly.

Gone Dutch

Ten

Shauna smiled as the call ended. She finished her wine and was heading to bed when her phone pinged. Vayenn had sent her a link in a message and she clicked on it to read about Harek's attack. Thankfully, Google translated the page from Dutch to English and she didn't like what she was reading.

S: He didn't mention the Maracheaussee. What are they?

V: Bit like your Serious Crime division, they're our military part of the Politie.

S: So he was targeted?! :o

V: Seems so.

S: Who? And why?!

V: Not sure. Sanne is being checked out.

S: Sanne?

V: Angry woman in red from the wedding.

S: Ah, yes. Saw her, didn't interact with her.

V: Best not to, she's a lot of trouble.

S: I saw that much!

V: Thought you'd want to know. Something tells me I should share things with you I would never have shared with Sanne. I trust you and I hardly know you.

Gone Dutch

  S: I'm glad you can trust me. Must be a Celtic Connection.
  V: Celtic Connection?
  S: Scots, invading Danes, England…
  V: Ah, I see. Maybe… Dutch aren't Danes, FYI. :P Anyway, I wanted to let you know. That is one of the better Dutch newspapers, worth keeping a link to.
  S: I understand. Good night!
  V: Goede nacht!
Shauna didn't need a translator for the last part. For once.

  They spoke the next day and Harek sounded more tired than the previous day.
  "What's wrong?" she asked, gently. She curled up in her favourite spot on the sofa, the boys were busy doing what they wanted to do most likely on their Xbox.
  "Just, dealing with company issues. I don't even know what's going on or why my contracts aren't renewing."
  "Really?" Shauna began to wonder if there was a connection to what happened in Rotterdam.
  "There's one order. He was willing to meet with me next week. I still hurt but the company might fold if I don't secure a few contracts for the next few years. Even two would secure us."
  "Where and when are they willing to meet with you?" she asked.

Gone Dutch

"He's at the Regency Hyatt, next week, but he's not confirmed any meeting."

"Sounds very posh," she said in reply, adjusting the phone on her ear.

"If he agrees, it'll be boring," was his reply. "I want to see you again, soon," he said, shifting slightly in his seat. He wanted to surprise her.

"I'd like that," she breathed back. "But your company is important." She shifted in her seat. "If I can help, I'll try to," she said.

"Talking with you helps," he said, shifting some papers on the desk before him.

"I try," she said, sighing. "It's getting late, I should let you go."

"A few more minutes, please," he said, settling back as a plan formed in his mind. "Do you own a cocktail dress?"

Shauna's eyes popped open. "Do I what?"

"Own a cocktail dress?" He asked again as he sat back, wondering what her reply would be. Helene had been very forthcoming with details about Shauna. He knew her birthday was coming up.

"No, I don't. I own dresses I could wear to one, but not something like out of Pretty Woman. I couldn't carry off a red dress like that," she laughed to hide her own embarrassment.

Gone Dutch

"Yes, you could" he replied, remembering just how her body had felt and looked like. "Fon's wedding shows you can."

"Thank you" she breathed. "But red just isn't my colour."

He chuckled. He now wondered what colour she would wear. "What colour would you wear?" he asked, being bold.

"I love purple, but a lilac or soft heather would work with me. Gold, black, navy, light blue. Red and orange just aren't in my colour spectrum," she said, taking a sip of something or other.

"What are you drinking?" he asked. He looked at his watch. It was ten pm his time, so it would be nine pm her time.

"An orange squash" she replied. "What about you?"

"Nothing alcoholic, I can't with this medication. But soon" he said. He was looking forward to having a beer but he was looking forward to lots of things now. "What do you like to eat, above all else?" he asked, making mental notes.

"I love Italian, but providing things aren't too spicy, I am open to most types of food. Just, I cannae be doing with spicy foods that insist on taking your head off!" she chuckled.

He smirked. Dutch food was not known to be spicy, though spicy food was enjoyed through other

Gone Dutch

cultural means. He could picture his favourite Indian restaurant in the heart of the old town of Rotterdam.

He sent a message as he spoke with Shauna, to his sister. She replied promptly. Now, he had his plan. Would she accept? Time would tell.

Tuesday evening came and Shauna arrived at her old dojo to be greeted by Julie.

Dressed in tight three-quarter length leggings, tank top and her hair pulled back into a ponytail, Shauna looked a little Lara Croft-ish.

"Not wearing your gi?" asked Julie, smiling as she booked Shauna and Michael in.
"I thought it would be rather rude, since I've not trained for years," she said, paying Julie the necessary fees.

Julie stood, showing off her black belt status. "Come on then," she said. "Let's get started. Mixed styles?" she said, smirking. She knew Shauna's skills.

Shauna smirked and then put on her poker face. "Everything," she said, beginning to warm up.

Two hours later, a shattered, hot, sweaty Shauna bowed herself off the dojo floor and finally gulped down a bottle of water. Michael joined her, just as hot and sweaty and as desperate for a drink.

"You've not forgotten much," exclaimed Julie as she and two other ladies bowed off the dojo floor.

"You're a killer," said another, smiling.

Gone Dutch

"I'm rusty," said Shauna smiling back at Julie. It had been good to train again. This was why Shauna had such an athletic build: she and Matt had trained for years, together, side by side.

A quick shower later, she was ready for her conversation with Harek. She emerged from her bathroom to see the light on her phone dim. Even diving across the bed, she couldn't get to it in time.
"Damn!" she cursed. She unlocked it and was about to check who it was (though she knew) and it lit up again, showing Harek's name.
"Hey!" she breathed.
"Hej!" he breathed back. "Are you okay?"
She laughed. "I was in the shower," she admitted. Maybe she could tease him from where she was. "Best I don't take my phone in there, I'm clumsy with technology near water!" she giggled, settling herself on her bed.
"And you're alone?" he asked. He closed his eyes, not that she could see that. He could see her in his mind's eye, naked in the shower.
"Of course I am alone in my bedroom," she smirked.
"How was your day?" he had to keep it boring, mundane. Everything going through his mind was to be played out in physical form only.

Gone Dutch

They spoke about their day, Shauna not telling him why she had a shower earlier in the evening than usual. He didn't ask either.

She asked about the painkillers. "I don't need them anymore. The ribs still hurt, but it's not as bad as the day after. Now that was pain."

She closed her eyes. She could still see him in the hospital bed, battered and bruised.

They spoke for a little while longer about mundane stuff, including his work.

"I'm trying to arrange to meet with him on Friday night, so I doubt I'll get the chance to speak with you until Saturday." He didn't like fibbing, but he wanted Friday to be something of a surprise, regardless of how his attempt to save his business went.

He could hear her sigh in reply. "I'll send you good luck vibes!" she said, twirling her dressing gown belt in her fingers.

"I'll need them, I think!" he replied.

Shauna looked at the clock. "I need to go," she whispered. She didn't want to, but she had lunches to prepare and the kitchen to clear down from dinner. She hadn't done that because of training.

"I need to rest too," he replied. His phone had binged and he was hoping it would give him the information that he wanted.

Gone Dutch

"We'll talk tomorrow?" she asked, unsure. He made her feel like a schoolgirl, talking with the good looking boy from the year above for the first time.

"Without a doubt," he replied. They bid each other goodnight, but both wishing it were in person.

Shauna was on a high after every conversation with Harek. Her boys commented on it each time the following morning.

"Did you get your call last night, mum?" asked Andrew, grinning like a teenager the following morning. "Did you make kissy noises?" He was hoping to embarrass his mother, but he should have known better.

"I did get my call and we did blow each other kisses." She blew one to Andrew, which made him squirm and hide under the breakfast counter.

Shauna chuckled and smirked. Michael laughed out loud, smacking the countertop as his mother turned the tables on the younger sibling. There was nothing more satisfying than a sibling getting bested by a parent to set another sibling off.

Shauna carried on with her chores for the day. For some reason, she was happier than she had been for nearly two weeks and she could offer no explanation of it.

Gone Dutch

Eleven

Friday was shopping day. She scowled as she drove up to her driveway, the boot full of food. Some idiot was parked over her drive entrance and there was a man with a cap in the driving seat. She whistled as she recognised a Tesla 6. What on earth was a chauffeur-driven T6 doing in front of her house? She motioned that she needed the driveway and the driver gave her a thumbs up. He carefully reversed and allowed her access to her drive, but only just.

"Gee, thanks!" she muttered under her breath.

She parked up and began unloading the car. Bryce came out of the house, leaving the door open so they could bring in the shopping.

"Hey, bro!" she said, as she handed him the heavier of the bags.

"Hey, sis. There's a package for you in the kitchen" he said.

"Okay," she said. She didn't look at him and he smiled as her back entered the house. He gave a thumbs-up to the chauffeur and grinned. Now, he needed to wait a few minutes. Placing the heavier bag at his feet, he rested against her car.

Gone Dutch

Shauna placed the bags onto the kitchen island and turned to see Harek standing at the entrance to her office. The kitchen ran the back width of the house and it had four doorways, so anyone could come and go as they pleased. Though, the office entrance was usually out of bounds.

It took her a few moments to realise someone was standing there, that he wasn't just in her imagination.

"Harek?!" she breathed, coming around to hug him. He met her in a stride, cupped her face in his hands and kissed her deeply.

"I've missed you!" he growled, between kisses.

"Same here!" she breathed, running her hands through his light brown hair.

It took a cough or two from Bryce to remind them both they weren't alone.

"How did… How the heck did you find me?!" she asked, holding his hand. 'He's here. Goddess, he's here!' she repeated to herself.

"It wasn't that hard," he replied, simply. "I asked Helene and Fons."

Shauna smirked. She'd have to thank Helene and Fons later on, but for now…
Then something struck her. "You said you had that meeting at the Regency Hyatt. How did it go?"

He smiled. "That is tonight, but he still won't confirm. I'd like for you to join me regardless. Let me

Gone Dutch

thank you for all you did that day." He kissed her again. "And to celebrate your birthday,"

She smiled. "You don't need to thank me and I can guess as to how you know that!" She then turned to her brother. "You're in on this, aren't ye?" she said, taking a seat at the island before she fell down.

"We've talked about you not being here tonight. I've got it covered sis. Away ye go."

"What?" she looked between her brother and her lover. "You two have come up in cahoots?" Bryce nodded, Harek merely shrugged.

"Bro, three kids?" she raised her eyebrows at her brother. "Are you going to be able to cope?"

Harek raised his eyebrows but Bryce replied. "My daughter begins her weekend stay with us, starting tonight. Seems Lynda wants to drop her off early." She knew that look on her brothers' face and the phrase. That was code for: Carrie's pissed at her mother again and her mother cannot cope.

Shauna shook her head as the chauffeur bought in more bags from her car. "Yeah, let's finish this chore off," smirked Bryce, following the suited gentleman back out to his sister's Leon.

Harek began unpacking the bags and looked at Shauna.

"Where do these…" he said, holding up two bags of pasta in each hand that Shauna would need two hands to hold.

Gone Dutch

She chuckled and made her way to the pantry cupboard.

"In here. Fresh stuff at the back" she said, smiling. Harek nodded. "Vayenn tells me the same. I do know how to unpack shopping" he said, smirking.

"How are your ribs?" asked Shauna, placing things on the shelves that Harek was handing her.

"They're still sore, but less than a few days ago."

She looked at his eyes. His face had healed. "Your eye is looking amazingly well-healed," she said, reaching up to touch that side. He grabbed her hand and kissed it.

"It is," he said, a matter of factly.

It didn't take long for them to put the food shopping away.

"Has Bryce given you the grand tour?" she asked as she put the kettle on.

Harek shook his head. "I was waiting for the lady of the house," he smirked. Shauna extended her hand and began the tour.

"This, we remodelled. It was partially in a lean-to, so we built the roof up properly and remodelled it to how we wanted it. We wanted it so we could entertain in here and spill out to the garden if the weather was nice." She opened the folding doors and Harek got to view the garden and the cricket pitch beyond the boundary hedge. One side of the garden was given over to growing food and a chicken run. The other side held a football goal.

Gone Dutch

There weren't many flowers in the rear garden. The patio deck nearest the house held a large picnic table under an open wooden pergola and half a dozen well-kept chairs. Near the house was a large storage box. The garden was quite functional and he could imagine many pleasant evenings were spent here.

He smiled. "You have green fingers?"

Shauna looked down at her hands. "Only if I forget to wear my gardening gloves," she said, pointing to a small basket on the window ledge that held a pair of gloves, gauntlets and two sets of pruning shears.

Harek smiled. He liked her sense of humour.

He closed the doors as they came back inside and Shauna took him to the office

"This is where I work, when I work from home."

There was a huge oak leather-bound desk in the far left, angled so that it commanded the whole of the room. There was a small table and two chairs in the corner nearest him and he pulled her into the office, pulling her close to him. "You put a spell on me, witch," he said.

Shauna froze, then followed his gaze. Behind her, in the corner nearest to the most northern point, was a dark wood Welsh dresser. The aloe vera plant on the very top of the arch sprawled out.

On the shelves below, were other ornaments of her craft, including the pot-bellied cauldron on the bottom shelf.

Gone Dutch

"Did I really put a spell on you?" she asked, smirking. She very much doubted he'd do something he didn't want to. "Or did you just answer Fate?"

Harek chuckled. "Even if you hadn't meant to, you did."

He leant in to kiss her but she pulled her head away.

"Does it bother you that I practice witchcraft?" she asked, glancing at her altar and tools. For her, this was going to be a deal-breaker.

Harek walked to her desk and picked up the Tarot deck that he'd spied earlier, when he had been curious, showing that it didn't bother him at all.

"No, it does not," he looked through the deck, and then looked at her with a small smile on his lips. Shauna relaxed slightly. Her being a witch and a widow hadn't fazed him.

"Do you read the cards too?" she asked. She didn't step towards him. She needed him to not reject her by coming to where she was. That gap was his to cross. Once he did, she knew she'd have let him totally into her life, as well as her heart.

He shook his head. "Vayenn did, for a while, it interested her." he turned to her. "I don't mind people who are witches, or people who read the cards. I don't mind that you are either, or both. We don't burn witches in the Netherlands anymore and even if we did, I'd keep that secret." He held his hand out and she reached out to

Gone Dutch

take it. He pulled her towards him and he pulled her into a kiss.

"Did you think it would bother me?" he asked, once she was breathless again. The look in her eyes told him it did. Her honesty backed it up.

She nodded. "It was something I had to show you. If you left because of it..." she paused. "I'd be sad, but I'd have gotten over it, eventually."

Harek smiled and lifted her chin so she looked deeply at him.

"I am not scared by it," he said, gently kissing her.

Shauna smiled. "Good," she sighed.

She took his hand again and guided him to the living room, where Bryce and the chauffeur were sat, watching television. The living room was long, the full length of the house and a good six metres wide. Shauna guided him back to the kitchen.

"That's the downstairs," she said, making her way through the fourth door towards the stairs.

She guided him up to the first floor. She pointed to another flight of stairs that went into the loft. "That's Bryce's suite. Large bedroom, en-suite and a mini kitchen. I tend not to go up there, unless Bryce says it needs hoovering and I have the hoover out. Usually, he takes care of it himself." Harek nodded.

"He's lucky you were able to help him," he said. "He told me while I waited for you."

Gone Dutch

"I'm lucky too, given what happened." she smiled.

"This is Carrie's room," she said, opening the door to show off her niece's room, changing the subject. One wall was baby pink, but the room was tastefully done to a young lady's taste. The dressing table, drawers and wardrobe still gave plenty of floor space for a pre-teen to utilise.

"That's your niece?" he asked, seeing a picture of Bryce and Carrie on Carrie's dresser. Shauna nodded. "She's only three months older than Andrew, so her having her own room was essential. I'm glad we extended over the garage when we had the chance at the start. It means that I get my own suite too, whilst the kids share the bathroom."

Harek smiled. She showed off Michael's room, who was getting to be Rugby mad. Andrew's room was next, which was Harry Potter in theme. Harek chuckled. "I've never read the books," he said as the door was closed.

"I can lend them to you, if you wish," Shauna said, smirking. The last room was hers.
It was a room Harek had already seen, mostly from one of their video chats but seeing Shauna's private room with his own eyes made him feel privileged.

Her bed was made up and Shauna stopped as she entered. Upon her bed, was a dress bag.

Gone Dutch

She turned to Harek. "You've been in my room already?" she asked, smirking. Harek stepped through and closed the door gently behind him.

He shook his head. "Bryce brought these up," he said, pointing to two boxes that lay next to the dress bag.

"I took a little liberty and bought you something to wear for tonight," he said. "The meeting still hasn't been confirmed, but I do have other plans for this evening," he waited until she turned to look at him. "For you." He walked to her bedroom chair, shifted her nightclothes and sat down.

"Oh!" she said, unzipping the dress bag first. Inside was a three-quarter length deep purple dress. It was strapped on one shoulder, cut at the legs and had many chiffon layers. One layer was sparkly and sat beneath the very top layer. The breast panel was rolled, maintaining modesty but hinting at more.

In one of the boxes, was a pair of shoes. They were low heel, black suede with a sequin pattern. In the final box, sat a torque necklace and matching earrings and bracelet, all in white gold.

"Oh my!" she exclaimed as she looked at them. The entire set had small purple amethyst pieces encrusted into them, whilst the necklace was a sweeping torque which made a figure of eight at the bottom and Harek stood as she lifted it out of the box.

"It's gorgeous," she exclaimed, looking at him then back at the necklace. He took it gently from her and

Gone Dutch

placed it around her neck. "Happy birthday, though, slightly early." He kissed her behind her ear, knowing that she'd melt. He felt her shiver and shudder as his touch sent fire through her.

"Do you like it?" he asked.

She nodded and made to take the necklace off.

"It is beautiful, thank you! I look forward to wearing it once I've showered," she said, carefully returning the torque to the box.

"We'll take them with us. Are you able to pack an overnight bag?" he said, taking in the smaller and finer details of Shauna's room. He noticed that she had an en-suite, made up of a walk-in shower, toilet and a double sink.

That threw him for a moment and Shauna saw the look he tried to hide. "Matt was a messy sod in the bathroom. He had products everywhere. He was worse than me!" she said. One sink was clearly not used anymore. Harek smiled as he imagined his own toiletries taking up that space. It felt right, somehow, though he couldn't understand why.

The sound of footsteps on the stairs stirred Shauna into life. "The boys!" she exclaimed, chuckling.

"Time for you to meet your toughest critics," she giggled. "My boys."

Harek smiled. "I am pleased to do so," he said, taking her offered hand as she guided them downstairs to the kitchen.

Gone Dutch

It took the boys not very long to realise they had a guest or two. The car had caught Michael's eye as soon as he laid eyes on it. Harek offered to show the young man the car, up close.

"A Tesla 6?" he breathed, his eyes wide.

"I believe in being economical," Harek replied.

Michael turned to Harek. "You're not going to hurt my mum, are you?" He was only twelve, very nearly a teenager but he was already the same height as Shauna and would be broad. He was a good looking lad, Harek had to admit. If he were to have a son, this is what he'd want.

"I don't intend on hurting her," he said, out of her earshot. "Has she been hurt badly before now?"

Michael shook his head. "No, and I'd like it to stay that way. The only way we're here now, is because she's tough; she's a fighter, strong. But she needs to be loved as only dad could have loved her. He's not here anymore. Did she tell you that?"

Harek nodded. He liked this boy's directness. "She told me how your dad passed. I'm sorry". Harek truly was. Losing someone you love in the blink of an eye changes you, hollows you out. Shauna deserved to not be hollow any more, he deeply wanted to change that.

Gone Dutch

Michael nodded. "I don't want to make this sound like a threat, but because, clearly you're bigger than I am. But I won't be happy if you hurt my mum."

Harek nodded. "Noted," he said.

"Okay," said Michael. "Try a sports car next time. Mum knows her supercars; well, most of them."

Harek smiled and stored that information for future reference. So, Shauna was a petrol head and a witch, added to what he knew about her. 'What a wonderfully complex woman' he thought as Michael tripped out over the T6. What would the child do with his car collection in Rotterdam? He couldn't wait to find out!

Gone Dutch

Twelve

Carrie arrived about half an hour later. She kept giggling as she snatched glances at Harek. Shauna lent in to have a word. "Hands off, missy. He's way too auld for you, you bairn."

Carrie sulked. She had her dad's dark hair and her mother's round face.

"Auntie Shaunie, you're a lucky lady!" she squeaked.

Shauna nodded. "So it seems. But anyway, behave. You're starting to embarrass yourself, and me!"

Carrie rolled her chocolate brown eyes, one of her best features, according to Shauna. "Sorry Shaunie!" quipped her niece.

"So, what's yer mum done to annoy you that you got dropped off two hours before normal?" Shauna knew that mentioning her ex-sister-in-law would bring her niece down to Earth. The question had the desired effect. "Eugh" Carrie rolled her eyes. "She wants to go spend the weekend with her boyfriend, but 'couldn't' arrange it for after I was supposed to be here. I don't like him anyway, he's creepy."

Shauna nodded as she grated some cheese for the pasta bake she wouldn't be joining in with. "Have you

Gone Dutch

liked any of your mum's partners?" asked Shauna. Carrie shook her head.

"Nope! Mum's taste has gone to pot." The girl sighed. "Why'd she have to cheat on dad?"

Shauna shrugged. "I have often wondered about that myself, kiddo, over the years. Being honest, I've no idea." Why her ex-sister-in-law cheated on her brother at least three times before he found out was beyond her. It was a deal-breaker and Lynda just didn't want to deal with the consequences of her actions.

"Well, it's pasta bake for you guys tonight. I'm off out."

Carrie, who was named after the actress Carrie Fisher, grinned. Didn't every male have a thing for Princess Leia once she was seen in "that" costume?

"I know! The Regency Hyatt! You're SO lucky Aunty Shaunie!"

Shauna grinned as she cleared the grater out of the last of the cheese.

"It might be a business meeting too, not sure yet. It's not just high-end food and polite chit chat."

"Daddy says he bought you a dress and stuff for your birthday!" she squealed.

Shauna smiled and nodded. "Wanna see it then?"

Carrie nodded. "I wanna see you wear it!"

Shauna laughed. "I'll have to take some photos, sweetie."

Gone Dutch

Carrie wasn't that convinced. "Can I at least see the necklace?"

Shauna nodded and smiled. "Sure. Help me finish this prep up then."

Carrie was as good as her word. One huge pasta dish was retrieved from the back of the cupboard. The garlic bread was placed near the top of the freezer. The jar of pasta sauce was placed on the worktop near the dish. Everything Bryce would need to feed the four of them for the main meal was set. Everything else, Bryce and the kids knew where to get it from.

"If there's any left after Michael's had his full," said Shauna, grinning at Carrie. "Put it in here and let it cool before it goes into the fridge, okay?"

Carrie nodded. "Right, come on then, let me go show you that torque."

Carrie wowed as Shauna showed off the torque necklace. It was a sweeping torque that wrapped itself into a figure of 8, or infinity symbol, with a large piece of amethyst hanging at the bottom, which would place it just below Shauna's throat.

"That's gorgeous!" said Carrie, stunned as Shauna re-packed it into her overnight bag.
"And a night at the Regency… I've been looking at pictures aunt Shaunie, it's amazing!" Carrie dragged out the "amazing" as only pre-teens can.

Gone Dutch

Shauna chuckled. "It should be. Not sure how I'm going to replay Harek for any of this though," she said.

"But, isn't this a birthday present and thank you?" Carrie sat bolt upright on the edge of her aunt's bed, a quizzical look on her sweet face.

Shauna looked at her niece. "He did say that, yes..."

Carrie rolled her eyes. "So say thank you and give him the night of his life!"

Shauna laughed. It was so easy being young. You just accept things as they are. That thought made Shauna stop. Why couldn't she do just that?

"Okay, but you're not supposed to know about the birds and bees stuff yet!" said Shauna, grabbing her bag and the dress.

"We've done sex education at school already and I do go to secondary school soon!!" Carrie rolled her eyes as if Shauna couldn't possibly understand. Shauna smiled at her niece. Sometimes, keeping things simple was the best.

Harek glanced at his watch and stood from the couch. He had loved talking with Michael and Andrew about cars and some of those in his small collection. The chauffeur was waiting in the Tesla and he heard Shauna come downstairs with her bags. He met her at the bottom of the stairs.

Gone Dutch

"Do you have a long coat?" he asked, taking her things from her. "You might need it."

"I do!" said Shauna nodding, remembering what was in her wardrobe. She danced around Carrie and headed back up to her room.

"I hope you realise just how lucky you are," said Carrie, standing with her arms folded across her, glaring at Harek.

Harek smiled. "I am beginning to," he winked as Shauna appeared at the top of the stairs with a long black dress coat in her hands. It didn't take too long to place them carefully in the boot.

"Now, you pair better behave for Bryce," she said.

"Mum!" the boys chorused. She smiled, hugged them, kissed them and headed to the car where Harek was waiting to help her get in. In a few moments, they were gone.

Harek watched Shauna as she sighed as the car was driven into Birmingham. The chauffeur, Johan, took the Wolverhampton Road down into Birmingham. Her shoulders were tense, her eyes alert and watching their route. He watched as she breathed out deeply when they reached a place called Bearwood.

"Are you okay?" asked Harek. He reached across and squeezed her hand. They were both in the back,

Gone Dutch

seated quite close to each other. Until now, Shauna's hands were on her lap.

"Just, I try to avoid the section of road where Matt died… It unnerves me when I come into Birmingham."

Harek nodded. This was the city she grew up knowing the most, he guessed. There were memories here he'd never be able to understand.

"To new memories," he said, taking her hand and kissing it.

She nodded, smiling broadly. "Yes. To new memories!"

Gone Dutch

Thirteen

They checked in and were escorted to their room somewhere near the top floor. The word room would be something of an understatement. The room was the same size as the whole of Shauna's house. The main doorway, and there were only two on this floor, brought you into an entranceway with a mirrored wardrobe on the left and a hallway console on the right. Beyond that, was a sitting room with a couch, two chairs, a dining table and access to views of the city.

There was a small kitchen to the right of the sitting area whilst the bedroom was up a small flight of stairs to the left. Shauna gasped as she saw the Queen-sized bed, silken sheets and an array of pillows arranged beautifully.

She turned to Harek as he tipped and thanked the porter, though she was sure he didn't need to; this wasn't America.

"He's going to do a few things later," he said, shrugging as if it was of no consequence.

Shauna went to hang her dress up, as well as unpack her small overnight bag. The bathroom, she discovered, boasted a whirlpool bath and a huge walk-in shower that would easily hold two people.

Gone Dutch

She smiled. "Harek…" she went to find him, to see him sitting on the sofa, his face crossed in frustration and puzzlement.

"What's wrong?" she asked, sitting next to him.

"Another possible loss of contract. I do not understand. They're suggesting that I sent them something yesterday, but I did not send any emails or correspondence yesterday, nor since before Fons was married."

He sighed. She took one of his hands in hers and kissed it.

Why did she, of all people, make him feel safe?

"Has he still not confirmed the meeting?" she asked.

He shook his head "Dinner isn't until quite late, but I have plans for us before that," he said, smiling. He closed his phone and put it down.

"So, what do we do until then? It's only late afternoon."

Harek sat back Knowingly. He was going to do this his way.

"Do you like the ballet?" he said, reaching into his jacket pocket and producing two tickets for the matinee production of Swan Lake at the Hippodrome.

"I've never seen a ballet live, though I've always wanted to," she said, smiling.

He stood, took off his jacket and held out his hand. He was going to treat her tonight, despite how

Gone Dutch

things were with his company. She had saved his life by appearing when she did. It was her voice that he had heard and had craved since. It was her that made him feel safe. No one had, except his mother. But, that's a mother's job.

"Then let's shower," he said, taking her to the bathroom and turning on the shower. It took a few moments for Shauna to realise he did actually mean, together.

She pulled away, heading for the bedroom area to undress. He watched as she undressed, wrapped herself in one of the huge fluffy dressing gowns that the hotel provided, and returned with her toiletries.

"Do I get to undress you too, or shall we make haste?" she said with a wink, letting the bathrobe fall to the floor and stepping into the shower. He smirked as he began to undress to join her.

They took turns to wash each other, Shauna being careful with the ribs on Harek's bad side as best she could, given that he was much taller than she was.

"What is your last name?" she asked as she carefully washed his back. She'd enjoy making it and him all dirty later.

"Have I not told you?" he asked, turning to face her as the shower washed off the soapy foam.

She tilted her head to the side. "I can't say that you have, no." She bit her lip in thought. "Nope, not a

Gone Dutch

clue." she continued, washing his pectoral muscles again.

"Van Meerloo"

"Is there a meaning behind it?" she asked.

"From the lake."

She smiled. "So, Harek from the lake, what other personal secrets do I need to know? I think you know all mine now," she said, smiling at him.

He paused to think as she began shampooing her hair. He held her hands, stopped her and carried on doing it for her. She moaned as he firmly massaged the liquid into her hair, her scalp before rinsing it off.

"My given name isn't Harek," he noted her eyebrows raised slightly, but then she schooled her expression. "I changed it when I was eighteen to my great-grandfather's name. I liked the sound of it more than Hendrick. I refused to answer to Hendrick even before then. My mother was not impressed with me."

Shauna smiled. "I think Harek suits you better, I have to agree," she said, allowing the water to wash away the shampoo.

He had to admire how she closed her eyes and let the water cascade her head. She was so close to him but he held himself in check. What he wanted was something he was willing to wait a few hours for. This seduction of her had to be the way he'd imagined it; it was his way to repay her, a personal gift.

Gone Dutch

Shauna opened her eyes and saw how he had looked at her. She was going to enjoy winding him up, so much so that she doubted they'd be able to return to the bedroom before they began exploring each other again.

After their shower, they dressed. Harek had once again bought his Tuxedo and he watched as Shauna grabbed some items from her bag and returned to the bathroom. When she emerged about ten minutes later, she was wearing stockings, suspenders and a skin-coloured strapless bra. Or something that was supposed to be a bra. Harek wasn't sure but he was sure when the dress went on, she looked amazing. His trousers were tight enough as it was and knowing that she was dressed as she was beneath that dress made him tent. It hugged her figure beautifully, her cleavage popped, making him stare and there was no hint of what he'd seen beneath.

"Shall I tie your bow-tie?" she offered, noticing that he wasn't putting the wretched thing on.

He smirked and handed it to her, sitting down on a bedroom stool. Sitting wasn't quite the word. He perched and balanced as she stood between his legs, smelling and looking amazing. In moments, she had the bowtie fastened, his collar tucked down and was smoothing out small wrinkles in his shirt.

He picked up his shoes and began to put them on.

Gone Dutch

"Err: what size shoe are you?" She looked at his feet; they were long and his shoes looked more like boats than shoes.

"In the UK, I'm a twelve."

She gaped, but only for a moment "I thought my feet were big at a seven," she chuckled.

"Your feet are dainty."

Shauna laughed. "Trust me, dainty is not a word that is used with me."

She went to her bag and removed the jewellery he had bought her. She put the earrings in and allowed him to put the torque around her neck. He helped her with the bracelet and she removed her sports watch. Turning her phone to silent, she quickly checked it then put it in her clutch bag with her watch and put on the shoes.

"Any problems?" asked Harek.

Shauna shook her head. "Bryce has plenty of experience with my boys and his daughter; he'll be fine. But, I did just check-in. I've been told to switch it off and enjoy myself." She smiled when his lip curled up into a smirk. Harek nodded and offered his arm. They were ready to go.

Shauna felt amazing as Harek helped her with the coat and she took his arm down to the lobby. They both turned heads as they walked through the reception area,

Gone Dutch

gaining a nod from the receptionist now on duty and the porter who had helped them earlier.

Johan was waiting with the car, who tipped his hat to both. Within moments, he had them heading to the Hippodrome.

Once Harek produced the tickets, they were escorted directly to the main box on the west wing, giving Shauna the view across the whole of the theatre. A few moments later, an ice bucket with an open bottle of champagne, two glasses and some mini chocolates were brought to them.

Shauna smiled. "I really shouldn't with the alcohol; not on an empty stomach." Harek nodded but offered her a half glass, which she accepted.

The performance was, in Shauna's view, amazing and breath-taking. She'd never seen Swan Lake live, though she knew of the story. The dramatics, the dancing, everything came together and it was beautiful.

"You enjoyed it?" he asked, leaning across and kissing her cheek gently.

"Yes, immensely," she breathed and sighed almost contentedly. "Thank you." Harek smiled. He stood and offered her his arm. Helping her with her coat, he too donned his and checked his watch.

"Shall we dine?" he asked. She nodded and smiled.

Gone Dutch

The Regency Hyatt had a floor for guests and their private diners, not just the function rooms for the weddings and receptions they hosted. Harek asked the porter to return their coats to their room and he merely nodded, took their coats and headed off.

Harek gave his name at the maître d' station and they were escorted to a table for two, lit by candles with a view over Birmingham that Shauna had never seen.

Shauna caught the eye of an older gentleman as she sat and she nodded a smile at him.
"Seems we've caught some attention?" she nodded across to the older gentleman. Harek turned, saw who it was and turned back to her, taking her hand in his. He held a thin smile.

"That's who I have been trying to meet. This... might get interesting," he said, smiling. "I apologise now if this becomes awkward. It was not my intention."

She smiled. She watched discreetly as a waiter attended the other table, looked to their table, nodded and vanished. Then, he appeared at their table, handing Harek a written note.

He smiled as he read the note. "He is inviting us for drinks when we have eaten. Will you join me in meeting him?"

Shauna nodded. "I did tell you I'd help if I could," she smiled and watched as the waiter returned with their reply. She nodded to the older of the two men,

Gone Dutch

and then turned her attention to Harek for the entirety of their meal.

Dinner was extended with dessert and a single coffee. Shauna declined the extra caffeine, sticking with her soda. She watched as the two men Harek had wanted to meet moved away to the bar section. She commented on it, thinking he'd want to know.

He breathed in deeply and set his shoulders. "Shall we?" he said, rising.

Shauna smirked. "Game on?" she asked.

He nodded with a smirk. That American term was well known to him too.

Fourteen

"Berend, Abbe. Nice to see you both. This is my date, Shauna. Shauna, two clients of mine, Berend and Abbe De Vries."

The waiter took their drink order and once the waiter had departed, the younger man began.

"I'm surprised to find you wanted to talk. Your email was quite clear."

Harek's jaw set. "What email was this? The last I emailed you was almost two weeks ago before my friend was married."

The younger man, Abbe, pulled out his phone and brought up the email in question. Shauna sipped her water, watching the older gentleman and keeping an eye on Harek.

Harek shook his head. "I did not send this," he placed Abbe's phone back onto the table firmly.

Abbe shook his head. "You did," he tapped his phone screen. "It says so at the top and that is your signature."

Harek shook his head. "I did not," Shauna noticed his jaw twitched. "I do not know what else to tell you, except that I do not communicate in that style via email."

Gone Dutch

Abbe looked like he was about to reply, loudly, when Shauna coughed, sensing that there was going to be a battle of wills. "It should be easy enough to work out if he did. May I? Please…" she smiled at Abbe and Harek clutched her knee. She squeezed his hand and he let go of her knee. Just as well, his grasp might have left a bruise.

Abbe gave her a puzzled look but handed his phone over to her when Berend nodded to him. Shauna put the phone flat on the table so Abbe could see. A few screen clicks and Shauna took a photo on her phone. Then she clicked through to find another email from Harek. A few more presses and she sat back, smiling directly at Berend.

"He didn't send it, as he said. The day the email that you're reacting over, he couldn't have sent it anyway. He was in hospital in Rotterdam, mostly unconscious." She took a sip of wine. "I know, I was there." She pursed her lips together. "How can I explain this in simple terms…" She thought for a moment, then smiled a small smile. "When an email is sent, it hides the path it took from the sent account to the inbox, but it's there in the background so you can reply to it. These two emails have very different paths. I'll try to show you."

She pulled up the older one, sent by Harek about a week before Helene's wedding, confirming timetables, expectations, start dates and courier information of the plans.

Gone Dutch

The second one was seemingly from Harek, but dates from when he was on morphine in the hospital with very different server paths hidden behind it.

"Here, this is the genuine one from Harek," she said, showing Abbe the older one and the photograph of the more recent one. "This more recent email, takes a very different server path, none of which are from his genuine email server and is only superficially showing Harek's company details. It's like phishing emails from the Tax office or PayPal." She pointed out other differences in the emails.

The younger man sat back, his lips thin as he looked to the older man, who Shauna assumed was his grandfather, maybe even father. They had the same bright eyes, the same jaw shape but otherwise, they were very different. Harek squeezed Shauna's knee and the older man sat back and chuckled. "You're quite the technical person, young lady."

Shauna smiled and acknowledged him with a nod. "Thank you, Berend. The truth is, I've dealt with this before and fairly recently too, so I knew what to look for. It's called ghosting and is very hard to prevent. It's how phishing emails work, they ghost or pretend to be from someone they're not. I'm sure you've had emails from Princes in Nigeria offering you millions?" Berend shrugged and topped up her wine glass, despite her protests.

Gone Dutch

"A toast," he said, raising his glass. Abbe retrieved his phone from the middle of the table and put it away. Shauna raised her glass, as did Harek. Abbe finally joined in, though his eyes still held a thunderstorm waiting to be released.

"To cleverness showing us the way," said the older man, and he drank.

"To cleverness," chimed the others.

He then said something in Dutch to Harek, who promptly responded: "In English, please. Shauna is not familiar with our tongue."

Berend nodded. "We'll stay with you. I do not want to be dealing with whoever sent *that*," and he nodded where Abbe's phone had been sat.

"Have you suggested or recommended Harek's company to anyone else?" she asked as the waiter checked on their drink levels.

"We have. What's the point?" said Abbe, still slightly bristling.

"My point is that if you have had such an email, I suspect others will have too. It would be a nice gesture on your part to let your friends and referred contacts know that you had received such a change of character but you've found out it was fake. As you said Berend, why do business with someone who is so unscrupulous?" She watched the old man carefully as she sipped some more wine.

Gone Dutch

He seemed to agree with her as he nodded in reply. "I certainly would not want my friends to do what I nearly did."

"But why do that?" asked Abbe.

"Why do what? Protect your friends, or send such an email as that?"

Shauna placed her hands on her lap. Morals were a good thing to go into battle over and she was right there.

"The email. Why send it? Why pretend to be someone else?" Abbe looked at Berend, then back at Shauna who had placed her hands back onto the table. Clearly, Abbe wasn't going to make this into a discussion on morals and ethics.

"That's a reason I cannot give you," replied Shauna as her tone exasperated. "Why do we have thieves and murderers?" Abbe nodded, though it didn't seem to make him any happier.

"I am glad you were able to show me how to do that with emails. Thank you."

Shauna smiled as Abbe visibly calmed down. "You're welcome," she said, taking a small sip of wine.

As they began to depart, it was Berend who first kissed her hand as she tried to shake his. Shauna blushed like a schoolgirl, though she had no idea why she reacted as she did to his gesture. They spoke quickly in Dutch then slowly he made his way to the exit. Abbe followed

Gone Dutch

after shaking Harek's hand and also kissed Shauna's hand. He winked at Harek and then followed Berend.

"What did they say?" she asked, rising and taking her bag from the back of her chair.

"They told me I was lucky to have you,"

Shauna chuckled. "They were nice. I'm glad they were willing to meet with you."

Harek shook his head. "Us. They agreed to meet." Shauna gave him a puzzled look. "If it were just me, they'd not sent that note. They would have, what's the English term? Blown me off?" Shauna smirked, her mind heading to the gutter for a moment. "I asked for a meeting even though I'd be on a date weekend with a beautiful woman. They didn't grant it to me until they saw you, I suspect they thought I was again lying to them, or something else." He leaned in and planted a small kiss near her ear. "You indeed are my good luck charm," he whispered.

"Just as well I was here then, isn't it?" she asked, taking his arm as he offered it to return to their room.

Gone Dutch

Fifteen

The room, when they returned, had music from Swan Lake playing lowly from somewhere, whilst a small platter of fresh fruits was placed on a table between the chairs. Rose petals were scattered on the silken sheets and across the floor by the bed. The small side lights were on, with lit candles cascading soft light in the bedroom, the curtains were drawn closed. Shauna smiled.

So that's what the porter was asked to take care of. Shauna began removing her shoes, but Harek shook his head, guided her to a chair, sat her down and removed them for her. He tidied them away into the bedroom and returned a few moments later, having removed his bow tie and his jacket. His top button was undone and he seemed more relaxed. He had his phone in his hand.

"Good news?" she asked as he sat on the other chair.

He nodded. "Some texts through from two others that Berend had referred me through to. They're disgusted by his update and have confirmed their contracts. We're saved, especially if they sign on Monday as they suggest they will here!" he said, leaning

Gone Dutch

forward. Shauna smiled and sighed happily as his lips met hers. Before she knew what was happening, he was kneeling between her legs, his hands cupping her face whilst kissing her passionately.

"That's twice you've done that to me," he breathed, pulling back for some air minutes later.

"Done what?" she whispered, caressing the back of his neck.

"Saved me," he whispered, kissing her deeply again. He broke the kiss and stood, taking her hand and making her stand. He held her close as music from Swan Lake reached their ears. Slowly, he began to dance with her in his arms. She rested a hand on his chest and tucked her head into the crook of his arm. He had one arm around her waist, he grasped her other hand, then sighed. Her touch calmed him and excited him at the same time. She brushed against him and he reacted to it. He looked down but her head was still against his chest, her hand in his, her eyes closed. He sighed contentedly.

The song changed and she broke away from him, aiming to sit down and eat some of the fruit. He grabbed her again and kissed her some more.

"I want you, Shauna," he whispered, grasping her hand and interlocking her fingers with her own. Her hand was much smaller than his, but it was strong. She reached up with her free hand, running her fingers through his hair, then she pulled his mouth down to hers and kissed him deeply. He began undressing her where

Gone Dutch

she stood. All it took was the strap across her shoulder to be slid down, and the dress pooled at her feet. She unwound her hand from his and began undoing his shirt, all whilst kissing him. She pushed the fabric aside and ran a hand over his chest. She loved that his chest hair was the same light brown as his hair, that he worked his body. He picked her up suddenly and she wrapped her legs around him to steady herself as her arms were flung around his neck. She could feel him pressing into her and suddenly, they both had too many clothes on. He somehow walked with her to the bed and he gently laid her down. He pulled away and quickly removed his lower garments.

"You are quite the specimen," she breathed, pushing herself back towards the pillows and kicking the quilt down the bed. He pulled the quilt off the bed, removed the last of his clothing and then began crawling towards her.

Watching him crawl towards her was intoxicating. He moved like a huge lion, his eyes had a hungry look about them. She began removing the holdup bra, but he got to her before she could. He had it removed in a few seconds and his hand was suddenly behind her head as he began kissing her deeply, laying her back onto the bed. She opened her legs and he nestled between them, kissing and murmuring words to her she didn't understand.

Gone Dutch

He kissed her jaw near her ears and she arched against him, moaning. That had to be his favourite spot on her. His lips moved over to her lips, to her other ear and slowly, down her throat, then the hollow of her neck to one of her breasts. He kissed the whole beautiful mound, licked and suckled on the nipple, making her writhe in pleasure. Then he did it to the other breast, teasing the first with his fingers. Her free hand ran through his hair in pleasure. He stopped and moved away, kissing her side and she jumped.

"Tickles!" she squealed, and she arched against him again as his kisses found another hot spot near her hips. He gently removed her knickers and kissed all around her hips, her groin. His tongue worked magic and before she could climax, he rose above her and kissed her. She was about to protest at tasting herself when he entered her.

Goddess, he felt amazing! She had no idea how else to describe how it felt, but she was surprised that she could take him in, given the length and breadth of him. He filled her, making her feel whole. As he slowly began to move, her mind became blank as more than their bodies bonded. He kissed her deeply and she felt his chest, twirling her fingers through the many hairs across his broad front. She used her legs to lift her hips towards him, making him go deeper and she moaned as he hit her g-spot.

Gone Dutch

The moan she gave out told him he had her at just the right angle. He grabbed her legs and bought them back towards her, so that her knees were nearer her breasts. Her cries told him this was a good move and when she breathed out "don't stop" he didn't. She climaxed but even then, he didn't stop. He eased off a little, keeping her in the position that she was in, but waiting until she opened her eyes.

"Shauna," he growled and she turned her eyes towards him. When she did, he increased his pace and he told her again to look at him as he brought both of them to ecstasy.

He let her knees fall back down to be either side of him and he kissed her as he slowly brought his full weight down on top of her. Her shudders took a few minutes to subside.

"That," she breathed a huge, contended sigh. "Was amazing."

She kissed him back and whimpered a little as he withdrew. He didn't move off her though, but somehow bought the quilt up over them and lay between and on top of her, kissing her, propping himself up on his arms. Eventually, he rolled over onto his back and he pulled her to him. He didn't stop showering kisses onto her and stroking her arms, hair.

Gone Dutch

"Where did you learn…?" she turned to look up at him, her nipples were still erect and they brushed against his side. "No, I don't wanna know."

He chuckled. "Why?" he asked, huskily.

"Because who you've been with before now, doesn't matter."

He smiled. "I've never had a woman in that position before. Until you, it was always the woman on her back, legs around me."

She looked up at him. "So you've never done it doggy style? Or been ridden?"
He shook his head. She pulled her head back and gave him a shocked look. "What? You poor boy! We so need to fix that situation." she leaned in and kissed him deeply. "But, later," she murmured as she nestled her head into the crook of his arm and he wrapped his arms around her.

"Is that a promise?" he asked.

"Sure is," she said, quietly. He looked down and saw that she was slowly drifting off to sleep. He closed his eyes, smiling in the candlelight.

Gone Dutch

Sixteen

The kisses wouldn't stop and he didn't want them to either. He moaned as the kisses became hot, as his nipples were sucked and nibbled. 'Best dream ever' he thought, then he opened his eyes. Shauna was lying between his legs and she was the one actually doing what his mind had thought was a dream.

"Moarn, famke," he croaked as she bestowed kisses near his hips. He was already standing to attention. She looked up at him with a wicked smile upon her lips. In a moment, she was kneeling near his groin and he pulled his arms up to behind his head. She wrapped her hand around the full length of him and seemed to be stacking her hands up his length.

"Goodness, how on earth did you fit this inside of me? No wonder you made me come as I did," she growled. In the next moment, her mouth was swallowing him. He moaned and arched backwards as he watched, causing more of him to fill her mouth. She knew he might do that, and moved as he did, so that she didn't gag. She played with him with her mouth whilst her hands played with his balls and she jerked the length of him. He had to be about a good ten inches in length and broad.

Gone Dutch

He was in heaven as she worked him, sucking, licking, swallowing him. His width began to increase as she brought him towards a climax, then suddenly, it stopped. As he opened his eyes, he saw her lower herself gently on top of him and he groaned in pleasure. He moved his arms to grab her hips as she worked out how he liked to be ridden. He did like the proper riding action, not just the grinding motion. He moved his hands to her breasts, tweaking her already erect nipples to a harder point. She reached behind them, found his balls and then found that smooth spot she knew he liked. He came as her fingers suddenly found that sweet spot. He swore.

"That's not fair!" he growled, grabbing her hips and staying inside her, flipped them over so she was underneath.

She chuckled and rose to meet his kiss. "Tough!" she huskily replied, taking his full kiss and giving back as much as she could. She found her hands pinned above her head and he lowered his head to kiss her breasts. He withdrew and turned her over so her back was to him. She rose onto all fours and looked behind her. He grinned at her wickedness and almost went hard again as she presented her rounded ass to him. He wasn't quite ready yet but moved into position behind and lowered his hand to find her deeply wet. As he fondled her sex, he pushed two, then three fingers as deep within her as he could. She cried out, begging him not to stop. He

Gone Dutch

didn't and he bought her to a climax with nothing more than his hand. She couldn't hold herself up and collapsed onto the bed, flat out, face down.

"Goodness," she said, as she turned to look at him. But he was full-on erect again now and he pushed her back down onto the bed. He placed himself between her legs and leaned in.

"Do you trust me?" he breathed into her ear and he kissed her ear's sweet spot. She nodded.

"Yes," she breathed and he smiled. What had he done to deserve someone as magical as her? He lifted her hips, kept her head down and placed himself at her entrance. In one swift thrust, he buried himself deep within her, her arse pushing against his hips. He easily held himself over her and he found her hands, then wrapped his fingers into hers. He used them as anchor points as he slowly but deeply ploughed into her again and again.

She couldn't move, she was totally at his disposal and it had been years since she had been loved like this. Matt was the only one she had been with, until Harek and she doubted she'd be with anyone else now.

His pace increased and she moaned in delight as again and again, he thrust himself home to the very depths she had to offer. As her climax built, her fingers tried to grab sheets, the mattress, anything but Harek held her hands and her body tightly beneath him. He

Gone Dutch

leaned into her head and she felt his hot breath on her ear. His breathing was shallow, quick and he didn't let himself release until he felt her shudder beneath him. She buried her face into the mattress and screamed in a climax as he groaned her name again and again into her hair, until he too, came in a flurry of thrusts and groans.

He slowly released her hands, giving them both time to find their circulation. He moved her hair to the side and kissed her cheek.

"Temptress" he breathed into her ear, not wanting to move since he was spent.

"Really? Me?" she moaned slightly. "You seem insatiable!" she chuckled, sighing contentedly.

He breathed into her neck. "You tempt me with this gorgeous body of yours," he said, stroking her ribs. He withdrew and turned so that he was now spooning her. He wound his fingers through hers again, keeping her close under the covers.

"Harek?" she said, turning her head to him.

"Hmm…" he murmured, nuzzling her neck.

"Thank you!" she said, kissing his hand.

"Why?" he asked, wondering what she was about to say.

"For an amazing evening, for making the night memorable,"

He nuzzled into her and murmured "Gjin dank" faintly as he drifted off to sleep.

Gone Dutch

It was a few hours later when they both stirred and they decided they needed a shower. Harek took Shauna's hand and together, they showered. Both were still spent and they spent time just showering each other and talking.

"You're sure?" he asked as they emerged from the bedroom to find room service had been. On the table between the two chairs, a breakfast platter was served.

She nodded. "I can't stay holed up in here, having my brains turned to mush all day. As appealing as that sounds," she sighed as sipping some coffee. It made him jealous. "I have two boys and I have responsibilities. Bryce has work to do later, his shifts got messed up. And Carrie has this weekend with us."

Harek nodded. "There are things I need to chase up, I was going to work here this morning," he said, looking around.

"I have an office," said Shauna. "You don't have to go back to Rotterdam tonight, do you?"

He shook his head. "I'll take my boat back on Monday."

She stopped eating and tilted her head. "Your boat?"

He nodded. "Yes, how do you think I got here?"

She paused. "Took a plane?" she said.

He chuckled. "You helped me save my boat building company last night. I'm not likely to take a plane unless the boat trip is too long, or there is a

Gone Dutch

hurricane," he motioned for her to continue eating "or other very bad weather." She watched as he devoured his food, though he chewed it, his appetite was rather large!

She loved the sound of his voice, his accent. It was deep, husky and sent shivers down her when he whispered.

"What about Johan?" she asked. He nodded.

"He will drive me back to the boat on Monday."

"And since you'll be at mine tonight, where will he stay? Here isn't going to be of use if he's meant to chauffeur you around and he's ten miles away."

He paused. "I'm open to suggestions," he said, pondering.

"There's a travel lodge not too far away if you want him to stay in a hotel. Or there's a foldout bed in the living room," she said.

"I'll ask him what he prefers," he said sitting back. Shauna gasped as she realised he'd finished his food.

"Did you even taste that?" she asked, trying not to gape at him in wonder. She wasn't even halfway through her breakfast. He simply nodded in reply and poured himself more coffee.

He watched her whilst she ate. She took her time and he wondered why she ate so slowly. He sent a text to Johan to organise the car and what he wanted to do for arrangements that night.

Gone Dutch

When they were finished, they cleared up, packed their things and checked out. Johan was waiting at the door to take them home. The two of them sat in the back holding hands and cuddling the entire way back to Shauna's house.

Gone Dutch

Seventeen

Harek had been impressed with Shauna's front garden when he had first arrived at her house only a few days before. There were roses, blue hydrangea and other flowering plants mixed in with various clumps of herbs such as mint, lemon balm and sage. The two huge rosemary and thyme bushes near the front door were quite impressive and the scattering of lavender added to the cottage appeal. It was cared for, that he knew and given that the back garden was turned over to the chickens, the small allotment and the boys play area, he was quite impressed. The front garden made sense now he understood Shauna a little more.

He turned as he heard a child's squeal and reproachful moans towards Shauna.

"You didn't send a picture!" cried Carrie as she admonished her aunt. Shauna stopped short and under her breath, he could tell she swore. He smiled.

"Carrie, I'm *so* sorry sweetie, I totally forgot!"

Carrie huffed. Shauna leaned in and whispered something to her niece that perked her right up.

"That'll be great! But…" she whispered something back to her aunt that made Shauna go rigid and stop smiling. What had the child said to get that

Gone Dutch

reaction from Shauna? Now he was intrigued and slightly more on guard. Bryce appeared at the door and ushered Carrie inside.

He decided to examine the garden more later, for now, he needed and wanted to be near Shauna.

"What the hell did she want?" asked Shauna as they stood in the front garden. Her fists were opening and closing slowly, which helped her keep her temper very much in check.

Bryce nodded towards Harek. "Take a wild guess," he said, his lips thin too.

"Who the hell told her?" sighed Shauna, finally letting the anger within her go.

"One of the kids, last night, before I could get to the phone."

Shauna nodded. One of the kids meant Carrie. She'd have blurted out that Shauna wasn't there and why before she had engaged her brain. Shauna shook her head.

"Great, just what I don't blooming need today. What did you tell her when you did manage to speak with her?"

"I just repeated what had been said. You were on an evening out with a guy and you'll be back today. When, I wasn't sure but before I needed to go to work. I ended up hanging up on her."

Shauna scoffed at the statement, then smirked at Bryce.

Gone Dutch

"Bet that went down well."

"Well enough for mam to call and say she'll be around this morning."

Shauna's shoulders slumped as she looked at Harek.

"I think we should've stayed in Birmingham!" she smirked, trying to put a good light on it.

"What is happening?" he asked. Johan had already taken the bags inside and had been given the rest of the day off, paid. The man seemed happy and said he would book into a local hotel for the remainder of the stay. He'd quietly driven away whilst Carrie had greeted and warned her aunt.

"I'll tell you inside. I'm so gonna need coffee." She scowled slightly. "A vat of coffee," she said, shaking her head and throwing her arms wide as she headed for her kitchen. Bryce shrugged and motioned for Harek to go first and when they were inside, Bryce locked the door.

The kids were watching Fast and The Furious on the TV. Shauna closed the door to the lounge to keep the noise level equal, then closed all the doors so that the adults were all in the kitchen, alone.

Shauna turned to Harek.

"It seems one of my younger sisters is going to be a pain in the arse today," she said, pointing to a portrait in the hall. Harek went to look. The picture was

Gone Dutch

of Shauna with her sisters and mother, in a women's only portrait. There was one with Bryce, clearly their father and the boys.

"Which one?" he asked. Discounting Shauna and the older lady, which left two other possible women who could cause issues.

"That's Cait," said Shauna, pointing to a woman who was smiling in her face only. "That's Isobel," she said. Isobel had a very similar look to Shauna, but stockier. "Cait's the one that likes to cause trouble, she always has, especially if she's in one of her phases, and I think she is given mam called." Shauna smiled. "I love her for the most part, but I don't get to choose my family. She'll probably try and get into your pants, just to warn you."

Harek's eyes widened at Shauna. "Why would she do that?"

Shauna laughed. "To cause trouble, test you perhaps. That's all Cait ever seems to want to do. She's very much like all three busy knights in a Tarot deck. Comes in, stirs things up, sods off and leaves you to deal with the mess she's made. I think the most recent time she didn't do that was when Matt died, but she must've been in a "take care of herself" phase."

Shauna poured coffee for the three of them that had been brewing for the last few minutes. Harek noticed she got his usual spot on with the tiniest amount of milk.

Gone Dutch

He noticed that she liked much more milk with no sugar: he'd have to remember that.

She signed and leaned against one of her kitchen counters. "Is she coming with mam and pa?"

Bryce shrugged. "I damn well hope so, since mam said she'd be seeing us this morning" he said, "Least they'll tell her off when she starts being a tit."

Shauna chuckled, then closed her eyes. "Argh!" she said in deep frustration. She put her cup down and ran her hands through her hair. Harek had seen enough.

"Famke," he whispered as he gently but firmly, grabbed her hands. She looked into his hazel eyes and he saw the worry in her soulful brown ones. "It will be okay. You've warned me, I can see she frustrates you, though I do not quite understand why. We'll play it simple and keep it light and not about her when she is here."

Shauna smiled and nodded, letting out a huge sigh. Only then, did he realise just how much stress Cait could cause her sister.

It didn't take long for the doorbell to ring. They'd taken the dress and suit bags, with Harek's overnight things up to her room whilst they waited. She told him that Cait would look through things if she could, so she placed the jewellery in her bedroom safe. Cait didn't know the combination, though she knew roughly where it was. The whole family did.

Gone Dutch

Bryce nodded to Shauna as the doorbell chime ended; trouble had arrived. However, so had the family police units: Shauna's parents were with her, which immediately calmed Shauna somewhat.

She welcomed her younger sister and parents, guiding them to the kitchen. The kids came to hug their grandparents, their other aunt, then they vanished up to Michael's room onto his Xbox. The kids had smarts!

"Mam, dad, let me introduce you to Harek. He was one of the best men at Helene's wedding."

Cait was immediately smarmy towards Harek, touching and purring over him. It didn't take long before Shauna's mother spoke up.

"Cait Jacqueline McInnes. Behave your damn self, you're being an embarrassment!"

Cait scowled but did as she was told, though she fluttered her eyelashes at Harek every time he happened to so much as look her way. Cait had worn a very short skirt and was forever crossing and uncrossing her legs to distract Harek. To his credit, he ignored her and focused on her parents.

Shauna quietly went to her sister's side as this behaviour went on, as her parents asked Harek what could only be classed as the inquisition. He answered their questions with grace and calmness.

"Cait, knock it off or get the hell out," Shauna growled quietly, aware that Cait might intentionally not take the hint in her tone of voice.

Gone Dutch

Cait turned to her and smarmily replied: "Whatever do you mean, sister dear?" Shauna squared her shoulders off, took a step back and ordered her sister to get out of her house.

Cait looked at her parents, to Harek, then to Bryce. The look on Bryce's face was enough. She didn't wait to see it echoed in Shauna's. Cait grabbed her bag, her coat and left without another word. Shauna stood at the door until Cait had walked away and around the corner. She lived with their parents, so walking five streets wasn't going to be a stretch for her. Shauna sighed, closed the door and returned to the kitchen.

Upstairs, Michael sat back triumphantly in his gaming chair.

"Thirteen minutes. That was quick, even for mam," he laughed. "Usually mum puts up with Cait for a good half hour before she makes Cait say goodbye!"

The others moaned and paid him in the sweets that they'd bet. They figured with the grandparents there, it would be a good hour before she showed herself up.

"I'm sorry about our other daughter," said Elspeth. "She gets a bit... jealous of Shauna and doesn't handle it well when she's off her meds."

Shauna scoffed. "Mam, that's an understatement." Shauna wanted to go on and say more, but there was enough tension in the air as it was. Booting

Gone Dutch

out your own sister from meeting your lover and boyfriend in front of your parents was just downright embarrassing.

"Why would she need to be jealous?" asked Harek, a little confused.

Bryce and Shauna shrugged. "She always has been. I never figured out what I did wrong to her. I doubt even she knows."

"Now now, Shauna," warned her mother.

"Mam, she's acted like that with anyone I bought home, even Matt. She grilled Lynda like she was a part of the Spanish Inquisition. Though, with Lynda, that was probably well deserved." Bryce chuckled at the memory.

"Anyway," said Shauna, taking charge again. "Let's talk about something else," she said.

"Harek was telling us about Friesland," said her dad, helping himself to another biscuit from the platter Shauna had put out. Elspeth scowled at him but he ate it anyway, knowing it would be his last one. Elspeth moved the plate back towards Harek, further away from her husband.

Harek continued his story of his homeland, the family house he was renovating, his business. Anything her parents wanted to know, he shared. His phone pinged and he politely excused himself to check on it. A few moments passed and he returned, smiling.

Gone Dutch

"Another confirmation, thanks to you," he said, kissing her gently on the lips. Shauna didn't respond the way she desperately wanted to, not in front of her parents.

"That's great!" she replied, smiling broadly. Her eyes sparkled and they explained what happened at the dinner the night before.

"You always were a clever lass," said her dad, smiling.

"I just paid attention when the tech guys explained it, dad," said Shauna, smiling. She felt Harek's hand reach for hers and she squeezed him tightly.

It was another half an hour before James and Elspeth McInness decided to leave.

"I'll have her call and apologise," whispered Elspeth as Shauna went to escort her parents out.

"No point. She'll no be sorry in the slightest," replied Shauna. "Not for about five days."

Elspeth sighed. "I wish you two would just get along."

Shauna signed. "I do too mam, but she's a grown woman, in charge of what she does and how she acts. She forgets she's not fourteen anymore and that we can't look after her like a bairn." Shauna held her mother's gaze. "Bet you she's stopped or reduced."

Elspeth held Shauna's stare, then sighed and closed her eyes for a moment longer than was needed.

Gone Dutch

She looked at her husband, a fresh fire alight. "Come on then, let's go deal with the brat."

    James sighed. "Ach, dae we have tae?" he asked, knowing full well that there was only one answer to that.

    "Come on!" called Elspeth, already twenty steps ahead of him.

    "Oh well, here we go again!" chuckled her dad, hugging his eldest daughter tightly. Shauna waited until her dad had caught up with her mother at the corner, before waving a final good-bye and then closing the door, heaving the biggest sigh of relief the world had ever heard.

    Harek smiled at Shauna as she came back into the kitchen. Bryce too let out a long, slow exhale.

    "I apologise deeply about Cait," began Shauna, but Harek just grinned and shook his head.

    "There is nothing to apologise for," he said, "You were not the one acting like a spoilt child."

    Shauna smiled. "No, that's true."

    Bryce checked the kitchen clock. "I need to go get ready and take Carrie out to that concert," he said, rolling his eyes and placing a hand on Shauna's shoulder, squeezing his sister in a half hug.

    Shauna glanced at the clock. "Oh, crikey! What time will you two be back?" she asked as she helped Harek load the dishwasher with the cups and plates from their gathering. He was domesticated, she liked that!

Gone Dutch

"Around midnight, maybe," he said. "I'll make sure I've got my keys," he said, grinning as he headed off to his room to wash and change.

"What is it Bryce does for a job?" asked Harek.

"Oh, he's one of the duty managers at the local supermarkets. But he usually takes the weekends Carrie is here off, to spend time with her doing stuff." They heard Carrie squeal as she was reminded about the pop concert. Her footsteps pounded on the floor above as she ran to claim the bathroom.

He knew his laptop bag was in the office and went to retrieve it. Shauna followed him and told him he could set it up on the oak desk.

"Don't you have work to do too?" he asked.

"Aye," she replied. "But mine doesn't have to be done on a laptop," she grinned. She watched as he adapted the plug of his to a British one and sat down behind her desk.

"This is quite comfortable!" he said, smiling as he settled into the huge chair. Shauna opened the blinds a little to let in some natural daylight, then left Harek to do his work whilst she did her usual Saturday chores around the house.

They heard Carrie and Bryce leave at some point, the girl's happy chatting faded away as they worked. After a while, she appeared with a fresh coffee for him and a tea for herself. She sat at the smaller table, on the

Gone Dutch

client chairs and unlocked her tablet. Harek watched her as she found a particular Tarot deck, a square piece of satin cloth, a Bluetooth keyboard and settled in. She did a routine of stretches and then began to type on the keyboard.

"Interesting," he said, from the corner of the room.

"It's an email reading," she said, smiling at him. He watched as she shuffled, riffled and dealt the cards. It was some minutes before she began typing her thoughts into the document. He smiled and returned to his emails. They worked side by side on their individual aspects for nearly ninety minutes before Shauna stretched and stood.

"Okay, time to sit with this for a while," she smiled. She locked the tablet and powered off the keyboard, heading to the kitchen. She left Harek talking on the phone in Dutch and decided to head out into the garden.

She had just about reached the greenhouse behind the garage when her phone rang. She knew who it was before she looked at the screen.

"Cait," she said as calmly as she could.

"Shauna," replied her sister, quietly. "I owe you an apology," she said a matter-of-factly.
Shauna sighed. "Aye, ye do. Accepted, ye big ninny," Shauna closed her eyes and sighed. Cait was a pain in the arse, true, but she *was* family. Cait sighed in relief.

Gone Dutch

Shauna could hold a grudge for months and often did with her. Not undeserved though.

"I hope he makes you happy," she said, waiting for Shauna to reply. Clearly, there was something else Cait wanted to say.

"So do I. It's early days, we'll see how it goes, aye?" she said, hoping Cait would make her point. It didn't take long.

"Do you want me to find out more about him?" asked Cait.

Shauna sighed. "If I want to know more about him, I'll ask him. The fact is, I'm not really that bothered about how many times he's been engaged, married or how much money he makes," she took a breath. "They're not at the top of my list of things to find out about people, most of the time. Usually, I work out if they're assholes. Your list comes much later." Shauna looked up and saw Harek leaning against the greenhouse door.

'Damn, he'd heard that!' she thought.

He smiled.

Cait lowered her voice. "Shauna, he's loaded!" she gasped.

Shauna smiled. So that was it. Money. Status. That was typical, bloody Cait.

"Is he?" Shauna feigned. She had already worked out he was quite well off; the car, the chauffeur, the Hyatt room, the ballet box office, not to mention the

Gone Dutch

dress and jewellery. "I hadn't figured that out already! But as I said, I'm not really interested in the numbers, though I'll take a wild guess that since it's been about three hours since I told you to go, you've done a full internet search on him."

Shauna shook her head. Cait didn't reply. "I thought so," said Shauna. "Go take yer meds. Bye Cait!" she hung up on her sister. She sighed and looked at Harek. "Some apology that bloody was!" Shauna wanted to throw her phone but Harek was standing before her and instantly hugged her tight.

"Ssshhh…" he whispered into her hair. "Kalm, famke, kalm," he whispered, over and over. He stroked her hair and rocked her gently until the fists stopped being hung at her side and her arms wrapped around him. She didn't need Google translate for that phrase.

Shauna sighed about ten minutes later, finally letting the rage of her sister's actions, vanish in a breeze. Harek hadn't moved, but he hadn't stopped stroking her hair or murmuring his calm phrase at her.

"Thank you," she said, trying to step away from him. He held her fast to him, not letting her go quite just yet.

"Err…" she said, looking up at him. "You can let me go now," she smiled.

Gone Dutch

Harek nodded. "I could, but you're hiding something obvious." Shauna wondered for a moment, then felt him press into her.

"Told you, incorrigible!" her chuckle increased and it became an outright laugh. Harek let her go as he too, chuckling at his own misfortune.

"We'll deal with your one-track mind later on," she said. "I need to get back inside, the kids…" He nodded and backed out of the greenhouse. Shauna was surprised he fit into it, though she wasn't surprised he did so carefully. He could only just stand up in it.

He had plenty of time to look around the small greenhouse as he held Shauna. The smell of her was enough to make him react but given that her hands had once again curled into fists, he decided he'd hold her until her anger diminished. He'd paid particular attention on the way out here to certain certificates on the wall in her office, items he hadn't paid attention to before. He was quite impressed by those and now understood what she meant when she said she was frustrated by being a few moments slower to reach his side that fateful morning. He was pretty sure more of his assailants would be quite seriously injured. He wasn't much for fighting, he preferred to watch such sports, not join in, but he appreciated all forms of fitness.

Gone Dutch

The greenhouse, he observed, was well used. A seed tray rack at the back housed trays that were now out of use, but the inner beds held cucumbers and peppers. Outside, in huge pots, grew tomatoes and some very healthy rhubarb roots were in full growth nearby. The greenhouse was the other side of the growing patch but it was in a heat trap. Inside the glass, Shauna was taking care of cuttings. Or maybe that's what she'd set out here to do. Then he noticed the automated watering system and realised she was checking on things in general. She had swirled past him a few moments before and he caught sight of her at the chickens. He watched as she threw in some corn from the food bin and collected eggs. He smiled. Fresh eggs were just the best.He heard Michael calling her from the house and he decided it was probably now safe enough to move back inside. He looked at the plants growing nice and healthy, fresh and vibrant. There were bunches of herbs drying from a length string in the greenhouse and if she weren't Celtic, she'd be Dutch, he decided. She was clearly someone that had similar opinions about the planet as he did. He smiled as he slid the greenhouse door over to go inside.

Gone Dutch

Eighteen

The kids were hungry, famished, complaining. At least, that's what they claimed: loudly. Shauna checked the clock and smiled.

"You kids ken the rules. Fruit and a biscuit. I'll delay dinner by half an hour, but no more." She pointed to the fruit bowl and the kids whined. Harek smiled. How often had he and his sister tried that trick on his parents? He hadn't realised it was something that was not unique to just the Netherlands. The kids thought that having him there would make Shauna more playable. How she held her nerve with them, amazed him.

Shauna chuckled as Andrew was the last to leave, winking at his mum.

"That child is as subtle as a ton of bricks!" she said, smiling at Harek. He'd seen the look Andrew had given her and he smiled. The child was direct, that was for sure!

"So, what is for dinner? Can I help?" he asked. Shauna looked up at him. "How about Hunter's chicken with potato wedges and vegetables?"

Harek nodded. "How can I help?" he asked, coming up behind her and kissing her right behind her ear. She shivered and turned to him.

Gone Dutch

"Behave whilst the kids are around," she giggled. "And yes, if you can wash up and grate the cheese, that'll be helpful." He kissed her forehead and went to wash his hands. Shauna pulled out the grater tower, the small block of cheese and a rather large bowl. He grated whilst she washed up and put the oven on to warm through.

In less than fifteen minutes, they had dinner prepared and in the oven. He was astounded that it didn't take much for the meal to be cooked. Chicken breasts were placed in the pan with bacon on top and a lump of brie beneath the bacon. Shauna made enough for the five of them, allocating Harek two portions of hunters chicken, having seen how much he ate at breakfast she was sure he'd be hungry. As the timer went off to signify the next stage, he noticed that she wasn't putting the wedges into the oven.

He watched from the breakfast bar as she finished the hunters chicken and returned it to the oven, then began cooking the wedges in an air-frier. The vegetables were fresh from the garden and whilst the main parts cooked, she sat down to begin preparing the vegetables. He chuckled, washed his hands again and grabbed another knife to begin helping her.

Together, they sat and chopped carrots, peeled sweetcorn cobs and tailed some mange-tout.

Gone Dutch

"Is there anything you don't like to eat?" she asked, suddenly aware that he may not like what she had planned.

He thought. "Not really. I eat a lot of different foods," he smiled. "There's nothing here I won't eat. You?"

She pondered. "Not keen on spam. Or tuna. Really don't like tuna. Other than that… I think I'm okay. I eat congealed pigs' blood in batter and offal in a sheep's stomach, so I can't claim to be a fussy eater." She held a poker face, but her nostrils flared slightly.

Harek stopped. "Congealed pigs blood? Offal in sheep stomach!" He thought for a moment. "Ah, blood pudding and Haggis!" he smiled and laughed.

Shauna finally chuckled too. "Aye, black pudding to us Scots. So no, I'm really not a fussy eater." She smiled.

They spoke of their favourite and least favourite foods whilst the dinner cooked. Shauna's phone pinged and she quickly checked it.

She looked at Harek. "There's one more sister to meet if you're up for it?" she said.
Harek nodded. Might as well get the whole meet and greet over with, he couldn't best Cait's little display earlier, nor did he want to.

"Okay, good. I've got a video chat with her around eight, if that's okay?"

Gone Dutch

He nodded. He wasn't planning on doing much until the kids went to bed anyway and any plans he had involved Shauna, her bedroom and the bed.

He flung her a smile as the timer went off, indicating that dinner was about ready.

He set the table as she used the house's smart speakers to call the kids to dinner. 'Smart' he thought. He'd have to suggest that system to Vayenn.

Dinner was a noisy affair with the kids chattering about the movie they watched, the games they played, who cheated or did something out of the rules. Harek had never seen anything like it, his niece and nephew weren't this loud he was sure!

Shauna laughed as silence descended on the kitchen again nearly forty minutes later.

"They're comfortable around you, that's good!" she said, clearing away the plates and preparing the dishwasher. Harek quietly helped her.

"What's that sound?" he said, leaning in and cocking his head. "Oh, silence!" he chuckled.

Shauna smirked and as she bent down to put plates in, he caught sight of her cleavage.

She saw that he was looking and shimmied her top half, giggling. He reached out to grab her but she backed away, wagging her finger at him.

"Kids!" she hissed, glancing at the hall door.

Gone Dutch

"Pleagje!" he growled back, grinning. He'd get her later.

They cleared things away and set the dishwasher going, then settled into the office. It was time to meet the last sister.

Shauna clicked on a link or two via her email and a Zoom chat began. It took all of three seconds before a lady, the spit of Shauna perhaps four years earlier, appeared on the tablet screen.

"Shauna!" squealed the other lady.

"Hey Izzy!" smiled Shauna, sitting back in her chair. She'd made Harek sit in the bigger chair but the tablet was turned to her for now.

"How are things?" asked Izzy, sitting back in her chair.

"Ach, they're good!" Shauna smiled. Izzy leaned forwards.

"Who is he?!" Izzy could tell that Shauna was happier.

Shauna laughed, throwing her head back. When she stopped, she wiped her eyes. "Izzy, you dinnae miss a trick sis!"

Izzy giggled. "Nope! Had you to train me and this job... Need my wits about me!" she said.

"Izzy, meet Harek. Harek, this is my youngest sister, Isobel. Or, as we call her, Izzy."

Gone Dutch

Shauna turned the tablet so that Harek was in view. Izzy gaped for a moment, then remembered to shut her mouth.

"Evening Harek!" chimed Izzy from where she was. "Hey, Shauna, protect him from Cait!"

Shauna winced at her youngest sister's words. Izzy saw her reaction.

"Oh, too late!" giggled Izzy. "Is she still alive?" she fake whispered, sitting back in her chair.

"Just about. I booted her out of the house. You ken she ran a full Internet search on him afterwards?" The last question was one of incredulity and more of a statement. Izzy gasped.

"She what?" Shauna nodded. Izzy's jaw dropped. "No way!"

"She damn well did."

Izzy was about to say something, then stopped herself. "I was going to swear, but I won't. Do mam and pa ken?" asked Izzy.

"Dinnae know. Even if they do, what are they going to be able to do? She's done it already. They'll no boot her oot, ye ken she has nowhere else to go and she can't look after herself long term."

Harek sat back and let the sisters catch up. The dynamic with Izzy and Shauna was similar to that with Bryce. It was clear that Cait was the odd one out of the four of them. It intrigued him that Shauna claimed Cait couldn't look after herself very well. He'd have to ask

Gone Dutch

about that, knowing it involved medication but at another time.

Izzy turned her attention to Harek and began asking questions. She also dropped a few hints about Shauna, which Shauna told her younger sister off for.

"Don't you be sharing my secrets, missy!" chuckled Shauna. Harek placed a hand on Shauna's knee and she wrapped her fingers through his.

"How's... Is it Dave?" asked Shauna. Izzy shook her head.

"He's out of the picture. Useless, good for nothing... I'm taking a break from "men" for a bit." Shauna chuckled that the word "men" was in inverted speech marks with her fingers.

"You mean boys?" replied Shauna, returning Harek's hand to her knee, not her inner thigh.

Izzy laughed. "Yeah, boys," she confirmed. "Not many men up here, or else I'm looking in the wrong places," she chuckled.

They spoke for a little longer, then Izzy said that she had to go due to work the following morning.

"Tomorrow's Sunday sis!" Shauna said, surprised.

Izzy nodded. "Yep! This whole Brexit thing has us pulling overtime, but I did take today off!" she smiled. "Anyway, gotta dash. Need my bath before bed. Night sis!"

Gone Dutch

Shauna blew her sister a kiss, they waved and the call ended.

Harek leaned back and sighed. Izzy was far easier to talk with than Cait had been. Shauna went to stand but he pulled her to him and made her sit on his lap.

"That's better," he said, gently kissing her lips.

Shauna moaned gently then whispered. "Not yet." She winked, stood and went to the kitchen. Harek smirked as she sashayed her way through to the breakfast island. She was such a tease.

Shauna retreated to the office and back to her tablet after things were cleared down in the kitchen.

"Working again?" he asked.

"I take the time from my initial thoughts to let the cards sit in my head. This is me double-checking, ensuring I've not messed up the reading, checking I've answered the question and then sending it off." She smiled as he nodded. He found the TV remote and settled down to watch something.

It was nearly nine pm before Shauna shooed Andrew to bed. Harek wasn't sure he would last until Michael was in bed, but he was going to have to. Shauna came to sit down on the sofa near him afterwards. He raised an arm to encourage her to snuggle in. She didn't need to be asked twice.

Gone Dutch

"So, what do you think of my crazy family?" she asked, breathing in his smell and entwining her hands through his.

"They're family," he replied. "I don't think mine are as loud as yours, but I can see you love them. Even the crazy ones."

She chuckled. "Aye, we do love each other!" she shook her head. "Just all in our different ways."

Harek shook his head. "No, we're a bit quieter, for sure. You've met my sister Vayenn already. We are more stubborn. The kids are similar to yours, my niece and nephew. They squabble, they pick fights, they love, they forgive, they do the same the following day. I don't get how you manage to do what you do and remain as calm as you do!"

Shauna smiled. "Practice. But in truth, I had no choice." She went very still and quiet. Harek waited, stroking her shoulder with his fingertips. It took a few moments for her to speak.

"When Matt died, what happened today, even something as simple as making the dinner we had, would've been near impossible. I simply didn't function for weeks, nearly months. Mam and pa held us together. Matt's parents came to help too, but we were all grieving, hurt, angry and lost. We were in it together. That bonded us differently. It is part of the reason I tolerate Cait when she's off her meds; She was just a rock at that time. She proved then that she can help, be

Gone Dutch

an asset and not be a spoiled wee selfish, indulgent brat. It took months for me to even get functioning after the funeral. When the boys returned to school, Cait was there, doing the school runs, making their lunches, keeping her job. Mam tried to get me to take over again, but I just couldn't, not that quickly. I did, eventually, but…" she paused for a moment. "It took a while. Longer than I'd have liked but the sudden grief, the pain, the loss… it was just too much."

She snuggled further into his arms. He wrapped his other around her shoulders and kissed her head. Harek began stroking her upper arm.

"You're cold!" he said, lifting her.

She shrugged as she looked into his eyes. She reached in for a kiss and the sparks flew.

His hand held her head in place as Harek deepened the kiss. She moved so she was straddling him and he groaned as she sat on his lap, facing him.

Despite where he was, he pulled back. He looked deep into her chocolate brown eyes. "Do you want this?" he asked, gently stroking her jaw, her cheek.

She nodded and leaned to kiss him deeply. He didn't need telling twice. His hands moved to her blouse and he began unbuttoning it as she lifted his to feel his chest, his torso. Her cold hands were like shocks to his system. He jumped but didn't stop the kissing. In a

Gone Dutch

moment, her blouse was undone, pushed to the side. He broke the kiss and leaned back, admiring the view. Somehow, she'd changed into a black lacy number.

"Famke," he breathed, forgetting that she didn't understand either Dutch or Frisian. His reaction to her made her not care.

He took a breast, lace and all, into his mouth and held her as she arched backwards slightly. His hands worked their way up her back and in moments, he'd unhooked the bra. He removed her blouse and sent her bra to meet it. Her breasts were full, her nipples dark and erect. They stood to attention and increased in size under his mouth's ministrations.

She groaned quietly, aware that the kids were only feet above them in their beds.

He didn't need the Hyatt rooms to hide her screams or to absorb them. Her small moans in this room were enough to drive him insane.

She arched back as his mouth switched from one breast to the other. His hands were tracing the lines around her collarbone, her shoulders. He appreciated just how toned she was as he observed the curve of her abs and her soft stomach mound. He wanted her, but he wanted her more than he had at the Hyatt. It was time to show her just what he could do to her.

He found her mouth and kissed her, holding her head with one hand whilst his other traced her body line

Gone Dutch

down to her skirt. He flicked the fabric away to stroke the inside of her thigh and he worked his way up to his prize. He stopped and pulled back, looking at her and then grinned. She'd removed her knickers and wasn't wearing any. When had she done that?!

"Minx," he breathed, sliding a finger into her. She grinned for a moment as he said "minx" but gasped quickly as one of his huge fingers inserted itself into her. She began rocking on his hand, still kissing him. She gasped as another finger joined the first, stretching her firmly but gently. He liked the fact she had very little underwear on.

It didn't take any translating software to work out what he hoarsely commanded of her as he continued to work his magic with his fingers.

"Can't..." she breathed between kisses. "Hold..." She dug her fingers, nails and whole palms into his shoulders as her body shuddered in climax. She bit her lip to stop her from crying out but Harek claimed her mouth as the convulsions rocketed. He absorbed her climatic screams with pleasure.

He let her calm down and he waited until she was looking at him before he took his hand out from inside her to lick it clean, like an ice-cream. He watched her as he did so and as she licked her lips, copying him. He held his fingers up for her, making her taste herself.

He wrapped both his hands behind her head, kissing her deeply.

Gone Dutch

"Did you mean what you said, last night?" he asked, planting more kisses on her jaw.

She nodded. "I never say things I don't mean," she replied, smirking. He grinned and lifted her from his lap, placing her on the ground. He turned her so that he was behind her and she leaned over the sofa. She turned her head and grinned at him, nodding. He quickly removed his trousers and pants, allowing himself to be free. Shauna sighed, knowing what was coming. Well, she thought she did.

The sight of Shauna's rear presenting herself made him throb in anticipation and he firmly grabbed her hips. He lined himself up to her sex and firmly pushed into her folds.

Her groans as he slid inside fully was almost enough to make him climax, but he had plans. Keeping a firm grip on her hips, he began thrusting slowly, deeply. He enjoyed watching her breasts bounce as he did so and he increased his pace, slowly. Her moans got stifled as she plunged her head into a cushion. Harek wrapped a hand around her hair and tugged her head back up to turn to him. He watched as she bit her lip to avoid making too loud a sound as she came for the first time. He didn't stop, he wanted to know just how many times he could unravel her before he too burnt out. His answer was twice. As she came for what was her third time, he

Gone Dutch

exploded into her, seeing stars for the first time, his muscles convulsing in places he hadn't realised could.

He slowly raised himself and kissed the back of Shauna's neck. She gasped as he withdrew, then tried to rise. Her arms and legs forgot how to work and she collapsed onto the sofa. It took a few moments for the blood to start circulating again. She saw the clock and began to gather their things.

"Bryce and Carrie will be home soon," she hissed. "I don't want either of them to see us like this," she grabbed their discarded clothing and together, they made their way to Shauna's bedroom, hiding giggles and trying to be quiet.

Harek smiled as he entered. Clearly, this is where she had wanted the action to be. Two tea lights cast a low glow across the room, the curtains were closed and the room was warm. He watched as Shauna tossed her discarded clothing into the laundry basket and went to the shower.

She motioned for him to follow. He noticed his wash bag was at the spare sink, waiting for him to unpack it. She turned the shower on and set all the shower heads to full blast. Stepping inside, she moved to the other end to let him join her.

Both were spent but they enjoyed washing each other, kissing each other, just being together. Neither

Gone Dutch

talked, there was no need. Shutting the shower off when they were done, they dried themselves and made their way to the bed. Shauna slipped on a chemise that came to her mid-thigh and climbed in. She was silken and cool to his touch as they found positions both were comfortable laying in.

"I've never seen stars before," he said.
"Stars?" she asked, confused. He kissed her. "Not when I've come, no. Tonight, I did."
She chuckled softly and smiled, stroking the strong arm that went behind her head and back across her breasts.

"I lost count of how many times you made me come tonight. I think it was three. It might have been four." He kissed her temple and mumbled "three" in response as the candles died, plunging them into contented darkness.

Gone Dutch

Nineteen

The dawn was not yet broken when Shauna stirred. She felt comfortable, content. Something strong and powerful held her and she opened her eyes trying to think. Oh, yes… Harek. She wiggled backwards to embrace him more and received a low groan for her troubles.

"Keep that up," he warned. She smiled in the darkness.

"You'll punish me?" She wiggled against him some more. "Oh, I think I can handle it," she said, turning to find his mouth. Leisurely, he rolled over into her, resting his arms on either side of her head, kissing her. His hand lifted her satin chemise and her hands found his shoulders. It took moments for her to wrap herself around him and guide him into her. Harek was amazed it took no effort at all but given their efforts the previous night and the ease of entering her now, clearly she was still aroused. So frankly, was he, thanks to finding her wrapped in his arms very early on a Sunday morning.

He took his time to love her there was no rush as there had been previously. He took all the time he could kissing her as he dove slowly into her time and time

Gone Dutch

again. He pulled her knees up to her and watched as she arched against him, trying to take more of him in. He had no more to offer her but enjoyed watching her react in the low dawn light. He felt her begin to convulse and it nearly sent him over the edge. He held onto her hips and thrust deeper, drawing each stroke out for as much as he could. When she thought she had finished, he increased his pace, sending her and himself back into oblivion.

Shauna came to with Harek resting fully on top of her. He was kissing her neck, her ears, her eyes. Eventually, he found her mouth and kissed her deeply as he withdrew.
"You're amazing," she said, breathlessly. He had pulled her across him and he was stroking her side her arm. His eyes were closed, but his touching never ceased.
"So are you," he whispered. Slowly, they drifted back to sleep.

Gone Dutch

Twenty

Daylight was assured when they awoke a second time. Shauna wondered where he was until she heard the shower running. She climbed out of bed and went to the bathroom, joining him in the shower. He smiled and kissed her leisurely as the water began to wet her hair. They washed each other, themselves and giggled like children doing so, recovering from their nightly activities.

Eventually, Shauna turned the shower off and handed Harek a towel. They dried and dressed, then headed down to the kitchen, holding hands.

Bryce smiled at his sister as she walked into the kitchen holding Harek's hand. It had been too long since he'd seen that look in her eyes. It had been too long for him too, but that was a different story.

"Morning sis!" he said, handing them both a mug of coffee.

"Kids are fed, they're in the lounge. Bagels are there and I'm off to work. My final shift then I'm off again for four days!" he said, cheerily. With that, he headed out the door.

Gone Dutch

It didn't take long for the kids to find her and ask the most important question of the day: "What are we doing today?!"

"Have each of you done the homework you need to?" She received nods all around, even from Carrie. "Show me," she said, settling onto a stool near Harek.

"So bossy!" he whispered into her ear, grinning.

"If they think they can get away with it, they will!" she replied, chuckling. "Michael is good at doing his work, and since he's got so many subjects, he knows he needs to. Carrie will try and wing it, Andrew does the subjects he likes. I know my kids," she said, winking at him.

It took all of ten minutes for her to verify that they had, in truth, completed all the homework that had been set, signing off their journals.

"So, what do you want to do today? Walk in the woods? Black Country Living Museum? Or something else?"

The kids looked at her and Harek. "Cannock Chase?" asked Michael after looking at his brother and cousin. "Can we take the bikes?"

Shauna shook her head. "Carrie's bike isn't here and Harek doesn't have one. Not fair to take three bikes with five of us, is it?" Michael frowned.

"Guess not," he said.

Gone Dutch

"But we can go up into The Chase anyway and walk. Go grab your boots, I'll pack snacks and stuf." Michael went to put on his boots.

"The Chase sounds nice," said Harek. "What is it?"

"Cannock Chase is a local forest. Well, local as in, it's within thirty miles," she sauntered up to stand before him, lowering her voice. "We could spend the day in bed, but I think the kids might do something that we'll regret." she pursed her lips together in reply. "Come on, let's get ready."

It only took them half an hour to change into suitable walking clothes, find their shoes, pack the snacks and load everyone into the car. However, they soon discovered that Harek didn't fit into small British cars. He didn't grumble though and was relieved when they finally parked up and clambered out.

Cannock Chase was, he decided, beautiful. It reminded him of parts of Friesland back home. It didn't have the watery edge the way Amsterdam, Rotterdam or Friesland did, even with the lake they'd found, but the smell of it was earthy, grounded. Shauna seemed to relax more as she breathed in the fresh air.

They secured the car and headed out along a track. The kids ran on, creating their own games. Harek and Shauna followed, hand in hand. Harek would quite often pin her against a tree, kiss her breathless and laugh

Gone Dutch

when the kids had to backtrack to find them. They spent hours exploring Cannock Chase.

The best moment, for all of them, was when Harek began tracking some deer. He quietly led them to where a small herd were grazing. Shauna captured photographs on her phone as quietly as she could. Everyone, including Carrie, stood perfectly still through the ten-minute encounter. The deer weren't skittish, so they were used to humans being near them. It was a memory they had encountered and shared.

That afternoon, when they were home again, Shauna began putting together the Sunday dinner. She squealed when Harek wrapped his arms behind her as she was preparing the lamb and potatoes.

"You are sexy," he said, kissing the sweet spot behind her ear, towards her neck.

"If I wore a bin bag, would I still be sexy?" she asked, laughing as she reached up for the jar of dried rosemary.

"Try it I'll let you know," he growled into her ear.

She placed the roasting dish with the food into the oven, then turned to Harek, her face slightly serious. She took a deep breath, watching him intently.

"This is my life. This," she said, sighing and motioning to all that was around her. "Is what my life

Gone Dutch

consists of. The kids, walks, work, the house. If there's anything more you expect of me," she shook her head slowly. "I can't deliver."

He sighed and pulled her in close. "Do you know when I first laid eyes on you?"

She nodded. "The wedding rehearsal."

He shook his head. "No, it was before then."

She leaned back. "Was it?" she looked to her left, trying to remember. "When?"

He smiled. "You were escorted onto Harmony Sea with Fons and Helene. We were in the far end of the main deck and you walked in with your friend."

She smiled. "Roo. I need to call her, but not right now." She made a mental note to catch up with the others during the week.

"I saw you then, confident, athletic and strong. Fons told us your name when he gathered us up to go to the apartments. I tried to catch your eye, but you didn't seem to focus on anything but Helene and your friend. I even suggested to Fons that we mingle the night before the rehearsal. He wouldn't dream of it, told me that you four had been promised one last night together with Helene," he rubbed her back as she stood between his legs, her head resting on his chest.

"I found your devotion to your friend endearing, touching. I knew you were loyal from that. You hardly seemed to smile though. I so wanted to change that."

Gone Dutch

She looked up at him. "I wasn't a sourpuss!" she poked him in the chest, firmly. "It was the first time I'd really left the boys since…" she swallowed. "Since Matt."

"Loyalty," he said, lifting her chin to kiss her gently. "You are so loyal, so involved. The most I usually get involved in," he sighed, "is the job. Our next contract, the finish of the current build. Even relationships didn't work out, or feel right," he kissed her head. "Until you. You've saved my business and reputation, not to mention my life." He paused and waited for her to look at him. When she did, he continued. "I want more than I have but until I met you, I didn't know what it was, exactly. My idea of what a family is doesn't match this. This is better; it's what my sister has, what my parents maybe had. I want that too, that connection. I want to share what I have, but I need to show you it all first before either of us decides that we're going to stick this, us, out."

She stepped back, looking into his hazel eyes. "Do you remember why we ended up talking on the outer deck?" she said, her hands folded before her. She leaned against the counter she'd not long been working at. This has been bugging her since and now she had the chance to ask why.

He nodded. "You told me off for it right away. I had forgotten what it was to be challenged, to be

Gone Dutch

accountable to someone. Other than Jon and work, I do my own thing, answering to no one else. Until now."

She sighed. "Why did my being a widow mean so much?"

He smiled and motioned around him. "This. As I said, you had something I hadn't even known I'd wanted, until Fons said you were a widow and had the weekend childfree. With all the others before, no one has ever gifted me the one thing I suddenly realised I wanted to be." He sighed. "That's why Sanne was there that night."

Shauna looked confused for a moment. "The angry woman in red." Shauna's mouth downturned as she moved towards a breakfast stool and sat down, making space between them, listening.

Harek nodded. "She came, uninvited, thinking she'd hang onto my arm for old times' sake, telling me she loved me that she'd get pregnant properly this time. She had already lied to me at least twice about being pregnant." His face darkened. "Twice," he growled. "I was angry at her and partially myself, which meant I wasn't as charming with you as I should have been. She tried to use me to stay at the reception, though she was only invited as my plus one, which I revoked weeks before. The others, Jon mainly, thankfully stepped up to set her straight and escort her out. Dirk helped too. She left, causing only that minor scene."

Gone Dutch

Shauna observed his shoulders and his deep breathing as he spoke. Suddenly, she ached for him. "So this family thing, that's what you want?" She focused on a junction of tiles on the floor as she spoke. Her voice shook and was only just audible.

He walked to her and stood before her, lifting her gaze to meet his. She stared into his hazel eyes and noticed how the colours changed slightly when he was thinking. He loved the intensity of her chocolate eyes, how he could almost see into her soul.

"Yes. But I want it with you," he watched her as he admitted what he knew, however quickly she had captured his heart. "Of that, I am so deeply sure," he leaned in to kiss her gently on the lips. He decided to speak to from the heart. "I have my half of the deal to show you. Your sister is right; I have wealth and plenty of it. I build boats for Arabs and other rich people all over the world. I employ people who are talented, hard-working, with families. They rely on me to ensure that they have a job. I rely on them to help build the business. They go home to families, their children, their wives or husbands, sometimes even together. I go home to a house that's empty, cold. It needs the sound of children, the smells of home cooking. I don't want my bed or my life to be empty, not anymore."

She reached her arms up behind his head and pulled him towards her for a deep kiss.

Gone Dutch

"Neither do I," she said, a few moments later. "I don't want to be alone anymore either" she breathed.

Harek smiled. "Then let's see where this goes," he kissed her lightly. "If you're up for the adventure?"

She nodded. "I am. Just, one favour," she stared into his eyes, holding his attention. "Don't hurt the boys."

He shook his head. "If I hurt you, I hurt them. I have no intention of hurting any of you. I'm in this for the whole journey Shauna, not just the wonderful weekends," he grinned "Or the fantastic sex," he watched as her lips slowly curved into a smile. "I want it all. With you." She sighed in contentment, knowing that now, they were at least on the same page.

Dinner was a lively affair. Harek had learned that it was either all or nothing with Shauna's family. He was happy to take it all. As they chatted and laughed, he wondered if his mundane, calm life was enough for her. He knew that there was only one way to find out.

Carrie went back home later that evening, but not before Shauna showed off the dress Harek had brought her for the ballet and dinner.

"Auntie Shaunie, that's gorgeous," squealed the girl, embracing her aunt.

Even Michael was speechless for a moment or two. "Darn mum, where'd the legs come from?" he asked after he remembered to close his mouth.

Gone Dutch

Andrew declared her "amazing" and Bryce just whispered "pretty woman," with a wink when the kids were out of earshot. She chuckled and sighed contentedly when she hung it all back up in her wardrobe. Harek smiled at her as he carefully helped her remove the dress and kept himself in check. At least, for now.

Lynda peered at Harek over her glasses at the front door when she collected Carrie. Lynda hardly stepped foot into the house anymore. It always ended in a fight somehow for neither Bryce nor Shauna could forgive her for cheating on Bryce.

It was much later, as they headed to bed just after the boys, that Harek and Shauna got their next chance to talk with each other.

Harek had quickly undressed and began warming the bed up whilst Shauna unwound in the bathroom. He watched as she appeared and disappeared from view, brushing her hair, her teeth. He smiled at her as she turned off the bathroom light. He'd lit some candles, knowing that she'd appreciate it. She smiled as she ducked under the quilt and cuddled up to him. He jumped.

"How can you be so cold, again?" he gasped, rubbing her shoulders as she sprawled across his chest. He loved holding her like this, caressing her, kissing her.

Gone Dutch

"Intentionally, this time," she giggled, kissing the nearest pectoral. He chuckled.

"You know I have to be up early?" he asked. Now the time was coming for him to go home, he found he didn't want to.

She sighed and closed her eyes. "I know," she whispered. "I know you need to go back, to get things going on the contracts and all that. I have to go to work tomorrow too, the kids have school." She looked up at him and he shifted slightly to look into her chocolate hinted eyes. In this light, there were almost pools of dark, swirling treacle. "Doesn't mean I have to be happy about it," she said, stroking the side of his face she wasn't leaning into.

He lifted her chin to kiss her mouth gently. "I don't want to, either. But I have a double reason to go home. I need to ensure that the building works at home are finalised and finished on time. That is harder to do when I can't check on it every day." He kissed her. "Tell me when you can bring the boys to Rotterdam. I want to show you everything you've helped save this weekend. I want to show you me."

He kissed her, breathing her in. "I warn you famke, my life is not as exciting as you think it might be."

She looked intently into his eyes as he stopped for a moment. "Two or three weeks is term break for Easter. I'll check the calendar in the morning," she

Gone Dutch

replied as his mouth finally left hers to kiss another part of her neck.

"Good," he mumbled, before claiming her mouth again. He moved slowly, climbing between her legs, kissing her all the while.

She tried to pull away and finally did so, asking; "What's been your favourite position?"

She grinned as he stopped for a moment. She'd indulged him all weekend, allowing him to play and fantasise beyond anything he had ever thought possible.

"Why?" he asked, stroking the hair back from her face.

"Because," she said, kissing him deeply, "That's what we do now," she tapped on his chest as she spoke. "Your favourite, your call."

He smiled at her. "My favourite?" he didn't want to move, he wanted to slip deeply into her and languishingly love her until they both saw stars. He swung his arm and hooked a knee of hers into it, kissing her mouth deeply as his hand fondled the breast on that side.

"My favourite is everything with you," he said, entering her. She gasped as he found his way to be deep within her, he tensed as he felt her inner walls clamp down on him. He waited until she relaxed a little, then began slowly thrusting into her. By the candlelight, he enjoyed watching her breasts bounce on each thrust, her moans and especially when she held back as much as she could. It took a lot of effort on his part to ensure that she erupted twice before he unleashed himself within her convulsing folds.

     He unhooked her leg and collapsed to the side of her. Finding her in the candlelight, he pulled her to him, kissing her face, her eyes, even her nose. He stroked her hair from her face as she quietly wept for a few moments. She sighed deeply, bringing herself back into some form of control. What she would do when he did leave, he had no idea. He realised there and then that he always wanted her by his side. Their countries, their origins were different but he had to find a way to make this work.
     'Bring it on' he thought in determination.
     He looked down at Shauna, not surprised to see she was drifting off to sleep. Holding her close, he closed his eyes and allowed sleep to claim him for a few hours.

Gone Dutch

Twenty-One

He glanced at the clock, aware that soon, he'd have to leave. He didn't want to cut and run and he wanted Shauna just more time before he left her warm oasis. He was spooning her currently, enabling him to access her softest of body parts.

He kissed her temple and she stirred. He gently called her name.

"Shauna?" he asked, stroking a breast, her ribs and kissing her ear. "Shauna…" he called. She stirred, nearly elbowing him in the head.

"Sorry," she whispered, reaching up to kiss him. "Is it that time already?" she asked. He didn't need to see her face to tell that she wasn't happy.

"Soon," he said, kissing her. "Too soon,"

He pulled her on top of him, still kissing her. He knew that having her on top would be simpler; she'd still be moist from a few hours ago. Had they really slept five hours? It felt like minutes.

Shauna knew this was the last time for a while and she hid a smile when he pulled her on top. She leant forwards, stroking and kissing his pectorals, suckling his nipples. She liked being in charge but she also liked the way he could control her. Goddess, she loved that!

Gone Dutch

  His hands pushed back her hair and she leaned forward to take his mouth into hers. She could feel his erection right beneath her. Rising, it took one hand to guide him into her and then she slid down him, taking every delicious inch of him within her already moist folds.
  She had learned how he liked to be ridden and she began slowly, rising and sliding down in gentle, long movements. His hands massaged her breasts, slid down to her hips, holding her firmly in place as he rose to meet her. Together, they found the perfect way to ride and be ridden.
  It wasn't long before the moans from Shauna indicated she was close to climax. Harek moved a hand and played with the nub of her clit, sending her over the edge. She breathed his name over and over again as she shook. He held her above him as he thrust upwards, once, twice, thrice before he too, moaned out her name in exhaustive breaths.
  She kissed him and slowly dismounted, but he had one more surprise up his sleeve. He pulled her up so she sat on his face and slowly, he tasted her and himself, making her cry out for him as he made her climax again on his face.
  She flopped to her side of the bed, unable to speak. He leaned her over and kissed her so that she tasted what he just had. Why men thought that this was sexy she wasn't sure but damn, it turned her on because

Gone Dutch

he reacted to it. He rose from the bed and pulled her to him, heading for the shower. He didn't turn on the bathroom light, the dawn light was enough to see each other by. In silence, between kisses that lingered, they washed each other's bodies, touching each other, as if to remember what the other felt and looked like, until the next time.

Twenty minutes later, Harek was in the kitchen with Johan, a steaming coffee in his hand. Shauna was wearing a chemise and a purple Japanese kimono, making Harek frustrated. Her hair was pinned up in a messy bun but the coffee was strong. She poured Johan's into a travel mug.

"You'll need it," she said, handing him the coffee and offering breakfast of fruit and bagels.

"Dank je," he said. Okay, that reply she could work out.

They ate in a semi-comfortable silence and when Johan had finished, he put his plate into the sink and spoke with Harek in Dutch. Harek nodded.

"Five minutes," he said. Johan nodded, tipped his hat to Shauna and quietly went to the car, taking Harek's bags with him.

Harek stood and opened his arms to Shauna. She went to hug him and rested her head against his chest, breathing him in.

Gone Dutch

He sighed. "You are a temptress!" he said, kissing her deeply. "I've left the contents of my wash bag here. I know I'll be back to use them."

Shauna chuckled. "You'd better be!" she said, rising to kiss him one last time. They sighed together as they broke apart.

"You'd better get going if you're going to catch the tides," she said. He kissed her quickly on the mouth one last time, then walked to the door with her following.

"I'll call when I'm back in Rotterdam," he said, holding her face. He stole one last deep kiss, then turned and walked to the car and climbed into the back. He waved at her as Johan drove him away. She only stopped waving when the car could no longer be seen.

Shauna sighed and closed the door, returning to the kitchen. It was a good half an hour before Bryce appeared, yawning. He stopped dead in his tracks when he saw his sister staring expressionless out into the garden.

"Sis?" he called gently. She was never up at this time.

She blinked and turned to her brother. "Morning!" she said.

"He had to go, huh?" he asked, spying the mugs and the depleted coffee pot. She nodded.

Gone Dutch

"I need to check when the schools are on holiday and the boys' passports. We'll be heading to Rotterdam for some of the term-break." She smiled. There was her target, a goal to aim for. Suddenly she was motivated, her despondent view cast away like the darkness at dawn.
She smiled broadly at her younger brother and thought, 'Hello Monday!'

Before her boys were even up, she had found and checked their passports. Checking the school holiday dates, she sent a text to Harek.
S: checked school holidays. We can do the first week in April for five days, maybe seven or eight maximum..
Harek's response was instant.
H: Great! We'll work out times for running the boat across to fetch you three. I will let you know when to be at Hull port. Miss you already.
S: Miss you too. Stay safe!
H: and you, famke!
He signed off with a kissing emoji. Shauna smiled. 'Monday's,' she thought, 'were great!'

She sent the boys off to school, aware that she was perhaps too perky for work on a Monday morning, but couldn't care less. They'd find out when she had the plans sorted. Bryce had promised not to say anything to

Gone Dutch

them and she walked into work happier than she had been in a long time. Jenny greeted her and instantly teased her about the peppiness.

Shauna shrugged. "I had a great weekend," was all she'd say with a twinkle in her eye.

Jenny laughed. "Well, bringing you back to Earth with a bump. Mr "I can't believe it!" from Trading Standards called. Ben and Adam want to chat with you when you have. There's a pile of invoices there" Jenny pointed to a small stack of papers, "and I'll get on with billing clients."

Shauna smirked. "Thanks, Jen!"

Getting comfortable in her chair, Shauna called Mr Wilson.

He answered the call on the second ring.

"Trading Standards, Mr Wilson speaking" he chirped.

"Mr Wilson," she chirped back happily.

"Ms Woodward? Glad you called me back. Wanted to check something with you about the case," he said. "Invoice 104234?"

Shauna switched the handset to her left side and typed with her right.

She sighed. "That's part of the missing invoice pad. So, you know who raised it. Not us."

Richard Wilson nodded, not that she could see that.

Gone Dutch

"I thought it would be. So you've not done any work for Mrs Hanratty In Tipton?"

"I'm pretty sure we haven't, but let me double-check our database." Several searches on the lady's name, her address or the type of job, and she came up blank.

"Nope, Richard, sorry. Didn't think it was one we invoiced for or done work for. Also, we're using the new pads and company logo, we have been since the start of February, so if and when you see the invoice it's got our old logo on it, it'll be a fake."

"Shauna, you're a star. I'm sorry that you guys have had to endure this idiot to build this case."

"Any idea when you guys can step in? This has cost us a fair bit in redesign and paperwork, vehicle rebranding etcetera that we'll never get back," she lowered her voice to a threatening tone, "and we'd like him shut down legally, in jail sooner rather than later. I know the two directors are going to ask me when the axe is going to fall."

She could tell Richard was smiling, even on the phone.

"I'm meeting this lady later today. But with all I have so far, I'll be handing it to the CPS this week. I doubt we'll be in need of an eyewitness. Every client has sworn a statement and signed it."

Gone Dutch

"That will be great. Four months of this is more than enough," she said, leaning back into her chair, knowing that Ben and Adam were going to be happier.

She stood outside the directors' office door and knocked confidently as soon as their call had ended. She'd known these guys since school, they'd been responsible for getting Matt to ask her out, even kiss her, which is why they had asked her to liaise with Trading Standards. She'd have had the task if Matt had been alive.

Ben's voice called out "Come" and Shauna strode in, taking her usual seat until both men were free. Adam finished his call quickly, keeping an eye on Shauna as she sat confidently in the chair between their desks.

Ben spoke as soon as Adam hung up. "So?" he asked, leaning forward eagerly.

"Another invoice from the missing pad. A Mrs Hanratty from Tipton." Shauna began. "Shocking Porch build, to say the least. Standards are looking to hand the file to CPS this week, as soon as her situation can be added."

Adam smiled. "Shauna, are you going to be OK going onto the stand to nail Brian?" He suspected that she'd be called as a witness.

Shauna gave him a look. "Can you pee standing up?" she asked. Adam and Ben laughed. "Honestly, guys, you both ken I hate twerps like him. You both ken

Gone Dutch

what Matt and I did for a hobby, for fun. But dark back streets and baseball bats aren't my thing." She remembered Rotterdam and she shivered. "Besides, with all the sworn statements from everyone he's screwed over so far, Wilson does not think they'll need me."

"You ok?" asked Ben, noticing the shudder she'd taken.

"Yeah, just, remembering something that happened too recently." She smiled at her old school friends; Matt's best friends.

"I suspect that the warrant will be issued later this week," she continued, "but it depends on how quickly the CPS work their magic. We might have a few more to add to the case file before they do." She shrugged slightly, but her lips were thinned. "But, I can't help that."

Ben looked at Adam and they both grinned. "You ask her, I am so not that brave," proclaimed Ben, holding his hands up and pushing his chair away. Shauna turned to Adam, then looked back at Ben. The mood had changed from sombre business to an old playful "don't piss off the Scotswoman". She hadn't felt Ben or Ad give off this vibe for years.

"Okay, what gives?" She knew Jen had probably gotten word to them already.

Adam swallowed. "You had a good weekend?" he asked, emphasising the word good.

Gone Dutch

Shauna rolled her eyes. "Is that it? You wanna ask if your best friend's widow got laid?" The look on Adam and Ben's faces told her yes.

She laughed. "Honestly! Okay, before I confess any details, when did Jen hint?"

Both men looked at each other. "She's a blabber," replied Shauna, shaking her head, but working out it they would have likely been told when Jen brought them their coffee. She looked back at the two men who were godfathers to her boys.

"Yes, I had a great weekend," her voice lifted as she spoke, "thank you both for asking. I went to the ballet, stayed at The Hyatt, ate a four-star restaurant dinner, helped save another construction business using knowledge gained by dealing with Brian and from our IT guys. It was a usual weekend for me," she said, watching them, her nostrils flaring as she pursed her lips.

Adam laughed. "Good for you! We were getting fed up with you not quite moping and the dates turning sour. You deserve to be happy, Shaunie."

She smiled. She knew he genuinely meant it. "Thanks, Ad."

"Have the boys met him?" asked Adam. Being one of their godfathers, he wanted to know.

"They have. They're rather taken by him."

"So," said Ben, leaning back in his chair. "Spill the details, Shaunie."

Gone Dutch

Shauna gave them an abridged version, minus the intimate details of the sex.

"So this guy, Harek, got beat up, you chase them away, get him the help he needs, start training again, hold down two jobs, raise three kids and take on dodgy builders?"

Ben sat back in his chair. "Shaunie, when we said to Matt you were a badass back in school, you weren't meant to prove it, babe!"

Shauna laughed. "Well, God may be gracious Ben, I'm not if I get crossed. You know that." She winked as she stood. "So, now that my love life has been discussed enough, can I get back to work? I've invoices to pay if you guys wanna keep the business and not get a summons." She left the men to their chuckles. Mates, eh?

Her phone pinged a little while later lifting her spirits as she saw who the message was from. She'd told Jen off for stirring with Ben and Adam, but in truth, she was glad that they still cared about her to ask. Harek told her he was safely in Rotterdam. She quickly texted him back and put her phone away, getting into paying their suppliers.

Harek smiled at her very quick, sassy response. He had thought about calling her but remembered she was also at work. She'd told him that she still did the

Gone Dutch

invoicing for the company Matt used to own, that the two men who still did were her boys' god-fathers. He hadn't expected any response for a little while, and was both pleased and surprised that she did so quickly.

    Smiling as his own company came into sight, he pushed her and her sexiness from the forefront of his mind. He pulled his shoulders back and prepared to stand tall.

Gone Dutch

Twenty-Two

Sweeping through the building area on the way to his office, he said his usual hellos to everyone and smiled at Jon when he reached their joined office. Over coffee, he bought Jon up to speed on what happened at the weekend with Berend.

"Unbelievable! I'm glad it's been sorted." Jon smiled at his friend and partner. "You seem happier," he said, relaxing a little.

"A beautiful woman does that to a man," he said, smirking. Jon threw his head back as he laughed.

"The same one from the wedding, who waited by your side at the hospital?" he asked, when he finally caught his breath.

Harek nodded. Jon stood, slapped his friend hard on the shoulder, offered congratulations and went to his desk.

"Honestly, my friend, I am pleased for you. I haven't seen you this happy since…" he pondered. "Forever!" he chuckled.

Harek grinned. "She's good for me." he paused. "She's amazing, talented, clever, witty and feisty. Not to mention, fit. She trains in martial arts," he added, watching Jon's face.

Gone Dutch

"Does she?" he asked, his face showing his interest. "Bet it got interesting in bed!" he teased. Harek gave him a one-finger reply, to which Jon laughed.

It took most of the morning to schedule the builds that had been confirmed from that weekend. Jon whistled at the end of it, hours later.

"That's nearly five years' worth of work from one dinner meeting," said Jon, amazed.

"Berend only granted it because I said I needed to talk to him face to face but I'd be on a date. He maybe wanted to be sure I was doing what I said before he'd meet with me. I think that caught his interest. I've never mixed my women with business before."

Jon nodded. "Speaking of women," he paused and swallowed. "Have you heard from Sanne since the wedding?"

Harek's face went dark. "No. I never want to see her again." He almost growled. "Or hear from her. Shauna has more character in her little toe than Sanne ever will. Why do you ask?"

Jon shrugged. "I wondered if she were behind the attack, that's all," he said. "Getting rid of her that night was a chore."

Harek had nodded. "I'm grateful you stepped in. The Polite are supposed to ask her, but I'm not aware of any update from them."

Gone Dutch

Jon nodded and smiled. "That's what friends do, isn't it?"

Harek grinned in reply.

Another two hours passed before both men were happy with their company plans for what would be the next five years of builds.

"We can call a company meeting tomorrow," Harek suggested, "Bring everyone up to date with our plans."

Jon nodded and checked his watch. "Time for me to go. You're not the only one who got lucky that weekend," he smirked.

Harek cast his mind back. "The curly blond?" he asked, remembering.

Jon nodded. "Amelie. She's Belgian but works in Amsterdam. She knows Fons because of the beer making," he stood with a sparkle in his eye. "I do love a good woman who knows her beers."

Harek's phone bleeped and he looked at it. Answering his building contractor quickly, he too stood and began packing away files.

"That her?" asked Jon from his desk as he tidied away their files. Nothing was left out overnight or if they were away from their desks for anything more than half an hour.

Harek shook his head. "Builder. I want the house finished before Shauna visits in a few weeks."

Gone Dutch

Jon stopped dead, looking at his friend. "You're serious about this one, aren't you? More than ever before!"

Harek nodded. "Yes. I never realised what I was missing until that night. I might still not have an idea if it weren't for her. Or for the attack."

Jon nodded. "Okay. Well, you go talk with the builder and whomever you need. I'm going to meet Amelie. What time shall I ask Anika to broadcast the meeting for?"

Harek thought for a moment. "How does ten am sound?"

Jon nodded. "I'll get her to do it tonight, so it's got time to cascade out." He picked up his phone to call their PA as he headed towards his car. A few moments later, Harek joined him, locking their office and handing over to the night security as he went.

Harek pulled into his driveway forty minutes later. He liked living outside the busy city of Rotterdam, preferring the quieter rural setting. Vayenn lived closer to the city, mainly due to the kids' school. Right now, he envied her that hub of noise. His house was too quiet after spending the weekend with Shauna and her lively family. The builder was waiting for him and together, they went into the house.

Gone Dutch

House was an understatement. To Harek, it was a house, the one in which he grew up. To anyone else, it was huge, which was why his mother had wanted something much smaller and much more manageable in her golden years.

Harek smiled. He could imagine the boys shouting from one room whilst he made love to Shauna in another, neither the wiser of what the other party was doing. The builder brought him back to his senses and together, they walked through Harek's plans.

The builder nodded. "It can be done. It will mean that I have crews here late at night. I know you'll pay the bill, so that is not a problem. Can you stand the noise?"

Harek nodded. "I'll stay with Vayenn or Jon when I have to, but will check in every other day. Leave my room sheeted off so that I can stay overnight when I stay here. Same for the library now that the door is hung."

The builder nodded. "If you want it done with everything I can muster, ten days, maybe eleven."

Harek shook on it. "Get them here and get it done," he set his jaw and a challenge. "I'll double your fee if you do it in those ten days."

The builder nodded, accepting the challenge. "Done!" They shook hands and the builder left, calling up everyone and anyone who would, could or had ever worked on a job for him. By the time he had arrived at his own house, he had the teams he needed.

Gone Dutch

Harek looked at the house as it was & began taking photos on his phone. It would be changed in what he hoped was ten days. The shell was there, but the interior left a lot to be desired and wasn't safe for two boys to live in. That left him just four days to make it into the home he'd be comfortable to show to Shauna. Challenges were his favourite thing.

Gone Dutch

Twenty-Three

Shauna stood cooking dinner whilst Harek was dealing with the builder. She and Bryce were speaking about her work whilst the boys finished off homework.

"The CPS might get a warrant and anything else they need this week," Shauna started boiling the peas. "I hope so, it's a pain in the arse finding his shoddy workmanship being done under our name. Matt would be livid if he were still here."

Bryce nodded, setting out the table for the four of them.

"But Ben and Adam asked you about him?" he grabbed the condiments from the side as she nodded a reply. "How'd they know?" he asked.

Shauna grinned. "Jen. I was too happy for her not to notice and since I hadn't told her last week that Harek even existed, she hinted to the guys that I maybe had a good weekend."

Bryce chuckled. "I'm surprised Becky and Jane haven't called to ask you what the heck."

Shauna's shoulders shook as she chuckled. "So am I, but well," Shauna shrugged. "I don't care." She checked her phone quickly but there was still no word from Harek.

"He'll call Shaunie," said her brother.

Gone Dutch

Shauna blushed. "Yep, probably still working, knowing him."

Harek was working, but in his private gym. Sitting at a desk most days meant that he needed to work the frustrations out in private. Whilst gym memberships were great, he didn't like the attraction that came with it when he exercised.

His personal trainer bought his attention back to what they were doing and Harek cursed. He had let his mind wander again. He growled and then focused on the task at hand.

It was nearly ten pm his time by the time his trainer had left, he'd showered and eaten something. Johan had ensured that there was fresh food in the fridge before he returned home. Sitting down finally in the library, he called Shauna's number. Two rings and he heard her happy voice greet him.

"Hoi, kreaze," she said happily, hoping she had gotten the translation right.

"Hoi, famke," he replied, settling back into the huge chair by the roaring fire. This was his favourite spot so far in the house. He had a feeling he'd have lots of them by the time he'd finished showing Shauna this place. "You have been busy with Google translate," he said, chuckling.

Gone Dutch

She loved the sound of his laughter. It was low and deep, like a big cat laughing.

"Well, I wasn't sure if I wanted the Dutch or the Frisian, but I figured you'd accept either. Besides, kreaze sounds a little better than knapperd!"

Harek chuckled again. He loved her honesty and he loved the fact that she was trying with his language. "What's wrong with knapperd?" he asked.

"It just sounds like knackered and I didn't like it that much!"

It took him a few moments to respond and when he caught his breath, he replied. "I have never thought of it that way!" letting his laughter subside. "How was your day, famke?" He sat with his feet towards the roaring fire, listening to her talk about mundane things, like work, the boys. He closed his eyes and paid attention to the lilt of her voice. He liked her attention to detail and her discretion when it came to what she called a small "work issue". He tried to draw details out of her about it, but she said because it was now getting legal, she couldn't go into details. He respected that and allowed her to change the subject.

"What have *you* been doing today?" she asked.

He told her about the plans Jon and himself had worked on for most of the day, and that he'd talked with the builder about finishing off a few things on the house before she came to visit with the boys in a few short weeks. He didn't want to tell her just how much work

Gone Dutch

was being done; she didn't need to know, though she probably would understand once she saw pictures of the place as it was right now.

They spoke for nearly another hour, even though they'd only said their good-byes that very morning.

"I should let you go and rest, you've got a company meeting tomorrow and I am back in tomorrow to finish off the invoices," she said, sighing.

"How long are you going to be at work for?" he asked.

"Until about two pm, as usual. There are some large invoices to pay and I have to ensure that they're done right. Jen's lovely, but I can't trust her to do these. Ben and Adam don't either, which is why they pay me to do it."

He nodded and then verbally replied, forgetting they were talking verbally, not video chat. The internet connection here wasn't great. That, he'd organise getting it sorting tomorrow, somehow.

"So I'll speak to you tomorrow evening?"

"Try and stop me! Though, I'll call you as I like to shower after training and I nearly missed your call last week."

Harek chuckled. "Yes, you did. But, I got you."

Shauna sighed breathlessly into the phone. "Yes, you did laddie!"

Gone Dutch

"Tease," he said, trying not to react to her saying that to him in the way she did. However, it was a pointless effort. "Now I need a cold shower,"

Shauna laughed. "Good night Harek," she whispered. God, his arms missed holding her.

"Good night famke!" he replied. The line went dead and he leaned back into the chair, groaning. It was going to be a long fortnight.

Gone Dutch

Twenty-Four

Harek was at the office earlier than Jon the following morning. Vayenn was surprised when her brother turned up at seven am and even more surprised when he offered to drop his niece and nephew to school. As they prepared their bags for the day, he managed to explain some of his plans to his sister.

"Do you think she'd appreciate it?" he asked, dancing from one foot to another. "It's not going to be too much?"

Vayenn nodded. "Yes, goodness yes she'll appreciate it and yes, it's too much, but she deserves it. She's saved your ass twice my dear brother," Vayenn slapped his shoulder. "Do it."

Harek nodded and grinned. "Right, I'll drop these two at school. You do what you have to do. Morning Reuben!" he called, ushering his niece and nephew out of the door, letting his sister and brother-in-law have five minutes of peace.

Reuben asked what was going on, to which Vayenn replied: "I'm not entirely sure!" and recounted the conversation with her brother.

"He's properly in love!" he said, holding his wife.

Gone Dutch

She chuckled. "He hasn't a clue," she replied, kissing her husband. The door shutting was the last thing Harek saw in his rear-view mirror.

Shauna had pretty much the same routine as Vayenn, though the boys walked themselves to school. Michael left first as he had further to go and Andrew left at half eight. Shauna left shortly after to get to the office for nine. She was talking with Ben and Adam when Jen knocked on the door mid-morning.

"Sorry to bother you, but there's a delivery here for Shauna. You need to sign for this."

Shauna stood and went to the front room where her desk and Jen's were located. On her desk, sat a huge vase with a dozen red roses, de-thorned and presented as if they were at Chelsea Royal. Shauna stopped dead, causing Jen, Ben and Adam to pile into the back of her. Ben grabbed a seat and made Shauna sit when he saw why she'd stopped dead. It took her a few moments to walk to the display and look for the card.

"Thought I had to sign?" whispered Shauna, looking at Jen.

Jen grinned. "I couldn't wait! Sorry," Jen was bouncing. "I signed for them and he left, but I wanted to see your face! Shauna those are amazing!"

Shauna finally hunted for the message card that usually comes with any Interflora delivery. She found it.

Gone Dutch

Written in the florist's neat handwriting was a simple message.

"Miss you, famke!
Wishing you a very happy birthday, H"

Shauna couldn't help the huge grin that she was now wearing. She had to move the vase to another surface so she could work. She sent him a message as soon as she was able to sit at her desk.

S: They're unbelievable, thank you!

H: They are not as gorgeous as you. I'm thinking of you often. Hope you have a great birthday!

S: So I see! Thank you! I'd kiss you if you were here!

H: Save them. I'll collect them later.

Shauna chuckled at the last message.

S: How's work?

H: Employees are happy. Jon is happy. I'm happy enough as they are all happy. I'll be happier when you're here.

S: Soon. Not taking kids out of school for a red hot interlude!

H: Wouldn't ask you to. Red hot huh? I must get the sauna working.

S: Sauna? Oh, now you're talking!

Her eyes danced as Harek sent back a laughing emoji.

Gone Dutch

H: We'll do more than talk, famke! Need to go, more to organise. Talk tonight.

Shauna smiled.

"So?!" squealed Jen. "What's Mr Handsome say?"

Shauna stuck her tongue out at Jen. "Just wishing me a happy birthday!" replied Shauna, smirking. "Your turn for the tea!" she said, pointing at the kitchenette. Jen scowled but she had a glint in her eye.

Shauna smiled as she called Harek after a tough two-hour training session. She doubted she'd get tired of seeing his name on her screen. They spoke every night, usually about their day and how much they missed each other.

The following night, Shauna video called the girls and everyone had plenty of things to say and ask. Shauna wasn't much of a drinker so sat with a cup of tea as she chatted with her friends.

"Harek's fine," said Shauna in reply to the enquiries of his health. Though, with Roo, that wasn't all she was asking about.

"Roo!" said Shauna, who then giggled. "Honestly girl, get your own longboat!" That sent Ellen and Helene into giggles.

"Hey, I've got a question for you three."

Gone Dutch

Silence fell and it made Shauna uncomfortable, but these women held her up and she needed them now. "Is it wrong to have a second chance at things? Or to want a second chance?" she asked.

"Why do you doubt yourself on this Shaunie?" asked Roo. Her directness was one thing Shauna appreciated, even if she didn't like it all the time. "This isn't you!"

"I just wonder..." she fought back tears.

"If you even deserve a second chance?" pipped up Ellen's quieter voice. She smiled as Shauna nodded in reply. "Been there, done that after I divorced. I wasn't brave enough to call you guys up and ask," said Ellen, glancing away. "And yes, you damn well deserve it Shaunie, we both do!" Helene and Ruth agreed.

"Hey, what's brought this on?" asked Helene.

Shauna sighed. "The weekend went well," Shauna breathed in deeply. "Really well. Even his business drink afterwards, though that was tense for a few moments." She shrugged. "I just wondered... well, am I allowed to be happy when things were okay before... when Matt isn't here?"

"That's just it," said Ruth. "Things were okay! They weren't bloody fantastic. We know you loved Matt, but a ghost doesn't keep your bed warm at night, lovely."

Gone Dutch

Shauna sighed. "I know. But, I'm wondering if I'm betraying him." She paused, fighting back the tears. "Am I?"

The collective no from the other three, along with supportive comments, did help to make her feel better.

"Knew you girls would help me get my head sorted!" she smiled. 'The rest of it I need time to build a bridge over' she thought, parking the rest of her concerns away.

"I have an announcement!" said Helene, smiling.

"When are you due?" asked Shauna, grateful for some good news to distract her mind and the others from her.

Helene smirked. "I knew you'd pick that up first. I'm nearly two months gone, so around New Year." The others chimed in with various congratulations and virtual hugs, all happy that Helene's dreams were being realised.

"Fons is ecstatic! Our parents are thrilled. I'm just... scared!" laughed Helene, nervously.

"Oh, Helene..." Shauna sighed, now returning the favour of holding up her friend. "Ellen and I will tell you; it's totally worth it! You'll be a brilliant mother and if it wasn't so important and wanted, you wouldn't feel this scared. I was the same, both times!"

"I was too!" Ellen picked up the reply. "I kept wondering if I'd be the world's worst... but I know plenty of others who are, so providing I got up, got

Gone Dutch

dressed, fed me, fed the baby and kept us clean, fed and safe, I realised I was doing well." added Ellen.

Helene smiled, dabbing tears away from her eyes.

"Thank you both!" she said. They spoke of other things, like where Helene was now living, her new job at the Rotterdam Botanical Gardens, learning Dutch. Taking an actual course to learn Dutch was something Shauna hadn't considered doing. She parked that thought for a rainy day and spoke with her friends for a little longer. Soon, they bid each other farewell and logged out of their Zoom chat.

The Wednesday before they visited Rotterdam, Shauna had the tidal details from Harek. He detailed where she was to drive her and the boys, where the boat would be moored and at what time they had to leave. At dinner that night, she told the boys.

"We're going on a boat, a private boat, to Rotterdam!?" screeched Andrew, who started bouncing up and down.

"Oi! Calm down, sit down and behave," she glared at her younger son as he bounced a little more, not listening to her. "Now." Shauna's commanding growl made her youngest sit down, though he was still itching to move from excitement. She was glad she'd told them now as he'd calm down by the time they were driving,

Gone Dutch

she wouldn't be able to deal with that energy as they drove to Hull.

"You both need to pack. Harek says we can leave what clothes we want there, so we don't need to worry about bringing back anything. But, you need to plan for about seven days."

"Which means take ten days' worth of stuff," said Michael, calmly.
Shauna could see by the twinkle in his eyes he was just as excited as his brother; he showed it differently though.

Shauna nodded. "Aye. But make sure it's not stuff you want to have here to go out meeting your friends with."

The boys nodded, shovelling food into their mouths.

"Chew your food!" she cried, admonishing them. Michael paid attention, she knew Andrew wouldn't.

Ten minutes later, food devoured, the boys went to start packing their bags. She smiled as she cleared the dinner plates away into the dishwasher, tidying the kitchen up.

She told the smart speaker to start some music and started dancing as she tidied up. Two songs later, Eye Level started playing and she laughed out loud. The theme for Van Der Valk seemed rather appropriate at the moment.

Gone Dutch

Twenty-Five

They made it to Hull that Friday afternoon, but Shauna became more anxious as the car started misbehaving as they neared the port. She smiled as they made their way to the private dock Harek had told her to go to. Sitting in the water tied to the pier, was a beautiful but large catamaran. Shauna was so awestruck she didn't see Harek come to hug her until his arms wrapped around her from behind. It took her a few moments to realise what was happening.

"Oh my gosh!" she said, turning to kiss him. The boys were already on the boat, exploring.

"That's... beautiful!" she said, looking at the cat.

He smiled. "You can leave the car in the owners' area. You'll need one of these on display so they don't tow it."

He handed her a security pass to the owners parking area and kissed her jaw. He watched as she drove the car to the lot. He followed her as the car rumbled and lurched, making horrid sounds. It didn't get as far as the owners parking spaces before steam emerged from the engine bay.

Something metal hit the floor and the car stopped dead where it was. Shauna got out and he saw she was

Gone Dutch

visibly shaking. She looked at the car, looked underneath and swore; lots. Harek reached her just as she started muttering that this was very bad. Michael and Andrew ran up to her and hugged her in a group as the realisation that the car was dead as the hot oil from the engine created a thick, slick river on the tarmac. Harek held her and stroked her hair, doing his best to calm her as he did back in the greenhouse weeks before. She sighed deeply, on the verge of tears.

"What the hell am I going to do about this?" she whispered.

He lifted her chin so that she faced him, her eyes swimming but not letting go.

"We get you a new one?" he offered. "I'll organise to have it towed."

Shauna shook her head. "It's a big expense! Damn it!"

Harek sighed. "Famke," he whispered. "It is an object, nothing more. It has served its time. We can have a new one waiting here for you for when you return. Or I can have Johan drive you and the kids home when you're back. There are options."

Security came over to see what the issue was and she could hear Harek speaking with them quickly and quietly.

They nodded and started making calls on his behalf. Another guard came up with a decent-sized cardboard box and handed it to Harek.

Gone Dutch

"Michael, Andrew: Please can you both empty everything out of the car that you can into this." He handed them the box and sent them to work emptying the car of smaller items whilst Shauna tried to remember to breathe.

It took a good quarter of an hour before Harek could persuade Shauna to come on board the cat. Harek ensured that all her bags were on board, that the boys had everything that they'd brought with them. Anything from the now-dead car that wouldn't go in the box, Harek had loaded into a hold in the Cat. The box included.

They made the tidal change and they were a good ten minutes out of Hull before Shauna realised what was happening.

"Oh, god!" she moaned, holding her heads in her hands. "What a clusterfuck!" she whispered, more to herself than anyone else. She mumbled words to herself then quietly but firmly talked herself around. "Come on lass, ye can't be acting like this! It's a problem: Sort it"

Harek had never seen her freak out before and in a way, he was glad that the car had died when he was around. At least he could help to sort things out. He took the boys to the control centre, handed them over to a crew member, and returned to where he'd left Shauna.

Gone Dutch

On the soft cream L shaped sofa, she had kicked off her shoes and was tapping figures into a small spreadsheet, working out what she could afford to spend. When the data died and she could no longer access her accounts, she stood to look around the Catamaran itself.

The glass roof and wall of windows allowed the sea view, the high-quality leather seats were comfortable, the breakfast bar was tidy, cleared down and the sun deck held a small amount of patio furniture. Her eyes glanced to the naming plaque on the wall. "Iris Rose" was the catamaran she was on. She then noticed the Iris' on the window engraving, the roses on the unit fronts, the door handles in the shape of iron iris. She smiled and sighed.

He came to stand beside her as she explored.

"This is a beautiful ship!" She somehow seemed like her normal self.

"Feeling better?" he asked, moving her hair away from her face.

She shook her head, still shaken but determined to build a bridge over it. "No, but I'll get there. I can replace it, but not easily," she said, keeping her voice low. "It's something I could well do without, but once I get decent data again, I can crunch my figures, see how much I can get together and have it at Hull for our return. The security guards were great and I must remember to thank them when I return."

Gone Dutch

"You don't have to do it alone," he replied. She looked at him, not understanding what he was saying.

"Meaning?" she inquired. He silenced her with the gentlest of kisses.

"Trust me," he said.

"Oh no. You can't," she whispered back, quickly understanding his intentions. "That's not why," she looked into his hazel eyes and saw the colours change, wondering how he did that. "It's not why I am here, or with you."

He didn't move. His eyes simply searched hers. "No one said it was. If you were on your own, you would find something suitable for you and the boys. It wouldn't be very well maintained until you got it and it would cost you to fix anything wrong with it. But you would do it, because you had to."

She couldn't argue with that. "But you are not on your own, not anymore. You don't have to do these things alone. Let me help. Let me be me and do what I know I can to help you."

She blinked but shook her head. "It's important for me to..." she began.

Harek sighed. "Famke, please, money is useless unless you use it to solve the problems it can. This is a problem money can fix."

"I am not comfortable asking you to do this. I don't even know how much I can get together properly, not yet."

Gone Dutch

Harek let his lips curl up into a half smile. "Okay, when you do, we will talk about it again. Perhaps over wine, and after the boys are in their beds. Okay?"

She nodded. That gave her a few hours. She just hoped it was long enough to work out how to do it without his help.

The boys were oblivious to the turmoil Shauna was putting herself through feet below them. Her pride and ethics were getting in the way and it had taken most of the journey to Rotterdam for Harek to convince her to even consider letting him funding a new car. He was pretty sure what she was aiming for and what he was capable of procuring was going to be very, very different.

A voice came out over the speakers in Dutch and Harek smiled. Shauna could hear her boys in the background and she smiled. They sounded cheerful, which meant they were having fun.

"They're with the captain?" she asked. Harek bent to put his shoes back on and handed Shauna hers.

He nodded. "Have been all trip. I'm sure they'll have lots to tell you." he smiled.

Shauna sighed. "I'm sorry I've been so preoccupied," She continued to pull on her shoes.

He chuckled and pulled her up to him. "You had good reasons," he said, kissing her. Losing the car like that was a shock, he knew. He'd never seen a car just die

Gone Dutch

like that. The Cat slowed and Harek walked Shauna up to the front of the Cat, giving her a front-row seat view of the city he called home.

Harek sat on one of the deck sofas, pulling Shauna to him. As they slowly travelled up the Rhine River, initial farmland gave way to boats and other industrial buildings which in turn gave way to Rotterdam. The river carried on through and up to the North of the Netherlands.

Shauna watched as the boat went under a huge bridge, then slowed and entered an industrial bay. It docked and Harek smiled at her. "Welcome to my town," he said, taking her hand and guiding her back inside the Cat.

Some of the crew were around, removing items here and there. Harek gave instructions to someone in rapid Dutch and they nodded, heading off to do as he had asked. He stepped onto the walkway and held his hand out for Shauna. He helped the boys off and the crew behind them had their luggage.

"We can get those!" said Shauna. Harek shook his head, smiling. "Come!" he said, motioning for the boys to follow too.

She saw Johan and she smiled at him. She was surprised when Harek swept her past the chauffeur and into the building behind.

When they walked through areas in the building that were screened off with industrial plastic, but had

Gone Dutch

workers behind it. "The screens are up because of the fibreglass," Harek said, guiding them onwards. "It flies about quite easily in the slightest breeze." They reached a set of stairs and he motioned for them to go up. They did and they entered an office type area.

People greeted Harek with waves and while he returned the greetings, he pushed on through to his own office. He motioned for them all to come through. As well as two decent sized desks that wouldn't look out of place in a mansion there was a large corner sofa. The boys bounced onto it as children do. Harek motioned for Shauna to sit. "I'll be back in five minutes," he said smiling, then left and closed the door.

Seeing the window look out onto the river, Shauna stood and went to look. Outside, as well as the Cat they'd come in on, were two others. One was of equal size, in a huge tent with two of the sides up. She was in the water and there were drop saws out on work benches, men walking about with tool belts, carrying wood and other fittings. The other was smaller and looked like she was nearly ready to go to whomever she had been built for. Harek appeared down at the two boats and he spoke with another man, equally as tall with blonde hair. Shauna recognised him and took a few moments to think where. "The wedding," she smiled, she was sure that was Jon. She saw Harek look up at the

Gone Dutch

window, Jon's gaze following them and both men began to head back to the building.

It didn't take long until both men entered the office. "I'm sorry, had to catch up about the business with Jon. Jon, you remember Shauna?"

Jon smiled and shook Shauna's hand as she offered it. Then he turned it over and kissed it. Shauna chuckled.

"I always remember a beautiful lady," said Jon, his eyes sparkling. Harek said something to him in Dutch and Jon laughed. He slapped Harek on his shoulder replying with something, obviously, the pair were teasing each other, as friends do.

Harek gathered paperwork together and with a smile, motioned for Shauna and the boys to follow him.

Harek walked them to the car Johan was waiting at. He opened the doors, not needing to encourage the kids to climb inside. The T6 comfortably held the five of them. "Mum, can I sit in the front, please?" asked Andrew. Shauna shrugged and turned to Harek. "Not my car sweetie, you'd need to ask Harek."

Johan answered for her with a nod from Harek. "Come on!" he said, motioning for Andrew to jump in. Harek held Shauna's hand quietly as Johan drove them home.

Gone Dutch

Harek sat up and paid attention to Shauna as the car wound its way down a drive. Nearly everywhere was near water, somehow. Small streams, lined here and there and it was strange for Shauna to see roads so near to the edge of the water. As the car turned up yet another corner, the boys said what her eyes did. "Wow!" they exclaimed. A huge windmill, easily two hundred and fifty feet tall, broke the skyline before them. The sails were stationary in an X and empty of cloth. There were several buildings attached to the old windmill that made it unclear what was what.

"Do you like it?" he asked as they alighted from the car. He was nervous. The boys were taken with it, but was Shauna?

"Like?" she turned to him, her eyes were wide in shock. "It looks amazing."

He smiled. "Come," He turned to Johan and said something in rapid Dutch. Johan nodded and waved them on, expecting the request. "Welcome to Mûne Roazen!" he said to her, unlocking the door and stepping inside.

The entranceway was easily three metres wide, wrapped in a climbing rose on the outside that was small and fragrant. As soon as they walked in, it was into the kitchen. Set into the base of the windmill and circular in design, the huge island in the middle of the room would easily seat half a dozen people, more if people were

Gone Dutch

standing. To the left of the kitchen, a sliding barn door was closed.

Harek walked to the stairs and motioned for them to follow. The stairs followed the outer wall on one side of the windmill and windows were placed to allow in light and give views of huge fields beyond. On the first floor, two bedrooms were nestled together. One was complete with two double beds in.

"We have to share?" whined Michael and Harek laughed. "You can sleep next door, if you wish," he motioned for the young man to go look and he stopped as soon as the door opened. Inside it were builders' tools, cuts of plasterboard. The floor had no carpet and a bare lightbulb hung from the ceiling. He backed out and smirked at Harek.

"Okay, we share," he said as he closed the door.

"I'm still renovating, though that room is closer now than two weeks ago. It didn't even have the electrics or walls in until this week."

He turned to Shauna. "Shall we continue?" he said, showing them the top floor, which would house a single bedroom. "These are meant for guests, not family." He looked at Michael.

"This is not where you're staying," he said. The single bedroom was as large as Shauna's suite, bathroom and all.

Gone Dutch

Leading them back to the kitchen, he continued through, guiding her to the back of the kitchen, which had glass sliding doors. Through there, was a lounge with large L shaped sofas, rugs and of course, a huge 65" TV. The boys spotted the Xbox in an instant and asked to play on it. Harek nodded and guided Shauna off to continue their private little tour. The boys would see where they were sleeping, later, he guessed. He knew Johan would have put their bags in the right rooms.

He swept her up another large spiral staircase to the first floor; his room. The balcony of which swept out onto the deck from the old windmill and around it. You could walk into his room and never set foot anywhere else in the house. His room was directly above the sitting area where her boys were but you couldn't hear the Xbox. As soon as she had stepped foot inside, he closed the door behind them, pulled her to him and pinned her against the door.

He leaned in and kissed her deeply, pinning her hands above her head so that her breasts perked into him. It was a few moments before he let her hands go and pulled away.

"I've wanted to do that to you since Hull," he said, searching into her swirling chocolate eyes.

She smiled. "I'm sorry," she said, but he held a finger to her lips.

Gone Dutch

"No more being sorry. You were allowed to geek out," his eyes narrowed. "Stop being sorry for being human, or you." She sighed and nodded, then kissed his finger.

He waved his finger in front of her and shook his head. "Later," he said, smiling. He moved and released her from the position against the door, so she could look around. "My home is yours, famke. Take it all in."

She pushed herself off the door and began looking around. The decking doors were folding and triple-glazed, hiding internal blackout blinds within. The en-suite bathroom was behind the queen-sized four-poster bed and held a claw rounded top bathtub, large enough for two to sit in, as well as a walk-in shower and again, a double sink.

"Recent addition," he said, coming up behind her to hold her. Everything in this room sparkled as if it were new. Or had at least, been scrubbed within an inch of its life. His hold on her was soft, comforting, assuring.

"You said you had the builders in?" she asked. She didn't need to turn to face him.

"I did. They did miracles in here, making the changes I wanted. The kitchen didn't even exist until a week ago. It's brand new."

"It is impressive," she gushed about it. "So much space and the range," he smiled when she mentioned the huge seven ring gas cooker he'd had installed. "I'm

Gone Dutch

envious." He puffed his chest out, he intended on that range getting an awful lot of use.

"Come," he said, releasing his hold on her before he carried out the thoughts that were in his head. "Let me show you what else there is."

In the new section, there were three more guest rooms. Two were set and ready to be used. The boys were sharing until the building work and decorating were complete.

He guided her back through the sitting area where the boys were still playing their game. "One more room," he said. "One of my favourites," his eyes shone as he held the sliding barn door. He tugged it and smoothly, it slid to reveal his office and library.

Shauna looked around, thinking that Belle would be jealous about this library. It climbed the outer wall of the mill, curving around. The shelves followed, filled with books. The glass roof pitched from the side down to the windows that were easily eight foot in height, flooding the space with light, even on the darkest days. Folding doors again gave access to the gardens but the huge fireplace with sheepskin rugs and a three-seater leather sofa made the room homely, warm.

Harek's desk sat so his back was to the window, cascading light over his work. He saw that his briefcase was on his desk, as requested. He went to sit down and

Gone Dutch

watch Shauna explore the many shelves that he'd finally filled with books.

He smiled as she slowly took in his favourite room in the house. He'd show her why later, when the fire was lit.

"This is amazing," she said, coming up to him and kissing him. He pulled her down onto his lap and kissed her deeply.

"I am glad you like," he said.

She smiled. "My favourite type of chair is Queen Anne," she pointed to a chair tucked into the corner, "they're perfect to curl up on with a book," she looked around to the fireplace. "Does that fireplace work?" she asked.

He nodded. "We'll have to christen it later," she smirked, kissing him again.

"I should let you work," she said, rising from his lap.

"I'll try to be quick," he said. "The kitchen should be stocked."

She nodded and headed out to find a kettle and call her parents.

Gone Dutch

Twenty-Six

"It's worse than that, it's dead Jim!" she said, chuckling at her father's question about how dead the car was. Sat at the kitchen island with Harek just off behind her, nursing a cup of green tea.

"Cylinder head and the oil sump off the crank I think, given how much oil flooded the car park!"

He swore gently. "How are you going to get home? Do you need me to come to pick you up?"

She sighed. "I'll start working that out tomorrow, or even tonight. I'm not sure yet what I'm going to do. I'm need to finish crunching my finances before I can tell you."

"Well," he said, "If you need me to come and get you three, let me know," he said. "Here's your mother" and the call switched to her mum. Shauna bought her up to speed and they spoke about options for a few minutes.

"Mam, I'll start looking tomorrow. Today, I just need to chill a wee bit."
"How will you look if you're in Rotterdam?" she asked.

"They'll have websites mam. I can look at their stock from anywhere," she laughed. "If they haven't got a website where I can even look at the cars, I'm not going to be getting one from them."

Gone Dutch

"Aye, well, okay," agreed Elspeth. "But you'll not see all of the car."

Shauna sighed. "Mam, they put up about twenty or thirty images per car, they'll be valeted to within an inch of their chrome plating. And I can drive just about anything with four wheels and an engine, uncle David taught me that. Save maybe a Fire Engine. My licence doesn't cover twenty-ton vehicles," she joked. Elspeth sighed in agreement.

"Okay, well, let us know what you want us to do to help you out. We can put towards a new one if needs be," she offered.

Shauna smiled. "I know mam. But, I'll think about that tomorrow. Just, let me do one thing at a time, aye?"

"Aye, okay dear!" she said. Shauna knew from her tone that her mother wasn't going to let it go.

"Mother," she scolded. "Don't you go window shopping for me. Ye hear?" She knew what her mother was like.

"But," replied Elspeth pleadingly.

"No "buts" mother. No. Do. Not. Do. That. To. Me." Shauna made herself perfectly clear. "Put dad back on, please?" she asked.

Her dad's voice scolded his wife for something. "Dad! Don't let mum go window shopping for cars, aye? What she thinks I want and what I need or even afford, are gonna be two different things, or even three," she

Gone Dutch

closed her eyes for a moment. "Please, don't let her. I just, don't need that kind of help right now."

James chuckled. "Aye, OK. I'll keep an eye," he said.

"Right, I've got to go. But we're here, in one piece, alive and intact. Thought you'd want to know." she said. Saying goodbye, she sensed Harek standing in the doorway and turned. He was leaning against the door frame with a smile on his lips, his eyes bright.

"You didn't wander far," he said, coming to join her at the island. He'd overheard her telling her mother not to go window shopping for cars. His heart leapt.

"I didn't need to. Have you finished work?" she asked.

He nodded. "In a way. Business work is finished. My other work depends on your choice. Come," he said, offering his hand. She took it and he guided her back to the library, to the large sofa and the fire that was now roaring in the fireplace. He motioned for her to sit on the sofa and he grabbed the laptop from his desk. Coming to join her, he placed it onto her lap, the screen on.

What she saw were cars. Not just any car, but a specific range and type. Audi Q7, not quite the latest model, used but practically new, hardly anything on the clock. There were three litre TDI models along with electric hybrid ones.

"Pick one of them," he said.

Gone Dutch

She looked at the screen and back at him. She saw the price tags.

Her eyes boggled. "That's way too much." She looked at him. "I know I don't have that amount," she said, sitting back, arms by her sides. She looked at the laptop screen, then back to him. "That's more than Bryce and I make in a year. And I've still got to insure it."

He smiled, turned her head to him and kissed her. "Too much?" he shook his head. "You need a safe, reliable, roadworthy car. Every one of those is well within my budget. Pick one," he said, insistently.

She shook her head. "That's a crazy amount for a car."

Harek took one of her hands and made her look at him.

"You need a car that will safely transport you and the boys from Hull to home and back again. I will be much happier knowing you have a decent, safe car to do so." He looked at her and saw her eyes dance. "Please pick one."

She sighed and arranged the list by price and then compared what features they had. When Michael told him that his mother knew cars, he hadn't expected her to know much of the difference in the list before her. Five minutes later, she bought a particular one up on the screen and scrolled through every picture that the car had. Twice. Then she checked the specifications again.

Gone Dutch

"This one," she said meekly. "But Harek…" he held a finger to her lips.

"Shauna, you need a car that will get you to and from Hull, to run the kids here, there and everywhere. I'll repeat myself: I'll be much happier knowing you're doing it in comfort. That you and the boys are as safe as your driving." He kissed her again, deeply this time and left her slightly breathless. "The benefits of wealth mean nothing if I have no one to share it with," he leaned his head into the side of hers gently. "Now, I do."

She heard what he was saying and her empathic side picked up on it. Could she say the three little words that he was trying to say? He felt so right in her arms and her bed. She'd missed having him just be near her, his voice not quite enough over the phone, them being so far away from the other that it hurt.

She relented. "Okay," she sighed. She closed her eyes and leaned her forehead against Harek's. He leaned back and kissed it, smiling.

"The caterers will be here soon."

"Caterers?" she said, sitting up. "For…?"

Harek smiled. "Tonight you meet my family. Vayenn and Reuben you've met, Evie and Luuk are my niece and nephew. My parents will be here too. Jon is bringing his girlfriend and there are a few others," he said.

Gone Dutch

She blinked. "Okay," she replied, tentatively. "This isn't a formal dinner or anything? It's just a family social?"

Harek nodded. "Just family and friends. The caterers are making it easy for us both. I can cook, but I was fetching you today and then the car happened. They were booked anyway, but I am sure that the kids will enjoy the party food, the Xbox, the gardens. We'll have time to cook and relax as a family, but tonight, no chores, not even the cleaning up." He smiled at her. She sighed and shook her head. He was bossy.

"I'll go freshen up then?" she suggested as he lifted the laptop from her lap.

"Good idea. There's a bathroom at the other end for the boys if they want to do the same."

Shauna nodded, standing. She watched Harek as he glided into his desk and picked up the phone with the laptop directly before him. She slid the library door partially closed and slowly made her way to the living room.

"Hey boys, dinner party time. We're meeting Harek's family tonight. Can you two go and get a shower?"

Michael and Andrew stopped their game. "We know. Harek said on the way over on the boat, but you were having a minor freak about the car," Michael nudged his brother playfully on the shoulder. "Come on Andy, race you!" Shauna sighed. The damn car had

Gone Dutch

caused a huge focus shift. She saw the boys to their room and the shower they were to use. Then she decided she was having a soak in that claw tub bath. So she did.

Gone Dutch

Twenty Seven

Harek found her half an hour later, up to her shoulders in bubbles. The boys had showered and returned to the Xbox in super-fast time. The catering company had arrived and were making preparations. Finally, his house was alive with the sounds and smells of home.

"There you are," he said, smiling at her. She smiled up at him.

"Here I am," she said.

"What's wrong?" he asked, placing the toilet lid down and sitting on it like a stool.

She shook her head. "Nothing I can't build a bridge over," she said, looking at him.

He gave her a curious look. "Just, overwhelmed with what's happened today. The car, the boat ride that I just clearly spaced out during, the plans for tonight that you told the boys about but couldn't tell me because I wasn't able to absorb it." she sighed. "I just feel like I've been…" she sighed and looked at him. "I've not exactly been supportive or myself today."

He smiled and went to kneel beside the bath. He lifted her face and kissed her. "Your world got turned upside down. I'm glad the car died where it did. Any

Gone Dutch

further away and you'd not be here, though I would have found you and the boys somehow." He kissed her again.

"It's hard," she breathed.

"What is?" he said, standing up. He undid a few buttons then removed his shirt and dropped his hand into the bath. He pulled the plug until half the bath had drained away. She squealed and he laughed. Then he turned the hot water on and began refilling the tub.

She watched as he undressed and despite his obvious erection, joined her in the bath. "Slide down," he commanded, getting in behind her.

Once the water was at the level he was happy with, he shut the water off.

He wrapped his arms around her and kissed her temple.

"What's hard?" he asked, rubbing warm water over her arms, drawing the conversation back to earlier.

"Opening up again." she signed. "I thought I had it down, that I was okay with there being an "us", I just freaked out back to me not having a handle on things when the going got tough."

He sighed and wrapped his legs around her, pinning her in the water to him.

"I've told you before, what you bring to me is something I didn't know I was missing. Until the chance to have it was suddenly there. I haven't worked out what I can bring to you, but I am working that out."

Gone Dutch

She turned to look at him as best she could. "You're unlocking a heart I didn't realise needed unlocking," she said. She rested her head against his chest and sighed. "I thought I had it all under control," she shook her head. "Today shows that one little thing goes pop and I melt. I never used to. I was always part of a team with Matt. I have just forgotten how to play like that, to trust the other member of the team."

He stroked her shoulder. "Your new teammate isn't sure either, so the trust goes both ways." He wrapped his arms around her. "When we met with Berend, I hadn't a clue how the meeting would go, or how I'd convince him to stay signed with us. I was ready for a confrontation, a legal one if needs be. You had it sorted in ten minutes and looking as gorgeous as hell doing it."

She voice lifted. "I do remember, I was there," she rubbed her left knee in memory. "My knee recovered quickly enough after dinner," she smirked.

Harek's voice went quiet as he opened up to her a little more. "In the hospital, even before then, when you found me, it was your voice I could hear above everyone else's. I heard you take charge until the ambulance turned up, I heard you tell people what to do, heard you tell me to stay with you. I don't remember much of the ride to the hospital but I remember Vayenn saying you had waited outside with her when you didn't have to. We'd only spent that one fabulous night together, but

Gone Dutch

you still stayed with me. It is that strength I want to be near."

She closed her eyes and wiggled against him.

Taking a deep breath, she whispered: "I in love with you".

Harek looked down at her. He was sure she'd said something. "Hmm?" he said. She turned in the water and knelt before him, bubbles everywhere.

"Harek, I love you," she said, slightly more forcefully.

He blinked, then smiled and reached for her to kiss her passionately. "And I know that I'm in love with you," he said, pulling her down towards him in the bathwater.

An alarm on his phone began chirping, calling their attention away from each other. They chuckled and began to climb out of the bath.

"My parents will be here soon, if they're not already. Johan is greeting everyone for me."

"Is he your butler?" she asked, wrapping a new bath towel around her.

Harek thought. "That's the best title for the job he does."

She smiled. "He's good at it. Come on, slowcoach, time to get dressed."

She padded out into the bedroom and pulled her bag up onto the bed. Finding casual but smart clothes,

Gone Dutch

she dressed in flowing trousers that showed off her arse and a lace cream blouse that showed off her bust.

"Here," he said, taking some of her clothes and putting them into a dresser he'd recently bought for her. "The closet is there," he said, pointing to a place on the wall.

"Where?" she asked as she looked around, missing where he had pointed but she couldn't see anything obvious. He smiled and pushed a panel and the door opened, revealing a huge walk-in closet behind one wall. "Oh!" she said, smiling. "I never even saw that!"

He chuckled. "If you didn't, then others won't either, I hope."
"Why do you hope?" she asked, finding something to slip her feet into. The black ballet style pumps went well with her choice.

"Because I had a rather good idea to hide a safe in there," he smiled and winked at her.

She chuckled and waited as he dressed in casual trousers and a dark blue button shirt. She applied a little makeup at the dressing mirror in the closet as he brushed his hair into place. Holding out his hand, he guided her down the stairs to meet his family.

Vayenn had indeed, already arrived. She hugged her brother, then Shauna and dragged Shauna away from Harek.

Gone Dutch

"Whew! Now, time for girl talk!" She led Shauna into the library and sat on the sofa, was Helene. Shauna was ecstatic to see her old friend and cried a little.

"Harek said he's been busy today, but not with work. What's going on?" asked Vayenn. Shauna sighed and stared into the fire for a moment. Helene shrugged at Vayenn as Shauna found the words. She looked at Helene.

"Carly died today."

Vayenn offered sympathy whilst Helene, knowing that the car was called Carly, gasped. "How?"

"Cylinder head blew as the oil sump blew off, I think. Might be the other way around, I'm not sure. The engine is totalled." Vayenn looked puzzled. "She'd been making weird noises all the way up the motorway to Hull."

"You're talking about a car?!" she said, grasping the terminology.

Shauna nodded and sighed. "The last car my husband and I bought together, the last big thing we did after Andrew, was to buy that car. It wasn't showroom new when we got it, but it has done us ten years, or more. But, yes, today it died. Just as I was going to drive it to the owners area."

Helene sat back. "Tell us about it."

So, Shauna did; again.

Helene sighed. "I'm sorry Shaunie. I know that car meant a lot."

Gone Dutch

Shauna shrugged. "As Harek pointed out; it's a thing, an item. It served its purpose and now it can't," she shrugged. "So, time to move onto a new one."

Helene looked concerned. She looked at Vayenn as she asked. "How?"

Shauna smiled. "I didn't get much of a say, though I was asked to pick it out of a list." She nodded towards Harek who could be seen in the kitchen.

"My brother brought you a car?" asked Vayenn as her jaw dropped.

Shauna's cheeks pinked. "Yes, why?"

Vayenn chortled as she threw her head back. "My stingy big, business head, stubborn ass of a brother, bought you a family car?"

Shauna nodded again. "Bullied me into it, almost." She shrank back a little. "I think I'm missing the point here though?" she said. Was she wrong to have let Harek push her into such a car? Or any car?

Vayenn wiped away her tears of laughter, rose and slid the library door shut.

"Let me tell you about my brother," she said, sitting back down. "When I was ten, he wouldn't buy me sweets because the ones I wanted was out of my pocket money amount. He wouldn't lend me the extra money either. Every girl he's been with, and I mean girl, has tried to get him to spend money on her like it was water out of the tap. Ever since he made his fortune with the boat business gramps built, he's been very careful where

Gone Dutch

he lays out. He needs a solid business reason to do so, even with general life things," she motioned around her. "Mûne Roazen was a shell for months, he only had a few rooms set up. This, his room and a bathroom," Vayenn smiled then shook her head. "Even then, he's a scrooge. To have him just do that is unlike him." Vayenn patted Shauna's knee.

"He is totally taken by you. He's never done anything like that for anyone that isn't family or a close friend." She sat back, grinning like a Cheshire cat. "You being in his life has changed that. He's made this place as it should have been months ago. So, I'll say it first: Welcome to the Van Meerloo family!"

Shauna sighed and smiled. "Here was me thinking you were going to say I'd tricked him or something."

Helene laughed. "Like you bewitched him?" asked Helene, making a point that Shauna would understand. Vayenn smiled. "He did claim I put a spell on him at your wedding," she said to Helene, grinning.

Vayenn laughed. "He told me you read the cards?" she said.

Shauna nodded. "He didn't seem bothered by it, thankfully" replied Shauna.

Vayenn smiled. "No, it won't bother him. He's interested and curious, but that's about it. He's quite tolerant and open-minded in that regard. He is however,

Gone Dutch

a stubborn ass in many, many other ways!" Vayenn rolled her eyes as she spoke, then shook her head.

Vayenn stood and motioned to the kitchen. "I think we need to get back to the party."

"He's not told me what we're celebrating." said Shauna as they headed to find food and drink.

Vayenn smiled. "He will," she said, winking.

Vayenn found a drink and went to find her husband, who was still chatting with Harek and Fons. She spoke to them both, looked at Shauna, poked her brother in the chest and dragged her husband away. Fons was suddenly busy with Helene at his side.

Shauna leaned against a kitchen counter, smirking as Harek came to find her.

"And what did Vayenn mean when she said you'd tell us what we're celebrating? I thought this was a family social?" She had a feeling something was afoot, Vayenn just confirmed that.

Harek smiled and cuddled her. "As I said before, it is. I've never had a house-warming party. The building work was never finished and I never got around to it. You and the boys gave me a reason to get the work pushed more to be finished. Next time, it should all be done and you can help me pick out furnishings."

"And that is all?" she asked, looking into his eyes. They didn't change into swirls of colour this time.

Gone Dutch

Were the eye colour changes a tell about his integrity? She'd have to watch for that.

He inclined his head slightly. "Yes, why?"

She smiled. "Your sister implied that there was something else going on."

He laughed. "I love my sister, I really do, but the truth is, she told me off for not introducing you to my parents and other guests."

She smiled. "Oh, okay. Where are the boys?" she asked, helping herself to a glass of something, she wasn't sure what but it didn't seem like alcohol.

"In the lounge, playing on the Xbox. I think Jon is being beaten at a racing game by Michael."

Michael was, indeed, winning at a racing game. Shauna recognised it as Forza, a game she knew Michael would rage at when he played it.

"Best of five?" asked Jon, having lost another race.

Michael laughed. "No! I'm going for some pizza, Drew can play with you"

Shauna hugged her eldest as he came past her. She noticed Andrew take up Michael's controller, his cheeks full of food.

"Boy is a damn hamster," she said to Harek, grinning.

Together they made their way through the guests, until Harek stopped before an older couple who were sitting at a small table that had been erected in the

Gone Dutch

kitchen. It took Shauna three seconds to recognise who they were: His parents.

"Mamma, Pappa, let me introduce you to Shauna. Shauna, these are my parents, Pieter and Hanna Van Meerloo."

Shauna shook Pieter's hand firmly. His father's height made it obvious he was Harek's father. Pieter was older and maybe not as broad, but certainly Harek was a chip off the old block. His eyes though, reflected in that of his mother.

His mother was more Vayenn's stature, now grey around the edges but still with the same light brown hair Harek had.

"Pleased to meet you," said Shauna, holding her hand out for Pieter. Instead, she found herself in a bear hug with him saying something in very fast Dutch.

Harek laughed and said something else that Shauna thought sounded like: "She doesn't speak Dutch yet Pappa!"

"Ah," he said, stepping back. English wasn't something he had grasped a lot of, but it was still a lot better than anything Dutch Shauna could say!

"Pleased to meet you," he said, finally. Shauna smiled.

"And I'm pleased to meet you, Pieter," said Shauna. His wife waved him out of the way and hugged Shauna too. "You make my boy happy," said Hanna,

Gone Dutch

smiling. It was clear that Hanna had a better grasp of English than Pieter.

"I'll try to!" said Shauna, smiling.

"Sit, sit!" said Hanna and Pieter pulled up another chair. For the next while, Shauna spoke with Harek's parents about her life, her boys and how she'd met him. Though they knew she'd found him after the attack, they didn't know why she had. Now they understood how.

Hanna rose after a while, saying something to Pieter in fluent Dutch. He nodded, said "Good night" in a bold voice, and carefully climbed the stairs with Hanna in the main part of the house.

Shauna smiled as they headed off to bed. She checked the time and decided to chase Michael and Andrew to bed, though, she hadn't needed to. They'd done that themselves and the Xbox was powered off. Fons and Helene bid their farewells. The catering staff began clearing things down, washing things up. Only a few of the many guests Shauna had met were still there, Vayenn and Reuben being the main two.

"Family are staying tonight. Mamma and Pappa have a room next to your boys. Vayenn and her family will be upstairs" he said, pointing to the windmill. Everyone else had or was, slowly making their way to their own homes. Shauna smiled.

"Harek," said Jon, grinning. "Good night and dank je!" He waved at everyone, taking his girlfriend

Gone Dutch

with him. Suddenly, it was only family and the catering staff left, who loaded their van with speed and departed.

Harek smiled and motioned those still awake to the sofa in the library.

Harek indicated that everyone sit where they wanted. Vayenn and Reuben cuddled into one side of the sofa, leaving Harek to claim the other end Shauna decided to snuggle into him.

"Your parents are nice," Shauna said, burrowing into him and nursing the drink that he'd placed there. She wasn't in the mood.

"They're good people, hard-working. How mamma ran this place I do not know."

Vayenn smiled. "She did it because she had to, that's why. And grand-mere was here. I like what you've changed," she added, nodding to her older brother. "The kitchen is a huge improvement."

He smiled. "I was lacking a reason to get all the work done." He kissed Shauna on the head. "Now I have one, or three!" he said, smiling.

"Did your parents meet the boys?" asked Shauna, looking at him.

He nodded. "They did. Pappa encouraged Michael to beat Jon. The boy has a poker face."

Shauna laughed. "When he's gaming, he's focused. I'm glad it extends to his studies too."

Gone Dutch

They chatted about the evening but it wasn't long until Vayenn said she needed sleep.
Bidding their goodnights to each other, Vayenn and Reuben left the library, sliding the door closed behind them.

Gone Dutch

Twenty-Eight

Harek pulled Shauna close in a hug, content to sit for a while before the roaring fire.

"How are you now?" he asked her quietly.

"I'm okay," she said. "I told Vayenn about the car," she said, wondering if Harek was going to be upset. He chuckled.

"What did she say?"

"She asked how on earth her stubborn, miserly, money pinching, business-focused big brother brought his new girlfriend a car when he wouldn't help her buy sweets when she was ten."

Harek laughed heartily. "She is never going to let me forget that, is she?"

Shauna giggled. "I doubt it. Siblings never do," she shifted slightly. "I still remember some of the things my siblings did to me. And things I did to them in revenge," she grimaced at some of the memories. "Not all of them great,"

Harek sipped his drink. "You did well tonight," he said, praising her.

"Well, I didn't save any companies, I didn't total anyone's car and I didn't embarrass myself," she looked up and then nodded. "I think I did okay."

Gone Dutch

The rumbles of laughter from Harek were more felt than heard.

She sighed in contentment and had no intention of moving. Neither did Harek. "Does it feel like home now?" she asked, stifling a yawn.

"Not quite, but it's more home now than it was last night."

She turned her head. "What will make it feel like home?" she asked, oblivious to what he was aiming for.

"Loving you, right here, now," he replied, huskily. He had placed his drink out of harms' way and took Shauna's from her, placing it on the table next to the sofa. She sat up allowing him to move and he rose swiftly, quietly to the sliding barn door. Finding the latch, he slung it locked.

"That's better," he said, his eyes dark and hooded. Shauna scooted back so that she was in the corner but he wasn't having that. He beckoned to her and she rose to him, grinning.

He grabbed her, spun her around and sat in the middle of the sofa. He pulled Shauna to him so she was straddling him and slowly, he reached in for a kiss. It was a slow, deep passionate kiss. With his hands behind her head and her hands on his upper arms, they moaned in pleasure just from the touching of one another.

He began to run his hands down her back and swiftly, he removed her blouse, aware of the bra that she wore which was front fastening. He had it unclipped and

Gone Dutch

removed in seconds, releasing her breasts from the confines of the supporting fabric.

His hands gently massaged her breasts and she moaned as his mouth took the whole nipple of one breast. He teased and licked it making the tip stand on edge. Her hands in his hair told him she liked that, so he did the same to the other. She began tugging at his shirt, demanding that it be removed. A few tugs here and his torso was bare for her to admire and tease. She ran her fingers across his bare chest, tweaking his nipples. His pectoral muscles twitched with the sensation, something she delighted in. He pushed himself forward and carefully, lowered them to the blanket of sheepskin rugs before the fireplace.

With her beneath him, he could move so that he could kiss her neck, her ribs and stomach. Kneeling up, he removed her trousers and knickers, revealing her very nakedness in one fell swoop.

He was about to work more kisses onto her body as she tried to undo his buckle. Smiling at her, he stood, removed the remainder of his clothes, and returned to the rugs and the roaring fire.

He began by kissing the ribs he intended earlier. Her hands played in his hair and she arched as he hit some ticklish spots that he knew he'd hit. Finding her wet folds, he began licking and playing her with his tongue, inserting two of his fingers deep within her. She

Gone Dutch

raised her hands above her head, clearly enjoying his touch. He turned his fingers within her and pulsed against the top of her walls, causing her to moan and squirm in response. He grinned as she responded to his touch. He kept moving his fingers as he licked and sucked, knowing that she wasn't too far from coming undone for the first time.

It took a good few minutes more before she shook, cried out and arched against him. He held her apart with one shoulder and his other hand, determined not to let her find her grounding.
He moved as the last of the shudders died away, he rose above her, placing himself at her entrance.

"Shauna," he whispered huskily. She looked at him and tried to reach up to kiss him.
"Say my name," he said, hovering over her. Only when she had said his name with her eyes wide open, did he slip himself into her folds, kissing her deeply as he did so. She arched up to greet him and scratched her nails across his back as he thrust into her time and time again.

He raised one of her knees to push it back against her side and breast as he found a way to thrust deep into her core. She cried out and arched up as he hit the same spot over and over again, causing her to climax before he could. He didn't stop. He didn't want to. He steadied his pace so that she would unravel again as he finally reached his peak.

Gone Dutch

They lay in a heap before the fire, which was now slowly dying. He leaned up to kiss her and found her weeping.

"Hej!" he said, kissing her tears. "Why?"

"Because I don't deserve you?" she asked, kissing him deeply. "But by the Goddess, I'm in love with you!" he smiled and stayed where he was, wrapped within her and kissed her until she had no more tears to cry.

She shuddered as he left her core empty but his kisses made up for it, at least partially.

"We need our bed," he said, standing. He had no idea what time it was and he didn't care. He, however, did want to do that to her again in bed. Their new bed, in their room, in private.

"Does it feel like home now?" she asked, finding her things by the firelight.

"Nearly," he replied as his eyes danced. The truth was, now it did feel like home. He unlocked the door and peered out. No one else was around. Leaving the fireguard up, he would let the fire burn itself out and escorted her up to their room.

Flinging the clothes onto the bedroom chair, he pulled back the covers for Shauna to climb under. Satin sheets and a heavy quilt would ensure neither got cold. Harek went to the folding doors, activated the blinds and tried to find his way to the bed in the pitch darkness. A

Gone Dutch

few stumbles later and he had found it. Climbing in with Shauna, he settled down with her in his arms, content. Shauna was already half asleep before his breathing had settled. Hearing her steady, gentle breathing sent him chasing after her to the land of nod.

Gone Dutch

Twenty-Nine

He awoke to a weak light coming from the doors and Shauna standing by them wrapped in something.

"Moan famke," he said, rubbing his face. She turned and smiled, leaving whatever it was she was looking at and coming back to their bed, dropping whatever she had been wrapped in onto the floor. The sheets on her side weren't cold, so she hadn't been standing there for long.

She was chilly though when she snuggled back in against him.

"What were you doing?" he asked, kissing her temple, her ear, her jaw.

"Welcoming the dawn," she said, reaching up and kissing his mouth deeply.

"Oh?" he said, between breaths of kisses.

"Yes," she whispered, working her way to being on top and suckling his nipples, kissing his pectoral muscles and working her way down his abs with many hot kisses.

She loved kissing his muscular body, seeing how his pecs jumped, his abs clench. She was never going to tire it, or seeing how fine he looked. She tossed the

Gone Dutch

covers back as she worked her way down to his ever-growing erection.

"Seriously, what is it with you Netherlanders and your manhood's? Your flag is always flying." He laughed and gasped a second later as she began licking and swallowing him. She grabbed the base of him and began thrusting him with her hand. She waited until there was a good amount of early jewels on his tip, before she worked her way to sit above him. She didn't need to line him up, she slid down onto him neatly, sweetly. Her insides clamped down as she took all of him in and he groaned in satisfaction.

"Zo goed!" he exclaimed. That she got that reaction in Dutch, made her smile. His guard was down with her now, there was no pretending. She began riding him, switching from entwining her fingers with his, teasing his nipples or running her nails across his abs. He never knew quite where her touch was going to land next. His large hands held onto her hips and at times, he thrust up as she landed down. She began to climax, feeling the heat build-up within her as she rode him, as he thrust into her from beneath. She reached around, stroking his balls just by his bum. As he shot his seed deep into her, he pulled her hips down to him, sending her to a full climax too.

She flopped down on top of him, unable to move.

Gone Dutch

"Stars," she whispered, knowing that he'd understand the reference.

He simply groaned in agreement and held onto her tightly. He switched them around so she was now beneath him, and he kissed her deeply.

"Now, I am home!" he said, lifting a leg of hers so it pushed against a breast.

"Really?!" she asked, going wide-eyed.

He nodded and began slowly building the rhythm up between them. It was only a few moments later that a small shudder and a groan escaped from Harek.

"How?" she breathed as he released her leg to lay between her.

"Needed to," he said, somehow managing to grab the covers and throw it over them.

He kissed her until he had to withdraw. He used his fingers to scoop the wetness out from within her and lick it. He didn't offer her any, for which she was thankful. He lay to her side, swinging her around to be on the side of him.

She closed her eyes, unable to keep them open. He joined her in a blissful sleep for another few hours.

She awoke later, still wrapped around Harek, content and for the first time since Matt had died, at peace. She looked up at him and stroked his hair away from his face. She smiled as he stirred and she moved off him to visit the bathroom.

Gone Dutch

He properly woke up when he heard the water running. He reached across for Shauna, but she wasn't there, though the bed was still warm. He lay back, listening then he understood that she was running a bath. The water shut off and he felt her presence a moment later.

"Join me?" she said, kissing him deeply. He stretched and decided a bath was a good way to wake up, given that they'd made love at least twice in eight hours. He got up and followed her to the bathroom.

The claw bath was full of bubbles, her wash things placed neatly at the sink he had built for her. She was already in the bubbles, leaning back against one edge with the taps to her left. She ignored him as he took care of his own needs and she didn't open an eye until he was stepping into the bath. She smiled.

"You need to flush that first," she said, pointing at the lavatory.

He grinned, leaned across and pressed flush, then proceeded to climb into the bath and join her. He slipped his legs around hers, placing his long legs on either side of her whilst she placed hers on top of his hips. He lifted one of her feet and began massaging her foot in the hot water. She moaned and leaned back, but didn't offer anything in return. He wasn't expecting her to, he was

Gone Dutch

sedated enough from last night, the thirst of having her in his arms again had been quenched.

They eventually emerged and dressed, then headed downstairs. Harek's parents were busy making breakfast for their grandchildren as well as Shauna's boys. Vayenn and Reuben were sitting on the sofa in the library, drinking something hot and talking quietly with the fire blazing in the hearth.

Harek smiled and greeted his parents, hugged his niece and nephew, Michael and Andrew, then poured himself a coffee. He went to join his sister and brother-in-law, leaving Shauna to talk to her children.

They squirmed as Shauna tickled them, checking that they were being polite. Hanna assured her that they were perfectly polite, "lovely boys," she said. Shauna noticed that Hanna and Pieter had everything under control. It was a much quieter affair with more children than it had been at her house only weeks before. Everyone was paired off, doing their own thing and Shauna was not.

"You look lost," said Vayenn, appearing at her side.

"I am, I guess," she said, slowly. "Not something that's usual for me!"

Vayenn chuckled. "Harek never got to show you Rotterdam that day. If you're okay with it, I can look

Gone Dutch

after the boys with my two. It seems that they're good at keeping each other out of mischief."

Shauna looked around and saw that the four of them were, indeed, interacting and playing nicely. Not that her boys were unruly, but they did like to wind each other up. Vayenn said the same about her two.

"I should give you something towards their keep for the day," she said, suddenly switching on to the agenda at hand. Vayenn shook her head and waved a no in reply.

"It's already taken care of. The Sea Life Centre at the Hague will keep them busy for the day. It will mean we'll be back fairly late tonight though. I thought the Sea Life Centre, the beach, some pizza and maybe a movie would be okay?"

Shauna laughed. "You're meant to tire them out, not you," she looked at Harek's sister with affection.

Vayenn smiled. "I don't think I need to worry about them wearing me out today," she motioned to the kids. Shauna turned to see all four of them playing Need for Speed on the Xbox. Evie was doing quite well, having never played it before.

Shauna smiled. "If you're sure?" she said, sipping the coffee whilst it was still warm. Vayenn smiled and touched Shauna's arm. "Of course I am."

Hanna placed a plate of food before Shauna could object.

Gone Dutch

"Wentelteefjes," said Hanna, expecting Shauna to know what that meant. The knife and fork appeared moments later and a small pot of fresh strawberries joined it with more coffee.

Shauna smiled. Well, this was food. Wenelteefjes was the Dutch take on french toast, served with fruit. The bread wasn't just normal white bread; it had swirls of cinnamon and sugar within it, wrapped in eggs. Shauna couldn't remember a sweeter start to the day.

Vayenn gathered the kids together and set off, leaving Harek and Shauna with Pieter and Hanna.

Pieter said something in Dutch, then repeated it in English.

"We are going to head back today my boy. Thank you for a lovely house-warming party." He hugged Harek then came to hug Shauna.

"And thank you for making him finally sort this place out!" he chuckled and kissed her on the side of her head. Hanna hugged her too, telling her again that she had very well behaved children. She smiled fondly at Harek, glanced at Shauna, grinned and walked to their car. In moments, it was just the two of them in a huge house, in the Dutch countryside, somewhere near Rotterdam.

Harek came and hugged her from behind. "Crazy enough for you?" he asked, grinning.

Gone Dutch

"Your parents are lovely" she said warmly, snuggling into him. "How did you get Vayenn to take the boys?"

He chuckled. "She offered. Her two are driving her mad as it's the school holidays here too. Your two have stopped the fights she'd have to break up."

Shauna smiled. "She said that to me, but I thought you'd twisted her arm somehow. She wouldn't take any money from me to cover their expenses for the day."

He turned her to face him. "I did take care of that. This week is my treat," Shauna's face scowled a little.

"What is wrong?" he asked.

"Just..." she stopped and shook her head. "I didn't come here to spend your money. I came to spend time, to get to " he kissed her lightly on the lips, ending her excuses.

"I know," he whispered. "They will have fun today, making memories and sharing an experience. They will tell you stories when you see them again tonight, or tomorrow when they can talk. If in having that fun, there's a little expense incurred that makes everyone happy, then so be it."

"You're a generous uncle," said Shauna, remembering what Vayenn had said the night before. *"He only spends money on family,"* she'd said. Did he consider her children family now? His words weren't

Gone Dutch

empty, this is what he meant. She was more than just a lover with kids in tow. Harek smiled.

"I try to be. It will bring smiles to their faces and I hope it gives you a much needed day off. Speaking of which," he said, drawing back and taking her hand. He guided her to the garage, something Harek hadn't yet shown her.

Parked within the walls, were five cars. The Tesla 6, which was different from the one she'd seen in England. A Tesla Roadster in hot red, a dark grey McLaren 720s, an Audi Q7 Electric car and a nineteen-thirty-three Singer Sports 4 in dove white.

"Wow," she said, stopping dead at the sight of the McLaren 720s.

She took the sight of the other cars but smiled deeply at the Singer Sports.

"Oh, an old classic!" she said, running her fingers along the wheel arches and roof.

"My grandfather's first car. I had it restored as she would have been and keep it here."

"That is beautiful! The McLaren and the Roadster… Michael will drool if he gets to see it."

Harek chuckled. "He can, tomorrow. I thought we might stick around here tomorrow, since it will be Sunday and we Dutch love our Sundays with family."

She nodded. That sounds just ideal.

Gone Dutch

"Which one would you like to ride into Rotterdam?" he asked, leaning against the garage door. She turned to him, her eyes still dancing.

"I'm not the one that is going to need to park it," she replied with a coy grin.

He laughed. "Okay. Roadster it is. Shall we?" he said, offering out his hand. Together they prepared themselves for a day in Rotterdam.

Gone Dutch

Thirty

Rotterdam was split into two parts, mainly because of the war. What had been destroyed in World War Two had now been rebuilt into newer and contemporary designs. Shauna couldn't believe the Cube Houses at the Blaak Station and was even more amazed that you could go into them. They did, however, make her uneasy and she was glad when her feet were back on solid ground outside.

The newer side of Central-East slowly gave way as they walked towards the old town. He stole several kisses under the Erasmus Bridge, enticed her with Dutch pancakes for a late lunch, laughed as she stepped into the biggest pair of clogs she'd ever seen, indulged her with visits to boutiques and cafe's in the old town near the river and held her close as dusk beckoned. They returned to the car and headed back as the street lights began to claim the city.

They were back before Vayenn and the kids, who, according to the texts for Vayenn, hadn't been a bother at all that day.

Harek helped her out of the Roadster then pinned her to it with a passionate kiss. She wrapped her arms

Gone Dutch

around his neck and kissed him back. She could feel his arousal through their coats and had caught his glances on the drive back from Rotterdam.

They heard a car pull up and Harek sighed. She placed a finger on his lips and whispered; "Later" to him as she went to greet Vayenn and the boys.

They were excited but very tired and it didn't take too long to get all four children into bed. Even Michael, who would normally stay up later, was ready for bed.

Vayenn and Reuben said they'd eaten pizza with the kids, so were not hungry. Harek nodded, then smiled. "I'll cook," he said kissing Shauna's jaw and nibbling her ear lobe very gently.

"Okay," she said, taking a cup of camomile tea to sit in the lounge and talk with Vayenn and Reuben.

Her tea was drunk before the food was ready. Vayenn and Reuben retired, saying that maybe the kids had tired them out. She joined Harek in the kitchen, watching him create a potato, carrot and onion mash with some steamed fish and a sauce. He seemed to be enjoying the cooking and was attentive enough to pour her a little white wine to go with their meal. When it was ready, they ate in comfortable silence, enjoying the company and the food.

Gone Dutch

They settled in the library before the wide-open fire, snuggled into the sofa, content and full.

"Rotterdam is beautiful and that bridge," She smiled. The giant clogs near the kiosk underneath the Erasmus Bridge had been the biggest giggle for them both today. Shauna yawned, unable to keep herself from yawning.

"Let's go to bed," she said, smiling at Harek. He smiled and spread the fire out so that it would die down slowly. Securing the doors for the night, he followed her to the bedroom.

Shauna wasted little time getting ready for bed. Harek snatched glances at her here and there as she cleaned her face, brushed her hair and teeth and changed into a half-length chemise. Of course, he had no intention of that staying on her for long. When she was finally ready, she lit a single candle on the nightstand and was wiggling under the covers, trying to warm them up.
Satin sheets, she decided, didn't warm up as well as fleece ones did!

He got into bed and reached for her, holding her in the crook of his arm as she stroked his chest gently. This, he decided, he could get very used to. He looked down when her fingers stopped their meanderings, to find Shauna was already asleep. Smiling at her, he held

Gone Dutch

her close, breathing in her scent and letting himself dream.

The following morning, she was up and dressed before he'd stirred. He felt a little lost and bewildered without her to wake up next to, so he quickly washed, dressed and sought her out. Not that she'd gone far, but she was at the eating island with Vayenn and the kids were on the Xbox already. Reuben had chosen to stay in bed a little while longer, having done all the driving yesterday.
He smiled as he watched his sister and his lover talk quietly. Shauna moved before Vayenn saw him and he joined them as Shauna poured him a coffee.
"Thank you," he said, snuggling in behind her and kissing her neck.
She smiled and snuggled into him, though she kept her eyes on Vayenn as she spoke.

Vayenn, Reuben and their children left mid-morning so that Harek could spend better time with Shauna and the boys. It felt quiet to have so few people in such a large house, but cosy at the same time. Shauna made herself a tea and then found her favourite spot on the sofa before the fireplace. The fire was out, there was no need for it but she liked to see it lit. Harek came to sit with her, smiling.

Gone Dutch

"Just us," he said, sitting close enough that she swung her legs into his lap.

"Yep. Just the four of us," she smiled.

She looked away at the fireplace for a moment, then asked: "Harek, you trust me, don't you?" His hazel eyes danced for a few moments, then calmed. "Yes." he nodded.

"Will you do something for me?" she asked, nibbling her bottom lip slightly.

"What is it?" he asked, shifting so that he turned towards her.

"Until I tell you to later tonight, don't reach for me to kiss me, touch me, anything sexual, until I ask. Can you?"

He had no idea what she'd ask that of him, so asked why.

She smiled. "Please?"

Her pleading made him grin slightly. "Is there something wrong?" he asked.

She chuckled. "No. But will you trust me enough to do this?"

He wondered what on earth he was being asked to do, and why. He checked his watch, it was around eleven am. Later tonight could be any time. He looked into her eyes to see that they weren't the swirling treacle he'd gotten used to, but a bark brown, twinkling back at him.

Gone Dutch

"I have no idea why you're asking. But," he said, letting go of a breath he didn't know he was holding, "I will."

She smiled, relieved. "Thank you" she whispered, swung her legs off his lap and leaned in. "Not until I say," she said, winking at him. How was he going to not touch her at all during the day?

She called the boys to the library, saying that Harek had to show them something in the garage. She winked and vanished, leaving him to entertain the boys with the cars.

Having Harek out of sight but not mind, focused her for a few hours on the task at hand. Taking a notebook and a pen she had found in his office, she mapped out the sunspots in the garden, the cooler areas. Stepping down from the patio outside the library down the half dozen brick stairs, she explored every aspect of the bare gardens Harek had created. She imagined what it would look like with herb beds, the flowers, roses; everything that she had back home, she wanted here but in a different way. She smiled as the sounds of the various cars reached her ears, or their tyres crunched the stones.

She stopped planning to make lunch and ate hers before the boys had finished. Finding a pair of scissors, she went to search in the garden to make up a small tie

Gone Dutch

of plants to hang in the shower. He might not have rosemary but he still had trees growing around that she created a small fragrant poesy. The pine trees helped.

She heard them return to the kitchen as she headed to the bathroom to shower. She smiled and wondered how Harek was faring at holding up her request. Tonight was certainly going to be interesting and her insides quivered in anticipation.

The boys pounced on the food Shauna had prepared and left on the breakfast island. They spoke about all the cars, which one was their favourite and how fast the car could go. It was a typical boy's morning and Harek preened at their knowledge, proud that he'd brought a smile to their faces just by sharing something he loved.

He looked up as Shauna came down, freshly showered. Her hair was wet and she was wearing a simple grey dress with pockets. She hugged the boys and winked at Harek. For a moment, he was jealous that her sons got a kiss and he did not. He only hoped that the reward later was worth it.

"I don't suppose you've some larger pieces of paper, say, A2 or so?" she asked, sipping a cup of tea she'd just made.

Gone Dutch

He pondered for a moment. "No, but I do have a roll of paper somewhere I think." He went to the library and in a drawer, he found what he was looking for.

"Mum, can I read some of these books?" asked Andrew.

"If you can find the English ones, I'm sure you can," replied Harek pointing to one end of the library, not missing a beat. Andrew shouted "cool" and explored the hundreds of books on offer where Harek had pointed. He stood and handed Shauna the roll of paper.

"Hier ben je," (here you are) he said, forgetting for a moment to use English.

"Thank you," she said, taking the roll from him with a sly smile.

He wanted to reach out and just kiss her, but he kept his word. It was going to be a long afternoon.

To pass the time, he showed the boys where the private gym was. Shauna had taken over his desk in the library by drawing something out, he wasn't sure what yet. "Later," was all she'd said to him and had hidden her notebook from his direct view. She had smiled her best smirk at him, but wouldn't reveal what she was planning or working on.

The boys loved the gym and tried out some of the equipment with Harek's supervision. Shauna found them there a few hours later, engrossed in one particular piece

Gone Dutch

of equipment. She looked around, appreciating the padded mats on the floor, the weights neatly stacked in one corner, rowing machines in another, the punch bag in another. Everything was laid out professionally as it would be in a high-end gym. She smiled, no wonder he had the figure that he did. She wondered when he found the time to work on that gorgeous body of his, he hadn't while she'd been here.

He noticed her in a reflection of a mirror and turned to look at her. She wore the black ballet pumps as she had the other day along with that simple grey dress that hugged her figure graciously. He got to wondering what underwear she had on under that dress. He sighed. He wasn't allowed to find out just now, but made a note to do so later.

She smiled at him as he gave her the once over, his hooded eyes betraying the hunger he was feeling. She pushed off the gym door and headed back to the library to finish up the drawing she was working on, pleased that her appearance in the gym had the desired effect on him. Making herself another camomile tea, she went back to her project.

Harek and the boys returned a short while later and he made them go shower because they'd done some physical work on the equipment. He watched her from the library door, engrossed in whatever it was she'd

Gone Dutch

undertaken today. He would have liked to go and see, to kiss her neck and have her show him, but his promise to her earlier made him stop. Shaking his head, he too headed for a shower; preferably cold.

She could feel the tension coming off him in waves and for her little plan to work, that's exactly where she needed him. He had trusted her and had only asked her why once. She had to admire his restraint and his will power. Smiling, she picked up the required coloured pencil and began adding to her plans.

The boys returned to their Xbox and Harek decided to begin preparing dinner. Shauna was still head down at his desk, engrossed in her little project and hadn't noticed the passing of time. Or, so he thought. He could envision her deck placed not too far from his, her chair facing the window, her face bathed in sunlight. It made him yearn for her and the boys to be here all the time.

The boys made dinner a noisy affair as they told Shauna about the cars, the drive Harek had taken each of them on, their favourite car and the bends they'd raced around.

"We did not race," replied Harek, reproachfully. "We might have taken a bend or two a little faster than normal, but we did not race."

Gone Dutch

"Don't care!" declared Andrew. "It was awesome!"

Shauna chuckled and motioned for Andrew to calm down. All too soon, the dinner was over.

"You're good at cooking," smiled Shauna as she began to clear dishes away.

"Thank you," said Harek, smiling. "You're a tease," he whispered to her as he handed her some dishes to put into the machine.

"I know," she said, smiling. "Just, keep your promise?" She stood up, shoulders back and raised her eyebrows slightly.

Harek sighed. "I will," he said, passing her some more dirty crockery.

She smiled at him from over her shoulder. He was wound up already, goodness knows how he was going to handle what she had planned for later.

Michael demanded that Harek watch a movie with them, picking out the latest Fast and Furious movie. Shauna vanished into the library again when the movie was on. Once it had finished and the boys were in bed, Harek went to find her, to find the library empty.

The sofa wasn't quite in the right place and the fire was blazing away. He was about to move it back when he noticed a note taped to it in Dutch. "Don't move this," He found that note on a few other items that

Gone Dutch

weren't quite in the right position too. The misplacement of furniture took him to the library patio doors. "Leave unlocked" was taped to one of the doors. Why were the doors unlocked?

    He now bore a very confused look on his face. He would have turned on the lights, but they had notes on them to leave them off. A movement on the grass caught his eye. Standing in the full light of the moon on the grass, stood Shauna, very naked. She had her arms and hands above her and she was slowly turning. Around her were items Harek knew weren't there hours before, formed a cross. Where she'd found fallen logs, a bucket with water, a huge candle and a toy windmill, he wasn't sure. She was turning in one direction, then another. His eye caught sight of another note left on the window:

    "Harek, blijf gewoon kijken, S."
Oh, he was certainly going to keep watching! He leaned back into his desk and with a growing sense of frustration and fascination, watched Shauna parade in the moonlight.

    After what seemed like hours, though it was probably twenty minutes, she picked up something from the floor, wrapped it around herself and returned indoors. Harek watched her intently from his vantage point. She returned, closing the doors quietly behind her and locking them. She didn't look at him nor glance in his direction. She walked to her favourite chair, removed the

Gone Dutch

coat that she'd borrowed from his wardrobe, draped it over the chair and then latched the library door shut. The fire was blazing but she bent and added a few extra logs to it carefully. She looked straight at him when she'd finished and beckoned him with one finger, her face showing no expression.

    He hadn't worked out how or even when, she'd say that he could touch her again. She still didn't now, but he went to her, as she asked. With nothing but hand movements to indicate what he should do, he stopped when she indicated that's what she wanted. "Beweeg niet" she whispered as she circled him. Goodness, what was she doing and why didn't she want him to move?
    He felt a tug at his jumper and she whispered "uitkleden voor mij" loud enough just so she could be heard. He appreciated her practising her Dutch, even if it was only simple instructions. He did as she commanded though, removing his clothes to meet his coat on the chair.
    She stopped him from removing more than his top half by removing his hands from his trousers. She wanted just the top half for now. She ran her fingers along his back, slowly, feeling every contour worshipping every muscle, dappling him with small hot kisses her and there. He tried to reach around for her, forgetting but she told him off, "Don't move," she snapped in Dutch. He stood on the sheepskin rug, hands

Gone Dutch

in fists by his side, trying to calm his breathing, just letting her feel hi, touch him. She felt his left arm, all the muscles twitching tightly as her cold fingers gently admired each hard angle and slowly, she came to stand before him.

"Good boy, beweeg niet," she smiled and slowly undid his jeans and slid them and his underpants down his legs. His leg muscles twitched and his erection stood out for the whole room to see and it was just as well it was only Shauna with him in the room. He stepped out of his clothes and she removed them to join the rest of the pile on the chair. Other than that, he did not move. His pectoral muscles twitched and vibrated as her fingers gently caressed them. She worked her way up, across, down his front, feeling, kissing and stroking almost every part of him, but the part of him that he desperately wanted her to. She had nearly circled him when her hands grabbed his bum cheeks and squeezed. He reacted, still rooted to the spot and he closed his eyes tightly to try and hold onto his promise to her.

He nearly broke his word as she squeezed the other cheek and circled behind him again. He opened his eyes, watching her as she came around before him, this time, she firmly took hold of him and squeezed him at the base whilst her other hand held his testicles like she was holding a precious, delicate item.

"Nog niet," (not yet) she reminded him. He closed his eyes in frustration and pleasure as she flicked

Gone Dutch

her tongue over his head. She teased him for a few moments, admiring the man she had before her, bending to her will.

"Now you can," she whispered and Harek reacted. Grabbing her, he forcefully kissed her, a day of sexual frustration and the latest teasing pouring out of him. She guided him to the floor, settling on the sheepskin rugs and like a hungry bear, he followed her down, hungrily kissing her and stroking her. His hardness pressed into her stomach and she raised her arms as she had in the garden, making Harek shift so that he could pin her arms above her. That's exactly what she wanted and she raised her hips against him slightly. Before he could stop himself, he was inside her and she pushed her hips up again to take him in. Not thinking, he began thrusting, as if he hadn't made love to her only the day before. He released her arms but she held them where they were.

Finding her mouth, he kissed her as he roughly plunged deep into her depth.

"Say my name," she commanded. He did. He called out her name as came in a heated rush, not thinking of her, just finally answering his own needs. He collapsed on top of her, his breathing heavy. It took him some time to realise what had happened.

"Why?" he said, kissing her.

"Because I could. I wanted to see if you'd trust me this way. I was only going to moon bathe, but seeing

Gone Dutch

your reaction every time I teased you today, just fed a power streak in me I didn't want to stop. I thought sex afterwards would be a good reward for excellent behaviour," she giggled. He kissed her, more gently this time then moved his kisses to the hollow of her throat.

"You enjoyed that power rush?" he asked, teasing a breast into his mouth and devouring it.

"Oh yes," she said. "Just as much as you enjoy making me do what you want me to."
He smiled. She had a point. He did enjoy that.

"Do you like it when I do this?" he asked, withdrawing and suckling the other breast whilst gently playing with the other.

"Oh yes," she groaned, arching up. He looked at this witchy woman beneath him as she allowed him to explore and enjoy her innermost secrets. Her folds were still wet and an idea came to him. He needed her to say his name, to shatter the windows. He needed her to be as subservient as he had just been, not from revenge, but because it turned them both on.
He got up and said; "Come here, tovenares!" he growled. He lowered a hand to help her up and then he sat on the sofa, facing the fire.

"Turn around," he said, "away from me."
She turned around, facing the fire with her back to Harek. He reached forward and pulled her down onto his lap. He wrapped one arm around her waist while his other found her core. It didn't take long to have her come

Gone Dutch

undone in his lap. Given his strength and size, she couldn't wiggle out of his grasp and his second erection stood proudly before her as her senses returned.

She grabbed him and began pumping the length of him. He raised her up and forward, spreading her legs with his own, then somehow, he was inside her again as he pulled her back onto him. She groaned in pleasure.

She rested her hands on his knees, using them to support her whilst his hands tweaked and played with her from behind her. He held onto her as she found her rhythm. It didn't take her long to come undone again but still, he held on. He eased them forwards so that she was standing but bent over. She twisted so that she at least had the arm of the sofa to hold onto as he thrust into her, sending sensations through her as she nearly collapsed into a heap on the floor. He held onto her hips, keeping her upright as he finally exploded into her, sending her into another series of orgasms.

He followed her down onto the rugs, listening to her laboured breathing. He pulled her to him, kissing her gently, making calming noises into her ear. Even spooning her like this, spent as they were, aroused and pleased him in equal measure.

"You are truly a tovenares," he whispered into her ear.

"What's that?" she said, pulling his hand tightly into her own and kissing it as he spoke.

"Enchantress" he whispered, kissing her again.

Gone Dutch

She turned her head towards him. "We need to go to bed, the boys…"
Harek nodded, unhappy that he was being made to move but he understood why. They grabbed all their clothes, banked the fire and turned to leave. Shauna smiled. The Moon had shone through the glass library roof at some point during their frantic and passionate lovemaking.

"Now this is a home," she whispered, taking Harek's offered hand and following him to the bedroom.

They awoke much later, limbs wrapped around each other under the satin sheets. Harek kissed her neck, her ear, her cheek and ran his hands seductively down her body. She moved so that his hands would reach between her legs. In moments, he had her pulled up onto all fours and was slowly, deeply, thrusting into her.

"Do you like it when I do this?" he said, breathing into her ear as much as he could.

"Oh yes, yes I do!" she breathed. This had to be one of her most favourite angles, he hit her just right at every thrust. "Do," she lowered her head as the orgasm began to build "not," she felt him pull her hair back so that her head had to lift. "stop!" she said as he increased the rhythm.

"Say my name," he said as he increased his pace again, growling. "Say it."

Gone Dutch

"Harek," she breathed and she repeated it again and again, louder and stronger until she screamed it in climax.

"Powertrip?" she asked, grinning when she could finally breathe.

His replying laugh stayed in his throat, but his shoulders gave way as to how much he enjoyed it.

"Oh yes," he said, holding her to him in a spoon fashion. He snuggled into her, content and happy. "Do you think the boys?" he asked. He wondered if they'd heard their mother scream his name.

"If they heard, they'll not say anything. Michael will tell Andrew not to."

He chuckled and sighed in happiness as he stroked her sides.

"Shauna, I love you. Everything about you, and I mean everything." He kissed her temple as she turned to him slightly.

"I love you too," she said, smiling. "I think we should shower though," she said, moving to get up. "Join me?"

"No," said Harek, locking his arms around her. "Stay here a while longer. I like this," he said. She laughed and snuggled back into him, dragging the sheets over herself again. They napped, wrapped in each other's embrace.

Gone Dutch

Thirty-One

The boys found their own breakfast and were playing on the Xbox when Jon called a short time later. Michael knocked on the bedroom door to say that he was here.

"Jon!" Harek called from the stairs. Quickly throwing on some sweatpants and his jumper from the previous evening, he went to greet his friend and business partner.

"I am not due in this week. Is something wrong?"

Jon nodded and pulled Harek into the library to speak with him privately. Shauna had showered and was in the kitchen brewing coffee when Harek's voice boomed out of the library.

Even in Dutch, swear words were swearing words and Harek swore like a mob of sailors. The boys smirked and shut the door to the kitchen. She ventured to the library door to see him pacing the length of the library.

"How?" he growled, but not at Jon. The conversation was in fluid, rapid Dutch, but she got the gist.

"I assume that you have company registers as we have in the UK?" she asked, handing both men a coffee.

"We do," Jon nodded.

Gone Dutch

"Start there. I'll meet you two in the offices in a bit, let me get the kids sorted out. We'll work out what's going on," she said, smiling. Harek smiled weakly and nodded.

"I need ten minutes," he said to Jon. He quickly kissed Shauna and headed off to grab a shower.

"I'm sorry," said Jon, sighing.

Shauna smiled. "Not your fault. I'm guessing that something isn't being delivered which is a key component?"

Jon nodded. "I thought you didn't understand Dutch?" he said, grinning.

"I don't, but there are some strong similarities with our languages, I figured the main part out."

He smiled. Harek appeared at the door and with a deep kiss to Shauna, he ran off to the office with Jon. Shauna found her mobile and called Vayenn.

His sister listened to the predicament Shauna was now in.

"Use one of his cars," she suggested.

"I'm not sure I'm insured to do so, so I can't even though I am capable of it."

Vayenn groaned in frustration. "I've got an idea," she said, pulling on her boots and grabbing her two kids. She sounded the idea out to Shauna.

"That would work," replied Shauna, grabbing her shoes and gathering the boys. "I'll get Harek to make it

Gone Dutch

up to you," she replied as she began to gather things together. Vayenn assured that he would.

Twenty minutes later, Shauna and the boys were on Vayenn's Q7 heading to Harek's business. Vayenn dropped Shauna off and then took the kids to her house. At least Harek knew where to go when they'd finished for the day.

Harek was surprised to see her, without the boys. Shauna told him what she'd arranged, then sat down with him and Jon to brainstorm and work out what was going on. More than an hour later, Shauna stretched cricked her neck muscles.

"These are the three companies that have bought out your suppliers or their entire stock of glass. Do you recognise them?"

Jon and Harek shook their heads.

Half an hour later, Shauna had more information about them. They were all new companies. "New companies shouldn't have this clout," she said. "It's a pity you haven't a billionaire who can do a hostile take-over in your back pockets, or who knows a new supplier who can sell you what you need," joked Shauna, sitting back with her neck stretched out. Now, she was stumped.

Harek looked at Jon and then they both looked at Shauna.

"What?" She retreated as Harek jumped up to kiss her.

Gone Dutch

"You are a genius!" exclaimed Jon, picking up the phone and talking to someone on the end. Five minutes later and a deep familiar voice spoke with them on the loudspeaker. Shauna smiled. It was Berend.

Harek quickly explained in Dutch that Shauna was present and they switched to English for her benefit.

"Good to hear from you, my dear!"

"Berend! Lovely to hear your voice again," she said. She had no idea that the man was a billionaire.

Harek quickly explained what was going on. "I know someone who can fix that," he said. "Give me half an hour or so," and he hung up.

Harek leaned back in his chair and sighed. Jon smiled and Shauna managed to sit back, working a crick out in her back. She hadn't been sitting in a very good position on the sofa while looking through paperwork. Harek came around to her to massage her back while they waited.

It took about forty-five minutes before Abbe called them back. "Opa is busy sorting something with the lawyers. But, there should be a delivery of supplies first thing tomorrow. He said he wants to go through some things with you all, he expects you for lunch in about half an hour." He read the address out and Harek nodded.

"We shall be there," he said.

Gone Dutch

Clearing away the paperwork, they drove to meet Berend at the SS Rotterdam.

Berend obviously liked boats. Not only did he have his private boats, which Harek had told her about, he liked to dine and be around them as much as was possible.

There was a large table, set for five, which quickly became six when Jon's girlfriend, Amelie joined them. Berend joined them about ten minutes after they'd been seated. Abbe was with him, flustered but keeping up with the older man.

"Well, that's been interesting," he said as he sat with a shortness of breath. He didn't need to order, the waiter brought him and Abbe the drink they always had.

"How so?" asked Shauna. What had the old man been doing whilst they were travelling to meet him?

"I've got a few… technical people?" he looked at Shauna. He was struggling with English because of her. She smiled.

"Feel free to speak Dutch. I'll catch on," she said. The old man shook his head.

"My English needs work," he said, smiling. His eyes danced and he carried on. "Computer people. They found out a few interesting facts already, such as who owns two of the companies, at least in the name." Harek and Jon sat up straighter in their chairs.

Gone Dutch

"They're owned by Sanne Kramer," stated Berend. Harek closed his eyes as his jaw twitched. Jon's face fell but he nodded an acknowledgement. Shauna turned to Harek, throwing him a questioning look, wondering if it were the same one. It was.

"Lady in red at the wedding," explained Jon, not realising Shauna would know who she was. So, the woman had a last name now. Shauna turned back to Berend.

"So, hang on, let me get this right. She's used three companies to buy the stock of fibreglass so that Harek and Jon can't fulfil their orders?"

Abbe nodded. "Not quite on all of the regular suppliers. We think she's bought the companies and won't fulfil the orders to Harek, in effect cancelling the orders. We ensured that Harek's company survived by giving them the orders. Your intervention over the emails made Opa intrigued. I know a few geeks from university, it wasn't hard to throw money at them to dig up more answers."

Shauna looked around the table. "Crazy lady strikes again," she said.

"Again?" asked Berend.

"I don't think the baseball attack on Harek was accidental. Your Polite do not seem to be as thorough as your hackers." She turned to Abbe. "How deep are they willing to go?" she asked him.

"Why?" he asked.

Gone Dutch

"The money. Follow the money, see where the trails go. Document it, send it to the Polite. I'll have the case details sent to you."

Berend nodded and Abbe quickly sent a message to a friend, then closed his phone off. Shauna sat back, sighed and thought. She looked at Harek. "We need to contact that Polite officer. Attack this from two ends, if not more." Harek squeezed Shauna's hand. It was time to have a chat with some nice policemen.

The "chat" lasted nearly two hours, though the Polite officers were nice, they were thorough in their questions. She was sure that they'd forgotten they were victims in this. Harek had called them when they left SS Rotterdam and they met at work after hours. Vayenn still had the boys and Shauna was getting more frustrated by the moment. The language barrier wasn't helping either.

The main officer, Inspector Steenstra sat back on the sofa and sighed, having gone over everything again. "I have more than I need. Except for the suspect."

Shauna nodded, her accent adding to the mix of frustrations on both sides. "That, I can't help you with. The motive, I can't help you with either. But, follow the money and you'll probably find her. You're no longer the only ones looking," she said. Abbe had spoken with his friends; because of Berend, they were willing to help.

"I need you to be careful," he said, looking at Shauna.

Gone Dutch

"We need you to catch her," she replied. Squaring her shoulders back, despite her tiredness, she'd fight.

"We'll try," he said, standing.

If you "Then try harder and I'll try to be careful," she quipped. He smirked, said something in Dutch to Harek and his officers, and left.

Harek sighed. "Brave hekse!" he whispered into her ear. She smiled.

"You'd think we were the ones in the wrong!" she growled as she got up to start filing the papers away they'd made that the Polite didn't take with them. Every policeman, Dutch, British or otherwise, made her feel like that. She could well believe it was their job to do that.

"What did he say to you when he left?" A lot of the language was still beyond her grasp, even though she was learning more day by day.

"That you're a feisty witch," he chuckled.

She threw her head back and cackled. "They've no idea!" she said.

Harek guided them to Vayenn's place and late though it was, they headed home with the boys. Shauna explained to the boys roughly what had happened. They simply nodded and said they had a great time with Vayenn and Reuben at the play park, riding bikes, doing outdoor things.

Gone Dutch

The boys went to bed as soon as they got in. Shauna found Harek on the sofa in the library, gazing into the roaring fire, even though it wasn't needed.

"I didn't get a chance to show you," she said, walking to his desk and picking up a roll of paper. She handed it to him and sat, watching. He unrolled it and then turned it around. He was confused for a moment, until he realised what she'd drawn. He was looking at plans she'd made for the garden.

He sat up, suddenly paying attention. There were rows of structured plants in certain areas, giving way to a more English scattered design in others. The herb garden, as Shauna had labelled it, was structured, with pathways and stonework, which was typically Dutch.

He looked at her, then back at the plans. "When did you do all this?" he asked. "This is amazing," he breathed as he traced her ideas on the plan.

"Yesterday, whilst I was teasing you and you tried to bury yourself in cars and gyms."

He chuckled. "The plans look amazing famke." He looked at it again, laying it out on the rug on the floor. "You've gone to a lot of detail here," he looked at her with admiration in his eyes. "I love it."

She smiled. "It was an idea I had. I can see it looking like that. But, it's your garden, your grounds, your home, your decision. It will need some of the older trees pruned back a little to let in enough light, but I love

Gone Dutch

the deciduous borders. It'll be amazing in the autumn when the leaves fall."

He smiled and leaned in to kiss her.

"I love that you can add to things here. Come," he said, holding his hand out. They retired to bed, content in holding each other in the darkness.

Gone Dutch

Thirty-Two

The week in Rotterdam was near to an end with no further update from the Polite or mishap occurring. On the morning of their last full day, Harek had one more thing he wanted to show them.

He pulled up not far from a tall structure, the Euromast.

Shauna shook her head and backed away, waving her hands.

"You are kidding me? You want us," she looked up. "To go up there?"

Harek looked at his watch. "Yes. Lunch is reserved here, but there are parks nearby to enjoy the fresh air afterwards. But, from up there," he said, "You can see how beautiful the City is."

"Come on mum!" laughed Andrew, running ahead and suddenly doing a cartwheel on one hand. She laughed and sighed, looking up.

"Heights and I…" she looked at Harek. He smiled, holding out a hand. Now she had to be brave. She sighed and relented.

The views from the Euromast were, she decided, amazing. Harek had the tickets already purchased and

Gone Dutch

before lunch, the restaurant and the platform were halfway up. Fighting her fear of heights, she forgot about them as the viewing platform rose, spiralling slowly around the mast, giving everyone inside the view of the river, the towers, the parks, the old town, the whole of the city and river for miles and miles.

The information that was pumped out whilst they slowly spun told them that on a clear day they could see all the way to Antwerp in Belgium, 80km away. Given the clear azure blue sky and the cloudless sky above them, Shauna was not surprised.

Shauna loved the brasserie and the food. She enjoyed the time spent with Harek and the boys. They found a park with a crazy golf course. Michael beat them overall, much to Andrew's disgust but they loved the sandy play area. Harek was happy to sit and hold her whilst sat on a bench as they watched the boys play with other children. Even though they had never met before, Harek was amazed at the games they came up with.

"One last family get together," he said, kissing her.

She nodded and smiled. Calling the boys from their play, they waved goodbye and set off for Mûne Roazen for the last time.

Vayenn, Reuben and the kids arrived shortly after they returned, followed by Pieter and Hanna. Jon and Amelie arrived at almost the same time and the barbeque

Gone Dutch

was lit. No matter their nationality, Shauna decided men and barbeques gave them an excuse to be all alpha over things. She chuckled and milled around in the library, showing the women the plans she'd drawn up for the garden.

Hanna smiled approvingly. Suddenly, songs began playing from hidden speakers. The first up was a Dutch band that Vayenn and Evie began dancing to. The Grand East, Vayenn had said they were called. A few others later and the music switched to something everyone got on board with. Abba.

Of course, that meant the music was turned up and the kitchen became a dance floor. Just as Shauna began wiggling her hips, Helene and Fons arrived. Helene's figure showed off her developing pregnancy, but her friend glowed! To the tune of Dancing Queen, Helene and Shauna danced. Helene sat down to Gimme Gimme, causing Vayenn to try and keep up with a now very happy Shauna!

Harek watched her dance and shake her hips to Dancing Queen, Gimme, Gimme, Gimme and quite a few others. He couldn't believe how she moved but he felt very happy at how content she was around his chosen and biological family. He loved how her skirt swayed, giving glimpses of her toned legs, barefoot as she was. He hated waiting, but the item he had planned wasn't ready and wouldn't be for weeks. He sighed,

Gone Dutch

having to apply patience, but smiled when Mamma Mia had Amelie and Vayenn dancing with her.

The kids were tucked in quite late, with the adults retiring as and when. Shauna and Harek saw Jon, Amelie, Fons and Helene off, leaving Vayenn's family and Harek's parents to settle into their rooms. Quietly, they retreated to their room.

Harek smiled and sighed happily as the door softly closed. He removed his shirt and felt Shauna's fingers trace his shoulders, and then come around to be before him. He pulled her into a kiss, grasping her head in his hand; he angled her mouth, holding her just right so he could taste all of her mouth. Her arms wrapped around his neck as his kisses moved to her jaw, her ears, down her neck to the hallow between her breasts. He stopped to help her remove her clothing, slowly undressing her as each item of clothing got in their way.

The items pooled at their feet or were flung to the chair that often housed their discarded clothing. Quietly, in the dimness of their room, they began to make love. The kisses from her on his torso made him hard whilst his suckling of her breasts, nipples and neck rose a heat within her. When she finally pulled his jeans off, taking his underwear with it, he groaned. He stepped out of it and gently removed her skirt, her knickers and immediately kissed her stomach working his way up to a breast. He knelt high, pulling her to him, wrapping his

Gone Dutch

strong arms around her waist like a vice as he kissed her torso, around her breast, not just the areola or nipple. She ran her hands through his hair as he worshipped her, scraped her nails across his shoulders and moaned quietly.

He picked her up and carefully took her to the bed. Flinging the sheets off in one hand, he laid her down, kissing her as much as he could, stroking her sides.

He worked his kisses lower and spread her legs apart slowly, kissing her inner thigh gently with many kisses. He blew on her sex, seeing them twitch in anticipation made him ache, but he'd be back for them soon enough. From the little light they had, he could see her arms above her head, pulling her breasts up, making her torso taunt. Taking her delicious nub in his mouth, he began to lick and suck, sending her writhing. He held her down as his tongue worked its magic, up, down, side to side. Moving an arm so that he still held her, he inserted a finger, then two into her, teasing her front walls gently with little flicks whilst his mouth still suckled and licked.

He sensed by her writhing that she was close and he was happy to drive her over that edge. Faster and deeper his tongue worked, quicker his fingers flicked and suddenly, he had to use his shoulders to stop her from crushing his head between her gorgeous thighs. She had barely calmed down and he was between her thighs, his full erection at her entrance, waiting.

Gone Dutch

"Shauna," he whispered. She looked at him, bringing her hands around his neck, stroking his head. She reached up to kiss him but he rose out of reach.

"Tell me you want me," he said.

"I want you," she said, voice raspy and husky. He tweaked a nipple and she arched. "Now, please," she begged. He kissed her.

"Say my name," he said, still holding back.

"Harek," she whispered into his ear. He lifted her right leg and slowly thrust himself into her wet folds. She clamped down her insides onto him and arched against him.

"Harek," she breathed, scratching his back as he began slowly thrusting in and out of her. She whispered his name over and over as he thrust deeply into her and he didn't stop when her climax made her arch in response. He grabbed her hips, lifting her onto his lap as she convulsed. He held back, determined to make her come for him again and she did, half on his lap, arched onto the bed before him like the Goddess she was. Her climaxes were close together now, not stopping. He lifted both her legs so they were up to her breasts and her arse cheeks were on his legs. She never saw what he saw when he was buried deep within her, up to his base. She climaxed again, begging him to not stop. Hearing his name on her lips as she arched, he finally gave in, thrusting himself deep within her and shooting whatever seed he had deep within her.

Gone Dutch

They languished in bed until midmorning, then enjoyed showering each other.

"I hate that you have to go," he said, kissing her forehead and hugging her.

"I know. But it has to be this way, least for now."

He smiled, an idea cementing in his mind.

"The boy's schooling," he said, smiling down at her.

She nodded. "Yep!" She smiled as she pulled away, heading to the bedroom door. "Come on, we can't stay up here all day!" She grinned as she headed downstairs, whistling a tune he'd heard before but couldn't place.

"Hey Google, play Eye Level," she said as she entered the kitchen. The built-in display he'd installed lit up and the tune she'd been whistling began playing. She danced around the kitchen to it as she pulled together their breakfast. Hanna smiled from the library as she danced around.

"You are happy," she said, smiling and coming to hug Shauna good morning.

Shauna paused and cocked her head to one side, pondering. "Yes. Yes, I am," she grinned boradly and continued swaying her hips as the music played on.

After breakfast, Harek called out to Shauna.

Gone Dutch

"The car company says they need your driver's licence?" he said, holding his phone out to her.

"Ah yes!" she said, taking the phone. In a few moments, she'd given them what they needed and given her the licence plate.

"Just need to get insurance her now," she said.

Harek nodded and handed her his credit card. "Pay on that, in full," he told her gently. Shauna squared her shoulders and paused for a moment, staring at him.

"Are you sure? I can afford the insurance,"

He nodded. "Very," he said smiling. She gently took the card from him, smiling softly. Half an hour later, with all the details done, she returned the card to him.

"Thank you," she whispered to him as he hugged her.

"What for?"

"The car. Insurance. All of it."

He kissed her. "I love you. What is mine, I share," he smiled.

All too soon, they were saying their goodbyes and everyone was departing. The kids said goodbye to each other, Michael even hugged Evie, which made Shauna smile.

With everyone departing, Mûne Roazen suddenly seemed quiet. Harek supposed he'd get used to it, but he had memories here now. Something he never had before.

Gone Dutch

Harek drove them to the works dock to load up onto Iris Rose. This time, Shauna paid attention to the scenery and the open sea. The day was warm, sunny with a few fluffy clouds scattered here and there. The catamaran cut through the water smoothly and in all too quick a time, they were back in England. Checking in with Customs at the docks, Harek joined Shauna and the boys at finding their new car.

Gone Dutch

Thirty-Three

It was electric blue in colour, not that Shauna cared much about the colour. What she was bothered about, what was under the hood, the gadgets and the mileage, reliability and ease of driving. The Q7 TDCi Quattro was huge. It was much bigger than she'd ever have picked out for just the three of them.

Harek had some of the boating crew bring out the boxes of stuff from their old car, but she simply asked that they put it in the boot. She'd sort that out during the week, either finding a new home for it or finally throwing it away. The old Seat was gone, though the stain from the oil leak it had made was still visible on the floor, even though it had been cleaned up as best it could have been.

"Mum, this is brilliant!" declared Andrew, taking a good look at the inside. The side steps would help him get in but it took Shauna a moment to work out which way round to put her feet to climb in, it was so tall. She managed it, but not without making Harek chuckle.

"Where does the fob go?" she said, holding it up.

"Its proximity, so it just needs to be on you or near you to work. If it goes too far from the car, the car stops."

Gone Dutch

"Oh!" She put her foot on the break and firmly pressed the start button. The engine roared to life and then settled, purring like a huge big cat. She smiled. She turned to Harek and smiled, kissing him briefly.

"Let me know when you get home, please?"

She nodded. "And you tell me. I think you'll be back in Rotterdam and at your desk at home before I'm even halfway home."

He rested his forehead against hers. It was insane, when he thought about it. He could be back in another country and at home before his fireplace before Shauna was even halfway home. The nearly three-hour drive from Hull Ferry Port to Amblecote included four motorways and various major roads. Roads he'd travelled on but it was still nearly three hours, not including a stop. He was sure that the boys would want to at about the half-way point.

"I need to let you get going," he said, reaching in to grab her head and pull her into a kiss that would have to last them for weeks.

She smiled. "I know. Talk to you when I'm home?" she said. He nodded and let Shauna drive away with the boys. He waited until she was out of the port and sight before he returned to Iris Rose.

It was indeed nearly three and a half hours later when Shauna finally called him to say that she was home.

Gone Dutch

"We didn't stop and I'm glad we didn't. The M1 was a nightmare!"

"But you're home and safe?" he reiterated.

"Yes," she breathed. "I haven't even gotten out of the car. It's such a pleasure to drive!" He smiled.

"You can't sleep in there," he joked.

"I could, if I get a double mattress in the back," she said, not quite joking. Thinking about it, you probably could get a double mattress into a Q7. He hadn't considered that.

"Okay, you could." he chuckled. "The house is so quiet without you and the boys," he said.

"It's quiet here too. The kids have retreated to their rooms. I take it you're in the library?" she asked.

"Yes. I won't ask how you knew. The fireplace is lit, I'm working on a few things for the builder's list when he gets back to it tomorrow."

"Sounds productive," her heard her sighing. "But, I need to go, fix supper and then get to bed. That was a shitty journey to do, though having this really nice car to do it was most welcome. Thank you again."

"Graach dien. Love you," he breathed.

"Love you too. Goodnight kreaze!" He held his eyes closed as she hung up.

Work was just a busy, usual Monday morning. Jen crooned over the Q7, Adam and Ben wondered who

Gone Dutch

the heck it belonged to and wanted the story of how Shauna had gotten it.

"You two were weird, naming cars and things!" chuckled Ben.

Shauna shrugged. "Least we know what item we meant when we used their names!" she chuckled. It had made sense to them, they didn't care what everyone else thought!

Elspeth and James called around that evening. Cait came too, mainly to be nosy about the car and how Shauna had paid for it. One look from Elspeth and Cait stopped asking questions. Clearly, words had been said and Elspeth had gotten through to her wayward, nosy, stubborn daughter.

"It's a pleasure to drive dad, and an automatic. That's going to take some getting used to, as is the cruise control. I'm not used to cars being a little like Knight Rider."

They chuckled at Shauna's description of the car doing things for itself, like keeping to the speed limit, changing gears and wiping the windshield automatically.

"Take us for a ride?" her dad asked.

Shauna laughed. "I knew you'd want a shot driving it," she handing him the keys, chuckling as she shook her head. She knew her dad.

Gone Dutch

They settled into their all too familiar distant routines of calls, texts and personal activities. Harek showed her pictures and shared video calls as the Mûne Roazen underwent more changes, more decorating and more improvemets.

She got excited when he showed her the beds in the garden being built as she'd planned out only a week after they'd returned home.

"You've had them start on it?" she gasped, excited.

"Yes. The machines can be gone before you and the boys return. I'll have the plants delivered when you're going to be here so you can put them in. But the paths, greenhouse, the beds, the building, should all be done by the time you're here next."

She covered her mouth in surprise. "That's going to be so amazing," the warmth in her voice reached his ears.

"There's something else," he said, turning the video back to him as he wandered back into the library.

"I've added you to the insurance on the Q7 here. You'll be able to drive it on your international licence. I do need some licence photographs for the insurance people though."

"A you sure?" she asked.

He nodded once. "Totally. I left you without a means to get around last time. I won't be doing that again," he scowled at the memory. "And, you like the

Gone Dutch

Q7. If you have Evie and Luuk with you, or you want to go out with Vayenn, you will need the Q7."

She smiled. "Thank you!" she said. She didn't know what else to say.

"I'll be able to see you in two weekends," he said, smiling at her.

"That'll be fabulous! Will you be coming here?"

He nodded. "Me coming to you is slightly less stressful than bringing the boys here. As much as I want you here, with the schools and timetables, it's the easiest and best option."

She nodded. "Sounds like it will be. Will Johan be joining you?"

He shook his head. "No, I'll drive down from Hull, I just need to organise the hire car out."

"I could come and fetch you?" she offered.

Harek shook his head. "That journey needs to be done once in a day, I don't know how you English put up with it,"

Shauna laughed. "We don't either! But we do!"

"Thank you, but no. I'll drive down from Hull. It's a shame that I can't park the Iris Rose at your doorstep!"

She laughed. "It's just as well, or I'd have very wet feet!"

He laughed. "Good night famke!" he said, "I miss you!"

"I miss you too," she whispered back.

Gone Dutch

Gone Dutch

Thirty-Four

The morning Harek was due to arrive, the smell of strong coffee hit her like a tidal wave. She looked around, expecting to see a coffee machine in her bedroom. But, there wasn't. The bedroom door was ajar as was the kitchen door to the hall. The smell reached her and smacked her senses firmly. Every smell that day was stronger and more intense. Even when Jen opened the fridge at work, Shauna gagged.

"Something in there is dying!" she said. They usually cleared it out on a Friday, but it wasn't unknown to have found something rotting in the back due to the guys leaving something behind.

Jen looked. "Everything is in date, Shauna. There's this French brie is close though…"

"Goddess, is that what stinks?" she said, scrunching up her nose.

"How come you can smell it from over there anyway?" asked Jen.

Shauna looked at her. "You can't?" she asked. Jen shook her head. "Seriously?!" she said. "That smell could fell an elephant!"

Gone Dutch

Jen chuckled. "Honestly, Shauna, I can't smell a thing!" she said, throwing the last of the brie away, then sitting back down at her desk.

Shauna carried on with her work, but the answer was already in the back of her mind. Later when she was checking for messages from Harek to say he'd left Rotterdam, she checked a few other things too. Jen interrupted her thoughts.

"Mr Wilson is on line one for you Shaunie," called Jen from the other side of the desks.

Shaun nodded and took the call.

"Mr Wilson! What can I do for you?"

"We have a court date. I'll be giving evidence as the TS Investigator; CPS doesn't think anyone else will be needed, including you. I'll let you know what the outcome is, if that's okay."

"Oh goodness, yes, please do! I'll let Ben and Adam know."

They talked for a few moments then hung up. Her mind immediately went back to its previous train of thought. 'Oh boy!' she pondered, realising the dates. Could she be? She didn't want to say anything to Jen, they weren't that close. There was only one way to find out. She smiled when she got the text to say Harek had left Rotterdam. That meant she had about four hours until she saw him again.

Gone Dutch

  She kept the rest of the day as normal as possible, updating Adam and Ben when she saw them. She did not say anything else about the smells of oil, mud, coffee, cigarette smoke, vaping, car fumes, wood… it was all horrendous and when home time came, she was glad to be out of there, hoping Jen didn't suspect anything. Stopping at a pharmacy on the way home, she purchased what she needed. She went to get changed out of her work gear and kept things at home simple. She drank some tea, squash and waited until she needed to pee. Then, she hid in her bathroom, and waited.

  The display on the countdown was new. She hadn't seen the digital testing sticks when she had the boys. She waited as the countdown did its thing, then saw the one word on the screen she strongly suspected she'd get: Pregnant.

  "Oh boy!" she said, closing her eyes. "There was a chance," she muttered.

  Shauna carried on with the rest of the day like it was any other. She made dinner for the kids, saying to them that she'd eat with Harek when he arrived. She prepared the dinner for the two of them. Bryce said he'd head out with friends for drinks, so wouldn't be eating with them.

  It was nearly eight pm by the time Harek's hire car pulled up out front. Andrew announced his arrival by running down the stairs, jumping the last few and

Gone Dutch

bouncing on to the sofa in the living room, excited that he was here. Everyone was all smiles, hugs, excited. She scooted the boys to bed when their dinner was ready, telling him that Harek still hadn't eaten and that they needed some time together. They hugged him and headed off to do their own thing and settle for bed.

Harek stood against the kitchen counter, watching as Shauna prepared their meal.
"That smells amazing," he said, sniffing the air appreciatively as she served up sausages, stamppot and steamed vegetables. This mixing of Dutch and English food appealed to him.

He helped set the table, pour some wine. "None for me, thank you!" she called, watching him as she filled their plates. She made gravy and he helped her carry the plates over to the table. She turned the main lights off and they sat to eat by candlelight.

"Are you okay?" he asked. Something had felt off since he arrived, though he couldn't put his finger on it.

"I'm very good, thank you!" she said, smiling. "What has been the biggest goal of your life that you've not achieved?" she asked.

'What a strange question!' he thought. He pondered for a moment. "I'm achieving it now," he said. He put down his cutlery and leaned back in the chair. "Shauna, what's wrong?"

Gone Dutch

"Nothing is wrong," she ran her tongue over her lips, the same way she always did when she was nervous. "Hold your hands out like this," she said, cupping her hands before her, "And close your eyes. I need to show you something."

He did as she asked, more from curiosity than anything else.

He felt her place something long and cold in his hands. "You can look now," she said.

The white stick before him was about a small ruler in length, not quite twenty centimetres, about two wide and tapered. He looked at the word on the digital screen and stopped.

'Pregnant'

He looked at the stick, then at Shauna. "Is this, what is it you call it?"

"A pregnancy test?" she nodded. "Yes, it is," she paused and looked at him staring at the stick in his hands. "A positive one," she said, slowly chewing her food. "I'm pregnant."

He stopped dead, looking at the stick and then back to Shauna.

"I did that test about three hours ago, probably about when you landed in Hull."

"Why? How?" he said. He couldn't believe what she was telling him.

Gone Dutch

"How? The same way nature has for decades!" she chuckled. 'How? Honestly!' she thought. He went to start speaking but no words came out.

"As for how I know?" She stopped eating for a moment to explain. "My sense of smell has gone through the roof. I awoke this morning to Bryce making coffee, but I thought he was making it in my room, the smell was so strong. Then at work, Jen opened up the fridge and the almost out of date French Brie hit me like a train. I was sitting at my desk on the other side of the office for crying out loud. I shouldn't have been able to smell the cheese. But, I did. Every smell has been intense today. I can even tell you used that green shower gel when you showered before you came over."

He really looked at her then. She wasn't lying. Not the way Sanne had. She knew the shower gel. He never told her he only used that when he came to visit her in the UK. It reminded him of how earthy and gorgeous she'd smelled the night she moon bathed. That night...

He began smiling, but she continued. "The pack comes with two tests; we can do it again in a bit if you want?"

He was smiling. "You're pregnant," he said as his voice dropped.

Her lips curled slightly. "That's what I just said," she said, taking one of his hands in hers and rubbing her current flat stomach.

Gone Dutch

He leaned forward, grabbing her head and gently, kissed her. "How long?" he asked, still confused but becoming excited at the same time.

"I'm quite early on, only about three weeks. I was due last week, but didn't think anything of my period not arriving. Until this morning…"

"So it was that night?" he recalled every detail of how she'd controlled him that night, owned him.

"Or the morning after. Or the other, many times after. Or the night before. Not really sure. But during that week, yes." She smiled and took a sip of her weak squash drink. No wonder she didn't want alcohol.

He smiled and began eating again, working through things in his mind.

"So can you?" He wasn't sure how to ask.

She chuckled. "I've done this a few times, you can ask!"

"Can we?" he made a hand motion between them.

"Can we still make love?" her lips curled up broadly and she licked her lips. "Oh yes, it'll be safe."

He smiled. Another lie Sanne had told him.

She sat back. "I thought, you'd be… somewhat more excited?" His lack of enthusiasm was concerning. Yes, this was a shock but they hadn't been using protection, she hadn't gone on the pill, so it was bound to happen.

Gone Dutch

"I'm…" He looked at her. "Sanne told me so many lies about her being pregnant…"

She nodded and sighed. Damn woman. "I know," she said, leaning across to hold his hand. "That's why I left one test to do with you. Later, when I'm ready to do it again." She smiled. He lifted her hand and kissed it.

It took about another hour before Shauna needed to relieve herself. She led Harek to her en-suite and had him watch.

"There's really nothing to it. I un-wrap it, I uncap it and then I pee on it for about five seconds." He watched as she described what she was doing as she was doing it. She left the latest test to the side as she finished up. She smiled and wiped the outer part of the test with some tissue and put the cap back on, before handing it to Harek. She washed her hands and by the time she had done, the results on the screen were in.

Pregnant.

Harek looked at the latest test, watched as it counted down and showed one word: Pregnant. She was pregnant. And he was the father.

"Oh mijn god!" he said, putting the test down and grabbing Shauna, twirling her around, laughing and then kissing her, deeply but gently.

She laughed. "I've not told the boys, yet, only you. For now, it's our little secret." He pulled back.

Gone Dutch

"Why?" he asked.

"The first trimester can sometimes be tricky. Not that I've had trouble before, but for now, I'd really like to just keep it our little secret. At least until at least after the first scan."

He smiled. "I want to be there for that," he said, excitedly, taking one of her hands in his.

"Good, because I want you there. I've been there before, with the boys. I know this is the first time you will have gone on this adventure."

"Will you let me know when the dates are? Do we need to do anything? Tell a doctor, book in to see one? I'm confused," he swept a hand through his hair, pacing up and down as he suddenly engaged with the news before him.

"Hey, baby daddy, slow down!" said Shauna, grabbing him by the hand. She smiled, now he was getting it "I'll call the surgery on Monday morning, get the ball rolling. They'll take these two tests as confirmation, because they'll have only made me pee on a stick if there was a chance and I go without having done one. I'll get referred through to maternity and prenatal, then it's all a question of things being done at certain points. The first thing is going to be the scan."

He kissed her, deeply. "Let's go to bed," he growled.

Gone Dutch

He made love with her, slowly, deeply, passionately. It was sweeter now, somehow, knowing she held within her the best thing he could ever hope to have in this world: A child.

He awoke the following morning with Shauna draped half across him, a leg wrapped around one of his, an arm of hers across his chest. He pulled the light quilt over them, kissing the top of her head. If he was able to wake up like this all the time, he'd be a contented man.

The weekend went too quickly for his liking and they spent it chilling. They went for a walk along the canals near her home and the boys rode their bikes. They were just happy to spend time together. He was surprised by the number of canals in the area and the ability to walk between the industrial canal, leisure and countryside in the space of a few simple miles. He was also puzzled as to why Bryce didn't pick up on anything being amiss, so to speak.

It was a bittersweet parting and he left departing as late as he dared, given the travel times to Hull and the tides. It was early June, so the darkness descended later now.

"I want you with me, always," he said, putting his forehead against hers, sighing.

"It's something we need to work out now, for sure," she said.

Gone Dutch

They kissed, not wanting to say goodbye, but knowing that they had to. She finally took a step back, letting him go.

"I'll let you know when the scan is happening. I want you there for that," she said quietly.

He stepped in to kiss her again. "Try and stop me," he replied, hoarsely.

She shook her head. "Never will," she said, walking back to her front door. "Now go, make the tides."

He thought about staying, having something really important to stay for. But the business was calling, employees, contracts. As he drove to Hull, a plan formed in his mind. Despite the late hour when he returned home, he called her. She answered immediately.

"You're back?" she asked, snuggling down into the bed.

"Yes, just. Where are you, tell me what you're doing?"

She chuckled. "I'm answering my phone late at night to some crazy Netherlander who decided to call," she chuckled, admonishing him in humour. He laughed. "As for where I am, I'm tucked up in bed, missing a sexy Netherlander hugging me close."

He sighed. "Damn, famke, I miss you and it hurts!" he growled. His bed was cold. This is not where he wanted to be when she was in the middle of England, pregnant with his child.

Gone Dutch

"I know. When you're here for the scan, we need to work out logistics and things. I'm not sure what the Dutch processes are for this, for scans and everything or birthing… all things we get to figure out," she said, switching to hold the phone to the ear nearest the pillow.

"And we will, famke, we will. Rest well. I love you."

"I will. I love you too," she said, slowly, unwillingly, ending the call.

Monday came and the call to her favourite GP was made. She knew that Dr Jen would call her back and twenty minutes later, she did.

Shauna explained why she was calling and after some congratulations, Dr Jen declared that the process of prenatal care had begun. Shauna's pregnancy was in the system, so all she could do now was wait for the scan dates.

Her next call was to Julie at the martial arts club. Whilst Michael could still attend, Shauna knew from experience it was not good for her to train. Her body disliked training when it was pregnant and she would hurt more. Every night, they spoke with each other, sharing their day. Sometimes it was a video call, especially when some of the building work was finished, or the greenhouse frame was erected.

Gone Dutch

The scan happened more towards ten weeks in than the eight Shauna was expecting. The main school holidays were right around the corner and the boys were surprised to see Harek at the end of their school day. Having made the morning tides, he was at Shauna's front door an hour before they needed to be at the hospital. With the folder in her arm, she smiled to herself as she drove Harek to his first-ever ultrasound appointment.

The maternity wing at Russells Hall Hospital was on the west side, accessed without going through the main entrance. Shauna guided them towards Outpatients on the lower floor and knew exactly where to go, where to check-in, so Harek followed her and held her hand as they waited to be called through. The waiting room was busy. Parents who already had children were there, clearly expecting their second or third. There were a few other couples who didn't have small people playing at their feet, cuddled up on uncomfortable plastic chairs sitting away from the main area.

Shauna stood as her name was called and Harek nervously followed.

The room was warm, small. Andrew's bedroom was just about as big. There was a bed, machines, monitors and a chair.

The nurse was polite, friendly and Shauna seemed to know exactly what to do. "Been here before,

Gone Dutch

remember?" she winked as she grabbed Harek's hand at one point.

Shauna lay down on the exam table and exposed her stomach. Some gel was squirted onto her and a wand was produced, attached to the machine. A few seconds later, a crazy black and white image of a head and little limbs appeared on the screen above Shauna, in front of Harek and on the sonographer's screen.

"There you are little one!" said the sonographer happily.

Harek held onto Shauna's hand as the checks were made.

"Well, Mrs Woodward! You are spot on with your dates! You're just under ten weeks gone, so we'll arrange a scan for about eleven weeks from now, if that's okay? How are you fixed…"

Harek zoned out the technician and looked at the little legs, feet, head of the child now growing inside Shauna. His miracle child.

He snapped into the moment again as the screen went blank and saw Shauna had wiped the gel off herself and had replaced her clothing

"Sorry," he said. "I'm… That was amazing to see!"

Shauna smiled at him. "First time will do that to you," she chuckled.

"Oh, is he not the father?!" asked the nurse, suddenly looking concerned.

Gone Dutch

"Oh, he is. I'm a widow," said Shauna, holding his hand. "It's his first, my third."

The nurse let out a small breath. "Well, congratulations to you both again," she beamed. "The baba looks nice and healthy, everything is there that needs to be and as it should be. I've printed you off two scans," she said, handing them to Shauna along with some cardboard frame thing that she put in her folder.

"Thanks again!" said Shauna, guiding Harek out of the door and the Outpatients clinic.

Outside on the way to the car park, he stopped, pulling Shauna back to him by her hand. He picked her up, swung her around and kissed her.

"I'm going to be a father!" he yelled, happily.

She tossed her head back and laughed. "Has it taken this long to sink in?"

He nodded. "Until now, I have been waiting for the worst because of…" he shook his head. "You're amazing," he kissed her passionately, his eyes becoming hooded and dark.

"Yeah, well…" she shrugged but smirked. "It ain't over yet. We've got parents and relations to tell yet," she said, heading towards the car. He grinned. He couldn't wait.

Gone Dutch

"Okay, so do you think your parents will be OK finding out on a Zoom call? Just, it will be easier if we tell them all at once, I think?"

She asked it like a question, wanting his input.

"Video call, verbal… I'm sure they won't mind."

She smiled. She got up to make hot drinks and left Harek sitting at the kitchen table, watching her. He checked his pocket, again. He waited until she was back at the table; drinks placed before them, before he leaned across the table and took her hand.

"Shauna?" he asked. She looked at him, squeezing his hand.

She watched as he reached down under the table and produced a small ring box. She froze, watching it. He lifted her chin to look into her eyes, watching her react.

"Shauna," he breathed. "I want to show you each day I love you. I need you and the boys with me. Will you move in with me, marry me?"

He opened the box to reveal a perfectly cut radiant clear diamond on a platinum ring. She gasped, frozen on the spot.

"Oh my!" she gasped. It was a few long minutes before she nodded and whispered "Yes" as she burst into tears. Taking the ring carefully out of the box, he placed it on her empty engagement finger.

"I love you!" he said, reaching for her and kissing her. "I need and want to spend the rest of my life

Gone Dutch

with you," he reached up and held her face. "When I said what I have I share, I meant it." She jumped up and hugged him, laughing. He pulled her onto his lap and was kissing her when the boys came home.

"Eugh, mum, go to your room!" said Michael.

"Boys," she said, smiling as she broke away from Harek. "We need to talk with you both before we talk to everyone else. Come and sit." She motioned for them to join them. Once they found snacks and drinks, they did.

"How would you two feel about moving to Rotterdam? Say, permanently?"

They looked at each other, then at Harek and her.

"Are you getting married?" squealed Andrew.

Shauna nodded, a smile playing on her lips as she showed the boys the engagement ring. They admired it, cheered and whooped, then started asking questions about schools and friends.

"Schools are one of the things we need to find out about, but we have all summer to look and find a good school where you can learn Dutch and do your GCSEs. You're not quite at the "don't move school" stage," she nodded to Michael. "But, this is going to be a one-way thing, boys. We'll be back for holidays and things, but," she held up the key Harek had given her moments before. "We have somewhere to go that we know. You will still have contact with your friends via the Xbox and visits, video calls, so you'll still chat to

Gone Dutch

them when you're not at school and the homework is done, same as here."

"What about your job, mum?"

Shauna shrugged. "I'll have to find a new one I guess, but I'm going to be busy for a few years. You see… You're both going to be big brothers."

They looked at her and Harek. "You're pregnant?" asked Michael.

Shauna nodded. "Yep," her eyes sparkled.

He folded his arms and looked at his mum and Harek. "So we get Harek as a step-dad?"

Shauna nodded again. "Is that a problem?" she asked.

"When's the wedding?" he asked.

"Not set a date yet son," she said, laughing. "Two big things first, eh?"

Michael stood motionless for a moment. So did Andrew.

"I could freak out here," he said. "But I like the house in Rotterdam. I like Rotterdam." He looked at Harek. "I know you make mum happy. I know she makes you happy…" he finally leaned back and sighed. "This is a hell of a lot to take in," he said.

"We know. Nothing is going to happen today, not about the schools or moving. We need to see the school year out and spend the summer sorting things like finding the right school for you both."

Gone Dutch

Harek spoke up. "We don't do secondary school until we're twelve, so Andrew, you'd get another year and Michael, you'd just be starting. But, that's the Dutch education system and you are both English educated. I'll look into it but I think an International school would save you both some frustration and time. We've got the summer to go and look at all the options Rotterdam has to offer, including private schooling if necessary."

Michael nodded. "Well, do gran and gramps know?" he asked. Shauna shook her head.

"You two are the first we've told. Everyone else will be here at about seven and we're on a call with Harek's parents and family too."

"They're gonna freak," cried Andrew, laughing.

"Calm down you!" she said, ruffling his hair. He took offence at having his hair messed up and ran when Harek threatened to do more than just ruffle his hair.

The boys had a few hours to digest the latest news and changes before grandparents, aunts, Bryce and tablets were set up for Zoom. Elspeth nudged James and whispered something as the tablets were brought connected to Zoom, showing Isobel, Vayenn and Reuben, Hanna and Pieter. Cait sat with her parents, but nodded as Elspeth said something quietly.

"I guess you can all take a wild guess as to why there's a huge family meeting?" asked Shauna to

Gone Dutch

everyone, once she'd introduced people digitally, or otherwise.

"You're pregnant?" asked Cait.

"You're getting married!" shouted Vayenn who clearly knew what her brother had planned.

Harek came and held Shauna's hand. They'd slipped the ring off whilst everyone arrived, lest their news was trumped before they were ready to tell everyone. They'd slipped it back on now.

"Both, as it happens," beamed Shauna. The cheers from the Zoom chat and in the living room was one of congratulations and deafening. Lots of hugs and tears abounded as the news was digested. It took a few moments for the noise level to be as such that questions could be asked.

Shauna walked the whole family through the day and why Harek was in England mid-week. The baby scans and how he proposed was shared. The boys came down to talk with their soon-to-be Dutch relatives. It was non-stop questions and answers for nearly an hour.

When the Zoom chat ended, it left just Harek with Shauna's family.

"Called it!" said Elspeth, grinning.

"Mam!" scolded Shauna. "Taking bets?" she asked.

Elspeth shook her head. "I said pregnant, then I said engaged, then I said both," she beamed from ear to ear. "But that was right after introductions when I

Gone Dutch

decided on both. Congratulations honey!" James too hugged his eldest daughter.

"What are you going to do with this place?" asked her dad.

"Well, Bryce still lives here. I'm not intending to sell it," she said, looking at her younger but very much taller brother.

He smiled, mouthed "Thank you" and went to chat with Harek.

Bryce found him on the patio under the pergola, holding a beer. Now he knew why all the beers available tonight were Dutch beers.

"You're a lucky son of a bitch you know that?" he asked, sitting down in the nearest chair to his soon to be brother-in-law.

Harek chuckled and nodded. "Yes, I am working that out every day. But, not having her and the boys at Mûne Roazen, it hurts. There's a lot of paperwork to come to make this all legal, but I can support her and the boys, so some of it is mitigated." He looked at the man who would be his brother-in-law as soon as they could set a date. "I need her, especially now."

"She's just told me she's not selling the house," said Bryce.

Harek nodded, understanding. "I wouldn't expect her to, you're family."

Gone Dutch

"How long have you known she's pregnant?" asked Bryce.

"Since she was three weeks pregnant. She found out pretty quickly."

Bryce noticed. "I got a rough idea when she told me off one morning for using half the jar of coffee grounds in a single pot. And then wouldn't drink any of it."

"Ja, what is that about the smell? I've not worked that out."

"It's to do with not putting poisonous things in your mouth when you're pregnant. A bit crazy but Lynda had the same," his jaw dropped and his eyes widened. "Oh, Christ, I've not told Carrie." Bryce ran a hand over his face. "She's gonna be so happy and annoyed we didn't include her tonight."

Harek chuckled. "I'm surprised the whole street and district do not now know," he said, watching the man who would be his brother-in-law. Bryce nodded and the lines near his eyes came together as his eyes lit up.

"There you are," said James, joining them. "Yer mum is already booking us in at your house in Rotterdam," he settled himself into one of the chairs. "I've come out to let them get on with it," he said, enjoying a beer. Harek smiled at his soon to be father-in-law.

Gone Dutch

"You're most welcome and as soon you can," he said.

"Aye, that's what Shauna said. Though, she said something about dates and checking with you about building works?" he said.

"I will have the house finished totally in a few more weeks. The gardens too should be done this summer. Shauna drew up lots of plans for the garden, I'm looking forward to them being realised. The boys like Mûne Roazen, there's lot of space to play, explore, run, hide…"

"Mûne Roazen," repeated James.

Harek nodded and took his phone out of his pocket. Bringing up photos of his home, he showed James and Bryce.

"Oh, Ellie's gonna love that," replied James. Harek began flicking through hundreds of photos, from the most recent to back when Mûne Roazen had been nothing but an empty mill and empty main shell, waiting to be rebuilt.

Harek went through what he'd had done to Mûne Roazen to modernise it, including the library. He leaned back in his chair, happy to share his life with Shauna and her family. He realised that they were now his family too.

"I am sorry I did not ask permission from you before asking Shauna to marry me. I assume you do not object?"

Gone Dutch

James shook his head, moisture gathering in his eyes. "One thing you'll learn about our Shauna, Harek. She's stubborn and strong, but she needs what you're offering. I want her to be happy again, really happy," he patted Harek's knee. "I'm happy for you both and ye have our blessing."

It was nearly midnight when Shauna and Harek finally closed the door to her parents leaving.

"Cait was well behaved," he said. Given the last time he had met her, she had been the perfect daughter and soon to be sister-in-law this evening.

"Yeah, she still has her moments though," she replied. "But yes, she was impeccable I agree." Shauna tilted her head to the right. "She must be taking her meds again."

"Meds?" he asked. Shauna had mentioned this before but he hadn't pried then.

Shauna nodded and sighed. "Cait suffers from high social anxiety and mental health, we're not sure why, but she does. It's like a switch in her that goes off every so often, hence why she can be a nosy bugger one minute and the supportive sister the next. It's not depression, as such, but she does take mood stabilising drugs." Harek nodded, aware now of why Cait is as she is and why Shauna does love her.

"Your mother is keen to visit," he chuckled as they headed up to bed, having secured the house.

Gone Dutch

Shauna rolled her eyes. "Ain't she just! Though, there's a lot of legal paperwork to do I think for us to be resident?" she asked.

Harek nodded. "Tomorrow's problem. Now, sleep. You need rest," he said, escorting her to the bedroom.

"So do you," she said, tapping each word out on his chest, but grinning.

He chuckled but was quite content to hold Shauna as she slept. It didn't take long for her to close her eyes and be asleep, hugging Harek with a small smile on her lips.

Gone Dutch

Thirty-Five

The following Monday, Shauna handed her notice to Ben and Adam. Jen of course, noticed the rock on her finger but let Shauna tell the guys her news. They were pleased for her but concerned about the boys and their needs, but only until Shauna had answered their questions. They then got about properly congratulating their best friends widow and her new adventure.

The school year finished out just ten days later. The boys decided what they wanted to take with them permanently to Rotterdam. Shauna was now showing her pregnancy, though only if you realised how slim she was before.

The boot of the Q7 was full, the spare back seat holding another suitcase of clothes and small boxes of stuff that they were taking to Rotterdam. The office was still full of boxes and other items that they wanted to take. Harek had said he'd meet them at Hull before their meeting later that week with the Embassy and the local municipality.

"So this is it," said Bryce, hugging her.

She nodded. "It feels weird to say bye to this place," she looked at the house she and Matt had built.

Gone Dutch

"But, I know you'll look after it," she buried her face in her brother's shoulder, hiding her tears in his jumper.

"We'll visit soon," she said hoarsely as she started her car, taking the first step to moving herself and the kids to Rotterdam.

She sent Harek a message as she stopped on the M1 for a break. Harek insisted on paying for the car to be stored at the port, so that she always had access to it when she needed it to bring the boys back to visit.

She told him where she was and his instant reply was: "On my way too!"

She smiled and told the boys, who wanted to grab a burger and a milkshake. Where they put the food, she had no idea, but since they'd want to unpack when they got to Mûne Roazen, she figured it wouldn't be a problem.

It turned out to be a good call, since it was nearly dinner time before the boys declared that their cases and boxes were unpacked.

Harek had helped Shauna move the first of her things into the house, but not before he'd carried her over the threshold. Now in his mind, she wasn't just a guest, she was home.

She sat in the chair nearest the bedroom windows, quietly later that evening. He struggled to find her once the boys had hidden themselves away in their

Gone Dutch

new bedrooms. When he did find her, even though he'd looked in the room twice before, he was relieved.

"Famke, There you are!" A moment later, "What's wrong?" he asked.

She smiled and sighed. "Just, it's been a long day and it's just hit me: what the hell do I do with my days when you're at work and they're at school, when I'm waddling around like a duck?"

"You'll be the sexiest duck waddling around Rotterdam," he said, taking one of her hands. She looked at him, shrugged and sighed. She closed her eyes.

"Look at me," he said, softly. She heard a click as a light was turned on and when she did look, his face was full of concern.

"There are many, many things you can do or be here. It is totally your choice. Once you have the BSN and you're on the BRP, you can work, have accounts, get access to the healthcare, the doctor, hospitals, dentists or whatever that you will need. You don't have to decide it all tonight. Or this month, even this year. Give yourself time to adjust, I've got you."

His hazel eyes reflected the light but they didn't sparkle or change like they did when he was planning something. They were filled with love and concern.

"Am I going to be good enough?" she whispered.

"What's caused this, Shauna? This is not you." He dragged over a stool and sat facing her, taking both her hands in his.

Gone Dutch

Shauna couldn't begin to explain how she was feeling, or voice the mind monkeys that were rattling around in her head, even though she wanted to. She tried to stop herself from crying, had been for ages, sitting in the dark. Until he'd walked in, looking for her, she'd been successful in that endeavour. Not any longer. He held her as she cried, telling her over and over again, she was more than good enough.

"You've been nothing but amazing, famke. Always."

It was a good half hour later that she was composed enough to go down to the dinner Harek had prepared. It was cold now, but a quick blast in the microwave heated it up for them. The boys, having been told that food was ready, had helped themselves to everything on offer and tidied away their mess.

He made Shauna sit on the library sofa, wrapped her in a blanket with the fire blazing whilst he tidied up and ensured the boys went to bed. He came to sit with her and found her dozing and sat at the other end, her feet in range. Taking off her slippers, he began massaging her feet gently.

She stirred and watched him as he cared for her. He looked up at her and smiled.

"Hej famke!" he whispered, leaning across to touch her face. She nuzzled his hand, held it to her, then kissed the palm. "Do you want to talk?" he asked.

Gone Dutch

She nodded and more tears threatened to fall. He lifted her feet and placed them on his lap, then he shuffled closer, wrapping her feet up in the blanket and taking her hands in his.

She made motions as if to speak, but stopped herself each time. Eventually, she managed to whisper. "I'm scared."

He lifted her legs, shuffled and lifted her so she was now sitting on his lap. He held her to him, wrapping his arms around her and she lay her head on his shoulder.

"Why?" he asked, softly.

"This is so fast!" she said and the tears fell again. He dried her tears with the blanket, his hands, his kisses.

"Two big things so close together, I know famke." He sighed into her hair. "Today has been a long day. It's the start of us being together, just the four of us, before we become five. Or more," she didn't react to him, which surprised him. "One day at a time, famke, one day." Twenty minutes later and he was carrying her up to bed, wrapped in the blanket from the library.

She awoke the following morning quite late. The room was still quite dark, the blackout blinds blocking out the light from the connecting deck enabled her to sleep for longer, but the light from the bathroom made it so she could see she was on her own. The other side of the bed had been slept in, but it was cold. Adding to her

Gone Dutch

fears from the previous day, she rubbed between her breasts and controlled her breathing.

      The door opened and Harek walked in, carrying a tray. The sound of kids playing reached her ears. The sound was of more than her kids playing on the Xbox.

      "Goeie moarn, famke!" he said smiling.

      She shuffled so she was sitting up, managing a weak smile. "I did it again, didn't I?" she said as the tray was placed across her lap.

      "Did what?" he said, kissing her gently on the lips.

      "Freaked out again," she said, sighing.

      He lifted her chin so she had to look at him. "Famke, you're pregnant and I think, beyond exhausted. Yesterday was hard and it's drained you. Rest today," he kissed her lightly on her head. "Things are in hand."

      He stood and opened up one of the blinds a little bit, allowing enough light in so she could see. Scrambled eggs with toast, jam, herbal tea and a bowl of fruit were presented beautifully to her. Along the top of the tray, were two flowers; a large sprig of heather, and a freshly cut red tulip.

      She softened as the gesture of the presentations before her. "Eat," he said, taking the coffee and joining her back in bed.

      She ate everything on the plate, slowly. When she'd finished, he cleared the tray away to the other side

Gone Dutch

of the door and called for Michael, asking him to take it to the kitchen.

"Who else is here?" she asked.

"Vayenn is, but don't you worry about getting up. You need to rest more. Come on," he gently commanded, making her lie back down. He tucked her in and closed the blinds again, sending the room into a comfortable darkness.

"Sleep my love, sleep. All is well." He kissed her lightly on the temple and she closed her eyes.

She hadn't intended to sleep for another three hours, but she had. However, she felt a little better for it. Getting up to take a shower, she didn't hear Harek come to see if she needed anything until she saw that the blinds were open, the bed covers were folded back and he was sitting in the Queen Anne chair, smiling.

"You look better! How do you feel?" He leaned forward, placing his arms on his knees, watching her.

"So much better. I hadn't realised that I was that tired and it was affecting me like that. I'm sorry." She came across to stand before him, naked.

He smiled up at her. He opened his legs, pulled her to him and held his head against her slowly expanding stomach as his arms wrapped around her middle.

Gone Dutch

"No need. I should have made you rest when you got here, instead of letting you unpack all those boxes," he nuzzled her bump gently. "I let you dictate the pace."

"I'm usually okay with things like this!" she said.

He shook his head. "Slowly, Shauna. We do this slowly," he kissed her gently on her forehead. "There's no rush, we do have all the time we want."

He breathed in her smell, the pink soap bar she liked to use, the way she pinned and twisted her hair up in a vicious looking clip, but letting wisps fall to frame her face. He walked her backwards a pace or two, then stood and kissed her gently.

"Come, chill downstairs with us. The day is warm, the sun is out and you can mooch about the gardens once you've eaten again."

She smiled at him. "Bossy, huh?"

He grinned, but his voice had dropped a baritone as he replied. "Right now, concerning you, I am becoming more so." He kissed her lips firmly. She nodded.

Vayenn smiled and came to hug her as she appeared downstairs. She'd been busy in the kitchen, baking something that had a distinct caramel scent. The worktops were clear, so whatever it was, it was either still in the oven or out somewhere.

Gone Dutch

Shauna was guided to a breakfast stool and made to sit by Harek, who began making her a huge sandwich with meat, cheese, chutney and a side bowl of fruit.

Vayenn took another stool but didn't ask any questions until Shauna had finished eating.

"Where are the kids?" she asked halfway through.

"Exploring the gardens," Vayenn smiled. "There's a good few hectares and a half out there. Reuben is with them," answered Vayenn.

The lack of questions from Vayenn made Shauna uneasy, but she ate the food.

Harek asked Vayenn something in what sounded like Dutch, but Shauna picked up a few Frisian words. Brother and sister didn't want Shauna to know what they were talking about.

Shauna looked from one to the other, wondering if either would tell her what was being said. Harek frowned and growled a reply. Vayenn stood, snapped out a reply that didn't sound nice, touched Shauna on her arm and walked out the front door to the gardens, but didn't slam the door behind her.

"Okay, what did I miss?" asked Shauna, finishing up her fruit.

Harek sighed. "She wanted to ask what else you wanted to bring with you from England. I told her not to push you on it today, or this week. She got, what's the

Gone Dutch

English term?" he paused for a moment. "Pissy? At me for it."

Shauna nodded. "I don't know what else I want to bring that's not in the office, is the answer. I just..."

Harek went to her and hugged her. "That's why I told her to give you time. She's excited, she likes you," he kissed the top of her head. "She's missed you and she's not seen you since the weekend you were here last. Now, we're making her an aunt and a sister-in-law, something we did not think would ever happen." He held her tightly. "It seems you both forget that you're human, like the rest of us, famke."

Shauna smiled. "Protective fiancé," she said, smiling up at him.

"I never want to see you that stressed or exhausted, again," he said, "especially when I can do something about it." He leaned down and kissed her deeply.

Harek held her hand as they walked through the gardens in the warm, bright sunshine. It amazed Shauna that her simple drawings were coming to life. The herb garden was built from stone, with the patterned paths connecting each of the beds. The beds were currently filled with soil, but no plants.

At the back of the herb garden, in a sunny corner, was the greenhouse. Newly built with the beds and the shelving she'd drawn in, it was larger than she had

Gone Dutch

drawn up. "Why not, you will make use of it, no?" was his reply when she asked why the much bigger size. The compost bins had been changed. "We reused the pallets, it was gardener's idea," he said and her jaw dropped slightly.

"Great upcycling!" she said, approvingly. There were three huge bins, so that it could all be rotated by forking it into the next one along. "Wait, you have a gardener?"

Harek nodded. "He usually just cuts the grass and keeps it tidy for me. He's loved making these plans of yours happen. He's been a taskmaster with the builders," he chuckled.

"You must introduce me," she commanded

"I will." he smiled and bent to kiss her gently. "Not today though, he is not here."

They spotted Vayenn, who threw a look of disgust at her brother, smiled at Shauna and went to head off in a different direction. "Vayenn!" Shauna called. She turned to Harek and held a palm to his chest. "Give us a few?" she said, then walked to her future sister-in-law.

"He said you were too tired." She glared at her brother.

Shauna nodded. "I still am, I think? I still feel weird, not quite myself, light-headed." she smiled slightly. "I've been burning the candle at both ends to get here with the stuff we needed. I don't usually turn

Gone Dutch

into a weeping mess that lets the mind monkeys tell me I'm useless. Or let my fears kick into overdrive."

Vayenn looked at her. "Really?"

Shauna nodded. "Really. I think I fell asleep crying on Harek's lap last night. I have no idea how on earth I got tucked into bed, though I can guess." Vayenn studied her for a moment, deciding after a moment that Shauna was telling her the truth.

"Then you do need to rest," she said, smiling gently.

"I know. But I needed to get up, move around, shower. Eat," she looked at the plants. "Again," Shauna smirked and glanced at Harek. "I think I worried him."

Vayenn shrugged. "Perhaps. He'll work it out."

"Don't be angry at him, please?" asked Shauna.

Vayenn smiled at Shauna, who had moved so Harek couldn't see her for Shauna. "He can stew for a while," she grinned.

Shauna shook her head. "Please?" she asked again, touching Vayenn on her shoulder.

Vayenn stopped planting some shrubs, and then looked at her brother, back to Shauna, who suddenly looked tired again. "Okay," she said, hugging Shauna. "Go, rest before he picks you up and takes you back to bed," Vayenn let her go. "I'll see you at dinner?"

Shauna nodded and headed back to where Harek was leaning against a tree. A simple nod between

Gone Dutch

brother and sister was all it took to have things back to normal.

Harek did guide her back to the bedroom, tucking her back into bed. Reuben and the kids were back in front of the TV, watching a movie that they'd brought with them. He shut the door and silence fell in their room. Ensuring she was tucked in, he lay on top of the covers, spooning her, helping her to settle. When she was asleep, he crept from the bed and joined the others for the movie.

The kisses on her cheeks, lips and eyes were feather-light, as was the soft deep voice calling her name.

"Hey you!" said Harek, smiling as she slowly awoke. She'd only been asleep for the rest of the movie, but it had been a deep sleep.

"Hey!" she said, stretching like a cat.

"Dinner won't be long. Vayenn's been busy. Care to join us?"

She nodded and smiled as he thoroughly kissed her. "Good!" He replied and chuckled as she wrapped an arm around his neck to hold him in the kiss. "Later, maybe," he replied, hoarsely, reading her intentions. He waited until she was ready to join them before walking behind her as they headed downstairs.

"Mum!" the boys cried, running to her and hugging her.

Gone Dutch

"Hey you two!" she said, laughing as she hugged them tightly. Goddess how they grounded her. "How's today been?" she asked.

"We've chilled out, unpacked a few more things," Andrew wouldn't let her go. "Why haven't you been down? What's wrong?" demanded Andrew.

Shauna chuckled. "I'm exhausted! You know, packing to move isn't as easy as you two think it is!"

"But," said Andrew. Michael poked him. "Mum's pregnant, you sausage. Mum's only got so much energy and she brought stuff we didn't think of."

She chuckled. "Well, we're here." She looked at the boys. "Not looking forward to fetching the rest of the stuff over!"

Harek hugged her from behind. "Let me deal with it," he said. It was more of a statement or a command, than a request or a question. She sighed. She didn't feel up for doing another dash either way of the M1. She nodded. "Okay," she said, relenting. He smiled, kissed her temple and waved them towards the dining island.

Several huge pancakes with bacon, sausages and other meats with many side dishes were consumed in a noisy filled kitchen. There was teasing between the kids, gentle admonishing from the grownups and family bonding time.

Gone Dutch

Harek pulled her close at one point, when the kids were busy playing a game, watched by Vayenn and Ruben.

"Come, let me show you the changes," he said, looking upstairs whilst standing in the kitchen.

"Okay," she said. She hadn't spent the time being inquisitive in her new home.

The guest rooms were changed around. The double room from before was still the same size, but with a shower room where a double bed would have been. The top bedroom now held the spare double bed and the other smaller guest room was now completed. It was unfurnished, but finished with plain walls, carpet and heating.

"Not sure what colours or how to do these rooms," he said, looking at her.

"You'd like me to help?" she asked. "Or do it?"

"We choose, together. I thought the larger room could be for parents, yours or mine, when they stay. The top one and this one, for other guests, such as Evie and Luuk, or Cait, Bryce…"

She smiled. "They've done a good job," she said, admiring the changes since she was there last.

He slowly led her through the rest of the house. The rooms that Vayenn's kids were staying in were now next to Michael and Andrew, while Vayenn and Reuben had some peace in the Mûne itself. The laundry room

Gone Dutch

was now finished and he finished the tour in the library, making her close her eyes. He turned her towards the folding doors, pulled them open and asked that she looked. In the grass, where she had moon bathed months before, was a circular large paved patio. Marked as a compass, the light grey stone circle was now partially in the evening shadows. The trees that once overhung it had been trimmed back and tidied.

"Oh, Harek, it's perfect!" she said, turning to him and hugging him, unable to express herself any more than she had.

They joined in one of the Xbox quizzes that now entertained the kids, getting some of the answers wrong! As the kids were herded to bed, she got a chance to chat with Vayenn. Harek and Reuben were in the TV room, so the women headed for the library. Harek had already lit the fire, closed the folding doors and left out some wine for them.

"Sneaky," said Shauna, declining a glass.

They talked about shopping, furniture and other things, the conversation eventually turned to what schools in the Netherlands were like, uniforms, school runs, the usual daily activities.

"There are plenty of places to pick up uniforms if you didn't or couldn't bring them from the UK. The school runs I imagine are just like you find them; busy, not enough parking, time-dependent…"

Gone Dutch

Shauna nodded. "That's why we picked a house within walking distance, Matt and I. It came into its own when I didn't have to move the car to go half a mile. It also meant I got fresh air and a little exercise, even in the rain," chuckled Shauna.

"Did you ever have to avoid certain parents at the gates?" asked Vayenn. Shauna nodded and her eyes went wide.

"Once or twice, yes. But you know, some people never really leave the playgrounds," they both chuckled. "Sometimes, I thought it would be easier if they were at a boarding school all the time?" Shauna shifted positions. "But, I'd miss them too much to do that. I need to be there for them, I can't do that if they're so far away all the time"

Vayenn nodded. Harek checked that they were okay, that Shauna was resting or at least, sat down with her feet up. Content that she was, he grabbed some more beers and headed back to the movie he was watching with Reuben.

Gone Dutch

Thirty-Six

She took it easy for the rest of the week. Vayenn and her family returned to their home mid-week, leaving Shauna and the boys to settle into their routine. The appointment with the local officials happened that Thursday and took most of the day. Shauna was happy she could keep her British drivers' licence, but understood she'd need a Dutch one. Bank accounts were created and Shauna gasped as Harek set up a monthly stipend for her directly to use as she wished.

    Medical appointments were then made for the twenty-week scan, Harek contacting his insurance directly, saying that though the basic level covered Shauna's care, he didn't have just the basic cover that every national had.

    It was a week to the day that Shauna and the boys moved in when Shauna discovered something that set her on edge. Clearing out a pile of papers in the library that had gathered, she found school application forms for the boys. Not just local schools or Internationals: Boarding Schools. Neither were near Rotterdam.

    She rubbed her expanding stomach, more out of habit than anything else. The prospectus for the school

Gone Dutch

was in Dutch, but a quick flick of Google translate and the camera function on her phone, showed it to her in English. The prospectus was for a boarding school. This form and the booklet was for a boarding school. The names on the form were her children's. She stood for a moment, going cold with anger, her mind slowly processing what was before her. Every limb was suddenly drained of heat and Shauna saw red.

Feeling rather empty and angry, she grabbed the forms back and went to find the boys. "Do you know where Harek is?" she asked them.

"In the gym, I think," said Michael as he jumped back from a shoot-them-up game he was playing. It looked like Fortnite.

"Okay." She vanished then double backed to them. "Stay here, aye?" She didn't wait for an answer from them.

She found him where the boys said he would be. She watched him with indifference in her eyes as he worked on his pectoral and shoulders, alternating between the two with some pull-down machine she'd seen The Rock use on one of his fitness videos. If she weren't white-hot angry, she'd have enjoyed the view.

He saw her watching him in a mirror, noticing the papers in her hand. He finished doing what he was doing and turned slowly to her.

"Shauna? What is it?"

Gone Dutch

She swallowed and strode towards him, taking her shoes off at the door.

"You!" She threw the school prospectus towards him. "You're planning on sending the boys away?" She thrust the admission papers into his chest. "My boys?" Her voice rose.

He stood there, stunned. Wiping the sweat off his face with the towel, he picked the papers up. "I forgot to shred these," he said, looking at them.

"What the hell were you thinking by doing that!" she spat.

"It was an option that I thought was on the table, that you might consider. Until I heard you talking with Vayenn last week. Then I put it in the pile to shred."

"What makes you think it's OK to send my boys to a boarding school and not even bother to discuss it with me?" Her voice lowered. "Just who the hell do you think you are?" He realised she hadn't heard him and was too angry to do so. She turned on her heel and left the gym, leaving her shoes behind.

He caught up with her in seconds, grabbing her arm and twisting her to face him.

"Shauna, listen! I didn't apply. Yes, they're partially filled out but you can't view the school without having the forms ready to be signed there and then. I didn't even fill in all their details." He held the forms out to her. "Read it again, famke."

Gone Dutch

He could see she was hurt, the set jaw and tears were a big give away. "I thought that the best International School in the Netherlands was what you wanted for the boys. Until I heard you talking with Vayenn. Then I knew it was never going to be an option because they'd be so far away from you with it being a boarding school. Every piece of paper in that pile is to be shredded to bits and burned. Look through it, there are work documents there that are wrong, draft contracts, first sketches of boat builds. This, was, is and will be, a part of that pile."

He came towards her, afraid that she'd run or worse if he touched her. He wanted to reach out to touch her, but pulled back. He wasn't sure what he wanted her to do. Acknowledge what he was saying. Look at him.

Huge breaking sobs suddenly wracked through her but all he could do was reach forward and hold her, rock her. He didn't tell her to be calm, like he would normally do. Michael appeared like a ninja with a box of tissues and then vanished back into the house.

It was a good fifteen minutes before Shauna could even speak. He held out the tissues as she tried to wipe her eyes, blow her nose. He kissed her forehead between wipes, muttering "I'm sorry," over and over.

He waited until she was able to listen before he said what came from the heart.

"Shauna. You, you the boys, our baby… you're the most important things in my life. You have been

Gone Dutch

since the day you saved my life. You've given me the chance to be something I really thought I'd never be. Not just a father figure to your boys, but an actual father. My own flesh and blood grows within you," he reached for her pregnant stomach, gently touching her, "and I need, want all of you in my life. I can't always promise I'll get it right, I can't promise I'll not screw up again but I will never knowingly do something to hurt you or the kids."

He leaned in to kiss her mouth, salty tears flooded his senses. He never wanted to see her cry like this or from pain, ever again.

"I love you," he whispered. She broke the kiss and she leaned into his forehead. "Ik hâld fan dy," he said again in Frisian. "I'll say it every day, every hour in as many ways and languages I can until you believe me again."

"This," she said, waving the forms in her hand. "This hurt," she swallowed and glared at him. "A lot. That you would even suggest…"

He held her wrist. "Yes, I screwed up. I am so sorry famke. Please, let me make it up to you. Tell me how, I'll do it."

She shrugged and let out a huge sigh. "I honestly do not know how."

He sighed. "As I've been saying since you arrived; slowly. We take it one day at a time. There are other great schools in the area, I have documents on the English Internationals waiting to be viewed. The boys

Gone Dutch

don't go to any school until you say that's the one we apply for. It's that simple. It's always been that simple."

She looked at him and nodded. "Thank you," she said.

"Feel free to burn them," he said, pointing at the documents clenched in her fist, his jaw ticking. "That way you know they're destroyed. I'll do the rest later."

She nodded and he walked with her back to the house. He watched as she burnt the forms in the library fire, making them catch on a corner. They watched as the flames travelled up and burned slowly. She threw the booklet onto the fire and breathed out slowly as it disintegrated in flames of blue, orange, white and green.

She went to sit with the boys afterwards, not looking at Harek unless she had to. He knew she was angry at him and he had no idea how to make it up to her. He showered and dressed, not liking the way things were now between them, terribly strained and awkward. What was a man to do? He did what the girls would do; he called his friend.

He explained to Jon what had happened. Amelie joined in via speakerphone. He was out on their private deck, keeping one eye on the bedroom door and an ear to their conversation.

"You keep it simple and heartfelt, Har," said Amelie, sweetly. "This whole month is a huge change

Gone Dutch

and being pregnant sure doesn't help. Those hormones must be raging!"

"I've tried to be heartfelt, but the hurt…"

Amelie scoffed. "Yeah, it's going to be raw. Flowers, chocolates, they work with a girl. Jewellery too. What are her favourites?"

Harek looked around to see Michael sneaking in to find him. "Hang on a moment," he said. He motioned for the boy to come and join him.

"What did you do?" he hissed. Harek quickly explained.

Michael's jaw dropped. "Oh. Darn." He folded his arms across his chest, but didn't look cross. "I'll try to help. This is the happiest I've seen mum since dad died. Andrew and I were, hell, are, happy you get to be a second dad to us, and not just because of the cars. You have the chance to fix it. Dad didn't."

"How the hell do I fix it?" he croaked, looking at Michael, but asking Jon and Amelie.

"I'd start with chocolate and flowers, her favourites," replied Amelie again. "What are her favourites?"

"Mint chocolates, any kind," replied Michael "As for the flowers, everything she's put into the garden. Fresia's, heather, tulips… if the plants were in, you could make a whole posy of them, put vases all around the house. But they're not all here yet."

"I have an idea then," said Amelie. "Listen."

Gone Dutch

Ten minutes later, Harek was making excuses to head out somewhere.

"I need to drop this paperwork off to Jon for this week. I'll be back in about an hour?" he said, kissing Shauna on the forehead. She simply nodded and watched as he headed out the door with his briefcase.

When he returned, she had gone to bed. He didn't know she'd cried herself to sleep.

She stretched and blinked several times. She reached across for Harek, but his side of the bed was empty, cold. She remembered the forms, the fight from yesterday and began crying again and got up to fetch some tissue. It wasn't until she came back to bed that she saw the single purple tulip on the other pillow. Attached with twine was a single handwritten note: "Mijn excuses" Taking out her phone and working the translate app, she saw that it said: I apologise. She saw another two in a vase on the nightstand nearest to her. Around the vase was another note: "it spyt my" (I'm sorry) it said. The floor creaked as she walked to the en-suite bathroom to check if there were any more purple tulips there. There were three in the sink, sitting in water.

"It spyt ma sa bot" (I'm so sorry)

"So you're sorry," she said, getting upset again. "So sorry you left me flowers and little notes…" She stopped, breathing deeply. "Actually," she said half to herself, "that's quite a gesture. Now, where are you?"

Gone Dutch

    She slipped on her dressing gown, her slippers, grabbed her phone and put it in her pocket.

    Rose petals were on the bedroom floor, guiding her not to the bedroom door, but the deck that connected the Mill to their room. She slid the door back, revealing a table and chairs, with a food dish and dome lid at the table. Various cushions were placed on one of the chairs. On the table was her huge splat vase, filled with her favourite flowers of tulips, hydrangea, fuchsia, lilac, heather and roses.

    A breakfast of ginger tea, toast with jam and some fresh fruit was upon the tray when she lifted the lid. She smiled and began to cry again. There was a note on the tray. "Asjebleaft ite" it said. She used her phone again to translate it. "Please eat".

    She sat down and did so, catching the first rays of the day as the sun came around to warm that side of the deck.

    She moved the plate as she slowly ate to find that there was an envelope there, containing a credit card. The covering letter was addressed to Harek, but the card had her name on it. On the table was a smart speaker and it began to play songs from the greatest showman. The first up was "From Now On". Not Shauna's favourite, but the message behind it, for her, was clear.

    Harek heard her open the sliding doors and he snuck into their room. He had been waiting outside their

Gone Dutch

bedroom door for half an hour or so, before he heard her get up. It had just been enough time for Michael and the boys to get things organised. He smiled as she sat down to eat breakfast. He was grateful that Michael knew his mother, especially as The Greatest Showman song began to play. He was also grateful for Amelie having access to these flowers in the middle of Rotterdam.

Thank goodness for shops being open late at night and her know where to find cuttings from the front of people's gardens. He just hoped they wouldn't mind missing a flower or two here and there.

As she ate, he quietly headed to the bathroom and began running her a bath. He kept an eye on her eating as the water filled the bath and the bubbles rose.

When he was ready, he walked out to the deck, determined to convince her it was just an error of judgement and not something more.

She turned as the sliding door opened a little more and Harek came to join her.

"Goeie moarn," he said, kissing her gently on the lips. She didn't pull away, so that was something!

"Good morning," she said, softly. "I'm sorry," she said, looking at him.

"I'm sorry," They both said it at the same time and chuckled at their synchronicity.

"I flew off the handle yesterday, I'm sorry." She reached across the table for his hand. He took it.

"I shouldn't have filled the forms in," he replied.

Gone Dutch

She chuckled. "What a pair we are, eh?"

He stood and pulled her up to him, kissing her deeply. "One day at a time," he said, holding her to him and nibbling her mouth. "Together."

She smiled. "Together," she said, warping an arm around his neck, pulling him close.

"And you're sure?" she said, holding up the credit card.

He nodded. "Yes, totally. Come," he said, breaking the kiss and leading her back inside.

He guided her to the bathroom, motioning to the bath. He checked the water temperature as she undressed, her little bump showing proudly before her. He waited until she was seated and comfortable, before vanishing to clear breakfast away.

He let her soak in the tub for half an hour before checking on her. He helped her out when she said she was done and dried her off, slowly dabbing the moisture away. She was surprised when he didn't try to make love to her.

"Later, when you trust me again," was his reply when she hinted.

She nodded and sighed. "You don't think make-up-sex is a thing?"

He chuckled as he dried her feet, his eyes dancing as he spoke. "Famke, I know it is. But, there are other ways to say sorry and the boys are very much

Gone Dutch

awake." He smiled and winked. She smirked back at him. So, maybe later then.

    He gathered them up into the Q7 and drove them into Rotterdam. Parking near a park, he tossed a football to the boys from the boot and they played as he and Shauna walked slowly through the park.

    "You know," he said as they walked past some block sculptures, "I have no idea what we need for the baby. Beyond a bed, or a cot and clothes…"

    She smiled. "All things to get in a few months," she said. "When the boys were small, they were with me for the first six or eight weeks, until they could sleep through six hours or so. Then, they were in their own room with baby monitors so I could rest and would hear them."

    He smiled. "Really? I thought they'd be in with momma for ages."

    She chuckled. "Maybe, but I've discovered I'm a greedy mother and I need my sleep." She watched the boys kick the ball to each other, trying to arc it rather than just straight boot it.

    "Which room is going to be the nursery?" she asked.

    "The one next to the boys," he said, "But we have space in ours for the first weeks."

    She nodded. They talked about pushchairs, car seats, bedroom colours, baby clothes.

Gone Dutch

"There are some things we can get that are neutral. The rest we can get when the gender is known. If, you want to know that is?" she said, looking up at him as they walked around the park.

"Do you want to know?" he asked.

"I'd like to, but if you don't," she shrugged slightly. "Then I'm okay with not knowing."

He pondered for a moment or two. "Did you know with each of the boys?" he said, glancing over at them.

She nodded. "It helped us come up with names, we started using the names before we saw them, helped the family get personal gifts made in advance, such as embroidered blankets and things."

He stopped walking and pulled her to him. "Then yes, I want to know."

She hopped on one foot. "Great! Because I really want to know!" He bent to kiss her and then carried on walking around, calling the boys so that they weren't left behind.

They talked baby stuff for the rest of the day. Snuggled up on the sofa in the library, they spoke quietly with each other. The boys had jumped back onto the Xbox. "There's a baby shop in town we can visit tomorrow, if you like?"

"What about work?" she asked.

Gone Dutch

"I've taken some time off," he said. "I did drop papers off to Jon last night, but I had some help in collecting the flowers," he said, motioning to the smaller vase he'd made up sitting in the library. The splat vase was in their room, on a small table near the bi-fold doors.

Harek's phone rang and he answered it. "Let me check," he said, looking at Shauna. "The removal company can collect the rest of your things tomorrow and have them here by the weekend, if you're OK with that?"

She smiled. "I'll check with Bryce, make sure he's going to be in."

Harek asked them to wait whilst they checked and a quick call to Bryce confirmed when he'd be available. With the details set, they snuggled back into each other, smiling.

Dinner was a quieter affair now they were getting into their own routine and used to the time change. Not that an hour made much difference, but it had taken some getting used to. They usually played a game or watched a movie after dinner. Tonight the boys decided, was movie night. Harek laughed when he saw the Teenage Mutant Teenage Turtles DVD. The boys, realising it was there, demanded to watch it. Popcorn at the ready, they settled down

Gone Dutch

"This is just as awkward as I recall!" he chuckled into Shauna's ear as the Turtles once again saved April from the evil Shredder.

The boys danced to "Ninjitsu" and Shauna reminded them that the tune was actually called Tequila. She brought up the tune by The Champs on YouTube and whistled it as it played. Then the boys got the reference and danced to it, replacing Tequila with Ninjitsu as they headed to bed.

She chuckled as she came downstairs from tucking them in and she fell into Harek's embrace on the sofa. "I thought something a little more… sedate?" he said, hitting play.

Mamma Mia came on and she chuckled as they joined in the songs. Hugging her as they headed to bed later, he smacked her bum gently as she climbed the stairs before him.

Lighting the candles he'd placed earlier that morning, closing the blinds, he beckoned to her.

"One more thing," he said, presenting her with a box of mint chocolates. She flung her arms around him, kissing him.

"I already told you, we were both fools." She looked at him, serious for a moment. "I'm sorry. Forgive me. I love you." Each statement was said differently; softly, gently, pleadingly.

Gone Dutch

He leaned against her forehead, repeating the same words back with just as much feeling.

"Thank you," she said, searching his eyes.

"Thank you?" he said, confused.

"For accepting my apology," she said, smiling. He nodded.

"Dankewol," he said, kissing her. "For accepting mine."

She ran her hands through his hair as the kiss continued, then she began tugging at his clothes. It wasn't taking much effort for him to undress her, being in the simple summer dresses she favoured that showed off her developing figure.

He pulled off his top, throwing it onto the chair. He picked Shauna up gently and carried her to the bed. Setting her down on it so she was before him, he let her stride him. It took all of three seconds for the dress to come off, for her small and perfect bump and her slowly enlarging breasts to be revealed in a lacy maternity bra. He unhooked it as he continued to kiss her, widening his legs so that she was open to any touch he wanted to bestow on her.

Taking a perfect breast into his mouth, he suckled and kissed, nipped and teased. Her groans were nothing more than encouraging. He teased the other, ensuring that she was supported. She held onto his shoulders with both her hands as one hand and mouth played with a breast, but the other gripped her butt.

Gone Dutch

His hands stopped gripping her arse, stroking her hips and slowly coming around to stroke her inner thighs, working around to her inner core. Wrapping one arm around her waist, he gently inserted a finger, then two, kissing and nipping her mouth as she writhed and moaned.

He played with her inner folds, flicking her walls until she came undone by his hand. He stood, grabbed her legs and gently laid her down.

He made quick work of removing the last of his clothes before coming back to her, kissing her mouth, her jaw, her neck, the hollow at her throat.

He kissed all around her bump, over it, all the way down to her now pulsing folds. Taking her in his mouth, he let his tongue do the talking, suckling, licking and made her come again. Stretching as she did now, it was impossible to work out she was pregnant.

She was just coming back to awareness when he gently pushed himself deep into her. She wrapped her legs around him as she arched at his invasion. She reached for his mouth, hungry kisses told him she wanted this, wanted him.

She opened her eyes, looking at him. "Harek," she breathed, making him look at her as he slowly began to thrust deeply into her. "I love you," she said, before arching at a thrust, taking him deeper into her.

His rhythm made it easy for her to shudder in climax. She knew he wasn't done, he hadn't got there

Gone Dutch

himself. She bit gently into a shoulder, scratched his back as he climbed towards his own and in doing so, took her with him again.

He kissed her as she settled down, his arms on either side of her head, supporting himself over her.

"Ik hâld fan dy, famke. Ik hâld fan dy," he said, kissing her deeply, not wanting to let her go. Slowly, he released her from his hips and swung her around to be on the side of him. He stroked her back, her arms as she cuddled into the crook of his neck. He kissed her head as she stroked his pectorals, happy to be wrapped up in bed with her.

He quietly slipped out of bed once Shauna was asleep, blew out the candles and came back to her, blowing out the last by his side once he was cuddled into her again.

That's how they were the following morning, tangled up, hugging. He awoke first, spooning her. One hand was on her bump whilst the other was holding one of Harek's hands. He kissed her temple and stroked an arm until she stirred.

"Goeie moarn!" she said, smiling, keeping her eyes closed as she turned towards him. He kissed her deeply before he huskily said the same words back to her.

Gone Dutch

He ran a hand over her bump; their bump. Then he pulled the covers back and kissed it. Then kissed her again.

She smiled and eventually, they got up, showered, dressed and headed downstairs.

"Mum!" whined Andrew when she appeared.

She hugged her youngest, ruffling his hair.

"What?" she said, using the same whining voice that he had used.

"Michael says we still have to go to school?" he pleaded. She laughed.

"Yes, you do," chuckled Harek as he joined them, placing Shauna's breakfast before her. She smiled in thanks and sat down to listen to Andrew complain about school.

"We can look at them on-line today, decide which ones we'd like to go and visit," said Harek, drinking his coffee and eating a bowl of muesli with yoghurt.

"Oh man!" moaned Andrew, stomping off to the Xbox and flouncing onto the sofa. Shauna chuckled.

"I think he was hoping we'd forget!" she laughed, slowly eating her toast.

"He should have maybe not said anything yet," he grinned.

The boys were invited to view the schools via their websites, to narrow down the number they wanted

Gone Dutch

to visit. Shauna based it on the travel times, travelling to each to gauge the time. Some took nearly an hour but there were a few options much closer.

Harek sent emails asking to view the schools, having worked on what the email should say with Shauna.

The week passed by far quicker than anyone wanted. The schools were viewed, decided upon and registration occurred, even during the school holidays. Admissions apparently worked through but they learned it was only on certain days and for a few hours. The rest of the belongings from England arrived a day earlier than expected, which pleased the boys.

Gone Dutch

Thirty-Seven

Jon and Amelie arrived that evening to help move the dresser into place in the library. Harek had moved furniture around so that Shauna's dresser was in the perfect northern spot. Amelie helped Shauna unpack the specific boxes Bryce had labelled. When they were done, Amelie stood back and was awed. "Really?" she said, looking at the antler candle holder, the cauldron, plants, bells.
Shauna smiled. "If you want to run, the front door is that way," she said, pointing. Amelie shook her head.

"No, I'm good. Just…" she paused. "Well, I expected witches to look like Morticia Addams!"

Shauna threw back her head and laughed. It took a few moments for her to compose herself. "Amelie, most of us only wish we looked as good as Morticia!"

Shauna rubbed her bump and Amelie made Shauna sit down. "You tell me what to put where," she said, attacking another box.

It took most of the rest of that day and the Friday to unbox what had come and place Shauna's dresser and desk. She was surprised Harek had got the removal men to bring it, but she was pleased when it was placed near

Gone Dutch

the window, so she'd have light when she sat there, working.

The girls sat on the sofa with drinks that Friday night, having unpacked everything Shauna had wanted to. The boys had been busy with their own unpacking. They weren't sure where Jon and Harek had vanished off to, but that was okay by them.

They chatted about everything and anything, bonding over life's similarities and adversities. Amelie was surprised that Shauna knew parts of Leuven, her hometown.

"Matrock was ace! The beer, the music, the bratwurst… The whole event was just fantastic," Shauna sighed, reminiscing over a favourite time. "And the chocolate shop on the corner of the square," Shauna made hmm noises that had Amelie agreeing with her. The chocolates from there truly were mouth-watering.

The boys were on the Xbox, playing one of their many racing games.

The men appeared after a while, carrying pizza boxes and beer. Harek put tubs of ice-cream into the freezer and together, the six of them feasted on pizza, various ice-creams and chilled out with a movie.

Jon and Amelie stayed over as guests so they were all enjoying Belgian waffles made by Amelie for breakfast the following morning.

Gone Dutch

"Shouldn't I be doing that?" chuckled Shauna as Amelie danced around the kitchen, clearly in charge for the morning. Harek admired the way Shauna dressed, the long flowing skirt that wrapped around her middle form, along with the light knitted jumper which fell off one shoulder, was so chic and Shauna.

"You could," she said, smiling. "But, this is what I do on a Saturday. Jon loves them but he says that I always make too many. Then, he wants to work it off in the gym and I don't see him until the evening! This way they," she nodded to the men, "can work it off and if they do and we can spend time together!" The boys liked having the extra sweet things for breakfast and Shauna was pleased to have a new friend.

Harek and Jon did vanish off late morning but they didn't say where to. Amelie shrugged.

"Don't care!" she said, smiling.

Shauna decided to show Amelie what plants had been planted so far and the grounds, so they all went into the garden. Shauna came back into the kitchen just after they'd left for a bottle of water, to find a man and a woman standing there, clearly waiting for someone.

The man grabbed her roughly and made her sit on a stool, pulling her hands behind her back. She felt a handcuff go onto a wrist and she fought. He growled quietly into her ear, restraining her. "I'm Politie, pretend," he said. Whilst he'd cuffed one hand, he

Gone Dutch

simply opened and closed the other band, then gave it to Shauna to hold.

"Who are you?" she barked. "What the hell do you want?" she glared at the uninvited guests. What the heck was the Politie doing here? The woman had brown hair and was slightly shorter than Shauna, certainly much thinner. She smirked and pulled her ponytail out. Shauna recognised her just by the hair.

"Sanne," she hissed. Where the hell was Harek and Jon? The guard in black came to stand near Sanne. He winked at Shauna once, who just scowled in reply.

"You know of me," said the other, her English forced.

"I ken of ye," replied Shauna, who shifted in her stool, her accent going deep Scottish brogue very quickly. "What do you want?"

"I want you, out of the picture," her lip turned into a snarl. "Out of here. Out of Harek's life."

Shauna threw her head back and laughed. Morticia would have been proud.

"You have nae idea, dae ye?" Shauna's accent got stronger. It would have been a tell to anyone who knew Shauna, to get the hell out of the way. To Sanne, the warning was unnoticed. The policeman though, shifted on his feet.

Sanne shrugged. "What do I not know that you'd like to tell me?" she said. "That you're engaged? Ha! It means nothing. That baby you're carrying, worthless.

Gone Dutch

He'll never accept it as his own. He can't father children, I made sure of it."

Shauna froze as the Politie officer stood more upright. "Really? How'd ye manage to do that?" Shauna had a feeling the Politie was waiting for something, a confession of sorts. Shauna decided she'd play along, though she'd happily floor the other woman in a heartbeat, pregnant or not.

Sanne scoffed. "It was easy, making him coffee each morning with the birth control drugs in. He never noticed. His count would never come up and it was easy to make him think I'd gotten pregnant but lost it each time," she puffed up a little. "So easy to destroy him."

Shauna sighed. That coffee had been thrown out when the kitchen had been renovated, before she'd come to Mune Roazen. "Okay, so before you decide you're going to do what you've planned, tell me one thing: Why?"

Sanne shrugged. "Because I can. Because I could. His grandfather made my father's company collapse. But, he's sold it on, made it a part of someone else's billions. I can't take that company back, but this boat building one," she scoffed. "So easy to plague, to destroy with failures," Sanne moved to another worktop, inspecting it. "How he keeps finding ways around it, I do not know."

Gone Dutch

Shauna looked around. There were no kids, no Amelie, no men. She looked at the Politie who gave nothing away.

Shauna aired her thoughts. "So it was you who had him beat up? They did quite the number on him," said Shauna, wiggling on the stool.

Sanne snarled. "They didn't do it well enough. He was back at work too quickly."

Shauna noticed the Polities fingers twitch. "Yeah, I got to him just in time. And the emails?" she pushed for facts and Sanne nodded. "Sorry, I didn't catch that?" said Shauna. She guessed that voice confirmation was needed.

"Yes," she spat. "That was easy."

Shauna chuckled. "Opening up the lower-level server ports always is. You know that they know to check for that now, don't you?"

Sanne bristled. "You, again?" she hissed. "I think I might just kill you myself," she hissed. The man in black nodded once. Shauna hoped he meant he'd heard enough, that this would help to convict her. Now they had to arrest her.

Shauna wiggled forward off the stool, keeping her hands behind her. She stretched her neck. "The weird thing about being pregnant and being this far along; it's very hard to sit still for long, or on hard surfaces." Shauna stretched as best she could with the "restraints" behind her back.

Gone Dutch

"Why would he have you living here?" scoffed Sanne, pushing herself off the counter to face Shauna. "You are insignificant to him."

"Ach, I dinnae ken," the policeman's fingers twitched again. "Maybe because we're engaged? Or maybe because this is his baby? Ye ken, I'm no you!" Sanne was close enough now and stunned enough at the news that the baby was Harek's, for Shauna to punch her. It took just the one to floor Sanne, the sound of cartilage breaking was distinctive, unmistakable and sickening. Shauna's right hand, fist and shoulder were all thrown into the punch the Dutchwoman wasn't expecting, thinking that Shauna was helpless and tied up.

Sanne hit the floor in a heap, blood pouring from her broken nose. The Politie motioned for Shauna to show him the cuffs, which he undid from the one wrist and then cuffed Sanne. It took a few moments for the Dutchwoman to wake up and realised what was happening.

The Politie officer read Sanne her rights and then people burst in all over. First, police in uniform entered, followed by Inspector Steenstra. Then Amelie and her boys appeared, closely followed by Harek and Jon.

"Where the hell were you all?" she asked after hugs and kisses were exchanged and Harek's strong arms pinned her to him.

"Held outside by the Politie. They didn't expect you to walk in as that officer was getting Sanne to talk."

Gone Dutch

"But why here?" she asked. The same officer came over to them.

"She was intending on hurting Mr Van Meerloo. I convinced her I was someone for hire and was asking her why, telling her that hurting children and pregnant women wasn't in the contract. But you came back in, got her to boast. I'm glad you played along," he smirked. "Nice punch!" he said as Sanne was taken away to be checked over before being put into a cell.

"Glad you growled that in my ear! And thanks for not doing up the cuffs too tight," she rubbed her left wrist. "Or in truth, at all!"

The policeman chuckled and bid them a good day, following Sanne out with the ambulance crews. Inspector Steenstra came over to speak with them as the rest of the teams cleared out.

"Thank you!" he said to Shauna. "Your goaded confession from her is just what we needed."

Shauna smiled. "Just, put her away for a long time, please?" she asked, snuggling into Harek as he held her close. Andrew was hugging the other side of Harek with Michael hovering close by.

When all the police teams finally cleared away and left, Shauna sighed.

"Goodness!" she said.

Harek refused to let Shauna go.

Gone Dutch

"Well, I don't know about anyone else, but I desperately need a cup of tea!" she said, going to the kettle to make herself and everyone, a cup.

Much later, after lots of praise from Michael, who had seen his mother punch Sanne and hi-fives from Andrew, Shauna relaxed on the sofa with Amelie, Jon and Harek. They offered to stay another night, using their car and the Q7 to block the driveway at the currently not functioning gate. Shauna gathered that Harek and Jon had been secured by the Politie first as they headed out to the gym. Amelie and the boys were next but they couldn't grab Shauna as she'd headed back into the kitchen.
"So what did they do with you?" she asked, grateful no one had been hurt.
"Made us wait in the gym itself. We could hear what was being said, Steenstra was clear we were to stay and that what he was recording would put her away. He said you were never in any danger, but when she said she'd kill you herself…" Harek let the sentence hang.
Shauna nodded but chuckled. "She didn't stand a chance. Maybe with a gun, but otherwise, not really," Shauna sat up straighter. "She was untrained, but determined. Nothing more than bravado." Harek held her hand.
"She," he began. Shauna cut him off.

Gone Dutch

"Isn't worth speaking or thinking about ever again. She's in jail, that's where she belongs and that's where she needs to stay."

He sighed. "I know. But you could've been hurt," he growled, his voice just about steady.

"With that amount of Politie there, recording her? Not a chance," she scoffed. "He made sure I knew he was a cop. If I didn't knock her out, I like to think he would've."

Amelie snuggled into Jon. "What she said she did to you though," Jon said to Harek.

"I never knew a thing," he said. "Not that it matters now, clearly it's all undone as we're very happy," he said, grabbing Shauna's hand as she rubbed her bump.

"Who did your grandfather sell his business to?" asked Shauna picking up on something else Sanne had said.

Harek chuckled. "Berend!"

Shauna laughed. No wonder she wouldn't go after the billionaire.

"We need to eat!" said Shauna, suddenly feeling not so great.

Harek jumped up and he and Jon vanished into the kitchen. They tossed the boys some crisps as they began making huge pancakes with every topping anyone wanted.

Gone Dutch

Thirty-Nine

"Shauna!" Jon hissed as she walked past the utility room a while later whilst clearing up. Shauna jumped, not expecting Jon to be hiding.

"Dinnae do that! What *are* you doing?" she asked, looking around. "Why are you hiding?" He ran a hand through his hair, clearly nervous.

"What happened earlier…" he said. "It's made me realise I love Amelie! I suddenly thought of proposing to her but…"

Shauna smiled. "So, ask."

"But I haven't a ring," he groaned.

Shauna chuckled. "You don't need a ring to ask the question bud," she smacked him lightly on his arm. "Just ask the woman."

He shook his head. "Let her choose the ring," Shauna continued. "It's perfectly acceptable these days. I don't have anything…" She stopped and Jon suddenly looked hopeful. "I might have… Finish tidying the kitchen for me, let me go scrounge. It'll not be perfect, but it might work." He grinned and stepped out of the utility to carry on tidying up the kitchen mess whilst Shauna went to scavenge around her jewellery boxes.

Gone Dutch

Slowly walking past Harek, the boys and Amelie, she headed to her bedroom to find the box she needed.

When she was sixteen, Matt had bought her a Claddagh ring, a symbol of love from the Irish legends. Her hands had changed shape and thickness since then, but she hoped it might fit Amelie's slender fingers for a time until she got to choose her ring. It wasn't one she wore these days, but one she still kept because of the memories it held.

Grabbing that and another dress ring, she made her way back to the kitchen. She popped her head into the library, to find Amelie sitting comfortably on the sofa before the fire, browsing the internet on her phone.

"Would you like another drink?" she asked. Amelie nodded, smiling.

"What will it be?" she asked.

"Stella," grinned Amelie. "Thank you!" she called as Shauna left.

Jon spun around as Shauna appeared in the kitchen, two rings in hand. The Claddagh and the other smaller dress ring that she had kept. She handed both to Jon and explained about the Claddagh ring and which way it was to go on. "Amelie is in the library and would like a Stella," she smiled, hinting that now would be a good time!

Jon shook his head. "Not now… later," he said, smiling. He gave her a quick hug, thanked her and

Gone Dutch

headed back to sit with Harek and the boys. Shauna smiled and headed back to sit with Amelie, taking the drinks with her.

"What are you looking up?" asked Shauna as she came to sit down next to her new friend.

"Oh, nothing important," she said.

Shauna raised her eyebrows slightly and tilted her head towards Amelie, who blushed. "Okay, I was looking up how you ask a man to marry you," she said.

Shauna laughed. "Just ask him," she replied, sitting in her favourite seat again on the sofa.

Amelie chuckled, then she examined her hands, quietly. "What if he says no?" she asked, quietly.

Shauna shook her head, already knowing the answer. "I doubt very much he'll do that."

Amelie looked at her in surprise. "You think he'll say yes?"

Shauna smirked. "Yes, I'm sure he will," Shauna tried hard not to say anything. "He'd be a fool to say no."

Amelie smiled. "I'll have to pick my time." she said. "Today... showed me I can't wait around for him to ask me."

Shauna smiled. "Tell him you love him," she encouraged. "Start there."

Amelie looked at Shauna with laughter in her eyes. "I will! How did Harek propose?"

Gone Dutch

Shauna retold that story, though she was sure Amelie had heard it before.

"Baby scans," smiled Amelie. "We're not there yet. But, one day."

Shauna smiled. "Carpe Diem. Seize the moment Amelie. Life's too short!"

Amelie grinned in reply. "Did Harek tell you that he nearly got restrained once he realised you were in the house with her?"

Shauna shook her head. "No, but I'd be the same."

"How did you keep so calm?"

Shaun shrugged. "I did martial arts with my first husband for years. Competitions, training. You learn how to handle the adrenaline, but muscle memory took over this time. It helped that the policeman whispered he was Politie and didn't cuff me properly." Shauna sighed. "I guessed that he was wired, his jaw was ticking too much and he didn't react when he should have, so I guessed he was acting under orders. I thought getting her to talk would help."

Amelie leaned over to hold Shauna's hand. "You were brave," she said, smiling.

"I didn't get much of a choice," chuckled Shauna. "Just, went with the flow and did it."

Amelie smiled. "We weren't sure who fell, all we heard was the sound of someone getting their nose broken and them hitting the floor. When we heard the

Gone Dutch

policeman say that Sanne was knocked down, we cheered. Everyone moved quickly after that."

Shauna chuckled. "It was like a swarm. One minute it was me, Sanne and that officer, the next everyone as in the kitchen," she rubbed her bump. "I was glad the boys were safe though, I knew they were with you."

Amelie smiled. "Michael cheered loudest I think when he heard you'd punched her, knocking her out. It was him that told Inspector Steenstra to tell you that the man in black was a Politie, and he tried to encourage Sanne to run when he heard your accent get stronger." Shauna nodded. Michael had already told her. "Everyone else was pleased though."

Shauna chuckled and sighed. "I'll be glad when I wake up tomorrow and we begin getting things back to normal. I've had enough talking about that woman for a lifetime."

Amelie agreed.

Jon popped his head around the door, asking if the girls wanted to watch The Greatest Showman now the boys were in bed. Banking the fire and locking the outer doors, Shauna and Amelie curled up on the sofa with their partners. Afterwards, they headed to bed, comforting each other as best they knew how.

Gone Dutch

The following morning, Shauna was making breakfast for the boys when Amelie appeared with Jon. On her engagement finger was the Claddagh ring.

"We're engaged!" announced Jon, even though you could have heard a pin drop when they walked into the kitchen. Harek hugged his friend and Amelie whilst other hugs and cheers were going on.

"Thank you," whispered Amelie as the girls hugged.

"You're welcome," Shauna replied, quietly. "Who asked who?" she coyly asked.

"He managed to ask me first, but only because I let him speak first," beamed Amelie.

Shauna chuckled and Jon brought over a cup of coffee for Amelie whilst Shauna made everyone the breakfast that they wanted.

Gone Dutch

Forty

School started not long after. Michael had gotten used to being in school on his birthday, September 4th and that weekend, he received a surprise as Shauna's parents and Cait arrived over to celebrate.

Shauna had decided to pick up a few new baby things that she had Harek had agreed on whilst Cait was around to help her ferry it all back.

They took a break from the shopping by finding a cafe in the old town, near the river. Shauna's parents had ventured out by themselves for the day, chauffeured around by Johan.

As they talked and ate, a huge figure of a man loomed over them, making Shauna jump.

"I'm so sorry," exclaimed Abbe, deeply apologetic. "I did not mean to make you jump and I had no idea you were pregnant." He kissed her cheek affectionately.

Shauna smiled. "I've not seen you since we needed the initial fibreglass shipment, so I am not surprised you didn't know," her eyes were soft, caring. "Abbe, this is my sister, Cait. She's staying with me for a few days, visiting from England."

Gone Dutch

Cait and Abbe shook hands, but Shauna hugged him. "Seriously, it's okay," she said, chuckling as he apologised yet again.

"How's your grandfather?" she asked, taking a bite of cake as she indicated for him to join them. Cait shuffled closer to him, impressed by the man before her.

"He is well, thank you! He'll be thrilled at your news. As am I. It is well deserved."
Shauna smiled as he spoke.

"Did my sister tell you that she floored that awful lady who was setting Harek up?" asked Cait as she fluttered her eyelashes at him. Shauna pulled her lips together tightly as Cait used the word "lady".

Abbe looked at Shauna, then to Cait. "No," he said. "What happened? We heard she'd been arrested and at Mûne Roazen," Abbe raised his eyebrows at Shauna, "but not that you were directly involved."

Shauna let Cait tell the story, partly because Shauna was tired of it, but because Cait obviously wanted to impress Abbe. Shauna felt for Abbe, but she knew he was adult enough to make his own choices, as was Cait. They chatted for ten minutes, Abbe giving Shauna another hug as he departed.

"So, who is he?" crooned Cait after he had departed with a look over his shoulder. Shauna sat back with a glint in her eyes.

"He had a hand in supplying Harek with the fibreglass when it was needed. He's quite well-

Gone Dutch

connected business-wise in the Netherlands." Shauna kept the fact he was a billionaire's grandson out of the description of him.

"He's a handsome Dutchman," drooled her sister.

"Netherlander," corrected Shauna quickly. "Dutchman is such an insult to some," Cait nodded, but she glanced again at the direction Abbe had taken. 'Poor Abbe!' she thought.

Later that evening, a huge array of flowers arrived from Berend to Shauna, congratulating her and Harek on becoming both engaged and their impending bundle of joy. A smaller bouquet was addressed to Cait, from Abbe. Shauna chuckled and smirked at her mother, a knowing glint in both their eyes.

Cait vanished for half an hour but was clearly pleased when she appeared just before dinner.

"Did he call you?" asked Shauna.

"No. I called him. He had his number put onto the card," said Cait as her eyes shone. Her family were on the Mûne side. Cait was in the smaller guest whilst her parents were in the larger double. It gave them privacy and quietness from the boys.

Michael and Andrew talked about their new life in Rotterdam, their school but how it wasn't that much different from life back in England. Sure, it was quieter but they had more room to play, explore and ride their bikes. They did their homework, they made new friends.

Gone Dutch

With nearly four hectares of land at Mûne Roazen, being outside was never so easy.

They celebrated Michael's teenage birthday with cake, a barbeque and a water fight. He appreciated the many gifts of cash, clothes and a new pushbike that fitted his ever-growing frame.

Cait and Shauna's parents departed that weekend, returning life at Mûne Roazen to some familiarity. The end of September arrived and with it the second scan.

Harek arranged to take the day off. The boys were dropped at school and they spent an hour in a coffee shop, talking about the prenatal care they wanted and going over the birthing plan that Shauna had laid out.

"You're sure you want it that open, so unplanned?" asked Harek. He'd seen Vayenn's. She had kept hers and it was more intricate than Shauna's.

Shauna nodded. "I delivered the boys on gas and air, only needing minor stitches. Things can change, I'm aware of that. What I want and what is safe for me and the baby when the time comes may not be the same things. I'm not going to be hung up about how it happens, if we both have to be kept safe." Harek had insisted she have a small bowl of fruit with her herbal tea and he watched as she slowly ate a single grape. She wasn't hungry but she loved how he insisted she keep her strength up, in a healthy way too.

Gone Dutch

Their time for the midwife appointment was drawing near and he led them to the midwife centre, as arranged.

Shauna was glad she had all her British birthing notes with her. Harek was nervous but buzzing as he held her hand for the second scan.

The midwife centre had a very different feel to the NHS back in England. Whilst the care in England had been excellent, Shauna decided that the English could learn from the lighter, airy, less stuffy feel the Dutch healthcare system seemed to give off. Nothing was conducted in a dark dingy room; the waiting areas were full of natural light, not just the bright lights of the bulbs above.

The decor too, wasn't NHS blue, this particular centre was in soft pinks, yellows, greens, depending on which part of the centre you were in. The blinds were also built into the windows, not cluttered with vertical blinds that were sometimes broken or just worn out as back in England.

Shauna felt rather warm and safe here. She had to ask Harek for a translation on some of the signs but "Birthing Suite" told her that this wasn't just a midwife centre. It was everything to do with prenatal care and delivery.

Harek stood as their name was called and he guided Shauna to the room they'd been called to. The sonographer smiled and asked Shauna a question. When

Gone Dutch

she looked confused, Harek quickly explained Shauna didn't yet understand Dutch.

The sonographer nodded. "That's OK. I get to practice English!" she said, smiling. The sonographer reminded Shauna of a much younger Agnetha Fältskog. Her name though, was Fenna and she walked them through everything as if they were at their ten-week scan.

By the time the actual scan was underway, Shauna wondered if this was how Harek had felt at the first scan. Slightly lost, excited but guided.

They watched the white screen show the 3D picture of their unborn child and Shauna chuckled as she saw their child had a pee.

"That's all three of you to show what gender you are by peeing," she chuckled with eyes bright and slightly teary. Harek looked confused. Shauna explained that the boys revealed themselves at the scan by doing the same. He still didn't get it, until Fenna explained what Harek had missed. The baby had urinated, but it had pooled, not arced. Shauna was clearly carrying a girl. The midwife carried on with her check as Shauna and Harek watched their unborn daughter in awe.

"Everything looks fabulous," Fenna declared. "Baby is healthy, you're on track and she's moving around well. How are you feeling momma?"

The midwife went through Shauna's mental as well as her physical health, her birth plan and Fenna

Gone Dutch

praised Shauna for the open plan. Given that Shauna had no issues as such with giving birth in England on nothing more than gas and air, the midwife signed off on the planned water birth at home for Shauna.

"You'll be assigned a specific midwife for the home birth," she said, tapping things into a computer to get what Shauna wanted. "I'll have her call to arrange a meeting and a visit, if that's okay?"

Harek nodded, replying in Dutch. Shauna poked him. "I am here ya know!" she said, grinning.

"I know," he said. "I just wanted them to contact me first. I want to be there."

Shauna smiled up at him. "Like I'd not tell you when I have a midwife appointment," she replied, giving him a sideways glance.

He chuckled and kissed her temple. "No, you would tell me, I know," he said. "But I make a good translator, no?" he asked, coyly.

Shauna chuckled. He certainly made a handsome one.

Shauna progressively got larger and struggled to do things more by herself. It was near Halloween, after Andrew's birthday and another set of family visits that it became obvious that being out in the countryside sometimes had its flaws.

Shauna liked to do the food shopping though Harek had told her he could get a maid service in to do

Gone Dutch

it, Shauna had told him she at least needed something to do during her days when he was at work and the boys were at school. Despite the online Dutch language course she had begun, the need to leave Mûne Roazen for other adult contact was necessary.

Putting the shopping away one time, Shauna got stuck on a set of small stairs. A fit of vertigo grabbed her, not letting go. Unable to move, she had the smart speaker call someone. Thinking it had called Harek, she waited. It had text Harek, but it was Johan's niece that helped.

"Hallo?"

Shauna heard a quiet little voice coming from behind her. But, she was unable to turn around whilst stuck on a two-step ladder as the world spun. She closed her eyes and called out hello back.

Shauna sensed someone standing near her but she had her eyes closed tightly to stop herself from falling.

"Wat is er mis?" asked the gentle voice.

"I'm stuck!" said Shauna.

"Laat me helpen!" said the voice. She felt a hand gently tap then guide one of hers to a shoulder, then a leg was tagged and helped down a step. A few minutes later, Shauna was sitting on one of the breakfast stools, the gentle voice jabbering away in rapid Dutch to someone. Suddenly, Johan's voice came out clearly over the girl's phone.

Gone Dutch

"Miss Shauna?" he said.

"Oh, Johan, thank goodness!"

"What happened?" he asked.

"Sudden case of vertigo from climbing a ladder whilst I was putting the shopping away," Shauna sighed. "The room is still spinning. Could you fetch the boys, please? I'm not going to be able to drive there right now.

"Mr Harek is already on his way. The school called him a few minutes ago."

Shauna swore gently under her breath. "Darn it, sorry Johan!"

"Are you all right now?" he asked.

"Yes, thanks to this young lady," she said. The image of the young lady before her slowly stopped swimming and spinning.

"Tanja, my niece," replied Johan.

"Thank you, Tanja!" smiled Shauna.

"She needs to practice her English Miss Shauna. I'll leave you both to talk, Mr Harek and I have the boys, and we'll be back soon!" The line went dead and Tanja smiled.

"Thee?" asked Tanja, holding up the kettle. "Yes please!" replied Shauna, holding her head. At least, she hoped that Tanja was asking if she wanted a cup of tea.

Shauna guided Tanja to where the tea was kept. When Shauna was finally able to see properly, Harek had the boys home. He dropped his case at the door as

Gone Dutch

Johan followed. Harek was at Shauna's side in moments, checking on her and hugging her.

"What happened famke?" his voice was low, husky.

Shauna sighed. "I'm sorry," she whispered as she looked up at him and suddenly everything spun again.

"I've been feeling funny and madam here is using me as a punch bag. I climbed the ladder to put some food cans away and got stuck… the whole room spun out, just like now."

Harek looked at her. "Do we need to get you to a doctor?" he asked, suddenly concerned.

Shauna shook her head. "No, I had this before with Andrew when he did his somersaults. It's common when babies are turning. I just need to sit and chill a bit, close my eyes, rest."

Harek nodded. "Come," he said, holding her as they walked to the library. He made her sit with her legs up on the sofa, covered her in a light blanket and lit the fire. When the fire was going properly, he noticed she'd dozed off. Smiling, he went back to the kitchen to speak with Johan and Tanja.

"Thank you," he said to Tanja, taking the cup of coffee Johan had made for him. "How did you get here so quickly?"

"I was coming to see uncle Johan, but he called me on the way, telling me something was wrong and to

Gone Dutch

let myself in. He gave me the door code and I found Miss Shauna," the young lady looked at Johan for the confirmation of Shauna's name, "unable to move on the ladder. I guided her down and made her a tea, then sat with her until you came home. I've just finished helping my uncle put the shopping away."

Harek nodded. Johan coughed.

"Yes, Johan?"

"My niece," he said, looking at Tanja, "is looking for a job. She needs to practice her English for university next year. Perhaps..." he let the sentence hang, wanting Harek to finish.

Harek knew what he was asking but wanted the question asked directly. "Go on," he said, leaning back against a counter and waiting for Johan to finish.

Johan looked at his niece and then to Harek. "I was thinking, perhaps she'd be able to help Miss Shauna, whilst she's pregnant and when the baby first arrives? Until Tanja is ready to go to University?"

Harek pondered for a moment. He looked at Tanja then beckoned her to follow him. He peeked in at Shauna, who was still asleep, then found the boys.

"Okay, let's see what you can do," he said to Tanja. "Let's see you make dinner and ensure they've done their homework."

Michael looked up. "We're getting a nanny?" he asked as his eyebrows rose.

Gone Dutch

Harek shook his head. "Shauna had a weird turn today, that's why I got called to pick you up. Clearly, your momma needs help around the house. I want to see how this young lady copes with doing what your mother would do at this time of day."

Michael nodded and smiled at Tanja. He tapped Andrew on the shoulder and they headed off to their rooms to do their homework.

Tanja smiled. "So this is an interview?" she asked in a small voice.

Harek nodded. "Pretend Johan and I are not here. Shauna is asleep, just like now. Help care for the boys, do the same chores Shauna would."

She nodded and Harek walked to the library, careful not to wake Shauna as he went to his desk to carry on working.

Johan followed and stayed out of Tanja's way, letting her get on with it. Harek monitored how Tanja did with handling the boys, the food and general house chores before he smiled at Johan. He went to Shauna and gently woke her from her slumber.

She stirred as her face was caressed, her lips lightly touched.

"Famke," he cooed softly. "Shauna," he said, coaxing her to wakefulness.

She smiled at him. "Hey!" she said, smiling and stretched out a little on the sofa.

Gone Dutch

Harek smiled. "Feeling better?" he asked, kissing her gently.

She nodded. "I think so?" she said, unsure.

"I have a proposition for you," he said.

"Oh?" She swung her legs down slowly and made herself sit up. "This sounds dangerous!" she added, finding her humour again.

He chuckled. "Come, hear me out." He stood and held out a hand for her to join him. Carefully, she found her feet and taking his hand, allowed him to lead her to the kitchen.

Tanja was at the kitchen island, serving up sausages, mashed potatoes, some cabbage and carrots with gravy. The boys were behaving more so than usual.

"I am wondering if you need a helping hand?" he said, watching Tanja as she cleared down the cooking area.

"Like a girl Friday?" asked Shauna, leaning into him.

"A what?" he asked, bemused.

"A girl Friday. A girl who does a lot of different jobs, helps out by doing what needs to be done."

Harek thought for a moment. "That sounds about right. Nanny sounds too old for the boys," he chuckled.

Shauna nodded. She stepped forward and smiled at Tanja. "I want to thank you," she hugged the boys tight "for helping me earlier," she finished.

Gone Dutch

"Graag gedaan," she said. Shauna knew that meant "you're welcome," but Shauna shook her head and smiled warmly. "In English, alstublieft."

Tanja stopped and thought, clearly she was struggling. "You welcome," she said a few moments later. Shauna smiled. It was closer than she got on her first attempt at it in Dutch.

"So, about that job?" Harek said to her in Dutch.

Tanja stopped and stared. "Yes?" she said, replying in English.

"How would you like to start tomorrow, at say seven o'clock? Can you be here for that time?" Harek switched to English, partly for Shauna but also to make Tanja think about it.

Tanja asked her uncle something in Dutch, Shauna thought it was about a lift, the word car (auto) was recognisable.

She turned to Harek as her uncle confirmed something, then she nodded. "Yes, I can."

"Do you drive?" asked Harek. "Can you drive?"

Tanja nodded and answered in broken English. "I have licence, but no car yet."

"I'll sort you a car you can use for transporting the boys. Let's talk about details," he said, motioning for Tanja and Johan to follow. He planted a kiss on Shauna's lips before heading to talk contracts and terms with Tanja.

Gone Dutch

An hour later, the deal was done. Harek made copies of the contract in both languages and had Shauna check over the English side before he asked Tanja to sign it.

"Thank you Mr Harek!" she said, dancing.

Shauna smiled. "I'll see you tomorrow morning," she said, pleased.

"Thank you, Miss Shauna!" Johan smiled and thanked Harek as he walked his niece to his car and took her home.

"So, I now have a girl Friday!" she said as they came back inside.

Harek nodded. "You need some help. I do not like you doing too much and hurting yourself in the process," he said, kissing her gently.

"I didn't mean to," she said, sighing, "but on shopping days, it will help to have extra hands to do things."

Harek smiled. "Good. Now, let's eat," his stomach growled in agreement. "Tanja made enough for us too. It's keeping warm in the oven."

Shauna sat down at Harek's insistence whilst he pulled dinner from the oven and poured Shauna a soft drink. They ate, talked and did what they usually did with half-grown children in the house. They played a game, then sent the boys to bed.

Gone Dutch

"I have an idea," said Harek, smirking in the candlelight as they prepared for bed.

"Oh? Two in one day? You're getting brave," teased Shauna.

Harek humphed at Shauna but smiled broadly. He enjoyed it when they teased each other but he particularly enjoyed the cuddles in bed, the lovemaking, the talking.

"Do you want to know what I thought of?" he asked as he held her. It was harder now for her to lay across him, but she snuggled into the crook of his arm with her back to him, giving him access to all her sensitive places. He enjoyed just placing a hand on the bump and feeling the baby kick or move. Shauna had told him she liked his hand being there too.

"I'm listening," she said, stroking that arm that held her to him.

"A date night," he stated in a slightly raised tone.

She stopped stroking his arm, thinking. "We haven't been out on a date by ourselves since we moved in," she said.

He nodded. "We've not had the chance, though I could have asked Vayenn to do that, it never occurred to me to do so, until now."

"Where would we go? What did you have in mind?" He smiled. She was getting excited by the idea.

"What would you like to do? What haven't you done since you arrived here?"

Gone Dutch

Shauna paused for a moment. "I'm not sure… We eat at home since you're a great cook. There's the cinema, I've not been to a Dutch cinema yet." She turned to look at him, propping herself up on an elbow.

"I have an idea that might combine a few of those, if you'll trust me?" he asked, raising to kiss her.

"Totally," she said, kissing him back.

"Then, Friday night is our date night. I'll ask Tanja to stay over so we don't have to worry about being back too early."

She smiled. "I'll make sure I have a nap before we go! I'd hate to fall asleep on a date!" she chuckled, kissing him. He lay back, encouraging her to straddle him and slowly, loved her until they were both spent.

Tanja was there the following morning, just before seven o'clock. Johan had a key and let himself and Tanja in. As Shauna, Harek and the boys descended, breakfast was being served.

"Good morning!" said Tanja, cheerfully.

"Goeie moarn!" replied Shauna and the boys, getting in their Dutch practice before coffee and food.

Harek had agreed with Shauna that she'd drive the boys to school, letting the school know that Tanja was permitted to collect the boys at any point. Johan would take Harek to work, as usual. With the plans set, they set off and soon, Johan went a different direction to Shauna.

Gone Dutch

Clearing Tanja's access to the boys with the school, left Tanja and Shauna to their own devices until the collection run.

"There's some paint I want to collect today for the nursery, before the baby's furniture arrives next week."

"Okay. Is baby boy or girl?" asked Tanja in broken English, but looking at Shauna's pregnant belly. Shauna smiled as Tanja's broken English was better than her broken Dutch.

"Girl," said Shauna, arriving at the paint store in the Blaak district.

They looked through the aisles but Shauna couldn't find what she was looking for.

"What is it you want?" asked Tanja, holding up two very different shades of pink, but both much bolder than Shauna wanted.

"Pale pink, soft pink. Like a rose," Shauna pulled out her phone and showed Tanja the pales pink roses from her English front garden.

"Ah! Wait," she said holding her hands up in a stop motion. She put the tins back on the shelves, then she vanished. A few moments later, she returned with a large tin of soft pale pink and the shopkeeper.

"Marc mix it for us," she said, handing the tin to Shauna.

Shauna grinned. It was the perfect shade "Oh, that's perfect! Dankewol!"

Gone Dutch

Shauna paid for the tin and spied a coffee shop across the way. Checking her watch, they had plenty of time still on the car parking meter, so Shauna suggested that they have some cake. Tanja smiled. "Love cake!"

So, they went to eat cake. It was lunchtime when they returned and Shauna told Tanja she was taking a nap. Setting her phone alarm for two pm, she went to lay down, leaving Tanya to prepare dinner.

At two pm, Shauna stirred with the alarm. Getting ready to fetch the boys, she found Tanja watching TV.

In the kitchen, dinner was organised as much as it could be, given it was still semi-frozen but wouldn't be by the time they were back from the school run. Vegetables were prepared and in pots, just waiting for the heat to be turned on. The kitchen was tidy, cleared down and Shauna could hear the washing machine spin a load.

"I make food," said Tanja, joining her. She unwrapped a plate with a toastie on it that though had gone cold, was still delicious.

With a cup of tea in a travel mug, they set out to fetch the boys back home.
Tanja was busy putting the dinner together whilst the boys did their homework and was serving it when Harek returned.

"We eat early in Netherlands," Tanja explained.

Gone Dutch

Shauna smiled. "In THE Netherlands," she gently corrected. Tanja had asked Shauna for help in her English whilst they ate cake earlier. Tanja thought, then nodded and repeated the sentence again with the correct definite article.

Harek said something to Tanja in Dutch and Shauna listened in. Harek noticed her attention.

"What did I just say, famke?" he said, smiling at her as he hugged her from behind.

"Something about a car, arriving on Friday?"

Harek grinned. "You're getting better," he praised. "There's an S1 arriving on Friday for Tanja to drive." He looked directly at Tanja. "I've spoken with the insurance, that is the only car you will be allowed to drive." He repeated it in Dutch so she understood.

Tanja nodded. "Dankewol," she said as she beamed from ear to ear.

Harek then began asking Tanja something else in Dutch, but Shauna recognising the word "Vrijdag", she knew this was about Friday evening's plans.

"I can stay, yes. Do boys know?"

"The boys know, yes," said Shauna. Tanja smiled, understanding that it was the word 'the' she kept on missing. She repeated the sentence again a few times, more to herself to get it right.

Shauna hugged her. "Your English is better than my Dutch," she said, smiling.

Gone Dutch

"We can work on your Dutch too," grinned Tanya. "But yes, Mr Harek, I can stay on Friday night. Where would I sleep?"

"Let me show you," said Shauna. She showed Tanya the top room in the Mill and Tanja nodded. "Beautiful room," she breathed. The soft yellows, distressed white furniture and floral curtains on the windows gave it something of an English charm that appealed to Tanja.

"Mooie kamer," said Shauna, in Dutch. Tanja nodded.

"Very good," she praised as Shauna got the "pretty room" phrase correct. "Heel goed!" she repeated.

Shauna smiled and she decided languages weren't so tough once you got into them.

Forty-One

Friday morning arrived and Tanja brought an overnight bag. It took her moments to place her bag under the bed and return to the kitchen to begin preparing the boys' lunches as well as the breakfasts, as per usual.

Shauna drove the boys to school whilst Tanja waited for the car to be delivered. It arrived near noon on the back of a small transport lorry. It was bright yellow and it took all of twenty minutes to unload it and have Shauna sign for it.

Tanja was quiet the rest of the afternoon though.

"What's wrong?" asked Shauna as they shared a cup of tea in the library.

"It's just so much," she whispered. "I have never had a car before."

Shauna smiled. She so knew what Tanja was feeling.

"You need a car as I might not always be able to drive. I'm getting bigger every day but I'm getting more tired too."

Tanja nodded. "But, it is so much," her voice took on a worried tone.

Gone Dutch

Shauna touched Tanja's arm gently. "It's a part of the job, so it is necessary, please don't worry about it."

Tanja shrugged and grinned. "No worry anymore," she said. "I'll start dinner for the boys. You, go rest Miss Shauna."

Shaun nodded. "Tanja, I want to go with you to collect the boys today, but you can drive."

Tanja nodded. "Sure Miss Shauna!" she said, smiling.

True to her word, Tanja woke Shauna up to do the school run. The boys were excited when they saw the S1 and loved the vibrant colour. Now the boys and the school teachers who supervised the pickups knew what car to look for, Shauna was happier to let Tanja pick them up.

Shauna napped for a bit longer when they returned home and was in the shower when Harek returned. He smiled and quietly joined her, making her jump.

"Harek!" she scolded, laughing at the same time!

He groaned quietly as she returned his kiss in the pouring warm water. He debated about being late for the booking he'd made or making love to his fiancé later; he decided he would do the latter.

"Come, otherwise we will be late."

Gone Dutch

She smiled. "Tease," she said, rubbing her slowly expanding stomach.

He kissed her mouth gently. "Later, myn leafed. Later."

"So, where are we going?" she asked. He'd chosen the Model X and it hummed along so quietly Shauna forgot about its quietness at some points.

He pulled into a car park and escorted her to a restaurant with subtle lighting, private booth tables and food served on plates that reminded Shauna of the Erasmusbrug.

They talked, held hands, touched, giggled and smiled at each other.

"I should have bought you here the first time," he said. "But, I was greedy," he winked.

"You weren't the only one that was greedy," she said, glancing at him coyly.

He looked out of the window and smiled. He pointed outside to Shauna and she saw the De Boeg lit up.

"What is that?" she asked, looking at a huge structure that had just been lit up.

"The De Boeg, or The Bow." He smiled at her as he watched her just enjoy the laser light show emanating from and upon De Boeg. "We lost a lot of ships in World War Two. That structure commemorates their

Gone Dutch

loss. There are human statues at the bottom, but you can't see them from here."

"It's impressive. There were a lot of boats lost from both our countries during that time. I'm not sure that we commemorate them in the same way." She turned to watch again as the laser took on a search beam-type show. "What's the date?" she asked.

"November eleventh," he replied.

"Remembrance Day," she said softly.

"Of course," he replied, bowing his head. Now the light show made sense.

They took their time to walk back to the car after such a delightful meal.

"That was my first Michelin Star meal ever, and you made it happen in Rotterdam," she said, hugging into him as they walked back to their car.

"It's not over yet, famke," he smiled as he guided her to a nearby cinema.

"Pick one," he said, motioning to the movie listings. She chose an action style one, something with The Rock and Jason Statham in it, and they snuggled into the very large seats Harek had paid for.

"This is my personal sofa!" she said, putting her sweets and drink in the various holders. He chuckled. "They're big enough to snuggle into for two people!" he suggested coyly. She wiggled over and motioned for him

Gone Dutch

to join her. A few minutes later, they were snuggled together, watching the movie.

However, Shauna didn't quite make it to the end. Wrapped in Harek's strong, warm arms, she missed the last third of the movie. He, however, smiled; holding the woman he loved, who was bearing him the greatest gift of all, in the dark whilst she slept, was magical.

"I'm so sorry! I didn't mean to!" she chuckled as the lights came on and Harek woke her.
He kissed her temple. "You didn't miss that much," he teased. He lifted Shauna's drink and sweets, taking them with them as they returned to the car. She sipped the fizzy drink on the way home, wrapping the sweets to share with the boys tomorrow. They talked about the parts of the movie Shauna did see.

It was gone midnight when the gates slid open, allowing Harek access. He'd had the gates installed after Sanne's 'visit' and only a select few had the five fobs that granted access. Two were in a safe, meaning three were active. Shauna's, his own and Johan's.

Jon, his parents and Vayenn had the gate code and he was pleased that the iron gates swept through the property, hidden in the tree line.

"When did you get the lights fitted?" she asked. She knew about the gates, but not the scenery, security lighting or the lights that lit up the Mûne Roazen and the grounds.

Gone Dutch

"At the same time as the gate was installed," he said, smiling. "Do you like it?" he asked. He'd never thought to ask her what she thought of the security he'd added to Mûne Roazen, but it was a suggestion from the Politie, given what had happened. He did more than the official report had recommended and took the direct advice of the very officer that had 'handcuffed' Shauna. When he had asked her if she was okay with it being installed, she had said that he needed to do what he thought would keep them safe. So, he did.

"I think it makes it more beautiful, especially at night," she breathed in the scene before her. Somehow, it made Mûne Roazen give off a romantic feel. "I didn't realise security would be this pretty." She spun around slowly, observing it all. "Did you add the cameras they suggested too?"

"Yes," he replied. The fact he'd followed the suggested hard line was neither here nor there. It was in. He would do his upmost to ensure that Shauna and the kids, all the kids, were never hurt again.

Shauna nodded. "Good," was all she said as she observed where the security camera were sited, though she was sure she didn't spot them all. The infra-red on the devices was clear but you had to look under walkways, eaves, sail arms and goodness knows what else to see them.

Gone Dutch

Harek helped her out of the car and into the Mûne. All was quiet. Every door was locked physically and otherwise.

Tanja had left on the under-counter lights in the kitchen and Harek whispered a command to the smart speaker in Dutch. A few moments later, the lights dimmed even more and music from Swan Lake played out lowly. Shauna smiled.

Harek reached out a hand and pulled Shauna to him, dancing as they had months before in Birmingham.

"Shauna," he said after they had been dancing for a little time. "I love you." He looked down at her as she gazed up at him. She was tall for a woman, still shorter than him and she was certainly hidden by his muscular frame.

"And I love you," she replied, reaching up to kiss him.

The kiss was passionate, deep, and persuasive. It wasn't desperate but it did contain a hunger. Shauna stopped the smart speaker and slowly guided Harek to their bedroom. Lighting the candles, they continued where they left off in the kitchen, slowly undressing each other, kissing all the time.

"Shauna," Harek breathed, holding her face in his hands. She silenced him with a kiss. "It's okay, I promise!" she breathed back, knowing what he was asking.

Gone Dutch

     He guided them to the bed and lay down, ensuring Shauna was on top. Slowly with as much care as he could, he made love with her until they were both spent. Laying against her, spooning her with a hand over her bump, he joined her in her in sleep as their baby kicked.

Gone Dutch

Forty-Two

Christmas beckoned and Shauna swore that Harek was a bigger child than her own two boys were combined. However, when the main Christmas tree was up and decorated by them all, with the second one in the library, it really did begin to feel a lot like Christmas.

Shauna and Tanja decorated the Mûne in a combination of Dutch and English traditions. The main tree, as it was family, was as Shauna and the boys would have had it in England. The library one was more traditional Dutch with blue and white ornaments, bows, ribbons and baubles. Everything that could have something hanging from it, or draped in tinsel, was decorated. Harek stopped counting the number of small lights and timers that appeared in the Mûne.

"You both did well," praised Harek. "I've never seen the Mûne like this." He looked at her. "You're not overly tired from it all?" he placed a hand on her bump, feeling their baby kick or elbow his hand. He was never sure. The baby's response softened his composure.

Shauna leaned into him as he hugged her. "It's our first one here. Bryce has a few days off and wanted to come to visit, bringing presents & taking ours back for everyone. I hope that's okay?"

Gone Dutch

Harek chuckled. "Of course," he nodded. "It will be good to see my brother-in-law!"

The weather turned colder as December drew on. Bryce made it before a sleeting storm shut down ports, making him stranded in Rotterdam with Shauna, the boys, Tanja and Harek.

"Looks like I made it in time," he said later that night as the sleet turned to heavy snow and the wind howled around the Mûne.

"Looks like you did," agreed Shauna, pulling her heavy cardigan closer to her. "The storm is due to break overnight, in the wee small hours, so you should be okay to get back on Friday as arranged." She handed her brother a hot drink. "The boys are happy the school has closed but not so happy they have to do on-line learning instead," Shauna chuckled.

Bryce nodded and smirked. "Well, if the power holds out, they'll complain. If it doesn't…" he winked and looked at the boys with a knowing smirk

Tanja joined them, offering homemade cookies. "Try?" she said, offering one to Bryce. He smiled and watched her as she offered the plate to the boys and Harek. Shauna caught him and nudged him.

"Oi wee brother," she said, smirking. "She's a good decade younger than you," Bryce looked abashed. "Seriously, take it slow?" She waited for a reaction. "Or not at all?" She carried on, knowing by his sly glance at

Gone Dutch

her he was listening. "I dinnae want her uncle, who has raised her, wanting to go after you or quitting here because of anything, all right? She's got University plans." Shauna raised her eyebrows at her brother, then tilted her head towards him as their mother had often done when they were in trouble.

Bryce snapped his head around to look at his sister. "Hmm?" he asked, not quite following. Shauna smacked his upper arm. "Ye ken what I said!" she growled.

He smirked and nodded. "Aye, sis, I heard ye." Shauna looked across the kitchen to see Tanja casting eyes at Bryce. Shauna sent up a prayer for strength. *'This is going to be a few long days!'*

The following morning, Tanja was up bright and early, making breakfast. So was Bryce, enjoying the coffee and talking with Tanja. Shauna noticed the twinkle in her brother's eye, smirked and bid them both good morning before taking a coffee upstairs for Harek to enjoy when he was out of the shower.

Shauna got back into bed whilst Harek finished his shower. He came to join her when he was done, leaving the coffee where it was.

"I think my brother likes Tanja," she said, smiling up at him.

Gone Dutch

Harek pulled back from kissing Shauna and looked at her. "You noticed too?" he replied with dancing amber eyes.

"Oh yes," she looked across at him. "Will Johan be upset if anything happens between them?" she wondered.

"I am not sure. I know she wants to go to University but an English one, which is why he wanted her to work with you. Beyond that…" Harek lay down beside her, caressing her arm and stroking her bump.

Shauna nodded. "I'll try to get Bryce to be respectful. Are there any dating traditions I need to know about so I can advise my darling brother?"

Harek thought. "Other than asking the parents for permission to marry her, not really. I guess you Brits have a similar code?"

Shauna smiled. "Some of us do, though it depends on who you ask and why," she said, snuggling into him to be held and caressed.

"I'll speak with him later, if you'd like? She's an adult in Dutch law; she can be with whomever she wants."

"I know. Same as in England but I'd still rather not have Johan upset because his niece got it together with my brother," she observed.

Harek moved to kiss her on the head. "I'll speak with Bryce later," he said, peppering Shauna's bump with little kisses, making their baby kick.

Gone Dutch

Harek gave Bryce the tour whilst Tanja and Shauna worked on lunch. The boys were doing schoolwork in the library, joining in their lessons via video conference. Both were displeased that they still had to "go" to school rather than play on their Xbox all the time.

Shauna eased herself onto a stool as Tanja prepared potatoes for the stamppot later.

"You like my brother then?" she asked. Tanja blushed and tried to hide her smiling face

"Hey, I don't mind," Shauna said, reaching for Tanja's hand. "I just don't want your uncle to be mad at you or us for anything you two get up to. And I'd like you to be safe." Tanja looked up.

"Safe?" she asked, confused. Shauna leaned across the island they were working at.

"No babies," Shauna said, quietly, rubbing her bump. Tanja smiled and blushed again.

"I have birth control," said Tanja, quietly.

"Tablets? The Pill?" asked Shauna, keeping her voice low so only Tanja could hear. Tanja nodded. "Bryce, already ask."

Shauna smiled as they heard the boys come back and she sat back in her chair to drink some tea whilst Tanja finished peeling the potatoes. The cabbage was already cut up finely, waiting to be part boiled and added to the mash to make the stamppot later.

Gone Dutch

Bryce didn't look annoyed when they returned, which pleased Shauna.

"Hey sis!" he said, hugging her. "I'm just going to get changed. I've got to try out that gym," he exclaimed at Tanja as he headed up to his room. Harek was already in gym type stuff, aiming to do that whilst the boys did their school video calls.

Five minutes later, Bryce was back downstairs and the men headed off to the gym.
Tanja blushed as she caught Shauna watching her as Bryce went past. Shauna chuckled and she winked at Tanja. She leaned over. "Just, be careful, okay? He hurts you, let me know." Tanja smiled and nodded.

Much later, Bryce got to speak with Shauna quietly. Tanja was calling home as she was stuck at Mûne Roazen. The boys were on the Xbox, beating Harek at one of their many games. Shauna had pulled the library door over, giving them a few moments of privacy.

"I dinnae want details brother, but please, don't hurt her? She's still a baba by our standards and her mother knows she's here."

Bryce nodded. "Aye, I know. She's a good few years younger but hell, sis, she knows what and who she wants," his smirk and sparkling eyes told Shauna all she wanted to know.

Gone Dutch

Shauna smiled. "Is there anything you need that we may have here?" she asked. She was meaning protection.

"Already taken care of," he said, nodding towards Harek and the boys.

She nodded and grinned. "Okay."

There was a moment of silence before Bryce spoke up. "Tell me something. Who is Abbe De Vries?"

"Grandson to one of Harek's most important business contacts. Why? Is he getting cosy with Cait?" Shauna shifted positions and winced a little as she found a new position. "He sent her flowers here the day he met her."

Bryce nodded and smiled. "He turned up at the house a few weeks ago, asking for her. But, at my house, not hers. She asked me to keep it quiet as she'd not told mam and pa he was over or seeing her. She told them the morning after though, as he walked into the kitchen. Then he asked dad's permission to date Cait," he grinned.

"Did he?" Shauna gasped. "Wow!" Bryce continued with details of the dating weekend and that Cait was rather subdued by the end.

"I just wonder how it worked out, but all she said was that it was great. It's hard to tell with Cait though," he shook his head.

Gone Dutch

Shauna nodded. "You want me to ask her about it?" she said, sipping a tea as the fire crackled in the hearth.

Bryce shrugged. "She's a grown woman, like Tanja, she can make her own mind up but I just want to know she's okay, that's all. She is family, though the biggest pain in the arse at times."

Shauna found her phone and fired off a quick message to Cait. The phone pinged a few seconds later.

C: Yeah, I'm fine. Why?

S: Heard Abbe was over that's all. Wondered how it went?

C: Expected this text last night! It went brilliantly! I was a bit tired and sad when he had to leave. And sore, in a good way!

Shauna showed Bryce the message and laughed. "Aye, right, okay!" he laughed, glad his sister was okay and her unusual quietness was down to something good.

S: Did you do to him what you did with Harek?

C: Yes, after the flowers. But he's nice too! A gentleMAN, if you get my drift ;)

S: You mean, he has manners and is respectful of a woman?

C: Yep. You know he asked pa permission to date me, the morning after…

S: Tad late by then, but at least there are no hidden agendas going on.

Gone Dutch

C: I thought it was so sweet. I've never had pa be asked that before, not about me. And I'm thirty!

S: Harek didn't ask pa, but it kinda hard to do when you're in hospital the day after :)

C: Yep! But, gotta run. That storm has hit us so need to get stuff done before it really kicks in. TTFN!

Shauna chuckled as Cait signed off. She showed the whole conversation to Bryce, who nodded. "I never thought to ask Tanja's uncle… Should I?"

Shauna shrugged. "I'm not sure, but it seems generational respect is a huge thing here, more so than we follow. Can't hurt to ask and be upfront about it."

Bryce nodded. "Not something I want to call him to ask about though! It's a wee bit awkward."

Shauna chuckled. "You'll get the inquisition, probably. Johan knows you have a daughter, he's met her. But when you get the chance, it's worth clearing the way first. Or well, before things get any further along," she grinned and winked at her brother.

The weather cleared a few days later, allowing the boys to go back to school and Bryce to return to England, though he wasn't in the mood to. It did give him a chance to speak quietly with Johan before Tanja did. Tanja pulled up in her car from doing the school run to see Johan and Bryce talking by the garage. Both men looked calm and collected, which made Tanja happy.

Gone Dutch

However, when she tried to join in, Johan told her firmly to go and help Shauna.

Tanja walked into Mûne Roazen, unhappily, to find Shauna at the kitchen island, deciding what to make for dinner.

"Johan is talking with Bryce but he won't let me join in."

Shauna nodded. "Figured that's what Bryce was doing. I'm sure it's nothing serious."

"It's about me," she said. Folding her arms across her chest crossly.

"Probably," comforted Shauna. "Which means, Bryce is getting a gentle but firm, third degree."

"Third-degree?" asked Tanja, running the hot water to wash up what the dishwasher couldn't take.

"Being asked lots of questions. Like a mini-interview."

Tanja turned the tap off and began heading back out to where her uncle and Bryce were, to run straight into Bryce.

"Hey," he said, smiling at her. "What's the hurry?"

"You're... finished talking?" asked Tanja, looking for her Uncle.

Bryce nodded. "We are," he said, pulling her in for a smouldering kiss. Shauna grinned. Concluding that at least the conversation had gone on well,

Gone Dutch

Bryce had to leave later that day, much to Tanja's dismay. Bryce let Tanja know he was home with a phone call about two whole minutes before Shauna got a simple text. The roads were now clear enough for Tanja to head back home, though they had agreed that as Shauna's due date got closer, Tanja would be at Mûne Roazen almost all the time.

Christmas arrived and because of Shauna's advanced pregnancy, Harek cooked the Christmas day dinner. Tanja had helped prepare it all into pots and pans the day before, leaving instructions in writing for Harek to follow about when to start cooking each dish. Harek had been home a few days, so everything was done as far as wrapping, gifts and preparations went. Between him and Tanja, Shauna hadn't had much to do.

Harek held her by the Christmas tree in the library, swaying to some soft Christmas music later that evening. The boys were playing one of their new games in a head to head on the Xbox. The kitchen was cleared down. How Harek made the boys help to clean up, Shauna never knew. She'd napped after the dinner, full of food and heavy with pregnancy. When she awoke, the mess was cleared and her little family were chilling out. She had intended to at least tidy up, but they were good intentions that never happened. They'd called their respective families that morning, to thank them for gifts

Gone Dutch

and catch up. Shauna learned that Cait was with Abbe for the holidays, not at home with her parents.

"You look beautiful," he whispered huskily into her ear. She'd chosen a red cowled tartan dress that came to her thighs over black maternity leggings. Her bump was evident now, no matter what she wore.

"I look pregnant," she chuckled as she swayed around the library slowly with him.

"You are both, famke!" he said, gently kissing her.

"You know, it's weird," she said as they swayed slowly back to be in front of the roaring fire. "Almost my whole family has come to the Dutch side somehow." The realisation made her chuckle. "Me with you, Cait with Abbe, Bryce with Tanja… poor Izzy is the one that's been left out, currently."

Harek chuckled. "I think we Dutch have a thing for you fiery, honest Scots," he said. "We like our women with fire, passion. Good people with good hearts." He looked down at her. "There is one other present I've not been able to give you, yet."

Shauna placed her hand on his chest. "You don't have to give me anything more! I've been spoiled enough as it is," she chuckled, looking up at him.

He shook his head. "Not in my eyes, famke." He nuzzled her neck gently. "It will be here in a few days, for what is it you call it? Hogmanay?"

Gone Dutch

Shauna nodded. "Aye, New Years. Is this going to be a surprise?" she asked, placing her head on his chest and closing her eyes.

"Yes, mym leafde, it is." He felt her nod against him and he smiled. He loved surprising her!

The surprise was indeed, unexpected. One mid winter's morning, after St Stephen's day, Harek's Model X pulled into the driveway, Johan at the wheel. Shauna thought that he'd brought Tanja to work but was amazed when Izzy alighted from the car.

"Surprise sis!" called her youngest sister.

"Izzy!" They hugged tightly for a few moments, happy to see each other after the longest of times. "I knew Harek said my "gift" would be here today, didn't ken it would be you," she exclaimed and began crying happy tears.

"Aye, well… I booked some time off. Wanted to see my big sis and my nephews." Izzy hugged Shauna tightly. "I cannae believe how well you're looking, or how tiny you are this time," Izzy reached out a hand to touch Shauna's bump, then withdrew it. Shauna grabbed her sisters hand and placed it on a particular known kick spot. Izzy's eyes widened and tears shone as her unborn niece pushed back.

Shauna looked down at her bump. "Aye, I can still see my toes" she wiggled her feet and looked at them without bending over to do so. "I couldn't with the

Gone Dutch

boys. Maybe it's due to having a girl or being pregnant in the winter. Who knows?" Shauna held her hands out for effect.

Johan had quietly taken Izzy's bags to her room and he touched Shauna on the arm. "Tanja has gone to see Bryce," he said, smiling.

Shauna nodded, grinning back at Harek's butler and confidant. "What's this, huh?" asked Izzy, clearly not in the loop.

"Come on! A cup of tea and I'll get ya caught up with the gossip," promised Shauna as they walked into Mûne Roazen arm in arm, giggling. The boys were pleased to see their aunt whilst Izzy awed about Mûne Roazen.

"Seriously sis, this place is amazing," Izzy gawped and spun around lots as she was shown around. "How do you look after it all and be pregnant?"

Shauna chuckled. "Tanja helps; she's my girl Friday," she explained, helping herself to a Christmas cookie that Tanja had made "But she's developed a thing for our Bryce."

"A thing?" asked Izzy.

Shauna nodded. "He asked her uncle, because her father is dead, permission to date her."

"Really? Wow!" Shauna nodded. "Serious stuff!" Izzy nibbled a cookie. "Did you hear that Abbe asked Pa to date Cait?"

Gone Dutch

Shauna nodded. "Aye, Bryce told me when he was here. He copied Abbe's example." Shauna leaned in "But, afterwards, if ye ken what I mean."

Izzy chuckled. "Aye, Abbe did the same with Cait, so mam said. Are you up for Hogmanay?" she asked.

"Harek's no said anything. Up for what?"

"A party, a small one. We've all been invited, including the boys," said Harek, coming into the library to find his fiancé and sister-in-law.

"Have we?" Harek noticed that Shauna's accent was stronger Scottish now, he guessed it was because she was talking with Izzy. He loved that she made subtle changes to blend in with life here, but he didn't want her to not be herself.

"We have. Berend is throwing a small New Year's Eve party, which might be more than we're being told. He's being more insistent that we attend this year than he ever has with me before." Shauna and Izzy looked at each other.

"Cait!" they exclaimed in unison. What was their other sister up to?

New Year's Eve arrived, bringing with it the party Berend insisted that they join in with. The sisters knew Cait was going to be there, but they'd no idea what else was planned.

Gone Dutch

The boys weren't sure about the party, but when they were told they were staying up to see in the New Year, they were excited but pushed back with the jeans and shirt dress code Shauna insisted they wear.

"You're coming and you're going to be smart casual about it," was her final word on the subject. Even though the boys appealed to Harek about the shirts, he just chuckled and told them what Shauna had already told them. Backed into a corner, they gave in and dressed up slightly.

Izzy and Shauna opted for blue dresses, though Shauna's was a wrap-around with stripes, Izzy's was far more elegant and off the shoulder. Shauna had called it corporate eveningwear.

They were greeted and escorted to the event by ushers. They found Cait talking with Abbe and Berend, who made a bee-line for the girls as soon as he saw them.

"Shauna!" said the older man, cooing over her. He patted her bump and kissed her on the cheek, smiling broadly.

"How are you? I see that you're about to make Harek a very proud papa," he said, smiling from ear to ear.

"I'm well, thank you! Berend, this is my other sister, Isobel."

Introductions were made, the boys introduced. Finally, Cait could get in to talk with both her sisters.

Gone Dutch

"Abbe said he had a surprise for me, but didn't tell me you'd both be here," she sighed happily. The girls hugged and chuckled. They chatted for a while before Abbe came to join them, wrapping an arm around her waist and smiling broadly.

"Excuse me ladies, but I would like to borrow my girlfriend for a moment or two," he said, whisking Cait away.

Izzy and Shauna watched intently as Abbe guided them to a private glass balcony. After a quick conversation, they watched as he dropped to one knee, producing a box from his jacket pocket.

They could see Cait begin to cry and nod, right before the ring was placed on her finger and they kissed. The whole room was watching by now and everyone cheered when the engagement ring was placed on her finger. Shauna and Izzy clapped, smiled and waited for Cait to come back to them. It took a while, but she did. Harek and the boys were told what was happening when they all met up.

"I think I need a drink," declared Cait, finally finding a stool near her sisters and sitting down.

"Let's have a look at it then," Shauna said holding her hand out for Cait to show off her ring. Shauna and Izzy admired the ring, a three-carat radiant cut diamond on an engraved Platinum band. The engraving was in a Celtic knot style, a nod to Cait's heritage.

Gone Dutch

"That's a serious ring sis," Shauna said in awe. "And I can tell you're in love."

Cait nodded. "Yes. Goodness, how could you bear to be apart from Harek, or even Matt?" She held Shauna's hand for a moment and squeezed it as she continued. "I realise now what you had, I just couldn't do it."

The girls talked and compared stories for a short while, before Cait was dragged off to be presented to someone else by Abbe. Izzy and Shauna had found a sofa whilst the boys had found the games room Berend had set up just for all the kids he had planned would attend. It was like a large family gathering; music played, people danced, did their own thing. Jon and Amelie were also in attendance, though they hadn't spoken much with Shauna or Harek yet.

"Shauna, we're being watched," muttered Izzy as she leaned into her sister

"Are we?" Shauna tried to look around. "By whom?" she asked.

"Creepy guy at your left, near the bar." Shauna turned and recognised who it was. She waved and motioned for him to come over.

"Oh, I know him," replied Shauna calmly. "He's the officer that "handcuffed" me when Sanne visited and was taken into custody. He's a good guy, a cop."

Izzy relaxed a little and Shauna smiled at the man as he approached. Shauna remembered he was tall but he

Gone Dutch

seemed broader dressed in black then he did right this moment. She went to stand but he motioned for her to continue to sit.

"Mrs Van Meerloo," he said. Shauna didn't want to correct him as she liked the sound of Harek's name after her own.

"I'm sorry," she apologised gently. "I really should remember your name but I am pretty sure I never got told it the day you managed to handcuff me," she said, grinning.

"Am I ever going to be able to live that down?" he chuckled.

Shauna made a point of thinking about it for a moment. "Nope, I don't think so," she said with a wink.

"Thomas Van der Velden," he said, extending his hand.

Shauna shook it and introduced Izzy. Thomas sat on the other side of Izzy and whilst trying to engage them both in conversation, Shauna could tell his focus was more on Izzy.

"I'm going to find Harek," Shauna whispered to her sister. Izzy nodded and Shauna carefully stood, heading off to find Harek who was now talking with Abbe and Cait whilst watching the boys play with some of the other kids in the games room.

She sighed as she joined him at his side. Despite the fact they were here to see in the New Year, she was starting to feel tired. She saw that they only had about

Gone Dutch

forty minutes to go, so she decided to just try and take it easy.

Cait pulled her away a few moments later. "I've had an idea. Shall we do what we traditionally did as kids, growing up?" Cait looked excited, wanting someone to join her. Shauna knew what she meant.

Shauna nodded. "You go find Izzy, she's with the copper that arrested that bloody awful woman. I can ask Michael if he'll do Bryce's bit."

Cait grinned, hugged her sister quickly and went to find Izzy. Shauna waddled off to find Michael in the games room.

She motioned for him to join her for a moment and she asked him if he wanted to join in.

"Singing Uncle Bryce's part?" he was nearly impersonating Tigger.

Shauna nodded. "If you want to, if not, that's okay. Your aunts and I can do it."

"No, I'd love to! Thanks mum!" he told his new friends he had to go for a few minutes and followed Shauna to meet with his aunts.

"Berend hired a piper," groaned Cait.

"Oh, okay." She looked around. "We're so going to need a microphone then," Shauna quickly organised things in her head. "Can you get us one Cait?" asked Shauna. Cait nodded. "I'll go ask. Who is going to lead?" she asked, looking at Shauna.

Gone Dutch

"Well, I can't," she grinned and rubbed her stomach. "I dinnae have the lung capacity. You do it. It'll be ninty-two all over again!"

Cait grinned, knowing full well what Shauna was saying.

"Ninty-two?" Michael looked between his mother and his aunts. "What?" he asked.

"I had a throat infection so couldn't sing. Cait, Izzy and Bryce sang the New Year in. I was told not to sing for six weeks or talk for three."

Michael chuckled. "You had to be quiet mum?" he asked, laughing. Shauna gave him a look that told him his comment had hit its mark.

Cait brought back a microphone after clearing it with the DJ. They spoke with the piper, who was glad to have them sing Auld Lang Syne as he was being paid for the time, not by the note.

As the last bell struck, Cait began singing. Abbe and Harek were close by, not quite sure what Cait and the girls were up to; until they sang. Cait sounded like Catherine Jenkins, taking the highest pitch, allowing Shauna, Izzy and Michael to sing the lower tones in harmony before the piper joined in on the second verse. They sang to the third verse, bringing the whole party to a standstill as Scotswomen and piper sang in the New Year. The Piper played one more verse, solo, before the

Gone Dutch

whole party clapped and cheered. Berend had tears in his eyes as he approached the sisters, hugging Cait first.

"That was amazing! Thank you, thank you!"

"You're welcome Opa," and Cait kissed Berend on the cheek affectionately.

Shauna smiled as Thomas whisked Izzy away, whilst Abbe took Cait off somewhere.

"Are you okay, famke?" asked Harek as her sisters were whisked away.

"Now, I'm tired. I'd like my bed," she said, allowing a yawn to escape. Harek nodded, gathered the boys and checked what Izzy was doing. Thomas promised he'd keep her safe and bring her back to Mûne Roazen the following afternoon and they returned home. It was nearly three am when Shauna got into bed. Harek corralled the boys to bed before he joined Shauna. He was sure she was asleep before her head had hit the pillow. Snuggling close to her, it took him only moments to join her.

They awoke late the following morning to the ping of text messages from Jon and Izzy on their mobiles. Both said they'd be there around noon. After a shower, they went down to greet their incoming guests. They were chilling out in the library when their guests arrived. Izzy was looking happy, Thomas looked a little apprehensive though.

Gone Dutch

"You're welcome here," said Shauna. "Come on in," she grinned, letting him follow Izzy as he saw fit.

Jon and Amelie arrived at their heels and Jon made a bee-line for Harek, pulling his friend and business partner aside. Amelie told Shauna why.

"We're planning a late March wedding and he wants Harek as the best man." Shauna smiled. That would be about two or three weeks after she'd given birth, if the birth went all right and things happened on time.

"Oh, that's exciting," said Izzy as she drank some tea.

Harek and Jon came out of the library to talk with Shauna and Amelie.

"Are you sure, famke?" he asked. He had taken her to the library to talk with her quietly. It would be close to after the birth, he didn't want to commit to something to then let Jon down.

She nodded. "He's been friends and partners with you since, goodness knows when. Yes. I'll have Tanja with me that day if needs be."

He nodded. "Only if you're sure?" he said, kissing her gently.

"I am very sure," she said, smiling. There was simply no way was he not going to be there for Jon.

They spent the rest of the day going through plans or chilling out. Izzy spent a few hours with her

Gone Dutch

nephews who entertained Thomas. They recognised him and were quite happy to show him their games. Andrew slinked off mid-way through and they found him in the library, on the sofa, reading a book. Shauna smiled. He was so like her; a bookworm.

Thomas asked Shauna for a few minutes of her time whilst Izzy was distracted by Michael and his games.

"I hope me being here isn't a problem?" he asked in a dead pan tone.

Shauna shook her head. "Not at all. Is there any reason why it should?"

"Because of what happened when I was here last," he said. Shauna nodded in understanding but had a glimmer in her eye.. She took in his blond hair, his tall frame, guessing him to be about six foot two. He was fit, athletic and quite handsome, but he didn't send a spark through her. Izzy, on the other hand...

"You were doing your job. Trust me, if I had a problem with you seeing my wee sister or being here, you'd know about it," she grinned at Thomas who visibly sighed. "Hurt her, and you'll know."

"So you're okay with us getting to know each other?"

Shauna stopped. "Are you asking me for permission to date my sister?" she asked, guessing that as he couldn't ask her father, she was the next best thing. He paused.

Gone Dutch

"I guess…" She watched as he stood more upright as his confidence in her company grew. "Yes. I am."

Shauna chuckled again. "Permission granted," smiled Shauna. Thomas smiled back, thanked her and headed back to sit with Izzy, pulling her close.

Izzy spent a few days with Thomas and a few with Shauna and the boys before she had to return to her job. Tanja returned from the UK and life returned to normal.

Gone Dutch

Forty-Three

They got news of Helene giving birth to a healthy boy at the end of January and Shauna sent across the new momma gift basket she had been putting together. She smiled as she received a message from Helene, thanking her, promising to try and meet up before Shauna too, popped. It didn't happen, despite them wanting it to.

It was on a cold, wet, early March morning that Shauna went into labour, waking Harek at three am with contractions beginning. The midwife arrived long before the dawn chorus sang-out, ruling out the water-birth when she learned that Shauna's water had already broken.

Lying on the bathroom floor on a bed of towels, dressing gowns and shower curtains to cushion her or protect the floor, Shauna quickly laboured through contraction after contraction.

"You're doing well Shauna," encouraged the midwife. "You're fully dilated, now to push. Are you ready?"

Shauna shook her head. "No choice," she sang out as a contraction hit, following the midwife's call to push. Harek held her hand, supporting her head.

Gone Dutch

"Watch her be born" growled Shauna at him when she was told the head was crowning. "You won't get another chance." By eight am, the cries of a new-born swept through Mûne Roazen. He was amazed how this little life had been born, cried when the baby did, kissed Shauna endlessly and he managed to cut the cord when he was told to with shaking hands.

"No stitches," declared the midwife proudly to Shauna. "Let's get you washed up and fed too momma," The midwife instructed Harek to help Shauna shower whilst she did the baby checks and gave Shauna a Vitamin K injection. By ten am, Tanja was bringing everyone breakfast. With the baby measured, washed, wrapped and fed for the first time, the food and hot tea were welcome.

The boys came to greet their baby sister when they came home from school. Shauna had managed a few hours of sleep, waking every few hours to feed her new-born daughter.

Shauna smiled at Harek as they introduced her to her big brothers. "Ailsa Ella Van Meerloo" he told the boys when they asked her if they'd named her. He called parents and those that needed to know, sharing the news. By the time he had finished cascading their news Shauna and his new-born daughter were once again asleep. He decided to join them, instructing the boys and Tanja as necessary.

Gone Dutch

Harek was kept busy between Shauna, his new daughter, the boys, work and Jon's impending wedding. Thankfully, Tanja was helping with the boys, the housework and caring for Shauna when his time didn't allow it. He did make sure that he was there on the day of Shauna's birthday, just a week after Ailsa was born.

March was still cold, wet and dismal. He often would find Shauna in her favourite chair, nursing their daughter or on the sofa in the office in front of the fire, which was lit daily.

He'd take to the gym early, do his exercises, return, shower then see family and business. He found Shauna before the fire in the library the morning in question, resting, drinking tea whilst their daughter slept in her bouncer, swaddled in a soft pink baby blanket before the roaring fire.

"Famke," he said, coming to sit next to her, pulling her close.

She snuggled into him, sighing contentedly.

"How are you?" he asked. She was walking better now and was able to move beyond the bedroom and the en-suite.

"I'm doing okay darling, thank you," she replied, snuggling into his embrace.

"Do you know what today is?" he asked, kissing her head.

Gone Dutch

"My birthday," she said, her eyes dancing as she looked up at him.

"Is there anything you'd like to do today?" he asked.

She shook her head. "Just, staying here with you is good. It's all I need." He smiled, he'd grant her wish.

"The boys and I have a few presents to give you. But there is one I'd like to give you now, before they come home" he said, kissing her head and stroking an arm.

"Okay," she said, sitting up and smiling at him. "But you don't have to."

Harek shook his head. "I do and I want to, for more reasons I can ever tell you," he said, kissing her gently on the lips. She sighed as he kissed her, making him check himself. Now was too soon to remind her just how full his heart was for her.

He guided her to the front door, making her put on her boots and coat. Sat either side of the front door, were four new royal blue plant pots. Two huge ones she was sure even Michael could get buried in, whilst there were two smaller ones. In the larger pots, large rosemary and sage bushes sat proudly, whilst parsley and thyme sat in the smaller pots. They were arranged in symmetry and wrapped in each, were soft warm fairy lights.

"Oh that is beautiful, thank you!" she said, hugging him.

Gone Dutch

He gently reached for her hand to make her follow him as he guided her around the garden, showing her the subtle changes that he'd had made. Standing over her circular patio, he'd had a huge white wrought iron pergola built.

"What would you like growing up on the arms, famke?"

She took it all in, eyes going wide, smiling broadly. "Oh my," was all she could say. That explained the tarp hiding this section from the library. He watched as she walked around the new structure, touching and breathing it in.

"I'd need to sit and think about it, is that okay?" she asked.

"Of course!" he said, kissing her gently, then hugging her.

"One last thing," he said, taking them back into the library. Ailsa slept on peacefully, warm and content before the fire. He sat Shauna down, went to a shelf and removed a package. A medium-sized white box was wrapped in a purple bow. He handed it to her, smiling as he gently sat down beside her.

She smiled "What's all this?" she asked as she opened it. It smelled beautiful and contained hand-cream, nipple cream, bath salts, a book on typical Dutch plants (In English) shampoo and various other self-care items. Contained within, was a handwritten note:

Gone Dutch

"To the love of my life, the mother of my child, the keeper of my heart.
Happy birthday! Love always, Harek."
Shauna cried a little as she read the note. Then she flung her arms around his neck and kissed him deeply.

"Thank you," she breathed, leaning into him as happy tears fell.

"How long before she wakes again?" he asked.

"About twenty minutes, I think? She's going longer between feeds, but slowly."

"You're doing amazing things with her," he whispered into her head. "You are amazing," he said, cuddling her and kissing her head as they gazed at their daughter.

"When she's fed again I'll run you a bath, let you rest. Cait said she was going to stop by today but later."

Shauna nodded. "It'll be nice to see her. Which is kind of weird to say and think," she chuckled.

Tanja brought them lunch to eat whilst they waited for Ailsa to awaken. Tanja fetched the boys and they cooed and cuddled their little sister whilst Harek supervised and Shauna indulged in a scented bath. The boys brought their mother a large box of her favourite British chocolates, thanks to Izzy's visit back at New Years.

The midwife checked in on them as Cait was arriving, suddenly making Mûne Roazen very busy. The

Gone Dutch

midwife did her baby and mother checks, praised Shauna and Harek for their efforts with the baby and each other and left them in peace.

Cait got to hold her niece, smiling at the little angel Shauna was blessed with. She watched as her big sister opened up a small present of amethyst stud earrings.

"They're beautiful Cait, thank you," Shauna whispered as she took them out of the box and inserted them into her ears.

Cait smiled at Shauna and proclaimed Aisla a darling quiet little thing. Shauna and Harek chuckled at Cait. "You don't hear her at two am when she's hungry sis," laughed Shauna, sipping a tea.

Cait shook her head and spoke gently in reply, as if to Ailsa herself. "You don't make a peep at all do you, my little angel?" Shauna continued to chuckle. Cait stayed for a few hours more, until Abbe called.

"On my way," she sang to him, chuckling. She kissed and hugged her sister goodbye. More presents arrived via the post or courier during the week as Harek got busy with Jon about his wedding. By the time Ailsa was three weeks old, the plans were pretty much done. The suits were decided upon, leaving just Amelie's dresses to finalise.

Amelie called on Shauna one day, only five days before her wedding, distraught.

Gone Dutch

"Hey, what's happened?" she asked as she nursed Ailsa one wet day.

Amelie cried in parts and paced in others, clearly equal parts upset and angry over something, switching languages with each profanity. Finally, it all came spilling out as Tanja left to collect the boys.

"Damn friend of mine," growled Amelie. "We've known each other through college, university and she bails on me five days before the wedding." The pacing worsened as she explained. "Five days."

Shauna cooed to Ailsa, keeping her calm. "That's not very good," observed Shauna as she burped Ailsa. "Did she give a good reason as to why?" asked Shauna

Amelie spat off responses in Flemish, English and Dutch. Finally, she seemed calm enough to tell the full tale, which wasn't much of a tale.

"So she's just said she's not willing to do the travel to Rotterdam, even though you've five days to your wedding, the fitting is tomorrow and the stag do is three days away?" Amelie nodded.

Shauna sighed. "What did Jon say?"

Amelie shrugged and her cheeks went red. "He's not said anything. I've…" she looked around. "I've not told him yet."

Shauna's eyes went wide. "Amelie, honey, you need to talk with him. He needs to know, you can't hide something that important from him."

Gone Dutch

Amelie sighed. "I know, but now I feel useless and worthless because I've been defending her actions and replies from Jon. He's been against her being my maid of honour since I mentioned it, but every time she's let me down, he grumbled." She began pacing again. "He thought she'd do something like this, she's never come to visit, despite being invited several times" She sat down on the sofa, putting her head in her hands.

"What do you want to have happen next?" asked Shauna gently.

Amelie sighed. "I want a true friend there, by my side. Someone that's been there since we met, though she probably doesn't remember."

Shauna chuckled. "Who could forget the first time they met you?" she asked, burping Ailsa on her shoulder after tucking a breast away.

"Do you remember when we met?" asked Amelie.

Shauna nodded. "The day Harek got beaten up. You were there with Jon. You sat on one side of me at some points, though some of that day is a blur. I do remember you fetched me some of that god awful coffee," she gagged at the memory.

Amelie smiled. "I wanted to ask you to begin with but I knew you'd have your hands full, especially if Harek was the best man." Amelie stood and paced again and Amelie wrung her hands as she did so.

Shauna held out her hand. "Amelie, ask."

Gone Dutch

Amelie sighed. "Shauna, I'd love for you to be my maid of honour. Please, could you?" She paused. "Will you?"

Shauna smiled. "If you can accommodate Tanja being there to help with Aisla and the boys on the day, yes."

Amelie tried hard not to cry at Shauna's reply. "Really?" she whispered.

Shauna nodded. Amelie hugged her as gently as she could around Aisla.

Harek and Jon arrived at Mûne Roazen on schedule. Tanja had prepared enough for all of them, having heard that Amelie had asked for Shauna's help, as well as her own.

"I'd love to!" she said, cooing over the baby. Everyone seemed to love Aisla.

Jon and Amelie went off to speak with each other, Jon was not happy with why Shauna was even asked.

"He was, how do you say, spitting feathers when Amelie said to meet him here, that she was going to ask you to be the maid of honour." He looked at Shauna with a frown. "Is this going to be too much, famke?"

Shauna shook her head. "I don't think so, not really. The main details are worked out already, I've helped you with some of them," she held one of Harek's hands in both of hers. "The final fitting for the wedding

Gone Dutch

dress is tomorrow. I need to get out of here at some point, I need to get around people that aren't family and be sociable." She looked up into Harek's eyes, full of concern and love. "I need to not be locked away anymore and if going dress shopping for one dress stresses me out, I need my butt kicked."

He looked at her arse, deciding that it was worth a squeeze. Shauna laughed.

"Besides, I want to use the new pushchair. I've not had a thing to do for the last three or four weeks, you and Tanja have made it so much easier for me with Aisla than I had it with the boys. If Jon's okay with Tanja being there to take over with Aisla when I have to do certain ceremonial, necessary things," she cast her mind back to Helene's wedding, "then I can do this for them, with you." She looked up at him.

"Jon's going to be there for you, when we marry, correct?" Harek nodded. "What example would it set if his best friend's fiancé can't step in to help? How does that make them family if we don't help when we can?" Harek sighed and Shauna continued. "Family isn't just DNA honey," she rubbed his arm and held his hand. "He knows more secrets and history about you than I'll ever get to know and I'm okay with that. Family is who we make it to be." Their eyes locked and Shauna spoke more softly. "They were there, with me, with Vayenn, when you got assaulted. Jon helped to look after me back on the boat when Vayenn took me back that night." He

Gone Dutch

hugged her, her words hitting home. "He didn't have to. But he did."

She paused for a moment. "It's one day, maybe two. If I do get stressed out with finding a dress, I won't do the hen do, though Amelie can come here the night you guys are out, wherever the heck you go, unless she has other plans she wants to do. We can have a girl's night in, movies, food, songs, dancing." Shauna pulled back and set her shoulders. "But I can make sure she walks up that aisle and dressed to her best."

Harek bent down to kiss Shauna. The cough behind them told them that Jon and Amelie had heard some of what Shauna had to say.

"Well, when you put it like that," said Jon, coming to hug her tightly. "Thank you my friend," he said, holding her close.

Aisla's cry bought them out of the quietness they'd found.

"Aww hell, boob time," joked Shauna, loosening Harek's fingers as she went to tend to their daughter. Shauna squeezed Amelie's arm and the women walked off, leaving the men to their discussions.

They talked of the wedding in more detail over dinner and with such things as flowers, catering and the cake already outsourced and organised, seating plan arranged, what national traditions they both wanted, it really was just the dresses to sort.

Gone Dutch

    The following morning, Shauna ventured out with Amelie and Ailsa for the first time. Tanja did the usual school runs and would take care of the basic chores, then have the rest of the day to chill or visit her family. Shauna loaded up the changing bag with what she knew she'd need and a few things that she thought she might. Having done this with the boys, she was adept at planning for more than one eventuality with babies.

    Ailsa however, was as good as gold. She seemed to enjoy the fresh air and was much less fractious than normal, so Shauna said to Harek when he called for the fourth time to check up on her.

    "Honestly, we're fine!" she said. "Now, stop callin' me!" she said, copying the phrase from Pretty Woman. She chuckled as she hung up shaking her head as Amelie laughed.

    They found a dress Shauna liked in Amelie's colours that would fit the rest of the colour scheme, flowers etc. that had already been picked out. It needed adjusting outward on the bodice to allow for Shauna's expanding bust due to her breastfeeding Aisla, but the seamstress said she could accommodate the maternal need and would do it that afternoon. At nearly five o'clock, the last fitting was made and the seamstress had done her job perfectly. Shauna tipped her handsomely and with the shoes having been picked out whilst they

Gone Dutch

waited for the dress, it was all loaded into the car and the girls headed home.

Vayenn offered to take the boys from Shauna for the night of the hen do, since Harek would be busy with the stag do in Amsterdam.

"I don't wanna ken what happens! Just, keep it clean and come back safe, all of you." was her last instruction to both Jon and Harek. Fons dropped Helene off with their son and he travelled with the other men to Amsterdam.

That night, with just the girls and babies, they danced to various songs, kick-starting it all off with some serious Christina Aguilera songs. Pink was up next and their little party continued until the small hours. Helene and Shauna drank very little, but Tanja and Amelie did have to call it a night.

"I think we did our job well!" said Helene, sharing Shuna's room and bed for the night. Both new mothers thought it would be easier if the babies were in the same room.

"You know," said Shauna happily as she settled down to feed Aisla one last time, "I think we did."

The wedding was held on what Shauna could only call a dreich day. Well, it started with fine misty rain but dried up before the car pulled up at the church.

Gone Dutch

Tanja took charge of Aisla and the boys during the ceremony, leaving Shauna to tend to Amelie who looked stunning in her tight sparkly mermaid gown. She held two single flowers; Shauna watched as Amelie gave her mother one of the flowers. Once the vows were exchanged and the first kiss happened, Amelie gave her new mother-in-law the other single flower.

The ceremony itself went without a hitch. The reception was slightly different, a mixture of Belgian traditions and Dutch ones intertwined, which made for it to be somewhat interesting.

Harek and Shauna weren't seated together and the women were seated first. The main meal was seafood-based, which was good for most of the guests, including Shauna. During the speeches, the happy couple were toasted twice; once at the start and again at the end. As the night drew on, the lights were lowered to reveal the table candles and hundreds of fairy lights that graced the eves of the hall in question.

The first dance or song was Cannemara, a French song about Ireland and the women had to twirl and throw their napkins. Shauna laughed as she twirled her napkin around and it escaped, flying off somewhere.

The Kransekage was one Dutch tradition Jon and Amelie said that they wanted to keep. Sparkling ice-cream cake towers weren't her thing, but the dessert buffet was certainly something that many enjoyed!

Gone Dutch

As Jon took Amelie to the dance floor for their first dance, Shauna and Helene found a quiet corner to quietly feed their children. Shielded by trellis and plants, they quietly talked as their babies fed. It was quite late when they found their hotel room and despite the lateness, it took a while for everyone to get to sleep.

The weather warmed up, the seasons changed and family visited, Shauna managed to visit the UK and drive her car again for a little while. The boys spent some of the summer weeks in England, visiting all their grandparents, aunts, uncles, godfathers, whilst Shauna and Aisla spent a week here and there visiting family. Shauna heard about the court case from Adam and Ben when they managed to catch up over a vast amount of coffee. The case had gone well and the builder was in prison for fraud.

Shauna's wedding to Harek slowly approached. They aimed for the Autumn Equinox, choosing autumn colours and silver for their wedding. Shauna visited a florist in Rotterdam, her Dutch having improved drastically enough for her to feel comfortable when ordering things. She held her list in front of her as she and baby Aisla waited to speak with the florist, who was getting a hard time from the customer in front for something that she hadn't even supplied. The woman

Gone Dutch

and her mother stormed out, nearly bashing into the pushchair but Shauna just shook her head.

"I'm sorry you had to endure that. Their issue isn't your fault."

The florist sighed. "I know. But, thank you!" The florist shook her head, said something in another language again, then smiled at Shauna.

Shauna struggled with what she wanted to say in Dutch, but managed it. The woman smiled and switched to English.

"So, tell me again what would you like? I need to make sure I understood" she asked, taking her notepad and pen.

Shauna went through the displays she wanted for the top table, the colours and saw the options available in both fresh and artificial flowers.

Shauna made her mind up instantly. "Providing each display is made up of flowers in autumn colours, have some heather, a tulip, some tartan ribbon," Shauna laid two reels of blue tartan ribbon on the counter. "And there's something silver in the display, I don't mind. It depends on what you can get on the day, or what is available." Shauna smiled. "You're the creative one, so I'll leave it to you."

The woman smiled. "I wish everyone would let me have carte blanche on these things sometimes." She looked thrilled at the gesture. "Do you need or want any larger displays?" she asked, making notes as they went.

Gone Dutch

Shauna shook her head. "No, but I do need a brides and two bridesmaid's bouquets, in the same colours and theme."

They spoke about the men's buttonholes, a mixture of a tulip and heather and the tartan, with Shauna showing the florist some idea's she had found on-line. The florist showed Shauna a few choices of how to arrange them. Picking one, the florist noted it down along with a photo. Taking a deposit, they shook hands and parted ways.

By the end of August, the plans were in place, the marquees ordered, catering and the licence organised. They were holding it at Mûne Roazen. Harek had hired several large caravans to be put on the site in an area that he never used. It allowed those that wanted to stay over to do so. Others brought their own tents and made it a huge camping, outdoor event. Shauna's parents were given a bedroom in Mûne Roazen whilst Harek's brought their caravan a few days before.

Shauna was surprised that there were water outlets for the caravans to hook up to for fresh water whilst on site. Close to fifty people, all family and friends were in attendance that day. Nature decided to add to their event by ensuring the sunshine and warmth were in abundance from sunrise to sunset.

Helene and Amelie were her bridesmaids, whilst little Aisla was a flower girl and held during the

Gone Dutch

ceremony by Izzy. Carrie was next to her father, beaming madly. Bryce and Tanja smiled as she walked past, escorted by her father to meet Harek at the altar, which was set up on the compass patio. Michael and Andrew, along with Jon, were "best men" and Shauna admitted that they looked rather dashing. She saw Berend, Abbe and Cait on the grooms' side and they were smiling. Ruth and Ellen had made it too, happy to see their friend marry for a second time.

The pergola was draped in golden vines, mixed in with yellow clematis, red roses, evergreens and willows. She had a huge smile as the same piper from the New Years' party played her down the library steps to the wedding official.

The legal official walked through the ceremony in both Dutch and English and it wasn't long until they were pronounced man and wife.

Shauna was both amazed and pleased that the day went without a hitch. The best man speech was funny, heartfelt and sincere. The father-of-the-bride speech was short and sweet. Harek made a speech at the cake cutting, reflecting back to Helene and Fons' wedding over eighteen months previously, Shauna's bravery and his love for her. By the end, Shauna was glad for waterproof makeup and her heart swelled with love.

After their first dance, the floor was busy with couples dancing, swaying or just being together and

Gone Dutch

everyone seemed happy. Slowly, everyone retired to tents or their bed.

Harek led Shauna to their front door and scooped her up before he walked her over the threshold.

"Welcome home, Mrs van Meerloo!" he said, planting a kiss on her lips as he gently set her down inside the kitchen. The catering staff were still clearing everything away and they ignored Harek and Shauna as they made their way to their bedroom. Little Aisla was in with Tanja and Bryce, but she was now sleeping through so wouldn't wake until the morning and Tanja knew what to do.

Jon and their sons had decorated their bedroom in warm fairy lights. They left a strawberry champagne supper on the table near the doors, decorated the bed in tulips and heather. Shauna felt loved when she saw the effort her sons and Jon had gone to. Harek kissed her as soon as their door was closed.

"You look amazing tonight, famke! Myn frou," he breathed, as he kissed her and slowly unzipped her dress, gently teasing the gorgeous satin dress from her shoulders. He kissed her shoulders, her neck and began kissing her down to her breasts, removing clothing slowly. He stood awestruck as once again, he undressed her to find stockings, suspenders and a garter belt that sang out Scotland the Brave when a button was pressed.

Gone Dutch

Any hopes he had of taking their marriage night slowly, went out of the window when he saw how Shauna was dressed beneath her dress. It didn't take them long to reduce him to his birthday suit, though he insisted that she keep on the suspenders and stockings as he ensured that they were thoroughly sated come morning.

Gone Dutch

Epilogue

Harek smiled as he pulled into Mûne Roazen just over a year later. He saw Aisla playing near the herb beds Shauna was tending to and smiled as his wife stood up, stretching her back. Her bump expanded before her, showing that she was due any day. So was Amelie. He and Jon had closed the company for a few weeks, giving everyone some needed paid time away and the directors, some time at home with their new families.

He unloaded the last purchase from the car as Shauna waddled towards him. Carrying twins was certainly harder than carrying one child. Whilst Shauna had a tiny bump with Aisla, she was much larger now in the hot Dutch weather and with two babies inside her.

"How are my two little ones?" he asked, rubbing her bump and kissing her.

"They're giving me grief," she rubbed her back and tried to ease her discomfort. "I'll be glad when they come out and join us, I tell you," She kissed him then twisted her back this way and that. "Did you get the pushchair?" she asked, trying to rub her own back again. Twins meant a new pushchair, a double one for when they did go out as a family.

Gone Dutch

He nodded. "Yes, I did. We can assemble it another day. How are you feeling?"

Shauna pulled a face. "Fat and twingy," she moaned. "The Braxton's are annoying," she said, scowling. Harek fished one of Shauna's favourite chocolate bars from his case and handed it to her, smiling. Kissing him, she retrieved it from him and encouraged Aisla to play nearer the garden swing whilst she savoured some of the bar.

"Where is momma?" he asked, hugging her close. His parents had come to spend time with them whilst Shauna gave birth and for a few weeks after. Tanja was now in England, preparing for her second year of University near Birmingham. Helped by Bryce, she had flourished in her English and his Dutch was getting quite good.

"In the house, I left her in the kitchen after I was told I wasn't allowed to help. She was helping Michael prepare something."

Shauna moved and then winced loudly. Harek grabbed and held her, but she only took another step before it was obvious she was in labour.

"But, I've got a month to go!" she wailed between contractions.

"Twins may come early, remember?" he reminded her gently, repeating the midwife's advice. Harek called the midwife as he guided Shauna to the birthing pool. He'd prepared it that morning, ensuring

Gone Dutch

that the water was the right temperature. He had noticed that her bump was dropping and deduced she was due sooner rather than later.

Helping her into the birthing pool between contractions, he never left her side. Andrew guided the midwife up to their room when she arrived. Hours later with only a few stitches to show for it (though utterly exhausted) Shauna held her two latest children. The eldest twin, a boy, was only three minutes older than his twin sister.

Smiling at their new-born children, they named them Sander and Yara.

"That's it, I quit!" she said after the midwife had left, putting on an American southern drawl and snuggling Yara whilst Harek held Sander. "I ain't bearin' anymore children!"

Harek chuckled. "Myn leafde," he said, reaching across and holding her hand. "Five is quite enough!" he agreed.

Gone Dutch

About The Author

Growing up, I was writing stories or making up stuff in my head. It often came out as fibs or tall tales. My imagination was active and anything could (and still does!) set my muse off. pInterest is a classic platform for allowing me to visualise the characters that live in my head.

I spent many years studying martial arts and being a displaced Scot that influence came into play in this book (more so in my darker duet, which will be out in late 2021/2022) I have three children (one is already taller than me) and I've been married for nearly twenty years now. Add in a cat, dog, chickens, friends… I'm a busy gal!

I spent one summer of my youth hooked on Mills & Boon, then YA, then fantasy. Playing Dungeons and Dragons when the hubby and I got together didn't help my muse, the poor lady went into overtime

I came back into writing after reading many good books and the lockdown of 2020 was certainly a platform to do something for me, creatively. So, my thanks to Karen Lynch (Her Relentless Series) for a huge muse, to Sandra Hill for her erotic Vampire Viking Series

Gone Dutch

(honestly, if broken Vikings chosen by the Archangel Michael can find love, anyone can) and for her rekindling my love of romance books.

Thanks too, to recent authors that have helped, guided, pointed and had me enthralled with their series of books: Jolie Vines (Marry The Scott series and all beyond), Catharina Maura (The Tie That Binds, Forever After All), Elle Thorpe (Her Cowboy series), Delta James (Tangled Vines series) and many others whose books I've picked up, enjoyed, met and reviewed on Amazon & Goodreads. (With these ladies, you bet I'm on their newsletter list!)

If you enjoyed this, feel free to stay in touch! Here's how:

My website: www.louisemurchie.com
Newsletter: Via website
Instagram: @louisemurchieauthor
Facebook: Author Page
Twitter: Tweet Me

Printed in Great Britain
by Amazon